FROM KNIGHT TO KNAVE

Cover design by Cathy Helms of

Also By Jae Malone

The Winterne Series

Silver Linings
Queen of Diamonds
Fool's Gold
Avaroc Returns

Short Stories

Sanctuary
One Hour Story – Leaving
One Hour Story - The Bus Station
A Stain in Time
Maisie
Kathy and Charlie
Freedom (Shortlisted for the King Lear Prize 2021)

Animal Stories for Younger Children

Lorna and the Loch Ness Monster
The Raven and the Thief
Blue Teaches A Lesson
Mrs Pringles Needs A Nurse
Tib and Tab Make A Friend
The Squirrel Who Missed Christmas

JAE MALONE

FROM KNIGHT TO KNAVE

The prequel to Silver Linings
Selected historical accounts of the folk of
Winterne Manor

NEW GENERATION PUBLISHING

Published by New Generation Publishing in 2021

Copyright © Jae Malone 2021

First Edition

The author asserts the moral right under the Copyright, Designs and Patents Act 1988 to be identified as the author of this work.

All Rights reserved. No part of this publication may be reproduced, stored in a retrieval system or transmitted, in any form or by any means without the prior consent of the author, nor be otherwise circulated in any form of binding or cover other than that in which it is published and without a similar condition being imposed on the subsequent purchaser.

ISBN: 978-1-80031-361-3

www.newgeneration-publishing.com

New Generation Publishing

Reviews for 'The Winterne Series'

Silver Linings :

'An intriguing read. This book would work well on the big screen.'
Alan Clifford – BBC Radio

'Trilogy's stirring start.'
Dawn Bond, Newark Advertiser

'An imaginative adventure with a dark streak.'
Jeremy Lewis, Nottingham Post

The book unfolds beautifully, with well-rounded characters and kept my daughter and I enchanted throughout. I'm just looking forward to the sequels!!!   *Amazon Reader*

Queen of Diamonds :

Jae gets better with every book she writes and could easily give J K Rowling a good run for her money.'
Newark Advertiser

'A loving and wholesome read.'
Jeremy Lewis, Nottingham Post

'Jae Malone's imagination is on the same wave length as legendary J R R Tolkien. She writes with vividness, intensity and sophistication.'
Amazon Reader

Fool's Gold:

Jae has a fluid, easily accessible writing style, while the stories feature richly layered plots where high fantasy, school-year tribulations and dark nefarious deeds interweave.
Steve Bowkett. Writer, storyteller, educational consultant, Member of Society of Authors & National Association of Writers in Education (NAWE)

'The author is a fine storyteller who seems effortlessly to combine the natural and the supernatural worlds.'
Editor: Nottinghamshire Today

'Wow. I can't wait to read this new book. I have so enjoyed reading the three previous books.'
Facebook Reader

Lorna and the Loch Ness Monster:

What a delightfully charming little story! Nicely written, beautifully illustrated and a pleasure to read. Absolutely ideal for any family with young children who are intending to visit Scotland for a holiday - but just as suitable for any family anywhere!
Helen Hollick, Best-selling and highly acclaimed author of historical fiction

*For David. Thank you for all your love and support.
This book is dedicated to you with all my love*

And to newly born Ace, for all the love ad laughter to come.

Acknowledgements

During this year of Covid 19, like so many others I have been at home, following the rules, but it provided the time to write the book that has nagged at me for a while. In the first two Winterne books, there are mentions of the tunnel, the curse on Winterne Manor, and the monk trapped within the priest hole, that had no explanation. So here are six stories giving the origins of the manor, and answers to who built the tunnel and why, who placed the curse and why the priest was never released.

The historical research has been great fun and so rewarding. It has been fascinating, for example, to discover that, during the Peasants Revolt in 1381 riots began in Bridgewater and at Ilchester. Ilchester is just seventeen miles from where I have based Winterne Manor, and the date fits perfectly with the timing of Part One.

I am indebted to Wikipedia for providing me with most of the information I needed. Not being able to get to our local library, or pay my usual annual visit to Somerset this year for research, the Internet and Wikipedia particularly have been a Godsend. I discovered a great deal of detail on the Battle of Poitiers, Judge Jeffreys and what happened to him following the Monmouth Rebellion, the Peasant's Revolt and much more.

However, it hasn't just been Wikipedia I have interrogated, and I would like to mention the following sources of very valuable information.

My thanks to **Somerset Live** for details of Witchcraft in Somerset through the centuries. **'Wells – A History and Celebration'** in which I found details about Italian Prisoners of War at Penleigh near Wookey Hole. **The Time chamber** gave an insight into the Somerset and Bath Asylum in Wells and the first Physician Dr Robert Boyd. **www.Mineheadonline.co.uk** was a remarkable source of information with regard to the number of martyrs executed by the Hanging Judge, Judge George Jeffreys.

My thanks too to dear friends. Firstly, historical author, Helen Hollick, who, since 2006, has been my mentor; a fabulous lady, always generous with her time and expertise and I'm so glad I know her.

Also, very dear friends who have supported and encouraged me are, Sally Holmes, Ellaine Monk, Shona Rowan, and Adrian Woods (who I believe is still seething at the conduct of Brother Matthew – in Part Three).

My lovely, long-time and long-suffering friends have generously given up their time to read through fairly sizeable sections of the book to look for typos etc. and given feedback on how it reads and where, perhaps, I have not made sense. Friends and constant supporters on whom, this time, I haven't dumped sections of this book are Amanda Boden, Karen Neil, Cheryl Hely, Sharlean Plummer. Cheryl, Sharlean and Adrian are members of the writing group I set up a few years ago. Over time, it has become more of a social gathering, and I look forward to when the Covid restrictions are relaxed, and we can meet up again.

Once again, the cover of this book has been created by the hugely talented Cathy Helms of Avalon Graphics. Working with Cathy is so easy. I don't always explain precisely what I would like but somehow Cathy just knows, and I thoroughly enjoy working with her.

Lastly, I want to thank Daniel Cooke, the Managing Director of New Generation Publishing and his team, David Walshaw and Saskia Osterloff for all their hard work on my behalf – especially with this book.

Contents Page

			Page
Part One	1356 In the time of the Black Prince: The Knight. From the Battle of Poitiers		1
Part Two	1510 In the time of Henry VIII: The First Earl		205
Part Three	1587 In the time of Elizabeth I: The Monk		213
Part Four:	1685 In the time of King James II: The Monmouth Rebellion		275
Part Five	1848 In the Time of Queen Victoria: The Curse		321
Part Six	1992 The Knave To buy a manor		391

Part One

1356
In the time of the Black Prince
The Knight.

Chapter One

September 1356: The Battle of Poitiers. The Hundred Years War.

With head bowed and knees cramped on the damp churned-up earth, all Will Hallett could see surrounding him were the armoured feet of a circle of bloodied and mud-spattered knights. On the ground beside him was his treasured longbow and bag of arrows; the longbow was actually longer than he was tall, reaching six and a half feet, made of the wood of the yew with a hardened hemp string. He swallowed hard. This was not how he expected things to turn out, for himself or the three other archers waiting behind him; they were probably just as scared as he was of what their changed destiny held in store for them and, he suspected, they had never been this close to royalty before.

The rough-skinned palms of his hands were damp with sweat while he waited, tense, for his moment. To give himself something to do, he removed his bascinet, a metal skullcap with chainmail at the sides and down the back of the neck. Most of the archers wore them for protection against overhead arrows. He tugged off his hood and ran his fingers through his short red-sandy hair to flatten it into place.

Shivering in his thin, clinging uniform, Will tried to control his trembling, not entirely caused by being where he was, or what was to come next. The chill autumn drizzle, left over from the torrential rainstorm the day before, had seeped through his clothes and into his body, and he was still recovering from a fever that had spread throughout the camp, leaving him

a little weaker than usual, and with muscles that ached so painfully he worried about being able to stand up again in front of all these important people. Of course, somehow he, like many others who had been unwell, had found the strength to fight in the battle. It was that or certain death. The French army was vast in comparison with Prince Edward's force; some said the enemy outnumbered them by ten to one. Like wildfire, word spread through the English force that they would be over-run and massacred, which was evidenced by the French flying the Oriflamme, their blood-red banner with the flaming sun. It was their message to the English army that no mercy would be shown, no prisoners would be taken. Anyone wounded on the battlefield would be put to death. It was meant to strike fear in the English hearts and although it did for many, conversely for the majority, it also strengthened the resolve, stiffened the spine, stirred the blood, and from somewhere they found the determination to fight through their feeble health and win the day, even though their number was so much smaller.

But now, he would have preferred to be sound asleep somewhere, his cloak tucked tight and warm around him, and not have to think about what the coming hours would bring.

He tried not to tremble as the tall man in black armour walked towards him and he raised his head just enough to see the razor-sharp, menacing sword coming closer, dried blood still clinging to the blade.

Will was just an archer who served his lord, William de Montacute, second Earl of Salisbury, and this did not happen to simple folk like himself. He had been prepared to die, expected to die in the service of his liege Lord, after all he was just an ordinary fighting man, like hundreds of others who got on with obeying orders, and did their duty.

For almost five years he had followed his lord and fought for him, and for England, believing God was on their side. That must have been right because the Archbishop had said so when he blessed them. But the horrors Will had witnessed over those years had made him question everything, silently. He kept those thoughts to himself, but he was sure others felt the same way, and there were many who had deserted even at the risk of being hanged if they were caught. But, the thing that puzzled him most was, if God *was* on their side, why did the French think the same thing? He could not fathom out why God was supporting both sides. If that was so and they

were both right, why were they fighting? To speak out, to give voice to those questions would mean punishment, so he held his tongue and continued doing his duty.

He had received wounds, there were very few of them who had none, but nothing serious, thank God; perhaps he had a guardian angel watching over him. In each battle he had been convinced his luck must run out and he would not see the end of that day. But here he still was and, apart from a few scars, some nasty recent bruises to his forehead and a cut to his cheek bone when a loose French destrier, one of the massive horses the knight's rode, had barged into him knocking him to the ground where he had landed face first on an abandoned shield. The fact that the horse was loose was evidence that the knight had probably come of far worse than he had and, through it all he had survived, thanks be to God, and mostly in one piece, so far anyway.

Beyond the circle of knights, from the vast field of battle, the cries of the wounded and dying men and horses joined with the shouts of stretcher-bearers, and the metallic clang of now redundant armour being removed from the dead by lucky survivors. Anyone who needed the protection of armour could always find some at the end of a battle, and no-one thought any the worse of anyone who helped themselves; needs must after all, and the dead had no more use for it.

From above the tents came the loud whip and crack sounds of colourful, damp pennants and banners as they flapped wildly in a strong breeze that kept changing direction, wafting sour-smelling smoke from campfires and funeral pyres – there was no time to bury the dead - making eyes water and seeping into clothing. Will coughed as it stung his throat, but the man in black armour seemed unaffected.

'I understand this man is one of your best archers, Salisbury.' From his low-level viewpoint, Will saw the greaves and sabatons covering the shins and feet of another man. William knew who the new arrival was, and he looked up into the smiling face of the Earl of Salisbury.

'Yes, my Lord. It pleases me to admit that is so.'

'I take it then that you would be somewhat *dis*pleased to lose him from your company?'

The Earl smiled and shrugged. 'Under these circumstances, Sire, and in view of our great friendship since childhood, I feel I have no choice.'

'Well said, my Lord Salisbury. Very well then. We will begin. William Hallett, raise your head.' Will did as he was told and stretched his neck to look up into the face of the incredibly tall Edward of Woodstock, Prince of Wales; at six foot four inches, he towered over most of the gathering.

'By the power invested in me from King Edward, the third of that name, in recognition of your service to the Crown and to me, personally, I hereby award you, William Hallett, with the accolade of Knight.' The Prince laid the flat of his sword on Will's right shoulder, then lifted it over Will's head to do the same on the left. 'Do you swear to uphold the virtues of Knighthood, protect the weak, defend ladies, obey God and the Church?'

'I do, my Lord,' Will replied, remaining on his knees that were now beginning to cramp from the cold damp earth seeping through his breeches.

A man standing a little behind the prince, handed him a scroll of parchment, bound by a red cord, which the prince then handed to Will. 'This document is indisputable evidence of your Knighthood. Let no man gainsay it.'

Then it was over. There followed a rousing cheer from the knights watching the ceremony, some of whom were gesturing for Will to stand, but he would not rise until he was given leave to do so, and wasn't even sure he still could.

'Salisbury.' The Prince began. 'I feel sure you must have some land within your domain that you have no use for, perhaps with a house and some woodland?'

The Earl of Salisbury, smiled at his close friend. 'Sire, for saving your life I am sure I can find something fitting for our young hero, in fact there is a property at a hamlet in Somerset...um...I believe it is called Winterne, but in all honesty, I have not visited there for some years now and cannot speak as to its condition. In addition, Sire, I am not eager to part with our new knight. He is far too good an archer.'

'Nevertheless, Salisbury...oh, Wi...Sir William Hallett, you may stand now,' the Prince added before turning back to the Earl. 'Even for you, my dear friend, I cannot allow a knight of the realm to return to the battle lines as an archer. So come, say your farewells to Sir William and let us move on. We have these other brave men to attend to, and I'm sure he could do with a rest.'

Having been on his knees for so long on the damp ground, Will's legs were stiff and numb, and it took him a few moments to struggle to his feet but, by now, the Prince and Earl had moved on to talk to Arthur Burnel, next in line to be rewarded for his act of heroism on the battlefield, and were unaware of Will's efforts to stand. But, as they moved on, he heard the Prince say, 'As I was saying, Salisbury, it is perhaps time the young man was allowed to return to England and survey his new property. Besides, as we agreed, he is no longer an archer and therefore your argument to keep him by your side falls flat, does it not, my friend?'

'You put his case too well, my Lord.'

The Prince turned back to Will, who was now trying to hide the discomfort of 'pins and needles' as the blood rushed back to fill the veins in his deadened legs.

'Sir William Hallett,' said the Prince, 'you, and the other heroes of today's battle who are yet to be knighted,' he gestured to Arthur and the two other young men Will had never seen until that moment, 'will dine with us this evening in my pavilion. I shall send a page for you...oh, and I would do something about those garments you're wearing. Perhaps change into something more...clean?'

Will looked down at his breeches and the white tabard with the red cross of St George on the front. Like everyone else his clothing was torn and smeared with mud and blood. He smiled back at the Prince. 'I would, my Lord, but I'm sorry to say, I have nothing but what I stand up in.'

'Then we must do something about that for you and these other fine fellows.' Edward turned to the Earl of Salisbury. 'Salisbury, you really must provide these brave men with clean uniforms.'

'Ha!' replied the Earl with a smirk. 'There seems to be little point in that, Sire, when you are releasing them from service after today...but,' he moved back to Will and wrinkled his nose, 'on closer inspection, I agree that they could do with bathing, and shaving...we will have some hot water provided for that to make it easier to scrape the whiskers away...and then they will need clean garments. Perhaps some rose water, or a rub down with cloves will help. Once we have completed our business here, Sire, I shall have two of my pages escort the four new knights to the river where they can bathe, and remove some of their body odour, together with the stains on their uniforms. My pages will also have some shear-scissors with

which to trim their hair. They will be issued with clean garments and, once the uniforms are dry, they can be mended and given to other archers in my company, and our new knights shall begin their journey to England on the morrow. When you see them again, they will appear as completely different men.'

The Prince smiled, 'Agreed, Salisbury. A good plan. Is it not, Sir William?'

Will bowed to Lord Edward, Prince of Wales. 'Yes, Sire and thank you, both.'

'You owe me no thanks, Will. Your skill with a bow, and your well-timed intervention, saved my life. To place that arrow so precisely in the gap of the French knight's armour as he raised his arm to cut me down, in the confusion of battle going on all around you, was nothing short of a miracle. We have won this day but there will be others, and I will not allow you to die or worse, to live maimed, perhaps as a beggar. Tonight you will have the respect of others and tomorrow you will begin a new life…oh, and we must have a crest designed for you with your coat of arms.'

Will smiled up at the Prince. 'I had never thought I would have my own crest, my Lord, and don't know what emblems to choose.'

'Well, give it some thought while you find refreshment and rest until the Earl's page comes for you, then perhaps our heraldic expert can help you choose which designs you would like and would be appropriate, then we shall have it prepared for you.'

The Prince turned to Salisbury. 'Good. Now for our other gallant heroes. Now, come Salisbury, let's not keep these good men waiting any longer. Advance Arthur Burnel and kneel.'

The Earl of Salisbury leaned in towards Will and said quietly, 'You have done the Kingdom a great service today and shall be further rewarded, but you must be hungry. You shall feast royally tonight, but for now go find yourself some nourishment, then get some rest until his Lordship's page comes for you. Your part here is done for now. We will send Master Roper, the Prince's heraldic authority, to discuss devices and their symbolic relevance with you and your fellow new knights. Once you have chosen, we can discuss them this evening when you have had time to decide. If my lord, the Prince approves them, they can be drawn up tonight to be included in your credentials.'

'Thank you, my Lord,' a relieved Will replied. His legs were now fully

recovered but weariness was beginning to overwhelm him, and he was glad to be dismissed, but it would have been disrespectful not to watch Arthur and the others receive their honours.

Chapter Two

Following Will's short and, for him, bewildering ceremony, the Earl of Salisbury gestured to him that he should move to one side of the circle to allow the Prince to perform the same procedure for the other three archers who had been awaiting their turn. He would have preferred to be alone, and needed to rest, but forced one foot in front of the other to take his place at the edge of the crowd while his three fellow archers went through the same procedure he had experienced.

Watching them he understood his fatigue was not unique; the strain showed clearly on the faces of all three. He looked at the Prince. He too, seemed pale and drawn, his smile genuine, but forced. Will, too exhausted, too battle-weary, too familiar with seeing wounded and dog-tired men, was relieved to still be alive, but filled with guilt that others who stood beside him in the lines had died and he had survived another day. Until then he had barely noticed the condition of those surrounding him, but now as he looked around, he saw the cut faces where permanent scars would be reminders of this day, bruises, blood stained clothes, bound heads, crutches, makeshift stretchers and many of those who stood in the circle had been helped to walk, or were being supported by others. He shook his head and wondered how many were still lying on the battlefield unable to ever join their fellow warriors again?

Archers were positioned at a distance from the enemy and, from the lines, rarely saw their faces, and were detached from the men at whom their arrows were intended to either kill, or at least put out of action.

On this day, the enemy had succeeded in breaking through the English ranks forcing the archers to defend themselves in hand to hand combat or run for their lives. Will had fought bravely for a while, striking out with his sturdy yew bow, and then had seen his opportunity to run but had found himself close to a group of English fighters surrounded by French and recognised the black armour and insignia of the Black Prince, the man who inspired the love and loyalty of his men, and Will could not desert him. The Prince stumbled and a French soldier was on him. Without hesitation, Will fired an arrow just as the Frenchman raised his arm exposing the gap in his armour; Will's arrow flew straight into the vulnerable spot and pierced the side of the man's chest killing him instantly.

At that point, more English soldiers burst through the small contingent of French fighters and put them to flight, capturing some in the process. The Prince and the remaining English close to him were safe and the battle was won.

The sudden thankfulness of being alive lifted Will's spirits; although his body might ache like the devil, if truth be told, he was one of the fortunate ones, he was unhurt and, now this battle was over, in a day or so he would feel better. There were those who lived but would be maimed for life; there were many who would never rise from the ground where they now lay. He smiled as the now *Sir* Arthur rose and was directed to stand beside Will. The third archer was beckoned forward for his investiture.

'Who knew we would survive this day and have this at the end,' Arthur said quietly as he joined Will.

Will leaned closer, keeping his voice low, 'There was never a day that I expected to see the end of since I joined the Earl's company. It seems fortune has smiled on us, my friend.'

Chapter Three

Dark ominous clouds and plumes of smoke rising upward, meant the waning sun struggled to break through the haze, creating an eerie early twilight to the hillside camp, and Will shivered as he, the bear-like Welshman Arthur Burnel and the other two new knights - who Will had finally discovered were Robin (now Sir Robert) Swinford and Hugh Armstrong - followed behind the young page, who was smartly dressed in the Earl of Salisbury's red and white uniform bearing the coat of arms on the right side of his chest. It consisted of four squares in the centre of a blue garter which was topped by a crown. Two of the squares showed the three joined armoured legs of the Isle of Man on a red setting, and the other two had red elongated diamond shapes, called lozenges, on a white background. Arthur looked tense and Will thought he was probably anxious about mingling with the nobility.

'You seem a little nervous, Arthur?'

Arthur pulled a face. 'I was brought up by my uncle, an educated man who taught me to read and write, hired a music teacher...I can play the lute, the recorder and the viol, I can count, I can tell you which stars are in the sky tonight and I can...'

'Then what are you doing here as an ordinary archer?' Will broke in. 'You are more educated than most of us, and I wager more than some of the lords we are to sup with tonight, so why are you worried?'

Arthur chuckled. 'Because, he never got around to teaching me courtly manners and I have no idea how to behave in such company.'

'I would not concern yourself with that, Sir Arthur.' The page had

overheard their conversation and decided to offer Arthur some advice. 'You are on the battlefield amongst soldiers of all ranks and our leaders have little care for how you conduct yourself at the table. What is more important is that you are careful of what you say. It would not do to upset any of the nobles. Some of the barons can be...prickly, and when wine and ale are flowing, tempers can fray. I would avoid too much strong drink if you can. It may help you guard your tongue and avoid trouble.'

Arthur smiled at the wise words from one so young who had obviously seen some bad behaviour from drunken noblemen.

'What is your name, lad?' Will asked.

'Thomas Granville, Sir.'

Will looked down at the page. He had not thought about it before but, in the light of the open fires and flaming torches, he became aware that this was just a young boy, probably no older than twelve or thirteen-years-old. Within a year or so, he would continue his training and move on to weaponry and combat. Soon this polite and gentle little person would take on a fighting role with his lord. Will's heart sank at the thought, but he said nothing. It was not his place. He knew Thomas was already aware of the future mapped out for him. But there was always the possibility that perhaps the wars would be over by the time Thomas would need to use weapons in battle, and there would be no need for him to experience the horrors of the battlefield.

The narrow lanes between the closely packed damp and dirty tents were still strewn with wounded or sick men lying uncared for on the cold dank ground; they were likely to die soon so no-one bothered tending to them, it would be a wasted effort. A small team of soldiers would patrol the lanes later that night and the dead would not be found there come sunrise.

Those who could survive were being nursed by wives or daughters who had followed husbands and fathers to the battlefields, or by some of the few soldiers who had experience and skill with treating wounds and cared enough to try. Most of those who were unhurt sat exhausted, trying to forget what they had seen and done by resting or eating or downing strong ale. A few played dice games or cleaned weapons. A young lad Will thought he recognised as the son of an archer who had stood near him on the battle-lines, threw a stick for one of the countless camp dogs to fetch, and

fed him small pieces of meat when he returned with it. He smiled at the clear affection the boy and the dog had for each other; both needing the warm companionship they gave each other. The dog had clearly attached itself to a human who would feed it, play with it, rather than throw stones at it to make it go away. Will could not see the boy's father and wondered whether he had survived the day.

Passing by open fires where stews and soups simmered in blackened pots suspended from metal frames, flatbreads baked on stones, and the smell of strong ale made Will feel hungry, but it was as they approached the Prince's grand pavilion that the appetising aroma of roasting pig rotating on a metal spit made his mouth water. At either end of the spit young boys turned the handles so the meat was evenly cooked on all sides. Soon, he and his fellow knights, would help themselves to slices of the meat to be eaten with flatbreads and washed down with ale and cider or whatever else they had been able to find in local houses and farms.

The sun was setting, the temperature had dropped but the fires warmed the company of soldiers and camp followers; having been the victors and survived the day, the mood was carefree, and spirits were lifted.

A rowdy crowd had gathered around the fire, chatting and laughing while waiting their turn to eat. This battle was over. They had won in spite of the enemy force being at least five times their size - it could even have been double that. The Black Prince and his Army should have been overwhelmed by sheer numbers, but they prevailed due to clever positioning on the higher ground above the French army where the longbow men carried the day. They would celebrate long into the night. On this night they loved their leader, their Prince. More battles were still to come, but not yet. For a few days they could sleep, eat, relax. Now there was plenty of food and drink for all and they were happy. Their dead were forgotten. They would not think of death that night, and Will understood.

The spear-wielding guards, wearing the badge of the Prince of Wales, on their uniforms, stood on either side of the entrance to the Prince's spacious and colourful pavilion. They eyed the group suspiciously as they approached, clearly ready to challenge anyone getting too close to their lord.

Will leaned in towards the page. 'Are we to be prevented from

entering?'

The page nodded. 'Yes, Sir William, but it is their duty to do so, so do not concern yourself. They will allow us to enter. It is just a formality.'

The long metal weapons had spiteful, pointed tips and, as the page walked up to the entrance, the guards stood to formal attention and reached out to bar the way by crossing their spears.

'Move aside,' ordered the page. 'These good knights are here by invitation of his Lordship, the Prince.'

The door flap of the pavilion was roughly pushed aside, and the Earl of Salisbury peered out. 'Put aside your weapons!' He commanded the guards and they quickly returned to their former position. 'Come inside,' said the Earl. 'His Lordship is waiting for you.' He turned to the page. 'Your duty is done for today. Thomas. You have leave to go and get your supper. We shall not need you again this night.'

'Thank you, Sire.' The page bowed and turned to go.

'Thank you,' Will whispered as Thomas made to leave.

'You are a knight, Sir William. I was just carrying out my orders. You do not have to thank me.' Thomas smiled and ran off looking like a young boy told to run off and play.

Later when the meal was over, Will took the opportunity of speaking to Arthur quietly where they were unlikely to be overheard.

'So, your thoughts on table manners now?'

'With what I have seen tonight,' Arthur laughed, 'from those who are supposed to be our betters, I am quite happy with my own table manners, thank you, Sir William.'

'William. A word, if you please.' The Prince beckoned for Will to join him.

'I wonder what he wants you for,' Arthur gave a puzzled frown.

'I will find out very soon.'

The Prince smiled as Will drew near. 'My Lord?'

'Come with me, William. I have something for you,' said the Prince, putting his arm around Will's shoulder and guiding him towards a corner at the back of the tent that was curtained off from the main room where the celebration was becoming noisier with each cup of wine, cider or ale guzzled.

In the centre of this small and more secluded chamber, stood a small,

square wooden table with two brown leather-topped stools on either side. Upon the table were two lit oil lamps, a simple wooden tray with two carved wooden goblets and a brown earthenware jug of red wine. Against the back wall was a small bed at the foot of which were, what Will took to be the Prince's two travelling chests which would contain a few items of clothing, and other personal belongings. One of the chests had nothing placed on the lid. Will knew this would be the more used one of the two. On top of the other chest were goblets, two more oil lamps, both unlit, a platter containing a half-eaten loaf of bread, a highly polished silver tray and three unrolled scrolls, their red ribbon ties laying unwanted, the wax seals broken. Will supposed these were messages received by the Prince from England.

The Prince picked up a goblet from the wooden table, poured wine into it and handed it to Will indicating that he should take a seat on one of the stools.

With the wine and ale that had been flowing throughout the meal, many of the nobles were already drunk and their celebrations, following their victory earlier, had become increasingly loud. Even the Earl of Salisbury and John de Vere, the Earl of Oxford, had been leaning against each other in a corner of the main tent, singing humorous songs; but now as they became more drunk, they began singing ballads about leaving loved ones behind and melancholy was setting in. Will thought he heard Arthur's deep baritone voice blending in with the pair of Earls and hoped Arthur would be up to travelling the next day. The last time Will had seen him he certainly looked the worse for ale.

The Prince smiled, poured himself some wine and sat opposite Will. 'They'll be asleep on the floor soon, but at least their singing, and the others talking at the top of their voices, will mask what I have to say to you.'

Will wrapped both his hands around the stem of the goblet and looked down as he raised it to sip some of the wine. It gave him something to do while he wondered what was coming his way.

'Yes, my Lord?'

'I believe the Earl has given you a large property with a lake, woodland and a baronial great hall but he cannot confirm what condition the house is in.'

Will looked up at the Prince. 'So I understand but I'm sure I can make it suitable to live in even if it takes me a while to do so.'

'I owe you a considerable debt and I wish to ensure that you have what you need to make the house habitable...comfortable, and that you have the funds to buy whatever materials you need, and you will have to pay builders and anyone else necessary to carry out the work needed in the house and on the land.'

Will was about to interrupt but the Prince raised his hand to silence him.

'Please, just hear me out.' The Prince stood and paced up and down the few feet of the floor within the chamber, then went to one of the wooden trunks, opened the lid and took out something Will could not see.

'I will ask the Earl to have his Steward visit you soon after you arrive at Winterne. He oversees all the Earl's properties but mainly stays at the manor at Donyatt where the Earl was born. It is only a journey of some thirty miles and therefore not too onerous. He will report to the Earl on the condition of the property and what is required to provide a suitable home for a knight and a...hero.' He walked back and sat down again then spoke so quietly it was difficult for Will to hear over an argument that was now beginning to flare up in the room beyond, and the loud but monotonous singing still coming from the two Earls as they repeated the same verse over and over again of a song they had sung at least six times.

'My Lord, I'm grateful for everythin' you've done but you don't have to do any more.'

'Ah but I do. You see I have to be seen in battle to be a figurehead. If I am seen to fall my followers would lose heart and, I did fall, but fortunately my guardian angel was watching over me, and sent you to save me in time to prevent many seeing. So you see you have done more for me and your fellow soldiers than you know. So, I do owe you. I want you to have a wife...you're not already married, are you?'

Will blushed: 'No, Sire.'

'Good, then we have time to get you settled in your new surroundings before you do find someone suitable.' He stopped for a moment, looking thoughtful. 'You know, it may be that the Earl of Salisbury may know of someone suitable...'

'Oh no, my Lord.' Will wanted to choose his own bride when the time came. The nobility married for wealth, land even to keep the peace

between enemies sometimes, but rarely for love and Will wanted a caring relationship with the woman he married; after all, it was for life. 'His Lordship and you, Sire, have done more than enough for me already...and I thank you both with all my heart, but...well, to be honest, I think that's something I would rather arrange for myself, with your leave, of course.'

The Prince chuckled. 'Yes, of course, Will. Perhaps we should not interfere in that side of your life. Now, you have your army pay which should be enough to get you back to England and to Winterne with perhaps a little left over but, here, take these.' He handed Will twelve pouches of a thick cloth, tied at the top with leather bindings. 'There is enough gold coin, nobles, to for you to pay for the materials and labour the Earl's steward feels are appropriate. He has a wealth of experience in these matters I am told. After that we will have a better idea of what more you need to make Winterne Manor a home fit for you and your future family.'

Will stared up at the Prince in astonishment. No-one had ever done anything like that for him and now this promise of a better life had come from a member of the Royal Family, the heir to the throne of England. Will was speechless.

'Do you have any family? How long have you served in my Lord Salisbury's troops?'

'I've been away for about five years now, Sire. I was a little over fifteen years old when I was called to join the levy. It was only to be for a short while but, during training I found I had some skill with a bow...'

'Ha! You certainly do if the shot you made that saved me was anything to go by.'

Will smiled. 'I trained as an archer and came out here with my brother, Albert. He died at Carcassonne last year.'

'I'm sorry to hear that,' said the Prince looking down into his goblet of wine. He paused, stood and seemed to be remembering. 'That was a sad day, a failure on our part...' he turned back to look down at Will, 'on my part...I had not anticipated so much resistance. Even though we took the lower part of the town, it was a disaster and I regret the loss of your brother and, of course, the other men who lost their lives there. Do you have any other brothers?'

'No, there was just me and Albert.'

'What about your parents?'

'Father died when I was ten and Albert was twelve and, since then Ma's been on her own. I don't know whether she's still alive either. My father was a blacksmith in our village of Westbury and we managed quite well. Albert had been father's apprentice and took over the smithy when our father died, but then we both answered the call to arms. The last I heard my mother was still living in the cottage attached to the smithy with Albert's wife, Agnes, and their children, but I have no knowledge of whether they still live or what happened to the smithy.'

The Prince stood and poured himself some more wine. 'Then I am happy to be sending you home. I hope your mother and sister-in-law are still well and able to welcome you home. But I brought you in here as I wanted to avoid prying eyes seeing me give you those pouches, and hear our conversation. Between you and me, the Earl of Salisbury is not as drunk as he sounds. We would usually make merry after a victory and what is going on out there is expected of us. He is doing me a favour by making sure they're all so drunk they will not notice we have left them or, if they do, will not recall it in the morning when they wake. I want no-one to know you have those coins, otherwise you will not have them by the time you are five miles down the road tomorrow. You may not even have your life. Hide them about your person before you leave this chamber and tell no-one what you have. I would not have your life in danger for trying to help you.'

'I understand, Sire.'

Chapter Four

The following morning Will was awoken early by a yawning Thomas Granville looking as though he had just dragged himself out of bed. 'His Lordship asks if you would like to break your fast with him before your journey, Sir William.'

Will had not yet become used to his new title and looked around to see who the young page was talking to. Then he remembered. He rubbed the sleep from his eyes, stretched, ran his hands through his messy bed-head hair, and instantly wished he had kept his head firmly on his small pillow. 'I must have had more wine than I thought.'

Thomas laughed. 'Perhaps you should stick to ale...next time.'

A cool, damp breeze blew through the opening flaps of the tent making Will shiver and he pulled his cloak, which he had used as a blanket, tighter around his neck and shoulders.

'Are you not cold, lad?'

'No, Sir William. My mother gave me two sheep's wool singlets before we left England. On cold days I wear one beneath my tunic, and so I am warmly dressed.'

'Huh! Next time, he says! But I suppose I must get out of my bed. Help me sit up please...oh, and there won't be a next time.' Thomas held his hand out to help pull the swaying Will to his feet, and held on until he seemed able to stand on his own.

'There is a jug of water and bowl on the table for you to wash, Sir William,' Thomas said with a sly grin.

Will looked up at the page under narrowed eyelids and gave a half

smile. 'I am delighted to give you something to smirk at my young friend, but I would stop now if I were you before that jug of water ends up over your own head.'

'Of course, *Sir* William. I would not like to cause offence,' Thomas replied with a chuckle he could no longer keep in.

Will stood, waited a moment until his head stopped spinning, then slowly walked towards the table gently pushing Thomas out of his way. With his head over the bowl, Will picked up the jug and poured some of the water over his aching head. Thomas threw a rough linen cloth over Will's head.

'And you can stop that!'

'Stop what, Sir William?' Thomas asked, trying not to laugh.

'Even from under this cloth, I can sense your amusement at my expense.'

That proved to be too much for Thomas and he finally gave up trying to contain his amusement and a moment later, after giving up trying to dry his hair, Will threw down the cloth and joined in the laughter until he remembered the question he had for Thomas.

'Do we know where Arthur is, I see he's not here?'

'Um, yes...we do know where he is...and you might find this even more amusing. One of the stable boys found him snoring and huddled up in the hay in one of the pavilions where the wagon horses are sheltered. I believe he's still there now. Apparently, they tried to wake him but with no success.'

Will reached into his bag and pulled out a clean tunic and breeches. 'He is still breathing I take it?'

'Well judging by the continued and very loud snoring, I would say so.'

Will chuckled as he pulled on his clean tunic over his head. 'I suppose *he'll* be there for this breakfast.'

'Who will be there, Sir William?'

As Will's head appeared through the neck of his tunic he frowned at Thomas. 'Firstly, I would be grateful if you would just call me Will while we are without company. I am a simple archer and unused to the title and, secondly, I meant the Prince.'

Thomas shook his head. 'I believe Sir...Will,' he looked a little discomfited at not using Will's title, and was obviously ill-at-ease at the lack

of respect being shown to a knight, no matter how newly invested, or that he was not from a highborn background.

Will smiled and laid his hand on the boy's shoulder. 'You'll get used to it. You'll need to if the Prince is going to continue his practice of knighting people like me on the battlefield.'

Thomas nodded as he bustled about collecting Will's belongings together. 'Yes, that's true and I hope they are all as friendly as yourself, Arthur and the other two new knights, but, no the Prince will not be there. I heard he will be in Council with his commanders discussing the ransoms to be demanded for some of the captured French nobles.'

'Were there many?'

Thomas nodded vigorously. 'Oh yes. It was so thrilling.' His eyes shone with excitement. 'To quote his Lordship, "There's enough of them to make things interesting and swell the English coffers." There was the French King himself, King John II, his youngest son, Philippe, the Comte de Toulouse, Comte de Rouen, the Duke of Burgundy, the King's youngest brother, Prince Henri, Lord John of Artois was wounded...I'm not sure how badly...then there was the Comte de Ponthieu, Louis the Comte de Etampes, the Archbishop of Melun and many others who are still alive. Then, let me think...who was it died ...oh, yes, the Duke de Bourbon, the Constable of France and the Marshal of France...yes, that's right, they were killed in the battle.'

Will's eyebrows rose higher as Thomas's list grew longer, and when he had finished naming everyone he could recall, Will shook his head and said: 'I had no notion the French were so heavily defeated. Of course, I was aware we had a solid victory but so many nobles...I think it unlikely they will ever rally again after this.'

'Of course, my Lord, the Prince, is delighted with the capture of so many high-ranking French nobles, but I believe this meeting will be cut short. I fear he did not look at all well this morning.'

'Too much wine?' Will smirked.

'Oh no, Sir William. Nothing like that!' Thomas, bending down to pick up a goblet from the floor, jerked upwards with an indignant expression. His eyes narrowed and Will could see that unwittingly he had clearly offended the boy with his casual remark. 'Were you not aware that His Grace has been unwell for some time?'

'No. I had heard nothing of it. What ails him?'

Thomas's animosity vanished as quickly as it had appeared. 'He contracted a condition that affects him from time to time and these episodes drain him of his strength...'

'But he was on the battlefield yesterday...he fought...'

'That is not unusual,' Thomas interrupted, 'but you may not have needed to save him if he had been in full health. It was his ailment returning that made him weaker than he would normally have been. We are now aware of the signs that another bout is threatening.

'Why did no-one try to stop him. It was only by good fortune that I was in the right place at the right time or he could have died there.' Will sat on the bed and stared at Thomas, scarcely believing what he was hearing. 'Why in God's name would the Earl of Salisbury have not stopped him?'

Thomas shook his head and sat down on the bed. 'You do not understand. You only met him a few hours ago, and you have come to admire him from a distance over the years. You see him, as many others do, powerful and splendid, but we who are closer to him see the truth he tries to hide from the men who fight for him. When the malady is upon him his friends try to make him rest...but he will listen to no-one...not unless the fever has taken him so badly he is unable to stand. Only then can we put him to bed until it passes, and he is stronger.' Thomas stood and walked to the tent entrance. He opened the flap and looked around, then turned back to Will. 'I wanted to make certain no-one was listening. It does not do to discuss this openly, but I felt you should understand to prevent you saying something...unknowingly.' With one last look around outside, Thomas returned to where Will was still sitting. 'Of course, there are times when, he may be too weak to fight, but not weak enough to be forced to take to his bed and, on those occasions, he will mount his horse and ensure the men see him. He inspires loyalty and courage.'

'I'll not speak to anyone about what you have told me, Thomas. I respect that you have spoken in confidence but thank you for telling me. Is it likely this condition will end his life?'

'As pages, unless our Lords speak to us directly, they tend to forget about us and we become invisible; servants hear nothing, see nothing, as far as our masters believe. But we do hear, and we do see and, yes, it is understood, although not discussed openly, that the Prince may not be with us for many more years.'

Will got to his feet and gravely said: 'It grieves me to hear that, I have a great liking for him, but I believe His Lordship, the Earl is waiting, and should not remain hungry any longer. Please understand though, that I am not making light of what you have told me, but time is rushing by and perhaps we had better get finished here.' Will laced his leather jerkin and tried to forget about his hammering headache.

Thomas, meanwhile, gathered Will's few belongings together on the bed, folded them carefully, wrapped them in a sheet and tied the four corners in a neat knot. While he was getting everything prepared for Will's departure, something was nagging at the back of Will's still fogged mind; there was something Thomas should not find, but what was it? Will looked around the tent searching for something to nudge his memory. Then he remembered. The coins the Prince had warned him to keep secret from everyone. For one gut-wrenching moment he could not recall what he had done with them, but then slowly the 'fog' lifted, and he realised he had not been as drunk as he thought, no matter how badly he felt this morning. He remembered hiding the coins, still in their pouch, in his boots which were under his canvas cot bed.

'Thomas, I am feeling better for the wash, but I have a dry mouth and throat this morning. Could you find me a cup of ale, please? Then I will be ready to join his Lordship to break our fast.'

'Of course, Sir...Will.' He almost forgot. 'I'll just be a moment.'

As soon as Thomas departed, Will pulled his boots out from under the bed, retrieved the coins and stowed them quickly in the pockets of his tunic and breeches. He had just pulled on his boots when Thomas returned with a leather tankard full, almost to the brim, with foaming ale. Will thanked him and began drinking, without stopping for breath, until the tankard was empty.

'You certainly were thirsty,' Thomas said. 'Would you like me to fetch you another?'

Will shook his head. 'No, thank you. That was enough and now I am ready to meet with the Earl. Lead the way, Thomas.'

Chapter Five

At one side of the Earl's cone-shaped pavilion, they passed a wooden trestle table upon which stood a metal-barred wickerwork cage that appeared to judder and Will saw something move inside. He stepped closer and was intrigued to see two pairs of orange-coloured eyes staring back at him. He had seen many pigeons before, scavenging for food, in a pie but never in a cage.

Thomas joined him. Will jokingly pointed towards the birds and asked: 'Is the Earl giving us pigeon pie for breakfast?'

The page laughed and shook his head. 'No, Sir William. They have a very different use and are far too valuable to eat, but come, my Lord awaits.'

Before Will could ask further, one of the Earl's sentries pulled back the door flap inviting him inside where he found the Earl sitting at a long table opposite two quite grandly-dressed men who stared rudely at Will, looking down their long noses in evident disdain.

'Ah, William, you join us at last,' said the Earl as he beckoned Will to join him at the long table set out with breads, apples, pears and various types of meats and cheeses. 'Come, sit with me.' He indicated a place beside him on the bench. Typically clean-shaven and his bushy mid-brown hair neatly styled, Will was surprised to see the tired-looking Earl had dark circles under his eyes and a growth of dark stubble about his face, and his hair looked as though it had not seen a comb for days. Had the Earl had been too busy with the Prince to attend to his own grooming? Had he been awake all night?

Will walked warily towards the table. Something in the way the two grandly dressed noblemen threw him hostile looks unnerved him, but the Earl beckoned him forward with a warmly welcoming smile, so he made his way to the table avoiding looking at either of the clearly vexed lords. The Earl turned towards them and said: 'Very well, gentlemen, we have concluded our discussions and I would speak alone with Sir William...you have my leave to go.'

Both lords rose to go. Will heard one of them grunt as he stood up, but he refused to look at Will. His comrade, however, made no pretence of his animosity and dislike of Will's presence as he glared down at him. At the entrance of the tent, they both turned to bow to the Earl and were about to exit, then the shorter one turned, stared at Will and spat on the floor, just as Sir Robert Swinford and Sir Hugh Armstrong entered and brushed passed the disagreeable courtier.

The Earl stood, and glared at them. Incensed. 'These men have been honoured by Prince Edward for their courage, so who are you to question his actions?' He indicated the astounded Will, Robin and Arthur. 'In fact I recall seeing little of either of you on the field of battle yesterday! Get out, Willoughby!' The Earl commanded. 'And do not show your face in my presence again today.'

'My Lord.' Willoughby knew better than to argue with the Earl. He bowed, pushed his companion out ahead of him and backed out.

'I must ask you all for your forgiveness of Lord Willoughby. Sadly, some of our nobles do not hold with the knighting of ordinary soldiers. There is an arrogance amongst many of our lords,' he smiled, 'especially from those whose titles were only bestowed one or two generations ago, so are somewhat new. Please, take no notice. They will not bother you again – they would not dare now they are aware of my displeasure – and you will be leaving us soon. I presume none of you have eaten anything as yet?'

The three knights shook their heads. 'No, my Lord.' They echoed each other.

'Good, that's good. So let us eat.'

'My Lord, we know nothing about our travel arrangements,' said Sir Robert.

'Ah, yes. I was going to tell you...but first help yourselves to whatever takes your fancy. There should be enough variety for all. There is ale in the jugs, but no wine. Ale is a better drink at breakfast and, by the look of all three of you, there was probably a little too much wine drinking last night.'

'Is Arthur not joining us, my Lord?'

The Earl smiled. 'I believe Sir Arthur is still sleeping somewhere,' he laughed, 'but we will have him join you before you leave. Now, you were asking about your travel arrangements but please enjoy your meal while I explain.'

Will filled his plate with slices of cold beef and lamb, a large chunk of cheese, then tore off a hunk of bread and half-filled a goblet with ale. The Earl waited for Robert and Hugh to select their choices and take their seat at the table, then he said: 'Firstly, you should know you will have an escort of forty guards.'

'*Forty guards!*' said Robin. 'But why, your Lordship? Surely there is no need to guard us that heavily.'

The Earl stood and walked over to one of the large wooden trunks and opened the lid. 'Inside this trunk are a number of treasures which the Prince would have returned to England for safe-keeping. The guards are for that reason, not to guard you. It just seems wise that you all travel together. Although we have re-taken a large expanse of France from the French and won a resounding victory, the roads may not be secure. Brigands, possibly deserting soldiers from both armies are likely to be anywhere along your road. With an escort of trained and well-armed guards, it is unlikely any roving band of robbers or cut-throats will think about making an attack.'

The three new knights looked at each other and nodded. Will asked: 'My Lord, where will we sail from?'

'You will travel to Honfleur where I have a ship that will take you to Newhaven. It would be customary for you to embark at Calais, but my cog...' He noticed the puzzled look that passed between the three listeners. 'That's a type of ship,' he explained. 'She's single-masted ship with upper decks at the prow and aft and can carry a considerable load. She is named the *Somerset* and is moored at Honfleur which is nearer than Calais. Although your sea journey will be longer, your road journey will be shorter, and the ship is idling in the harbour. It had been my intention to join you but, with the Prince unwell at present, I am unable to leave my post. Take this letter and give it to the ship's Master. I have already sent him a message to inform to look out for you. He is Master Walter Smith, a somewhat cheerless man, but he knows the sea and how to handle a ship and crew. When you arrive at Honfleur, half the escort party will sail with you to Newhaven before taking the wagons on to London, and those who wish to do so may continue with them.' He turned to Hugh. 'I anticipate this applies more to you, Sir Hugh. You will have a longer journey than your friends here, all the way back to Nottinghamshire. I would recommend you find a group of travellers to join for the sake of safety when you leave London.'

'I will, my Lord. Thank you.' Hugh nodded.

'And depending on their route, my Lord, it would possibly be wise for me to stay with them for part of the journey as my home is in Kent,' said Robin.

'Indeed it would, Sir Robert,' the Earl agreed. 'When you have disembarked and the wagons are unloaded, the ship will be re-provisioned and return to Honfleur to await my orders.

'I am optimistic that, by the time the *Somerset* returns, the Prince will have recovered his usual good health and, perhaps then, I can visit my family for a while and inspect my lands which I trust will not have suffered for my absence.' He handed a rolled parchment to Will sealed by red wax and indented with the Salisbury family crest. Will thanked him and tucked it inside his jerkin for safe-keeping.

The Earl continued speaking. 'I have an excellent steward who takes care of my property and business matters. Now, that letter will confirm your credentials and should be handed to Walter Smith. We estimate your journey to Honfleur will take around two weeks, depending on incidents, weather and hopefully no accidents, and you will be given provisions for the journey. Anything else, for instance fresh meat or fish, will have to be found along the way.' The Earl walked back to the table and sat down beside Will again. 'You will be provided with tents, bedding and any other necessities such as we can spare but, thankfully, with the battles being over, for the time being anyway, we should…hopefully, be able to supply you adequately.' He took a gulp of ale. 'One thing I must impress on you though,' he held out his fisted hand and pointed at them all in turn, 'is that you must not discuss the shipment with anyone. We cannot afford for word to get out amongst the company. We would have more men deserting just to get their hands on these riches, and I am trusting you with the confidentiality of this information.'

'But surely, my Lord, the escort will have been told what they are guarding,' said Hugh.

The Earl leaned forward, planting his elbows on the table. He looked at Hugh. 'They have been told nothing more than they are escorting yourselves, and some...personal items belonging to the Prince that, now the worst is over, he no longer needs.'

'Forgive me, my Lord,' Hugh persisted, 'but won't it appear that there may be something more...valuable...with that large a company.'

The Earl shook his head. 'You must remember, some of these men have been with us for years. They are tired, jaded, battle weary. Many have families at home and have no knowledge of how they fare. They are ready to go home and will be so relieved to return, that it is likely they will think of little else other than boarding that ship and seeing the white cliffs again. We estimate you can travel via Le Mans, at between sixteen to twenty miles per day. You will have the wagons to haul, which will slow your progress and it would take longer if you are attacked, but possibly less if your escort hurries you along in their haste to leave France,' he chuckled.

'Well, I at least, will feel safe travelling through unsafe country with such a large company,' said Robert.

The sound of rattling weapons, shouts and the whinnying of horses, which earlier had been in the distance became louder. Hugh walked to the entrance, opened the tent flap and looked out. 'It seems our escort has come to collect us.'

'What about Arthur?' Will asked. 'Can you see him?'

Hugh laughed. 'Yes. I can see him. He's snoring on the back of a hay covered wagon. He seems comfortable enough.'

The Earl said: 'Then, if you have finished your meal, I suggest you make final preparations for your journey. I believe they will want to leave within the next hour.'

The three men thanked the Earl for his kindness and generosity but, just as they were about to depart, Will asked: 'Your Lordship, will it be possible to say our farewells to the Prince?'

The Earl looked down at the ground, then back at Will. 'I think not, Sir William, he is...in conference.'

Will knew from his conversation with Thomas earlier, that this was probably untrue. 'That's a pity, my Lord, I would have liked to thank him for his kindness to us all.'

'I will pass your message on.'

'Thank you. I am grateful.' Will turned to go and was outside the tent when the Earl called him back. 'Will, stay a moment please.' He looked over at where Robert and Hugh stood waiting for Will. 'Carry on gentlemen, please. William will join you momentarily, but I wish to speak to him about Winterne first.'

Robert nodded, but a puzzled expression flickered across Hugh's face and then was gone as quickly as it appeared. He hesitated a moment before following Robin outside.

'I needed to speak to you alone. Unfortunately, Willoughby and Berkeley stayed over-long and your fellow knights arrived before I had the opportunity.'

Will wondered what was coming. 'And my lateness did not help...'

The Earl smiled. '...No. Indeed. But I believe we can forgive that...under the circumstances. But we have little time, so to business. Take a seat again.' He indicated that Will should sit opposite him. 'The Prince informed me...in confidence of course...of the...um...reward he has given you for your service to him, and that he has advised you to speak to no-one of it. That is wise counsel, but I would also add some comments of my own to his. Will...Sir William Hallett, you will have need of at least one good friend when you begin your life at Winterne and, although at present he would not seem to be the best of companions, I would suggest Arthur Burnel. He is strong, amenable, reliable...usually,' he gave a little chuckle, 'moreover, he is educated and generally experienced in many aspects, but most of all he has no family ties and will need somewhere to call home. He does not have the...um...donation the Prince gave you for Winterne Manor, and will be seeking good employment, even though he be a knight. We have many impoverished knights who are willing to sell their weaponry skill and other talents for the right...um...employer. Although you barely know each other, Burnel had already formed a good opinion of you. He spoke highly of you to me while you were with the Prince yesterday, and he seems amiable enough.'

Will said nothing while he thought about the Earl's suggestion without answering. His silence surprised the Earl.

'Do I take it you disapprove of my suggestion?'

'Oh no, my Lord, I believe it may well be a good suggestion, for both Arthur and myself, but I had expected we would all go our separate ways when we arrive back in England, and had not really considered asking him about his future plans, but may I ask what will happen to Robin and Hugh?'

The Earl stood and walked over to a small trestle table, poured some ale from a jug into an earthenware goblet then pointed to the vessel Will had used earlier, held the jug over it and looked questioningly at Will.

'No thank you, my Lord. I have had enough for now.'

Taking a mouthful of ale, the Earl swallowed and sat down again. 'They both have homes and families to return to, but Robin...Sir Robert, is the older of you all at two and thirty years and, unlike the rest of you, is a family man. He is also a craftsman fletcher, his arrows are strong, straight and they fly true. Although we have our victories, this war is not won entirely, and the fight will likely continue for many more years. Robin can employ apprentices to train others in his skill, he will then make a good living and, he has a farm, with a considerable amount of land in Kent, although it is not alike to Winterne Manor, of course,' the Earl smiled, 'but it is probably in a better condition. I understand it is his birthplace, has fertile land and tenant farmers which will yield him a good living from rents. I believe it is those rents that have been an income for his family while he has been with us. He is a quiet man but does not lack confidence or experience, and I feel will do well on his return. With his knighthood he will also gain respect in his vicinity and more doors will open for him which will enable his business to grow. In turn, his profits will grow and he will be able to keep those three young children of his in a much better life than they have had thus far.'

'I didn't know anything of this but, of course, until yesterday I don't believe any of us had actually spoken to each other, although we had seen each other in the lines and in camp. But you make no mention of Robin's wife.'

'Ah, you are not aware then that she died giving birth to their last child, a boy I believe. The children have been cared for by his wife's mother, a widow. I understand she will stay with the family until he marries again, if he ever does.'

'And Hugh, my Lord?'

'Now Hugh is another matter entirely. He hails from the north...now where was it...begins with an B...Bi...Bli...yes, I have it...Blidworth or

Bliddorth, as he calls it...a village in the shire of Nottingham, and he wants to return. He is the son of a farmer and has family in the area. It seems the farm is quite small but, again this in in confidence, there has been a...small... financial gift which will allow him to purchase some land that adjoins his own and will increase his property. He is more than content with his plans for the future, and I believe he has a young woman waiting for him. They will be able to marry...if she is still waiting for him...and I hope she is. He can now offer her a better life than he would have hoped for as a result of his courage on the field.' The Earl drained his goblet and set it back down on the table but kept his hand wrapped around the stem. He looked back at Will who sat silently, waiting for the Earl to continue. 'Alas, his future with the lady is not confirmed. It seems her father did not approve of the match, holding the view that the Armstrong farm was too small and its income was too little. For Hugh to return with a title – making her Lady whatever-her-name-is – and as owner of a farm of significant size, should put her father well and truly in his place. He cannot object to their marriage now.'

Will laughed. 'It seems we are all destined to enjoy better times ahead.'

The Earl compressed his lips. 'Make no mistake, my friend, Winterne Manor is situated in a beautiful part of the country,' he paused and looked down at the goblet, seemingly deep in thought, 'hmm, beautiful it is...and sometimes some would call it um...mystical.' For a moment, the Earl seemed to have drifted away into a world of his own, but then he looked back at Will. 'But I digress, the manor has been empty and run down for some considerable time, It will be hard work to make it an impressive place to live again. It is habitable though...well, parts of it are.'

'Then it's a good job I will have Arthur with me, but can I ask my Lord, what did you mean by mystical?'

Again, seemingly uncomfortable with Will's question, the Earl looked away while he tried to find a way to put what he meant into words. 'It is hard to explain...there's a certain feeling about the area, nothing that is easy to define...and I assure you it is nothing malign...quite the opposite in fact...and some of this is merely gossip. You understand, of course, that the common folk can be...superstitious.' He chuckled. 'Some leave food out for the little people...little people, I ask you. How gullible some people are.' He brought his hand up to his face and cradled his chin between his thumb and forefinger. 'My Steward, Edwin Cheeseman, has said there have been occasions when he feels as though he is being watched, but not by anything that means him harm. In fact, the feeling he gleans from it is one of benefaction. It is as though he were being protected. He assures me he has no concerns about visiting the area and that residents of the village are happy to be there.'

Will listened intently. Winterne was now sounding more interesting… and puzzling.

'I hope I have not worried you,' said the Earl.

'No, my Lord. If anything I look forward to finding out about the place even more and with Arthur for company, I am sure we will manage very well.'

'From our conversation last night I suspect he may be glad of somewhere to lay his head, and to have something where he can be of use, but now you must go.' He and Will stood at the same time, the Earl took Will's arm and began guiding him towards the tent doorway. 'It sounds as if your escort team is busy with preparations for your journey to Honfleur. Let's see how they are getting on.'

Behind the row of tents opposite, they caught glimpses of the bustle of activity at the far end of the camp where a tall hedge separated the camp field from the one beyond. A number of soldiers – a combination of Welsh and English, and mainly archers – prepared for the journey. Liveried in white sleeveless tabards with the red cross of St George and the insignia of Edward, the Prince of Wales, many of their uniforms were tattered and shabby, and stained mostly with blood and dirt, but what any other soiling was, was anyone's guess.

The whinnying of excited draught horses being tethered to the wagons, rounceys and coursers being saddled, men lugging heavy goods and loading them on the open-topped wagons, told the Earl that the preparations were well underway.

Turning to Will, he said: 'I think it is unlikely we will meet again, but I give you my oath I will send Master Cheeseman to see what your requirements are at Winterne, and I hope it becomes a comfortable home for you.' He turned to re-enter the tent, 'You have my promise that, if I am ever in the area, I will visit you to see what you have done with the manor, after all it is still within my estate and…' he gave an wry smirk and wagged his finger at Will, '...I can always take it back if you fail to restore it. Or, perhaps on second thoughts, if you make it so attractive...' He laughed at the dismayed look on Will's face. 'I spoke in jest, Will. Winterne Manor is yours entirely.'

Will relaxed. 'I will not fail you, and you would be most welcome, my Lord,' Will chuckled, possibly with relief, 'but please send a messenger first to give us time to make ready for you.'

The Earl looked long and hard at what had been an English archer from a simple village family background just the day before. 'I will indeed, my boy, for that is what you are still and, even though you have been elevated to knighthood, stay the same young man you have always been. Try not to let your new position in life change the person you are, even though you will have greater responsibilities than you could ever imagine.'

Will was shocked by this speech from the Earl. He would never have expected anything that sounded so compassionate from this young, just a few years older than himself, but battle-scarred nobleman. 'I...will try to do as you say, my Lord...and thank you.'

The captain of the Earl's guard made his way across the busy traffic of soldiers and groups of camp followers to approach the Earl. 'My Lord, the escort is ready, both *Sir* Robert and *Sir* Hugh are ready,' the Earl frowned at the guard, 'and *Sir* Arthur is soundly...if not deafeningly asleep on one of the wagons.' There was sarcasm in his tone and he did not try to hide his arrogant and unkind smirk.

'Thank you, Captain.' The Earl moved closer to the guard who stood poker-straight to attention. 'I would remind you Captain, that these men have been bestowed their knighthoods for acts of valour on the battlefield, and I would have you show them respect.'

The captain gulped, looked down at his feet, shamed and embarrassed. 'I apologise if my manner caused offence, my Lord. I did not mean to insult Sir William or...'

'Yes, yes,' said the Earl, impatiently. 'Remember, had it not been for this young man here, our Prince would not be with us today. Keep that in mind in future when you address young men such as these.' He looked over at Will who seemed somewhat ill at ease at the Earl's public reproach of the captain.

'I regret any offence I may have caused, Sir William.'

'No matter, Captain.' Will smiled. 'Your apology is accepted, and I believe it is time I took my leave, my Lord.' He bowed to the Earl who nodded his approval, and was about to leave when the Earl cleared his throat. 'Hhhrrmph. I am pleased you survived to take Winterne off my hands.' He seemed a little uncomfortable at speaking about his personal feelings and Will could understand that. It was a rare thing for fighting men to show close friendship or any emotion; friends and relatives could die at any time, as Will knew very well and it didn't do to get too close to anyone.

'Right. Now get along with you. You have things to do and your companions will be waiting. You have a long road to travel before you make camp tonight.'

Will bowed and left, headed to where the escort soldiers were readying the horses for the journey. There was nothing more to say. The Earl had said it all.

Chapter Six

Outside the tent and now alone, Will took a deep breath and prepared himself to face the chaos ahead as he weaved his way between tents, to join the hustle and bustle of preparing for the journey. The lanes between tents were crowded with people scurrying about carrying out the orders of their commanders, others were using the rest time to practise archery aiming their arrows at targets on wooden boards propped up on hay bales. There was loud laughter as many of the archers, having enjoyed themselves a little too much the night before, missed the board when their aim went wide and the arrows landed in the supporting hay bales.

Behind one tent, on a clear space of the field, a group of soldiers were training with the use of wooden swords; these would not kill or maim but they could still give nasty bruising and cut skin if they landed on a bony part of the body. Will watched for a few moments as the supervising Man-at-Arms, separated the group into pairs and demonstrated what he wanted them do then stood back to watch while they tried to copy his instructions. Soon the air was filled with yelps, curses and angry shouts as wooden swords landed on much softer flesh and bone.

Will moved on, and stepped over several prone bodies of men, some cuddled up to their women, who were all noisily sleeping off last night's ale, just as Arthur was doing in the back of one of the wagons. All in all, thought Will, this morning was no different to any other after a successful battle; the only difference was that he would not be amongst his fellow archers on the following morning.

He turned away and stood back to allow a stable-hand, leading two draught-horses to go by, then found Robin and Hugh already seated in the second wagon. Before he could talk to them, a shout went up and they turned around to see, a large bay draught horse give a deep, throaty squeal – almost a roar - and rear angrily as a young stable-hand, who Will guessed was only about thirteen or fourteen years old and probably inexperienced, tried to manoeuvre him into position. The horse kicked out with his right foreleg. Stunned, the boy screamed and fell to the ground, struck on the forehead by a flying hoof, blood pouring from the injury down the ashen face. Within seconds, a crowd had gathered around the boy, and shortly after Will saw the lad being helped to a bench where an older man, who Will took to be his father, took a handkerchief from his pocket, dipped it in one of the horses drinking buckets, before dabbing the wound gently to clean it. Two older men then calmed the frightened horse by loosening his reins and talking to him softly.

Once calmed and backed into the shafts, they secured his harness to the wooden frame. Still uneasy but more settled, the horse softly snorted, blew down his nose and a few moments later he seemed quite relaxed.

When Will saw the boy a little later, he had a grubby bandage edged with yellow thread around his head that had probably been torn from a petticoat worn by one of the female camp followers. Clean dressings were rare amongst such a large army.

In total there were four large wooden wagons, each one laden with and packed with goods few people knew about. Will found Arthur in the back of the last of the four wagons, and wondered which of the four contained the Prince's 'special' items that were to be sent back to England.

'Move out the way!' Will felt himself being shoved to one side as two stable-hands struggled to lead two strings of five large horses in each. These were a mix of draught horses and mounts for the soldiers. He stood back to let them pass by and watched as they tied the animals, in fours, to the fence. These would be 'spares' used to rest tired horses who had pulled the wagons or had been ridden for long hours by the escort soldiers; walking without rider or burden would help keep them fresher during the journey. One of the stable-hands approached the serjeant. 'Sir, it is the Earl's orders that you select ten men from your party to care for one of the spare horses in addition to their own.' The serjeant nodded and said something Will could not hear, and the two stable-hands walked away.

Thomas Granville emerged from the tent in which Will had slept overnight and Will walked over to join him. He was holding the tied bundle containing Will's few clothes and personal items and, more importantly, he also had Will's treasured bow and quiver full of arrows. Will took the bundle from him.

'I left this behind when I went to the Prince's gathering last evening and somehow forgot about it. I am grateful to you for finding it for me. I would not have liked to leave without it, and I should not have been so careless. Perhaps I should take you with me to make sure I am well looked after.'

Thomas laughed. 'If my Lord ever decides to dispense with my services, I shall come to see you at Winterne Manor and ask for employment.'

Will put his arm around the boy's shoulder, 'And you would be very welcome,' he replied as they made their way through the lane now rutted by wagon wheels and horses hooves, toward the third wagon in which Arthur still snored.

The sky that had been an almost clear blue, was now threaded with puffy grey streaks and Will hoped their journey was not going to be hampered by bad weather just as they were heading out. He did not expect to have sunshine and clear skies for the entire journey; that would be very unlikely, but he hoped they could at least get a good start before the weather changed.

He and Thomas walked through the muddy lines of wagons, horses, soldiers and the throng of women, children and the ever-scrounging dogs who ran around the camp searching for scraps of food from anyone kind enough to spare something for them. At the front of the line they saw Robin and Hugh, both unused to riding horses, sitting on the front seat of one of the wagons. Both being from farming stock, they knew well how to drive horse pulled wagons.

Thomas pointed out a very tall man, not in military uniform, but wearing the badge of the Earl of Salisbury on his leather jerkin, heading in their direction with a large grey horse, and Will was surprised when he stopped in front of him and bowed.

'Sir William, my name is Edgar Hayward, and I am the of the Earl of Salisbury's stable master. His lordship requested horses for yourself and your colleagues. This is your mount.'

Will's face drained of colour as Edgar handed over the reins of a very sturdy grey horse that stood behind him. Like Robin and Hugh, Will was unused to riding. Archers walked for many miles each day, or if they were lucky they could ride on wagons, but very few were wealthy enough to own horses of their own, and there were never enough horses within the army for everyone to ride. Panic seized Will as the horse stared back at him with what he took to be a challenging glare, but not wanting to show his terror, Will wondered how he could find a way to refuse the ride. Quick-thinking Thomas sensed Will's unease and kind-heartedly came to his aid.

'Sir William,' Thomas began, 'might it not be more practical for you to follow the example of Sir Robert and Sir Hugh? Sir Arthur may not be feeling quite himself at present. You see, he sleeps soundly still in that last wagon. I am sure he will wake before long, and could share driving the wagon if you travel together.' He turned to the guard. 'Perhaps you could tie the steed to Sir William's wagon and, if he wishes he, or Sir Arthur, could ride it later.'

'That seems to be a good plan, Thomas,' said Will, gratefully. 'I can keep a watch on Arthur until he wakes and...now I think of it, it might be as well to have two more horses. We will have need of them when we reach England.' Will, on finding out they would have horses of their own, realised the journey to Honfleur would give him ample time to get in some riding practice. 'Edgar, could you bring the mount you have set aside for Arth...Sir Arthur, please. We can tether it to the wagon as well and I'm sure Sir Arthur will be grateful to you for having dealt with this on his behalf.'

'We do have a mare set aside for Sir Arthur, but as he is...unwell, I only brought yours as I was unsure what to do about the other, but certainly I will fetch the other mount directly.'

Immediately Will felt a little more reassured that there was a mare available and hoped she would have a less hostile attitude. 'Yes, thank you. We shall be departing soon and seeing the present activity amongst the troop, I believe the sooner the better. Thank you.'

Silently Will and Thomas watched Edgar as he walked back towards the wooden-fenced pen where the horses were tethered but, when Will looked around at Thomas, they both laughed at Will's obvious apprehension. 'That horse terrifies me, he's so big, Do you think Edgar noticed?'

'No. I thought you hid it very well.' Thomas smiled. 'But I must get back to my duties. It has been a great pleasure to have met you. I wish all knights were as friendly as you.'

'And I shall ever be grateful for your help...especially with regard to the horse. I have no knowledge of how good a horseman Arthur is, but I hope we both will be more at ease around the beasts when we reach England. It is a long way from Newhaven to Winterne.'

'God speed, Sir William,' said Thomas, and he walked away towards the Prince's pavilion.

'Oh, Thomas,' Will called.

Thomas turned around.

'Don't forget, if ever you need new employment, come and find me.'

Thomas laughed and waved. 'I will. Take care and good fortune.'

With Edgar and Thomas having left him on his own, Arthur dead to the world in his drunken stupor, and the escort team occupied with their own preparations, this was a perfect time to find somewhere secure for his pouches of gold coins. It would be impossible to keep them about his person, without having them noticed. By wearing his cloak, he had managed so far is keeping them hidden, but their bulk within the pockets of his tunic and breeches would he noticed before long, and to continually wear his cloak, would surely make some people suspicious. Of course he had his saddle bag, but it would be better not to have anything of value left in them; they were for belongings he could afford to lose if stolen. No, saddle bags were too insecure.

He hunkered down to inspect the underside of the wagon. If anyone did see and wondered what he was doing, he felt it would explain that he wanted to ensure the structure of the wagon was sound for a long journey, that the wheels were correctly attached, the spokes were not cracked and the metal rims were complete: a pre-travel inspection that was entirely plausible. He could then argue that he would have thought that all the wagons should have gone through a thorough final inspection.

Thankfully while he was looking, Arthur slept through. There was nothing underneath that would have been useful as a secure and safe place, but he noticed that the sides of the wagon were built of two layers of long planks with a gap between them. He stood up, lifted the wagon cover, and examined the gap between the planks. To his joy he discovered it had been filled with wool. Wondering why, he supposed might be a way of giving some kind of insulation to the wagon, preventing draughts coming through any gaps when people were sleeping onboard, and perhaps the wool and double thickness made the sides a little stronger by bulking out the wood.

Concealed by the wagon cover and the hedge behind him, Will began to pick out some of the wool and, to his relief found the gap would be just wide enough to squeeze in the pouches side by side and deep enough to be able to re-cover them with wool. He also realised that the narrow gap would stop the coins from making any jingling sounds as they moved and the wool would also muffle any noise. This could not have been any better.

The wagon swayed a little as Will climbed up onto the seat. Arthur continued snoring completely oblivious to the movement or the noise and bustle going on around him. Some of his jaw length dark brown hair had flopped over his face and his moustache still had some ale froth dried on the bristles.

A few moments later, Will saw, Edgar returning through the crowd, leading a tall chestnut horse. Her coat gleamed in the sunlight and her black mane and tail shone. She looked at Will with soft brown eyes framed by long black eyelashes and Will decided she was the one he wanted.

'Does she have a name?' he asked.

'Her name is Chataigne, Sir William. She is a French horse we took from a prisoner. He appeared to care about her...seemed quite concerned about her safety if we took her. He told us she is four years old, has always been a gentle and safe ride and that her name, in English, means Chestnut.'

'And the grey?'

'Hmm. Well apparently he is a little more...shall we say...spirited. He, too, was taken from a prisoner after we captured Narbonne.' He looked around at the large gelding with, what Will thought was admiration but then realised it was actually more like affection. 'There is very little information I can give you about him, Sir William, other than we named him after the town. We believe him to be about five or six years old. He's strong, needs good handling, but will obey when he knows his rider is master.' He patted Narbonne's neck, gently and the horse responded by nudging Edgar's hand with his nose; there was a true friendship between Edgar and this animal and Will wondered whether it was fair to take him from Edgar.

'Thank you. That's been very helpful, but would you not prefer to keep him? I can see he likes you.'

Edgar shook his head. 'Bless you, Sir William,' he stroked Narbonne's velvet ears, 'I am fond of him. We have grown quite close during the time I have been looking after him and, for that reason, I do not want him here. If he stays he will probably die in the next battle or the one after that, and I would have him away from here.' He looked at Will, pain reflected in his eyes. 'Truth be known, I would have them all away from here. They are gentle, intelligent and loyal beasts who should not be on a battlefield. No take him, Sir William, and treat him gently.'

Will looked at the horse who eyed him warily. He found it hard to believe the horse had a good nature but he nodded and said: 'Then I am happy to take him and I promise we will look after him.' Will hoped that Arthur would know what he was doing with horses, as he had made up his mind that the mare would be the one for him.

Just then a feminine cry caught their attention. They both turned to see a young woman with long raven-black hair trying to push her way through a group of seven or eight young laughing soldiers who were pestering her, deliberately getting in her way, making a grab for her cloak and the loaves of bread she was carrying. She struggled to get passed them but they circled around her teasing and humiliating, spinning her around and jostling her from one to another. At first she angrily chided them for their rudeness and tried to retain her dignity but the more they continued pestering her, the more distressed she became. The girl was almost in tears when Will jumped down from the wagon seat and pushed his way through the group, took her by the elbow, and began steering her through the group of ruffians. Their leader moved to stand in front of Will, challenging him to try and take the girl passed him. Two more came to stand on either side of him. Facing them, Will could see what they had not. Edgar had approached them quietly and without warning he grasped the right arm of the chief tormentor and twisted it behind the man's back, pulling it as high as he could without actually breaking it or disjointing the shoulder. The man yelled in pain and his companions hastily retreated to join the others. By now they had attracted a large group of spectators and Will, unused to being involved in a public display, wondered what to do next.

He need not have worried. Edgar knew exactly what to do. 'What would you like me to do with this scoundrel, Sir William?' asked Edgar, emphasising the *'Sir'* to impress on his wriggling captive that this man was no regular archer. 'Should I hand him over to the Earl?' At that the rogue's associates looked at each other, clearly aware they had overstepped the mark and mistaken Will for a just another soldier. Realising they were in danger of upsetting one of the Earl's friends, they began to slip away, one or two at a time, from their now former leader who was still squirming against Edgar's strength and groaning each time his moves caused Edgar to tighten his grip.

Will thought for a moment, 'No. I believe this was just a case of drunken high spirits and I am sure our *friend* here will apologise to the lady.'

'I will, Sir. I *will! Ow! Lemmego!'*

'Are you alright, Mistress...?' Will asked the girl, whose elbow he realised he was still holding.

She looked up at him through long-lashed dark eyes and smiled shyly. 'I am, Sir...Sir. I thank thee but now I must go. My mother is waiting for the bread.'

'Very well. I have to leave now but my friend here...' He smiled at Edgar. 'You can let him go. I do not believe he will cause the lady any more trouble and perhaps you would escort the young lady safely back to her mother.'

Edgar leaned forward and whispered very closely to the ruffian's ear. 'You can go now, lad, and Sir William may not be around, but I will. So any more trouble and you'll have me to answer to.' He released his hold and the man walked off rubbing his arm and muttering under his breath. 'Come, young lady,' he held out his arm, 'I'll escort you back to the family section of the camp. Let me carry that bread for you.'

The girl handed over her bundle of loaves and turned to Will. 'Thank you both for your kindness.' Then, without looking at Edgar she slipped her arm through his and they began to walk away. With her left hand she lifted the front of her mud-splashed long blue woollen skirt; mud and animal mess were a hazard of the camp, and it paid to keep your eyes fixed on where you were walking. Will watched them walk away, pleased that he had been able to help her, but a few paces on she looked back at Will and flashed him a warm smile, her dark eyes warm and Inviting.

Reluctantly, he waved and turned away. It was time to go. Perhaps it may have been different if he had been staying with the Earl's company, but there were numerous young men amongst the gathered crowd, and it was no surprise to see many of them stare after her admiringly as she passed through the throng. Their attraction to her very apparent, but their fear of Edgar was more obvious.

'She likes you.' Thomas had been on his way back to the Prince's pavilion when he heard the commotion and pushed his way through the crowd to see what had happened. While Will's attention had been held on watching the girl walk away with Edgar, Thomas had returned unnoticed and when Will heard him speak, he found Thomas grinning widely. 'And I take it you have a liking for her?'

The girl looked back and to her obvious disappointment, saw Will was busy talking to Thomas as he fastened the straps on his saddlebag and was no longer looking in her direction. Will glanced in her direction, just as she looked away. Yes, she was lovely and appeared to like him, although he was fully aware that might just have been because he was her rescuer. But there was no point in thinking about her, he was leaving in just a few minutes. It was a shame they had not met before. If he had been staying, it might have been different, but after taking last look, he gloomily watched her walk away.

All around him soldiers wearing black woollen chausses or leggings and chainmail shirts over which some wore red and blue quartered tabards – the primary colours of the Black Prince, while others wore quartered tabards in yellow and red – the colours of the Earl of Salisbury, were mounting. Loads on wagons were covered with waxed sheeting and fastened, and soon the column was ready to leave. A whistle blew and twenty mounted soldiers at the head of the line began to move forward, then came the wagons followed, at the end of the line, by another twenty mounted soldiers. Arthur's snoring was not interrupted by the jolt when Will urged the two wagon horses forward and, looking down at this drink-befuddled fool about whom he knew very little, Will questioned why the Earl had suggested he would be a good man to have with him at Winterne. He was still wondering about that when the column began to pick up pace and, as they passed the Earl of Salisbury's pavilion, Will was surprised to see his Lordship emerge and wave him a salute as he went by. Will, both hands on the reins, could only nod back in acknowledgement.

Chapter Seven

It was two hours later when Arthur eventually awoke, opened one bloodshot eye, closed it again, groaned and then rubbed both eyes and tried to sit up.

'Wha...what's all the noise?' Pushing himself up into a sitting position he rested his elbows on his knees and propped up his head with both hands. 'Why are we moving?' He tried to fully open his eyes but the daylight filtering through his half-closed lids hurt too much. He closed them again.

'It's good to see you're still alive,' came a voice from somewhere above him.

'Oh, it's you, Will. I think I'd rather be dead...then it wouldn't hurt,' moaned Arthur. 'Where are we going?' He propped himself up on his elbows, eyes still firmly shut. 'Stop the wagon?'

'What?'

'Stop the wagon. *Now!*'

Will pulled on the reins and the horses slowly came to a halt. Eyes now half-open, Arthur struggled to his feet, clambered down from his comfortable hay bed, half fell, half crawled over the tailboard before staggering into the bushes to vomit into the ditch. Will waved to the driver of the wagon behind to overtake them while Arthur crouched on the roadside, waiting for the spasms to end.

The two men on board the wagon laughed as they passed Arthur. Arthur gave them a rude sign. 'Too much ale, eh?' said the driver. 'He'll know better another time,' he said to Will as they went by.

After a few moments Arthur got to his feet and wiped his mouth. Will thought he looked a little like a scarecrow with his dark, hay strewn hair trailing across his sweat-beaded forehead, as he swayed, leant against the wagon until his head stopped spinning, took a few deep breaths and lurched towards where Will sat patiently waiting for him.

'Why don't you climb back on the hay and sleep off the rest of the ale?'

'Hmm. Maybe I will. I was going to join you up there, but my head feels as though a herd of horses are running through it.'

'Go. Sleep it off.' He handed Arthur a flask. 'Have some ale.' Arthur turned his head away and blanched at the thought of more ale.

'Too much may have caused your problem,' said Will, 'but a little of it might help make you feel better and it will freshen your mouth.'

Arthur took a long swig from the flask, gasped for air, and handed it back. 'Thank you my friend.' He walked the length of the wagon, stopped to give a quizzical glance at the two horses tethered to the tailboard that he had not noticed when he clambered down, then hoisted himself back into the wagon, dropped to his knees on to the hay, lay down and covered himself with his cloak pulling it right up over his face, shutting out the light. Will grinned, urged the horses to walk on and the wagon trundled forward.

'Where are we heading?' Arthur mumbled.

'To Honfleur, then a ship to Newhaven.'

'Ugh. A sea voyage. The thought of that makes me feel so much better.' He said nothing for a few moments and Will thought he had fallen asleep again. Then...

'And how do we go on from there?'

'The horses tied at the back of the wagon. They belonged to the Earl, but he gave them to us.'

'I had a terrible feeling you were going to say that.'

Will smiled. The grey, Narbonne, was the larger horse and therefore more suitable to carry the also large Arthur, but Arthur could find out later just how strong-willed Narbonne was. He was not going to let Arthur have Chataigne under any circumstances. A few moments later the rattling of the wagon was drowned out by the loud snoring of Arthur.

Although their relationship was quite amiable, during the early part of the journey Will saw little to change his mind about the wisdom of keeping Arthur with him when they reached England. Arthur had awoken after a further three hours of sleep feeling much better, although he still looked very pale, and had joined Will on the seat. The following day he took turns in driving the wagon and, when not driving, spent an hour getting to know Narbonne – Will had persuaded him that the size of the grey horse would be more suitable for him. When Arthur mounted, Will fully expected Narbonne to object and waited for Arthur to be thrown off, or for Narbonne to buck and resist but, to his surprise, and he had to admit, admiration, Arthur turned out to be an experienced horseman, and soon had Narbonne walking along like a docile lamb.

It had been estimated they would aim to travel sixteen to twenty miles each day but, if the weather was good and travelling conditions allowed, they would set off at first light to try to exceed that distance. If they arrived at Honfleur early, that would be an advantage, but if the weather or other events prevented them from achieving their expected mileage, the good days would give the benefit of being further along which would, hopefully, prevent any delay in the ship sailing on time.

When the sun began to go down, they would stop for the night setting up a makeshift camp which would be quick to take down at sunrise for the next leg of their journey. Each night, if the weather permitted, the men would sleep under the stars to allow a fast break up of the camp the following morning, getting them back on the road without unnecessary delay. Will and his three companions would select a quiet corner, under a tree if there was one available, or close to a hedge when they settled down to sleep, and it became a routine for Will to wait until he was certain no-one was watching, to check the pouches of gold coins were safe.

If the weather was inclement, crude, rough-and-ready tents with waxed groundsheets would be erected for the soldiers which would afford them some protection from the weather, but the serjeant insisted Will, Hugh, Robin and Arthur sleep within the wagons as befitted their elevated status to the knighthood.

When Will was released from his driving duty he spent time getting to know Chataigne and practised riding her; Arthur helped with giving him instruction on how to sit, how to hold the reins correctly, and how to make Chataigne at ease with her new owner. She was a lovely mare, obedient and well-behaved and a bond of trust soon developed between her and Will. In addition, Will began to see that there was far more to Arthur than he thought and developed a grudging respect for the man he originally had thought to be a fool.

Most days they saw fires in the distance. As he rode alongside Will and Arthur on his heavy-set dappled grey horse named Ash, the escort serjeant told them they were likely to be the campfires of the bands of brigands the Earl had warned Will about, or of people now homeless after the opposing armies had pillaged the towns or villages, but the large group of well-armed soldiers had obviously deterred any incidents.

For one dreadful week it rained incessantly and it was some help that the wagons had covers that could be put up to give some shelter to the men on board, and waxed sheets to keep the cargo or hay dry but, when the wind blew strongly from the north, the force of the rain stung faces, made it difficult to see ahead and those on horseback or on wagon seats were soaked to the skin.

One wagon had to be unloaded and abandoned when it became embedded in mud. Using four horses to pull it and some strong men to push they attempted to save it but, with the heavy cargo on board, as the mud released its hold and the wagon began to move forward it collapsed. Abandoning it they transferred the cargo to the remaining three wagons.

Will and Arthur took two hourly turns in front of their wagon giving one of them time to get dry and warm up a little inside, and when they found some more sheltered spot to camp, they were glad of a pot of warming soup or stew.

With now three wagons and additional horses, the days were slow and monotonous. Their waking hours were filled with travelling along seemingly endless, scarcely-used roads with little to cheer them as they passed ravaged villages and farms, some with curling, acrid blackened smoke attesting to the fact that brigands had been there very recently. Arthur made a point of pointing out the scarcity of birds in these areas, and the silence; there was no birdsong, and the sinister effect made him shudder. Will crossed himself, many of the soldiers did the same. Other than those tragic sights, there was nothing but fields, hedgerows and what remained of forests after the armies had cut down vast tracts of woodland for firewood, wagon repairs and even weapons. As they rode through the devastation there was little conversation; seasoned soldiers though they were, each of them was silently occupied with his own thoughts.

A common sight was the decomposing bodies, mostly of animals, but sometimes of people, lying in fields or on the grass verge at the side of the road. Although nothing was said, many of the escort covered their mouths with kerchiefs or scarves, clearly concerned about disease. Blackened remains of what had been thriving villages were a common sight and apart from the odd deer or wild boar they managed to hunt for their own fresh meat, there was very little food to be had to vary or supplement their supplies. Many silent prayers of thanks were given to the Earl for having the foresight to stock the party with enough wheat, grain and dried or salted bacon and fish to give them basic nutrition during the journey.

Wherever possible, when they stopped for the night they would look for the shelter of woodland near streams or rivers. There were nights when this was not possible due to the destruction of woodland, leaving just a barren, mutilated landscape scarred by clusters of tree-stumps, reducing the company to a brooding silence at the tragedy of war.

One night they found the kind of location they were looking for where part of a small, clean rock and gravel bed stream ran alongside a gently-sloped clearing large enough to accommodate the company. On checking the condition of the ground, they found the soil was largely sand-based which had allowed the recent heavy rains to drains away leaving it dry enough for camping. Ideal. A wind had picked up clattering the almost bare branches at the top of trees, forcing the last of the dead and dying leaves from the deciduous trees leaving a fluttering covering of red, gold and brown on the ground. The pine-trees clung tightly to their green spines but below them were bundles of dead needles. Hugh decided that wrapping an oiled cover-sheet around a flattened pile of pine-needles would make a good bed. Robin tried to talk him out of it reasoning that needles tended to be sharp, but Hugh was not to be dissuaded. His argument was that the stiff linen sheet would protect him from the prickles and the pile was thick enough to provide a good mattress of sorts. Having settled down to sleep, he was unaware of Arthur, Will, Robin and the serjeant laying wagers on how quickly he would give up trying to sleep on the spikey bed. For a while they listened to Hugh's snoring and watched as he moved around in his sleep. Will was struggling to stay awake himself and his head was nodding down towards his chest when a groan roused him. Arthur nudged him.

'Hugh's awake.' Hugh stifled a laugh.

'Ouch!' Hugh tried to scratch his shoulders through his shirt, but as he sat up shifting his weight, the needles moved pricking through the sheet and his hose, into his bottom and legs.

'Strewth! That's sore.' Clambering up onto his feet, he picked up his cover sheet and cloak and headed towards his three companions and the serjeant, who by now were struggling not to laugh. It was only when he saw coins changing hands from Will, Arthur and the serjeant to Robin, that he realised what had been going on.

He stood and glared at them for a moment: 'I am delighted to be the reason for your mirth, my friends.' But when Robin offered to share his winning with him, Hugh saw the funny side and joined them on the grassy bank where they had chosen to sleep. 'No, Robin. You keep your booty, my friend,' he chuckled. 'You tried to warn me and I was a fool.'

The next morning, Hugh asked Arthur to look at his back while he inspected his legs. On examination it was clear that the pine-needles had indeed been uncomfortable. Hugh had what appeared to be several bands and clusters of bright red pin pricks across his back, shoulders, and the back of his arms, legs and buttocks that looked very sore.

'I think you will not make that mistake again, Hugh,' said Arthur.

'No. I was convinced the sheet was thick enough to stop the needles getting through. How wrong I was.' It took a few days before the damage to Hugh's skin healed as the rash disappeared and he never did try to sleep on pine-needles again.

There came a morning when, both seated at the front of the wagon with Arthur taking the reins of the horses and deep in his own thoughts, he became aware that Will had not spoken for some time.

'Is there something bothering you, my friend?'

Will turned to Arthur, his brows knitted in a deep frown. 'I confess I do have worries, in the main concerning Winterne.'

'In what respect?'

'Arthur, I have no wish to burden you with my problems.'

'We have yet a long way to travel, I have no particular concerns of my own and nothing else to occupy my mind. It may be that I can help if you would like me to.'

Will smiled. 'Thank you. It would ease my mind if I can find an answer to what bothers me.' He looked down at the horses steadily walking in front of them. Arthur said nothing, waited while Will put his thoughts in order.

'As you know,' Will began, still looking ahead, 'I come from common folk, at least on my father's side, I do. As the village blacksmith he made a reasonable living but I have had little schooling.' He turned to Arthur and gave a faraway smile. 'My mother was...is...the daughter of a merchant in carpets and was destined to marry whoever her father chose for her but she and my father fell in love and eloped...'

'She was a brave lady to do that,' Arthur cut in.

Will nodded. 'Indeed she was but she was never to quite let go of her more cultured way of life...not completely. They were happy of course, but she ensured, quite strictly, I might add, that Albert and I spoke well. She used to say that it was to be sure that we could mix with all levels of company as we didn't know what the future held.'

'Perhaps she foresaw your knighthood.'

Will compressed his lips. 'Perhaps she did.' He paused, frowned and looked ahead again. 'I hope though that she did not foresee Albert's death. It would have broken her heart if she had.' After a moment's silence, he went on. 'For a while, my father paid one of the monks at a nearby abbey to tutor me, but I had little interest in reading or writing, I was good with numbers though. My talents, such as they are, are practical and I have no knowledge of how to oversee others, and my mother would be ashamed to hear me say it, but I have no knowledge of how to lead people or even speak to servants.'

'But neither do Robin or Hugh...'

'That's right, Arthur, but they will be returning to their farms and families. I am to take over a manor and rebuild it where necessary. I am to manage an estate...be the lord of a village and its people.'

Arthur nodded. He was beginning to understand Will's predicament. 'What would help you feel more confident? And remember, the Earl promised to send you his steward to help with your needs at Winterne. That should help.'

'That is true, and indeed it will take some of the concern from my shoulders but, perhaps being able to read more skilfully would be the first step. People have respect for those who can read and write.'

'Yes, it is a good skill to have and, more than others having respect for you, it would give you more confidence in your own abilities. Perhaps I could help you with that.' Arthur was aware that those who had been raised to knighthood and the nobility, instead of being born into that social class, could indeed be at a disadvantage when it came to mixing with those more highborn than themselves, or even in gaining the respect of those who were lower born. Will would have to prove himself worthy to be an equal with the gentry, and worthy of high regard from the folk in and around Winterne. It may be that the prince had not done Will any favours when trying to reward him for saving his life, and some other way of showing his gratitude may have been more appropriate.

'I would be grateful for your help but, if possible, I would prefer not to have anyone see. I would like to hide my shame.'

'Then we can wait until a suitable time but, tis no shame not to be able to read. I would wager that many a noble lord, born into the aristocracy has the same lack.'

Will laughed. ' That may be so...but they have nothing to prove.'

The surface of the road suddenly became rough and pitted and Arthur did not speak for a few moments as he tried to concentrate on how to avoid running the wagon into the deeper ruts. Robin and Hugh in the wagon ahead were a good guide as to what was ahead of them, and Arthur steered the horses accordingly. Will held onto the seat with both hands as the wagon bumped across the uneven gravel and rock-strewn lane that was more of an untended path than a road. Behind them and tethered to the wagon Chataigne and Narbonne plodded along without complaint, and Will decided to find a spare carrot for them when they stopped for the night.

Arthur looked over the side of the wagon to check how close they were to what appeared to be a deep ditch close to the tall privet hedge. 'I think we have enough room to avoid those ruts on the right and this muddy furrow, and we can talk later about your worries. If you have no objections, I have no plans for when we reach England and I wonder if it would be of any help if I stay with you for a while at Winterne. I may be able to help you with reading and some other social skills.'

Will agreed readily, and wondered if perhaps that was what the Earl had in mind all along.

Chapter Eight

A little before sundown on a pleasantly warm evening, having found a small bridge to cross the L'Obriquet river, they skirted the small town of Beuvillers, a little under twenty five miles from their journey's end, looking for a suitable place to camp. For some distance, the road they had been travelling ran parallel to the river edged with a steep bank. Most of the time they could catch glimpses of the river through the trees or over the dry stone wall that ran alongside the road and three of the escort were ordered to ride ahead to seek an opening in the wall, and for a suitable place to camp for the night. A short while later they returned having found a break in the wall and surrounded by trees just beyond, was a flat grassy area wide enough to accommodate their company, that led down to the river and they thought it fitting place to stay for the night.

The usual routine followed of a small party sent off into the forest to hunt, another went to find wood for the campfires, some were given the job of gathering large stones to enclose the open fires, and to set up the cast iron equipment on which the blackened cooking pots would be suspended. Their remaining vegetables and whatever meat their hunting party were able to find would all be tossed into the pot to heat and simmer in a mix of ale to give it more flavour and water.

Beyond the camp site, those of the escort who had not been given a job, would unfasten the horses from the wagons, remove saddles from the mounts, feed and brush the animals, then leave them hobbled, using a short length of rope tied at either end to their front legs, which would enable them to walk and safely graze without being able to run off.

Will reached into one of the wagons to pick up a bucket, intending to fetch water from the nearby stream, but a young soldier ran after him. 'I'll fetch the water, Sir William,' he said, with a huge smile. 'Forgive my boldness, Sir, but it does not do for a knight to fetch water when someone else can do it for him.'

Will shrugged and handed over the bucket. The lad was friendly and willing, and this was something he would have to get used to; he was now a knight and would not be expected to serve others in the future. His life had changed, and he had to change with it, but it made him nervous; could he learn how not to be one of the ordinary folk? Perhaps Arthur could advise him. Each day he discovered more about Arthur, and had begun to see why the Earl had thought it would be good for Arthur to be with him at Winterne.

As the sun went down, four fires were lit, two under the cooking pots where purple carrots, onions, cabbage and leeks were bubbling away and soon the hunters returned with several rabbits, five chickens, a goose and a brace of pheasants that would all be shared out amongst the four cauldrons, together with herbs parsley and sage and chunks of salted bacon. The other two fires had a trivet placed on them with a flat stone on which simple flatbreads of rye or barley flour mixed with salt and water were baked which were then eaten with the stew. With hunger being the motive, the animals and birds were soon skinned and plucked and cut into pieces small enough to cook quickly. Before long, a delicious smell wafted into the air around them, if they were not particularly hungry before, that all changed as the aroma reached their nostrils and each man held their pottery or wooden bowl impatiently waiting until the food was ready.

'Oi!' One of the Welsh archers, a small and stocky dark-eyed, dark-haired man called Gwilim, raced towards the trees and vanished into the undergrowth. The shriek of a young voice reached them and a second or two later Gwilim reappeared tugging the ear of a struggling barefooted young boy in ragged clothing.

Gwilim was usually a quiet man given to being solitary unless he had too many cups of ale or managed to get hold of something stronger. It was then that a fiery temper overtook him, and he could be brutal. Will had seen him earlier in the day taking swigs from a flask when he thought no-one was watching, and was certain the flask contained something other than ale. Now, seeing his mistreatment of a lad that could be no more than nine or ten years of age, Will knew his instinct had been right, and Gwilim had to be stopped. He moved towards Gwilim, but Arthur stepped in front of him and called out, 'Gwilim, my friend, what have you caught there?' Arthur moved closer. He was a big man and now Gwilim did not seem quite so sure of himself, but puffed himself out with bravado and said: 'E'll be after our food, tha's wha' 'e'll wan'.' Gwilim slurred. Still holding the wriggling and crying boy by the ear, and pinching harder than before, Gwilim looked around for support from the nearby group of men. But they were busy concentrating on their game of knucklebones, an ancient game played with five small goat or sheep bones. Sitting around one of the fires, the men took it in turns and made bets on how many of the stones they could throw up in the air and catch on the back of their hands. Being ignored just fuelled Gwilim's anger, making him more unpredictable.

Arthur inched closer still while Will, keeping to the shadows crept cautiously nearer. Both of them aware Gwilim's humiliation had made him more dangerous.

'The poor lad's probably starving...' said Arthur in a soft, soothing voice.

'Mebbe so, but it's our food and...well...e's one o' them, ain't 'e? An' there'll be more o' them waitin' in them woods, you mark my words.'

'One of them?' Arthur enquired amiably, now almost within arm's length of Gwilim.

'Yeh, 'e's a Frenchie ain't 'e?' Gwilim seemed to have shrunk and looked around searching for support from anyone as the approaching, imposing figure of Arthur towered over him.

Arthur was within reach of the boy but made no move and this calmness unnerved Gwilim who stepped backwards towards the tree-line dragging the boy with him. Without taking his eyes off Arthur, Gwilim retreated and Arthur slowly moved forward until Gwilim stumbled backwards over a raised tree root losing his grip on the boy, and landing clumsily on the ground. Arthur darted forward and grabbed the boy holding him away from Gwilim who had quickly regained his feet and tried to make a grab for him.

Without speaking to Gwilim, Arthur turned and walked the trembling boy away towards the campfire where he wrapped his cloak around him. 'As-tu faim?' Arthur asked *('Are you hungry?')*

The boy nodded. In the glow of the dancing firelight Arthur could see the dirt on the boy's face and limbs and how thin he was. Picking up a bowl and ladle, aware that the entire camp was now watching, Arthur filled the bowl and handed it to the boy. Will watched in admiration at the way Arthur had taken control of the situation.

The serjeant walked across to join them, glaring at the other men as if daring them to object, and gave the boy a wooden spoon. The boy devoured the hot stew with quick glances across at Gwilim who was quite clearly fuming, but powerless without support from his fellows.

Arthur hunkered down as the boy finished his meal, wiping a dirty finger around the bowl and sucking off the last of the savoury stew. Will approached and gave him a hunk of dark rye flatbread. The boy took it greedily but then tried to run off, but Arthur held him firmly.

'N'ayez pas peur. Y a-t-il plus d'entre vous dans les bois? Comment vous appelez-vous?' *(Do not be frightened. Are there more of you in the woods? What is your name?)*

'Mon nom est Jehan,' *(My name is Jehan),* said the boy, glumly looking down at his cold and scratched bare feet. Arthur felt a surge of pity for the boy.

'I can't believe yer feedin' 'im an' givin' 'im our food,' yelled a still mutinous Gwilim. He had been humiliated by this new so-called knight and was not about to back down. "E's givin' the Frenchie our food, lads. What yer gonna do abou' it?'

'Thass enuff, Gwilim,' said one of the Knucklebones players. 'Go and sleep it orf,' said another.

Will walked up to Gwilim, whose bad temper was building.

'That's a good notion, Gwilim. Why not find your bed roll and...'

Gwilim spun round and thrust a fist towards Will's face but Will sidestepped, Gwilim lost his footing and fell to the ground again. He lay, dazed, for a few moments then stood and it appeared that he was going to walk away but he suddenly pulled out a knife and sprang in Arthur's direction. Someone gave a warning shout. Arthur turned in time to deflect the knife and punched Gwilim hard on the chin. Gwilim fell backwards poleaxed and, with an awful cracking sound that everyone nearby heard, he hit the side of his head on one of the large stones that encircled the fire. There was a smell of scorched hair. Gwilim was dead. No-one spoke or moved for a few moments, stunned by what had occurred. Then the serjeant moved towards Gwilim's body, hunkered down to check there was no pulse. 'I want some volunteers to bury this man. He's beyond all help now.'

Jehan burst into tears. 'Il est mort?' *(Is he dead?)*

Arthur nodded. 'Oui. Il ne te fera plus de mal.' *(He will not hurt you anymore).*

With an unsteady voice Jehan said: 'C'est ma faute.' *(It is my fault)*

Will joined Arthur and Jehan. He was unable to speak French, but he understood from the expression on the Jehan's face what he had said. 'Tell him it is not his fault, Arthur. Gwilim was being cruel. Local townsfolk are starving, we have seen enough evidence of that. Armies of both sides have stripped the land, taken what they wanted and left them nothing. We are to blame, not them and Gwilim should have had more pity for their suffering.'

All the time Will was talking, Jehan was studying his face, trying hard to understand what he was saying. Will smiled down at him but then a movement at the edge of the trees caught his eye.

'Arthur, look!'

A woman and a smaller boy who, in his terror of the soldiers was trying to cling to the woman's ragged skirt as she hurried towards them. Although the mother appeared tense; the English soldiers had her older son after all, she had watched from the safety of the trees as Jehan had been caught. She had wanted to go to his aid, but she also had her younger son to think of.

Gwilim's cruelty to Jehan was not a surprise. She expected it from soldiers. What surprised her was that one had tried to protect Jehan. Further, she watched in disbelief when Jehan was offered food, and the big man was kind to him. Horrified, she had seen the small man pull out a knife and thought Jehan would die, but he had lunged at the other man who knocked him to the ground. She was convinced this would lead to a general brawl and Jehan would be hurt but, again, the soldiers astounded her. The man in charge shouted something and four men had carried the small man away. She had no idea whether he was dead or just unconscious, but when they took two shovels from one of the wagons and headed to the far end of the clearing, by the dry stone wall close to the roadside, she had the answer. She decided that, whatever resulted, she was going to try to reclaim her son from the soldiers and left their hiding place.

'*Maman! Etienne!*' Jehan ran towards them, followed slowly by Arthur, Will and the serjeant.

'Viens. Tu es le bienvenu.' *(Come. You are welcome.)* Arthur offered to give them some food and Jehan's face lit up in a beaming smile; it was very clear to the mother that her son trusted this man, but she was still unsure.

'Oui. Merci, Monsieur,' Jehan replied for her, with a smile from ear to ear.

Soon, Arthur and Will were joined by Hugh and Robert, the serjeant and several other of the soldiers who had some sympathy with the woman and her young sons. Etienne, now with a full belly had snuggled up to his mother – who had introduced herself as Jeanne – in the warmth radiated by the campfire, and was sleeping soundly. Jehan sat on her other side, holding her arm, his eyes glowing and his mouth formed into an perpetual smile.

In the flickering glow of the fire, Will studied the woman. Grateful for the food and warmth, but still clearly apprehensive and untrusting, she seemed to flinch at every sudden movement, every shout or sudden noise – even from the horses. The only visible parts of her body were her face, where dark shadows under eyes revealed her fatigue and suffering, and her hands; both face and hands were pale and thin.

With Arthur translating, they learned that Jeanne and her boys had been trying to return to her parents village in the north, but then Etienne had developed a fever and she had been fortunate in finding a cave with a narrow opening and dry floor, where they could shelter and keep warm while she nursed him. They had lived on what little food she had salvaged from the farm and fish from the stream, which also gave them fresh water and she only lit a fire at dusk when the dull light cloaked smoke more easily.

But Etienne had recovered enough to move on, she had been reluctant to risk them being found by marauding bands of deserters from armies and others who had no longer had homes or possessions, and they had stayed a little longer than she head meant to.

It had been a little over a week ago when a small group of some twenty French deserters had come through her village and found her family farm on the road out. Her husband had sent her and the boys to hide on the top floor of the barn. The soldiers had thrown ropes around their four pigs, their only cow and her calf and rounded up their chickens, killing the entire flock. Peering through a crack in the wall, she saw her husband remonstrate with one of the soldiers and stopped herself from screaming as a crossbow bolt fired from somewhere she could not see, entered his chest killing him instantly. But she had no time to grieve; she had her boys to think about. Smoke billowed up from the back of their cottage. The swine were burning their house. Fully expecting the barn to be next, she helped Etienne onto her back, telling him to hold on tightly across her neck, and stepped down the ladder to the floor watching Jehan climb down above her at the same time as keeping an eye on the barn door. Once on the ground, staying low, she hurried the boys into a corner of the barn where they hid behind bags of grain listening to the loud voices of the soldiers and the crackling sounds as the fire took hold of their home. She shushed Etienne who had begun to cry and cuddled him closely while she prayed they would be able to escape before they were seen, and she explained how terrified she was that the barn would be set alight while she and the boys were inside. But, then a shout had gone up and, to her relief the men ran to their horses and rode off in a hurry dragging her pigs and cattle with them. But her relief was short lived as she realised why the group had left in such a hurry. Coming across the fields, but thankfully some way off still was a large contingent of English soldiers.

Grabbing a knife, and a basket into which she put all the eggs they could find, and then snatching what clothes had been drying in the garden, she had piled those few possessions into a small wheelbarrow, lifted Etienne into it and with her pushing the wheelbarrow, they had run off into the nearby woods, where they had hidden until the all the soldiers had gone. They had been on the road ever since. It was her intention to take the boys back to her father's farm outside Lisieux, but the roads being blocked by brigands, the terrible rains, together with Etienne's fever, had forced them to wait until he was better before travelling on.

'Did I 'ear 'er say Lisieux?' asked the serjeant.

'Yes, she has family there. That's where she and the boys are trying to get to. Why?' asked Arthur.

'Well, if I'm right, I think we go quite near there.' The serjeant smiled, something he did rarely. 'Don't seem right them 'avin' to keep walkin' when we could let them travel with us, do it?'

When Arthur explained to Jeanne what the serjeant had said, she hugged her boys and cried for joy, her relief obvious. They would have food, protection and comfort for the remainder of their journey. They were going home.

Soon after, in keeping with their usual routine, the serjeant appointed four of the company as lookouts around the camp site for the first four hours, and another four to relieve them for the last watch until sunrise.

That night Jeanne and the boys slept in Will and Arthur's covered wagon on a bed of hay and wrapped in cloaks and the next morning, the boys were running about the camp, playing as children should, while Jeanne helped with preparing and baking flatbreads, then with packing up the site.

The following evening, a little out of their way, they approached the village of Lisieux. From a few miles out Jeanne had become very quiet, and Will noticed how she gripped Jehan's hand more tightly the nearer they approached. They passed some empty villages on the route that had been devastated, by passing armies and both Will and Arthur understood her anxiety. They had seen some atrocities during their time in France, and so had Jeanne and her boys. She was clearly anxious about what she would find when they reached their destination. Were her family still alive and, if so, would they still be there?

During their last stop to change the horses, Will and Arthur had quietly discussed what they could do if Jeanne found her family home abandoned and unable to find relatives. Eventually they agreed that, if the worst came to the worst, they would offer the family a home and work at Winterne but, that would only be as a last resort; they felt the English would not take too kindly to having someone they considered to be the enemy living nearby. As it transpired, it was not necessary to make the offer.

The approach to Lisieux proved more promising than they had expected, and her hopes rose. The serjeant advised that a small party of Jeanne, her boys, four of the escort company, plus Will and Arthur should go on horseback to Jeanne's family home; if the full troop went, it would frighten the villagers who might think they were about to be raided. Keeping the group small would be less intimidating. Having Jeanne with them, who insisted she was well known by everyone locally, having lived there all her life until she married Geoffroi, should make their arrival less frightening.

Approaching the outskirts of the village, most houses appeared undamaged, but although there were a few people seen on the street, some ran to their homes as the small party walked their horses through.

Jehan rode behind Arthur, his hands gripping the big man's jacket as his little arms were not long enough to go around Arthur's waist. Jeanne, riding one of the escort horses had little Etienne sitting in front of her, happily pretending he was in control of the reins.

Although the people they saw were nervous it did not seem to concern Jeanne unduly. She turned around in the saddle to talk to Arthur and pointed to a house a little separated from the others. 'Il. Il y a la maison de mon père'. *(There. There is my father's house.).*

The house appeared to be unscathed. Jeanne made the sign of the Cross over her chest and said a quiet prayer. Just at that moment a young man came out of the low front door. Clearly taken by surprise at the sight of seven large horses approaching him, he jumped back in alarm.

'Bertran! C'est moi! Jeanne!' *(Bertran. It is me! Jeanne!)* She urged the horse on. Etienne nestled in closer to her. He did not know this man.

The man looked puzzled, suspicious, but then looked more closely and a huge smile spread across his face, his eyes glittered. 'Jeanne? Ma sœur?' *(Jeanne! My sister?).*

'Oui, Bertran. C'est moi.' *(Yes, Bertran. It is me.).*

Etienne raised his huge blue eyes to look up at his overjoyed mother; he had not seen her like this since the day the men came to their farm. Her wide smile and happiness on seeing this man, who he had no memory of ever meeting before, surprised him. He looked around at Jehan and saw that he too seemed happy, so he decided to trust this man and, when his uncle reached up to Etienne, he allowed himself to be lifted down in his uncle's strong arms, and stood beside him as Jeanne dismounted unaided. When they hugged each other tightly, he wrapped his arms around his uncle's legs not wanting to be left out. But still he was a little confused. If adults were happy, why did they cry? Arthur dismounted and helped Jehan down from the saddle just as the door opened again and a grey-haired woman came out to see what all the fuss was about.

'Jeanne! Ma fille! Dieu merci!' *(Jeanne! My daughter! Thank God.)* Crying, she hurried over to join in the embrace then saw her grandsons, both waiting patiently for their turn as the adults hugged, kissed and cried joyously at finding each other again. Grand-mère called them to her and the boys ran into her open arms.

Arthur looked over at Will. 'I think our job is done. Come, let's leave them to their reunion.' He signalled to the escort to turn the horses. 'We'll re-join our party and head on to Honfleur. It's only a few miles now. It will be very late when we arrive there but that will give us a good start on the day tomorrow.'

'Monsieur!' Jeanne and Jehan ran up to Arthur. 'T'ank you all,' Jeanne struggled with her English. Arthur dismounted and hugged Jehan. 'I am...am....'

'Tu ne nous dois aucun merci, Jeanne. On n'a fait que ce que les hommes décents devraient faire. Vous avez votre famille maintenant et nous vous souhaitons bonne chance pour l'avenir. Au revoir Jehan. Occupe-toi de ta mère. C'est une dame courageuse. *('You owe us no thanks, Jeanne. We only did what any decent men should do. You have your family now and we wish you all luck for the future. Goodbye Jehan. Look after your mother. She is a brave lady.).*

Arthur remounted and Jehan looked as though he was going to cry, but Arthur winked at him, shook his head and smiled. 'No tears,' he said. Jehan seemed to understand and blinked his tears away as Arthur, Will and the escort soldiers rode away with a last salute to Jeanne and the boys. When Arthur risked a look back he saw the boys being led into the house by their grandmother as Jeanne and her brother walked arm in arm behind them. He never did find out if Jeanne's father was still alive, but she would have the warmth of family around her now, and he fervently hoped the boys would have a good life and die at a peaceful old age when their time came. God forbid, these delightful boys should ever be forced into the army.

Will saw Arthur's the wistful expression. He had clearly been very taken with Jeanne. Will wondered if Arthur would have preferred to have her and the boys join them in Winterne. But it was not to be.

Perhaps Arthur would find happiness once they were settled. He had learned so much more about Arthur's generous personality and his skills during this journey, that he was now determined to have Arthur join him in Somerset.

Hugh and Robin had their own plans, but Arthur had not mentioned anything about what he wanted to do, or where he wanted to go. They could talk about it during the voyage.

The rest of the escort party had waited in a field a little way outside the village. Having decided to move on to Honfleur that night, they had no camp to erect yet, so they had little to do until their mission had been completed one way or the other.

As Will, Arthur and the small party arrived, they found some of the group relaxing around a campfire, a few were wrapped in their cloaks leaning against the dry stone wall and catching up on some sleep, and the horses were untied from the wagon traces but hobbled. The serjeant rose to greet them as the rest of the troop roused themselves and began preparations to leave.

'The lady found 'er family then?'

Arthur gave a brief nod.

'Yes, her brother and mother were at home and the village appeared to be mostly untouched.

The serjeant nodded and smiled. 'Well, thass just as it should be, home wi' 'er family. Tis better fer the boys than livin' in another country, wi' strange folk like us.'

They began the last leg of their journey to Honfleur under an inky blue starlit sky and, with the aid of a full moon, were able to see their way clearly for the last few miles to the harbour at Honfleur.

A little way beyond the outskirts of Lisieux, Will became convinced he could smell the sea. The air felt fresher, cleaner and the breeze held a salty tang. The horses appeared to have noticed something different as well. It seemed that their plodding ceased, their heads lifted, and they trotted more jauntily.

Chapter Nine

Having made camp on the outskirts of Honfleur, aware that this was the last night they would all spend together, Will knew he had to remove his coin pouches from their wagon, and he pulled up in a corner of the field where the hedge would obscure him from sight while he retrieved the coins after dark when everyone was asleep.

Once settled, the four new knights gathered together around the campfire. Most evenings the serjeant would join them, but on this night he decided to stay with his men.

The sea breeze was fresh, and the night was not as pleasantly warm as the one before. As they talked they realised, if the wind was favourable, this could the last night they would be together.

'I have been away from my family for so long I doubt my children will remember me...' Robin's eyes misted and he looked away. 'And I've never seen my new son.' He shivered and reached down to throw another log on the fire, pulled his cloak a little tighter around his neck. 'The only thing I know about him is that my...my late wife...' He paused, turning his face away. Will and Arthur exchanged sympathetic glances and Hugh poured Robin a cup of ale and handed it to him. Robin took a mouthful of the frothing drink before continuing. 'Al...Alice named him Stephen. He will be almost four years of age now.'

'What about your other children?' asked Will. 'You know it seems strange that after all this time we have spent together, we still know very little about each other.'

Hugh chuckled. 'In war it doesn't do to know too much about your neighbour in the ranks. You might get to like them, or they you, but then they die...'

'Or you do,' added Arthur.

Robin smiled, the glow of the fire reflecting in his brown eyes. 'My children are very precious to me and I have missed them. My daughter, Cecilia, is eight years old and the image of her mother, whose flaxen hair, when loosed, hung to her waist, but her eyes were a deep blue. The only feature Cecilia seems to have inherited from me is her brown eyes. Edward, is nine years old and folk say he is a small version of me, the same eyes and straw coloured hair and will be tall, like me. He is a good boy, strong of character and a willing worker on the farm, so my mother-in-law says. She had been looking after my family since...well, since Alice died, but she is ageing and will be glad to have me home to allow her to rest. What about you? What plans do you have?'

Arthur replied first with a shrug. 'I have not yet really thought what I will do, but I am free to go where I wish and will decide when we arrive in Newhaven.'

Hugh, put another log on the fire and used a long stick to move some dying embers to the side, answered. 'I am going home to Bliddorth. I too have a family farm and it is time I went back to work it. I hope to be betrothed if Margaret will still have me.' He rubbed his unshaven chin. 'Hmm, mayhap I too have been away too long, but I still have hopes.'

Will took time to study Hugh in the light of the flickering fire. He was broad shouldered and strong, with solid well-muscled legs and arms and a mop of abundant wavy dark-blond hair that fell to his shoulders, and his laughing bright blue eyes glittered in the firelight. Will had never realised what a cheerful, affable sort of man Hugh was, and wished he had made a friend of him before it was too late. Once they arrived in England the distance between their homes would be much too long for them to keep in contact.

Although he had seen both Hugh and Robin around the camp, they had never spoken until they made this journey, and even then he had spent little time with either of them. They had more in common with each other through their background in farming, and he thought it strange that, on this probable last night they would be together, they were spending more time talking and getting to know each other than they ever had. The only detail he knew about them before had been from the Earl of Salisbury. And he found he liked them both.

Hugh continued. 'Of course, Margaret's father wanted nothing to do with me. He said I was a poor suitor for his daughter's hand in marriage and I was leaving to go to war. I had no intention of being killed and thought I might make my fortune. Margaret promised to wait for me; she said she knew I would return. I had no thought, and I am sure it was the same for you, that I would return as *Sir* Hugh with additional lands.'

The clattering of hooves approaching on the stone-paved road near their camp caught their attention and interrupted their conversation. The serjeant, who had been sitting with a group of his men, stood and unsheathed his sword, his soldiers did the same as three men on horseback entered the camp. They reined the horses and the front rider dismounted and approached the serjeant, who returned his sword to its sheath. 'I am looking for Sir William Hallett, Sir Arthur Burnel, Sir Robert Swinford and Sir Hugh Armstrong.'

'And who may you be, sir?' asked the serjeant.

'Walter Smith, Master of his Lordship the Earl of Salisbury's ship, the *Somerset*.'

Will and his friends stood to greet the stranger as the serjeant guided him and his two companions towards them.

'Sir Arthur,' said the serjeant, 'I'll leave yer ter make the introductions,' he turned to the master, 'an' fer the moment, I will take my leave of you, sir. We' meet agen in the harbour tomorrer.' He bowed and walked away to join his men around the campfire where he gave an order to two of the men that neither Will or Arthur could hear. The two guards walked over to one of the wagons, took out a number of large cushions and laid them on the ground around the fire where the knights had been sitting before the visitors had arrived.

The two men with the master were introduced as Kelvin Smith, the master's son who was the Steersman on the ship, and a small dark-haired man with a small, pointed beard and Will could barely take his eyes off him. His clothing was unlike anything he had ever seen before. A loose sleeved, long blue tunic reached to his knees, tied in the middle with a wide piece of off-white material, that Will thought was probably linen, and over which lay a slim chain belt with several leather pouches in various sizes hooked on to it. Beneath the tunic he wore wide black trousers that reached to his knees and gathered at the ankle. Over these he had a loose-fitting outer garment, a type of roomy coat with baggy sleeves with two black stripes that wound around them. On his head was, what to Will appeared to be nothing more than another piece of linen wrapped around several times, concealing most of his hair. Will, fascinated, stared. He had never seen anyone like him. From his neck hung several slim chains, from each dangled a single amulet, a full moon, a star, an open book, a bee and a key.

Will had never seen anyone quite like this strange little man and had been so captivated with him, that he only became aware that the master had been speaking when Arthur nudged him.

'...physician from the East, Isaac ben Abadi, a man of learning and friend of the Earl's.'

The little man moved forward and bowed to Will. 'Greetings to you, Sir William Hallett.' He moved along to Arthur, Robin and Hugh, greeting them all by name.

Puzzled, Will leaned towards Arthur and whispered. 'How did he know which of us was which?'

'I have no idea,' Arthur whispered in reply. 'Perhaps it is magic.'

Doctor ben Abadi had heard Will's question. He smiled and walked back to Arthur. 'No, my friend,' he laughed. 'It is not magic. It is good communication. I received a message a few days ago from my friend, the Earl, informing me of your journey to Honfleur and, contained within the message were brief descriptions of each of you.' He shook his head, 'There is no such thing as magic, it is science in which I believe.'

Will looked relieved. 'Will you gentlemen join us for a cup of ale?' Will asked indicating the cushion seating placed around the fire.

Master Smith, and his son eagerly agreed. 'We have not come far,' said the master, 'but we will be grateful to join you, riding always makes me thirsty.'

'Thank you but I do not drink ale,' said Doctor ben Abadi. 'However, I do partake of wine and have a leather bota bag on my mount. You are welcome to join me in a cup. It is a good, sweet vintage.'

Will, Robin and Hugh politely refused the offer of wine as it was something they were unused to, but Arthur readily accepted saying he enjoyed wine, but had not had the opportunity to taste it for a long time. Again, this was another aspect of Arthur's character that surprised Will;

common folk did not drink wine; he was finding out more about Arthur all the time and he wondered what more there was to know.

Once the guests were as comfortably seated as could be provided, and wine and ale poured, Arthur asked Doctor ben Abadi how long the messenger the Earl had sent him had taken to journey from Poitiers to Honfleur. He understood a single rider would be able to travel faster than they could, but it was a long journey, through unsafe land and presumably with just one horse.

Dr ben Abadi smiled. 'Did anyone say it was a human messenger?'

Arthur looked puzzled. 'How could it be otherwise?'

'Have you never heard of messages being sent by pigeon? No? Well let me explain. At my home in Honfleur I have a what we call a pigeon loft. It is a safe home for pigeons to fly back to. They have an instinct to return to their homes and the pigeons the Earl has with him come from my flock. He took a number of the birds with him and, when he wishes to communicate with me, he ties a coded message to the leg of one of them, or two in case something happens to one of them if it is a particularly important message.'

All four of the young knights listened to the doctor's explanation with increasing incredulity.

'And we thought he kept the birds to eat,' said Will.

'Oh no, my friend. These birds are far too valuable to have such a dishonourable end.'

A noisy group of soldiers sitting nearby playing knucklebones suddenly roared with laughter. Kelvin stood up, an angry expression on his face, but the doctor reached out, took him by the hand and pulled him back to his seat. 'Do not be offended, my friend. It is very unlikely that with the amount of noise they were making, they would have heard our conversation. I do not believe they were laughing at me.'

Kelvin grudgingly sat back down on his folded blanket next to his father, an ugly scowl still etched on his face; Will noted that he appeared to be a little hot-tempered and wondered why his father had not stepped in to calm him. He decided he would be careful in his dealings with Kelvin during the voyage home.

'Master Smith, there must have been some reason for your visit to us tonight. We had not anticipated seeing you until our arrival at the harbour tomorrow.'

'Indeed, Sir Arthur, I do have a reason to see you this evening. High tide in the morning is at thirty minutes after nine of the clock. In order to give time to load the wagons, the escort and thirty horses, you must be at the harbour shortly after sunrise.'

'Thirty horses?' Will asked. He had expected the entire company to make the crossing.

'That is correct, Sir William,' said Doctor ben Abadi. 'Only half the contingent will be returning to England. The other half will be returning to Poitiers. In view of the danger on the roads between Poitiers and Honfleur, the Earl ordered a full escort for yourselves and the wagons, but feels that an escort of twenty will be ample for the journey from Newhaven to London. In addition, I shall be travelling to Poitiers with the returning escort for two reasons. Firstly, my pigeons need to be returned to the Earl and I shall accompany them. I do not actually need to return them myself as the escort could take them, but the Earl tells me that His Lordship, the Prince has a recurrence of the malady that afflicts him and this is the main reason for my visit. I invited myself to accompany Master Smith and Kelvin as I was eager to meet you and, with travel preparations for the birds in the morning, and loading the ship for your voyage, it is unlikely we shall have time to meet then.'

At the mention of the voyage, Will looked down at his feet and even in the glow of the firelight, the doctor noted a draining of colour from his face. He would find an opportunity to talk to Sir William alone before they returned to the town.

Over the following hour, the seven chatted amiably, ale and wine flowed, and the knights learned a great deal more about the sea and medicine than they had ever known before. Will was enjoying the conversation but, during a quiet moment, the master drained his cup and got to his feet.

'It is time we took our leave. We all need a good night's rest before our voyage.'

Once again, the doctor saw a flicker of apprehension cross Will's face. Robin, Hugh and Arthur, together with the Walter and Kelvin, walked back to where the three horses were grazing contentedly. Spotting the movement, the serjeant rose and joined them; he had some questions for the master about the arrangements for the following morning. The doctor though, took a little longer about getting up, blamed his old bones, and asked Will for his help to stand, then took a few moments to shake his feet saying that he need to get the blood circulating again. Will had no idea what he was talking about...did blood circulate? Will lifted the bota wine bag and carried it for the doctor, who was walking much slower than he had when they arrived, to where the others were waiting.

Before they came into earshot, without looking at Will, the doctor said: 'Sir William, I believe I detect a certain lack of enthusiasm on your part regarding your sea journey on the morrow.'

Will stopped walking and looked down at the little man with the extraordinary insight.

'I was not aware I had been that obvious.'

'Is you're problem mal de mare?'

'What's that? I have not heard of it.'

'Are you seasick?'

'Oh, yes, that I understand.' Will took a deep breath. 'I have only sailed once before, when we came to join the Earl's company of archers and, yes, I was violently sick. The crossing was shorter, from Dover to Calais. The journey we take tomorrow will be longer...if the wind is strong enough to blow us home quickly, the sea may be rough. Then again, the lower the strength of the wind and the journey will take longer. Either way I shall be glad when it is over.'

The doctor reached for one of the leather pouches hanging from the chain belt around his waist. He opened it and pulled out a lump of something twisted and brown. He broke a piece off revealing a pale-yellow centre. 'Take this and chew a little of it while you are on your way to the harbour.'

Will reached out to take the strange looking object from the doctor. 'What is it?'

'It is ginger root. People in the Orient use it as a medicine and to flavour food. It has a strong flavour which some people like, some do not. However, it is an effective anti-emetic which means it will help to stop the nausea.'

Will turned the odd looking knobbly root over in his hand, his brows knitted in a frown. The doctor smiled. 'I agree it does not look very attractive but, even if you find you do not like the flavour, tolerate it if you can as it will certainly help. Oh, and do not be put off by the odour. It has a rather powerful, heady quality but that indicates the root is fresh, which is the way it should be.'

Will smiled broadly. 'Thank you doctor. I am most grateful to you for your help. This may make the voyage more pleasant.'

They walked on towards where Walter and Kelvin were waiting for the doctor. 'As I understand it, the master is expecting a fresh breeze tomorrow which should take you along at a reasonable speed, so you are fortunate your voyage will be a kind one, maybe some spray but no large waves, and will take you to Newhaven within around seven hours or so.'

'Thank the Lord for that,' sighed Will.

'Oh, Sir William. Just one thing more about that piece of ginger...only chew the yellow flesh, not the skin. You might find that a little too tough to chew.'

'I will remember that Doctor, and thank you again. Have a safe journey to Poitiers and I hope we will meet again.'

'I wish you well, my friend, and it would indeed be a happy occurrence for us to meet again sometime in the future, but I think it unlikely.'

Having helped the doctor, who was surprising heavy for such a small man, into the saddle, Will thanked him again. The three riders were just about to set off when the doctor turned back to Will.

'Having said that, we have no knowledge of what God has in mind for us, and where my travels may take me in the future. As a friend of the Earl it is not impossible I could find my way to England and we may meet again.'

Will stood and watched until the three visitors were out of sight before going back to the fire to join the others for a short while, until he began yawning. 'We will awake early and have a long day ahead of us. I think it best if I retire for the night.'

'It is time we all did, I think, Will,' said Hugh. 'But perhaps one more small ale before we do.'

Chapter Ten

'Yes, why not,' Will agreed and sat down again. 'If all goes smoothly it will only be two days before we go our separate ways and, while travelling we have had little time to talk.'

'How long were you in service to the Earl?' asked Robin.

'Five very long years,' said Will staring down into his ale. He looked up at Robin. 'I was not aware of how long those years were until I was released. And you?'

'A little over four years,' Robin said, wistfully, gathering his thoughts. He went to speak then paused, looked up at Hugh and Will. 'Alice discovered she was with child again not long after I left, but she managed to get a message to me through her brother who joined us at Calais a few weeks later. I wish I could have gone home to her, to be with her,' he paused again and looked around, his lips compressed in a thin line, 'but I would have been a deserter...'

'...And would never have been safe at home,' added Arthur.

Robin nodded. He had no need to do more.

Hugh looked down into the dying embers of the fire, glad of its remaining warmth. 'Like yourselves, I was visiting my cousins in Derbyshire when my Lord, Sir John Chandos, called in his levy of fighting men. I tried to explain that my home was in Nottinghamshire and I had no allegiance to Sir John, but I was taken with my cousins. I alone survived. One died at Castelnaudary, the other Carcassonne.

'Arthur?' Robin looked across the fire to their quiet companion. 'And you? How come you to this army?'

Arthur gave a little smile. 'My story is a little different. It was no levy or conscription that brought me here. I volunteered. I was looking for adventure, glory and, perhaps, some riches along the way.' He gave a scornful chuckle. 'As you can see, up until now I found none but I have experienced life, have thought I was going to die many times...and I appreciate life more now than I did. I am also privileged to have found friends.' He raised his cup to all three men sitting around the fire.

One of the soldiers, sleeping under a tree and warmly wrapped in his bed roll began to snore, very loudly. Robin laughed. 'That sounds like Hugh.'

'I do *not* snore!' protested Hugh, looking very affronted.

'Oh my friend,' laughed Robin. 'You do indeed snore...and very loudly, but please do not take offence, at least it proves you're alive.'

'Then tonight I shall sleep under the wagon.'

'And I shall still hear you,' Robin said with a sly smile to Will and Arthur.

'To change the subject,' said Arthur hurriedly, 'we know what circumstances brought about Will's knighthood, but do you mind telling us for what action you received yours? An act of bravery should be celebrated by us all and, just as we should be ashamed of our misdeeds, we should be proud of our achievements.' Neither Hugh or Robin seemed to want to speak up so, after a few moments Arthur said: 'Then, if you will permit me, I will go first.

'I was with my group of archers amongst Lord Richard of Pembroke's contingent. We had been fighting the French for almost two hours before they gave up and retreated but, some of their number surrounded and killed our Lord's standard bearer before they could be stopped. Being preoccupied with staying alive I had been unaware of this happening but my nearest companion had seen six of the French soldiers snatch the standard and head towards a small wood. Of course, if they had reached it there was no knowing where they would have gone from there, and the two of us gave chase.'

'Just the two of you?' asked Hugh.

'Yes, we had no time to think of trying to gather help...and with everyone around us battling to stay alive...you understand how it was in the midst of...you...have to act, think, in an instant.'

Hugh nodded, recalling his own battle ordeals.

'Well, we hurried towards the trees and, just inside the treeline, we saw them. I am certain they had not realised they were pursued...they had not seen us...obviously thought they were safe and were spitting on the flag, two of them trampled it. Neither of us spoke but we both reached for arrows...it was as if some signal had passed between us. We were in an elevated position looking down on the French disrespecting our Earl's standard. Again, with a mutual understanding we chose our targets, the two stamping on the flag. We fired simultaneously. They fell. Dead. The other four left the standard where it was and ran at us but we killed two more with our arrows. The last two hesitated but it was clear they realised they would have to fight us. If they fled we could kill them as they ran. Their only choice was to put us out of action. They charged, swords at the ready. I threw down my bow and drew my sword. My companion had no sword, but he had his bow and a long knife. I don't know how he died, I was too preoccupied fighting off my opponent.' Arthur stopped talking and took a sup of his ale. None of the group pressed him to continue. They knew he would when he was ready. 'I slipped and fell. He lunged towards me, and he must have felt over confident as he raised his arm for a downward strike. I reached up and jabbed my sword between his ribs. He was done. I got to my feet and saw my companion...I never knew his name...lying dead close to the dying Frenchman. It was over. I left them all just where they lay and walked down to where the standard, now filthy and somewhat tattered, lay in the mud, picked it up and began walking back to the field. As I reached the edge of the trees, my serjeant and four of our company approached me...I explained what had happened. He had been informed of the incident, we had been seen running towards the trees after the French, the skirmish we had been involved in earlier was over and he had wanted to see the result of our actions...it seems he had expected to be burying us both. At a nod from the serjeant two of the group walked into the wood as the rest of us began walking back up the hill. I heard a scream and knew they had put the Frenchman out of his...pain. The serjeant took the standard from me and thanked me for my efforts. He then told me the name of my companion was Stephen Carter and he was from Chester. It felt better knowing something about who he was. I lit a candle for him at the next church we passed.' Arthur took another gulp of his ale and drained the cup. 'That's my story. It seems the serjeant informed our Captain of my...our action as he handed him the standard. The captain then returned

the standard to the Earl's Marshal, the story reached the ears of the Earl who spoke to the Prince...and the rest you know.' He gave a little chuckle and looked at Will. 'Nothing quite so outstanding as saving the life of our prince but what Will did showed decisive thinking and skill.'

All eyes turned to Will, who felt uncomfortable. He never wanted to be a hero; never expected to be a knight and was unsure if he would ever be one in the proper sense. He expected to die at each battle and had survived by the Grace of God, but would he have rather stayed an archer? Yes. He would. He knew his place there. He was amongst people he understood there. The future baffled him and anyone would have done what he did, surely? Change the subject. Move on to someone else.

'So, Hugh, it's your turn,' Will said.

'Hmm. Well, from our position we were firing arrows down onto the French knights but we could see that, with the thickness of their armour, our arrows were bouncing off, having no effect. I suggested to our Captain that perhaps a better vantage point, where the arrows could be more effective would be from the side rather than from above. He sent that message up the line to Sir John and to the Earl of Warwick. It was approved and we moved. You will have seen the result. As with yourself, Arthur, the prince was informed and, as you say...you know the rest. My knighthood was a strategy reward. Robin?'

Robin smiled, good naturedly. Whenever Robin smiled, it showed in his eyes. He had a warmth about him, a gentle kindness and Will had wondered how such a good man could cope with the horrors of war and killing, but like so many others, he had been called up to do his duty and had done so with courage and endurance.

'We put two enemy cannons out of action. We saw them being brought up to fire at our men-at-arms and knights who were preparing to mount for their charge at the French. Two of their divisions had already seemingly withdrawn, and the prince wanted them pursued. The cannon had been placed where they would not be seen by our mounted force so, without waiting for orders from our serjeant or captain, I asked three of my companions to follow me, under the cover of a ridge, down the hill to where the cannons had been placed.

'We watched as they primed them and set the elevation, and we saw a cartload of cannon balls being brought up as we crawled through the undergrowth towards them. There were four men to a cannon and four of us. When we got into position we knelt in the long grass and fired our arrows, killing five of their men outright but, of course, that gave us away to the other three...one was wounded...and they called out for help, whereupon more men came to help them. We fired again and again, killing most of them, but those who were left rushed us and we fought, hand to hand.' He paused, sighed. 'But although we won, we lost two of our number. There was no-one left at their cannon, so the pair of us went forward, scattered their gunpowder underneath the cannon carriages and used their fuses. They were just hollow cords infused with gunpowder and waxed to make waterproof and burn faster. We used the longest lengths we could find, found their smouldering match, lit the fuses we had placed under both carriages and ran, all the while praying the fuses would work...but hoping we had time to get far enough away.

'We had just returned to the protection of the ridge, when the cannon blew up sending pieces of wooden carriage and metal flying everywhere, but we were safe behind the ridge. The explosion obviously caught the attention of our officers and our captain saw us re-joining our team. He could tell by the mud on our breeches and the specks of black powder on our tunics that we had something to do with destroying the cannon and... again...just as with yourselves, the message was passed upwards...and the rest you know.'

'Well, wha' a brave bunch o' lads you are, sir knights,' said a voice from behind them. The serjeant had laid out his bedroll under a nearby tree and, unable to sleep, had been listening to their respective stories. When Robin finished relating his story, the serjeant emerged from behind the tree and walked over to join them. Cup in hand he sat down on the ground beside Arthur, filled his cup with ale from the flask and said: 'I salute you, gennelmen. You 'ave performed some courageous acts an' deserve your 'onours an' yer retirement.' He raised his cup. 'To you, Sir Knights.'

As the fire died down, leaving just a few smoky embers showing an orange glow, Hugh, who had fallen asleep began snoring softly. Robin gave a weary smile, wrapped his cloak around him and sat back against the wheel of their wagon. Soon he too was asleep.

Will, keen to recover his coins, from their own wagon lay down, and through half-closed eyes watched as Arthur's head began nodding. Staying awake, tired as he was, was not easy but the knowledge that time was running out kept him alert. It would have been easier if the three of them had gone to their usual sleeping places, under their wagons or in tents, but the long day, the food and ale had worn them out.

Slowly Will sat up, looked around to see where the guards on watch were placed and could see that one of them was also slumped against a tree, his head flopping forward. The serjeant had better not see him like that when he was meant to be on duty, thought Will, but it makes things easier for me. The other guard was awake but facing the other way which was very convenient.

Taking one more good look around to make sure he was not going to be seen, Will got to his feet, hunkered down and ran towards their wagon, all the time looking in the direction of the awake guard. He did not turn around. At the wagon, Will climbed inside, pulled out the wool from between the two side panels, and reached down for the pouches. Although he had no reason to believe they had been stolen, he was apprehensive as he slid his fingers inside the cavity until they felt the drawstring cords at the neck of each pouch. They were still there. His heart beat a little more slowly.

Sitting back on his haunches, Will bundled all twelve pouches together onto a large cloth and knotted the top, before edging his way to the opening at the back of the wagon hood. Just before he climbed out he reached for a handful of hay. Shrouded by the shadows of the hedge and the wagon, he crept over to where Chataigne dozed standing up. Instantly aware of him she made a nickering sound in welcome, but Will covered her mouth with his hand to calm her, then gave her the sweet hay to munch on to keep her quiet and busy. Behind her, on the ground was his saddle and saddlebags. Kneeling, but on edge, and continually looking up to see if anyone was awake and watching him, Will slipped six of the pouches into each of the saddlebags and concealed them under the saddle. Satisfied, nothing appeared any different than it had before, he patted Chataigne on the neck then worked his way back around the wagon and walked slowly back to where the others were sleeping. If anyone saw him now he could always say his bladder had been full.

Chapter Eleven

Will awoke as the sun was rising behind the hills, its rose-coloured glimmer showing promise of a beautiful but chill autumn day. He had slept fitfully, and a nightmare where he was on board ship on rough seas close to rocks on which he was shipwrecked, left him drenched in pungent-smelling sweat. Relieved to be awake and find himself on dry land, he rose from his bedding watched by the nearest sentry, rummaged amongst his small pile of clothes to find his other hose, then carefully picking his way across the sharp stony ground, walked barefoot to the nearby slow-flowing stream. On the bank he stripped off his undershirt and, wearing only his hose, took a moment to steel himself against the shock of cold water that would take his breath away. Wading in up to his waist, he shuddered in the crystal clear water. Fish in a variety of colours and sizes swam around him all seemingly heading in the direction of the flow. He stood still, up to his waist in the stream waiting for his body to become accustomed to the cold, then moved further into the midstream where the water reached his shoulders. He stood, preparing himself for the second shock, took a deep breath then, before he could change his mind, plunged under the water until he could hold his breath no longer. Chilled, but refreshed and cleansed of the sweat, he turned to wade back to the bank.

'If I did not know better I would have thought there was a full moon last night and you have become a lunatic.' Robin stood on the bank holding out one of the cover-sheets he had taken from a wagon. He looked worried. 'You are too thin, Will. Your ribs are too evident and you are so pale, your blue veins stand out within your skin as though they are streams on a parchment map. It is only now when you are without your shirt and tunic that this is evident. You need some good meals inside you.' Robin hunkered down holding out the sheet as Will slowly waded towards him, a huge smile on his face.

Will smiled as he waded towards Robin. 'Have done with chiding me, for pity's sake. I thought you were a friend not a critic.' But he took Robin's comments in good part.

'Tis no criticism, my friend.' Robin waited until Will was closer and watched as he carefully stepped over the rocks and sharp gravel at the edge of the bank, before he reached out his hand to help Will up the bank. 'Tis concern for your welfare. You have much work to do at Winterne, so I understand.'

'I know you mean well, Robin, and I agree my body is thin but my arms are strong from working the bow.' Will reached out to take the sheet as he clambered up the bank and began rubbing himself dry. 'My legs are muscled from all the walking, my bruises are healing, I have survived the battles and...' he stopped speaking while he rubbed most of the water from his hair, 'I am fortunate, my health is good. Do not worry on my account, Robin. Camp food is not good as you will know, and you eat what you can get, but once we are back in England I intend to grow so fat you will not recognise me, and as for being pale, my father and my brother were the same. Pale skin, red hair and light freckles on face and arms but we go red in the heat of the summer sun.' As Will's arms and legs warmed up from the force of rubbing himself dry, his skin began turning pink again.

'Your feet are still blue. That water must have been icy.'

Will pulled on his shirt, then his tunic. 'It is cold but not that bad. I have known worse. Once the sun is fully up it will be a good day. But why are you awake so early? Could you not sleep?'

'I slept well enough for a while, but have been restless for the last hour or so.'

'Is there anything worrying you?'

Robin reached down to pick up a round flat pebble and threw it skimming across the stream. Then he sat down on the bank as Will finished drying himself and changed into his dry hose.. 'Not worrying exactly, but I do feel a little uneasy...no, you are right...worried is the right word, about how my children will receive me when I return home, and it has been so long since I have seen them, my older children that is, it is so close now.'

'Your farm is in Kent, I believe.'

'Yes, near Ashford. It is a pretty place and I look forward to being home but have misgivings. It will not be the same without Alice there and I have so many fond memories of her and, although I hate to admit it, I am unsure how I will respond to Stephen.' As he picked up another stone and stood to skim it across the stream, Will saw the melancholy in Robin's eyes. Many marriages were made to increase the size of a business or farm but Will could see how much Robin had loved his wife; there was a genuine pain there.

'Because you lost her through his birth?'

Robin's eyes glittered a little too brightly, he tried to speak but something caught in his throat and he nodded by way of answer. He took a deep breath. 'If he is like Cecilia, he will have the appearance of Alice and I think it will break my heart.' Tears rolled over his lower eyelids and Will stayed silent, not knowing what to say.

Behind them in the camp men began to rouse from their sleep, horses became restless at the sounds and movement, fires were lit, rye flatbreads were prepared and the bakestones laid on the fires to heat.

Robin wiped his eyes with his sleeve and stood up. 'Come, Will. I believe it is time you were properly dressed and I can smell bread and ale and we shall soon be at sea. Are you eager to be up and on our way?' asked Robin.

'Not the voyage, perhaps, but I shall be glad to see Winterne although I understand there is much work to be done. How long will it take you to reach Ashford after we leave Newhaven?' Will asked as they walked back to where Hugh and Arthur were now awake, and waiting for them.

'I will travel some of the way with the troop and leave them when they head onwards to London. My estimate is three days.'

'Will you be safe to travel onwards without company?'

'I think it would only be for one day's journey and I will look out for other travellers to join for the most part, but once I reach the approaches to Ashford I know many people and my safety should not be in question. How will you travel to Winterne?'

'We will look for a company of travellers. There are many towns to travel through so there should be no great difficulty in finding company.'

'We?' Robin seemed puzzled.

Will stopped and looked at Robin. 'Oh yes, and of course this is no secret, we just have not thought to mention it before. Arthur will be coming to Winterne with me. He has no family, no home as such, nothing to go back to where he comes from, and offered his services to assist with the renovation of Winterne. From what we understand it will be a sizeable undertaking and, to be honest, I will be grateful for his help.'

Robin nodded. 'It sounds like a very reasonable plan. I was wondering what was to become of Arthur. I had thought he might try to find his fortune in London, but this may well satisfy him more. But come, see, the camp is almost disassembled and you are still shivering. It would also appear that the flatbreads are ready.'

As they walked back to the join the others it occurred to Will that all four of them had worries and concerns, and they were more alike than he would ever have thought.

Chapter Twelve

With his usual efficiency and booming barking out of orders, once mounted on Ash, the serjeant soon had the convoy of horses and wagons in order. Eighteen soldiers rode in pairs in the front with the three wagons following. Two of the escort soldiers drove the first wagon, and the rest of those on horseback brought up the rear. The serjeant positioned himself at the head of the column as they made ready to head off. The group knew he would not be there long. If he kept to his usual habit he would soon be moving around the column, riding amongst the men and alongside the wagons talking to Will and the other three knights.

Aware of the responsibility of his rank, he tried to maintain a certain reserve from his men, but once they were on the road, his detachment from his men rarely lasted long.

In the second wagon in line, with Arthur at the reins, Will peered around the side of the wagon hood at Robin who was holding the reins of the third wagon. He was waiting for Will and Arthur to shift forward before moving their wagon in behind. The draught horses were so well trained that when one wagon team moved forward, the others followed. Robin seemed to have regained his normal cheerful disposition, and was laughing about something Hugh had said as they moved into line. Will felt relieved that, for now anyway, Robin appeared to have forgotten his worries.

A few moments later they were heading away from the field and entering the walled town of Honfleur. It was then Will remembered the ginger root.

'Arthur, do you have a knife or something sharp within reach? Mine is in my pack at the back of the wagon.'

Arthur reached into his pocket and pulled out a small knife. 'Here. Will this suffice? Be careful though, I sharpened it yesterday.'

Will smiled. 'Indeed it will, thank you.' In his hand he had the lumpy, rough textured piece of ginger and he began carefully cutting away some of the rind which he threw onto the grass verge. Its pungent, spicy smell wafted upwards.

'What is that?' Arthur grimaced.

Will explained that Doctor ben Abadi had assured him it would help him to avoid seasickness.

'Either that or the smell will make you sick which will take your mind off your seasickness!'

Will cut away a piece of the pale yellow flesh of the root and lifted it to his nose, sniffed at it, then to his mouth, but hesitated. 'I am unsure about this, Arthur. What think you? Would you try it?'

'Thankfully, I do not need to try it. I do not suffer with Mal de Mare. Be brave my friend. After all what is the worst that could happen?' Arthur shrugged. 'I doubt that the good doctor would give you something that would do you harm...although it does emit a very strong...um...aroma?'

Will held the smelly root away for a moment, then pinching his nose with his left hand, he popped a piece of ginger into his mouth with the right. His comical grimace and shudder made Arthur laugh. 'Cheer up, William, and think of the pleasant crossing you will have.'

'If this doesn't make me sick first!' But he refrained from spitting it out and unenthusiastically began chewing. Arthur tried hard, but could not stifle his laughter.

It was market day, and even though the escort of forty soldiers and wagons should have been impressive enough to have people move out of their way, the nearer they drew to the harbour where traders had their stalls, the sheer number of people crowding the narrow streets between tightly-packed three and four storey houses, with unusual grey-slate frontages, held up their progress to the harbour.

The serjeant, at the head of the party, ordered six of his men to dismount, walk ahead and where people showed a reluctance to stand aside and allow the cavalcade through, they were to *gently* encourage them to move out of the way. But his troop seemed to have their own idea of the meaning of 'gently' and when manhandled out of the way, some of the men of the town forcefully objected, leading to scuffles breaking out. Mothers hauled their children out of the way, and older people bellowed at the soldiers that they should show some respect. The situation deteriorated rapidly and grudgingly the serjeant recalled his men, ordering them to re-mount.

When the wagon in front, being driven by two of the serjeant's men, came to a halt, Arthur reined in their own two horses. Chataigne whinnied, panicked at all the noise. Will clambered over the hay to calm and reassure her and Narbonne, and to ensure Robin and Hugh in the wagon behind had realised they had to stop.

'What's wrong?' shouted Hugh, but his spoken English resulted in him being spat at by a man walking in the narrow gap between the wagon and house walls. He glared at Hugh and Robin and said something clearly meant as an insult to the English, while sullenly and silently challenging Hugh to react to his insults. Infuriated Hugh stood up so quickly the wagon rocked, and was about to jump down, clearly ready for a fight, but Robin tugged at his jerkin pulling him back onto the seat.

'Leave him. It will only make the situation worse.'

Hugh grudgingly obeyed and stayed where he was.

Having been forced to halt during the disturbance, Will and Arthur, in the middle wagon, hoped the situation would not worsen. Due to the narrowness of the street, and the press of the crowd on both sides, they were unable to see much of what was happening through the covering of the wagon in front. But the noise coming from somewhere ahead, clearly indicated that the townsfolk were furious. It was fairly obvious just how tense the situation was.

The crowd cheered having thought they had won the dispute, until the serjeant ordered the first eighteen men to ride six abreast instead of in twos. His thinking was that the sheer size of the horses walking in a tight formation, should be enough to intimidate people into moving aside and allowing the procession to move through. Then, to impress upon the townsfolk that he meant business, the serjeant ordered the first line of soldiers to lower their pikes to point directly in front of them; anyone who refused to move then ran the risk of being skewered and trampled. Unfortunately, it did nothing to ease the tension although those who had been blocking the way did move aside,

As the riders at the front found themselves able to proceed, the wagons behind followed on slowly, too slowly for Will's liking; the sooner they were beyond this point, the happier he would be. He and Arthur were both fully aware of the hostility in the air albeit now silent, although it felt more menacing, and they kept their eyes firmly fixed ahead of them, looking neither left or right as they passed by the sullen and threatening townsfolk. The antagonism was very evident, it would take very little to re-ignite this tinder box.

As the procession of soldiers and wagons made its way through the narrow street, someone in the crowd behind them began hissing. The sound was taken up by others and grew louder, spreading through the crowd behind and before the troop.

The serjeant manoeuvred Ash to the front line of his men. 'Do not look at anyone in the crowd. Do not make eye contact. Do not *react*. Continue to move forward and we shall be out of this in a few minutes. I do not want this to spiral out of control. Some of you will be boarding the ship. Some will not. Those who remain on French soil will be half of this company and therefore in a weaker position on their return through the town. Raise your halberds but continue moving forward.'

Raising the weapons did appear to calm the crowd a little, as the threat of weapons being used against them lessened. In the main, the hissing ceased other than from a few diehards, who were ignored by the soldiers.

Soon the front line of horses reached the end of the street and trotted out onto the quay where the air was fresh and the aromas of bread, fish, spices, oily sheep's wool and staple products such as eggs, butter, cheeses, poultry, and ale from the market stalls mingled with the tang of salt sea air. The serjeant held back until all his escort party and the wagons had emerged from the street and entered the quay. He sighed with relief. They had avoided what could have been a dangerous incident and before long, the ship would be loaded and the knights on their way back to England. All he had to do after that was get his remaining men back out of the town with the doctor...and his pigeons...and return to the Earl at Poitiers, without any further trouble. He turned his horse to follow the last pair of soldiers when it bucked, squealed loudly and reared up. Having been relaxed and deep in thought about what the next hours would bring, the serjeant was unprepared and was thrown to the ground, hitting his head against a step.

Taken by surprise, the soldiers in the last group, rushed back to help their officer. One brave man made a grab for Ash's reins. As the panicked stallion kicked out, the sharp hard hooves of the distressed animal were dangerously close to the soldier's face. As Ash began to calm, and the others attended to the serjeant, the young soldier stood beside the horse's shoulder, held the reins loosely and talked to him until he gradually relaxed and his squealing stopped. The horse snorted and blew down its nose, his strong muscles rippled and he tried several times to pull away, but he soon tired and, being an experienced warhorse used to being commanded, within a few more minutes he settled down.

By this time, Robin and Hugh had realised something had happened behind them. They reined in their horses and called out to Will and Arthur, who in turn shouted to the wagon drivers in front of them, and the whole company came to a halt.

The quayside bustled with noises, smells and colours. Market traders, surrounded by groups of prospective buyers, were unaware of the incident. Their stalls covered by vibrant striped blue and white oilcloths, they continued to shout invitations to likely buyers inviting them to inspect their wares. Brightly coloured small birds in cages tweeted and screeched, while street dogs chased around scavenging for scraps of anything edible. A flock of nuns garbed in grey habits entered the market from one of the side streets and glided amongst the stalls in pairs buying bread and other necessities. Two younger ones in white, clearly novices, covertly eyed bales of cloth dyed in vivid colours they were no longer allowed to wear. Even occupied with the tragedy of the serjeant's sudden death, Will found a moment to smile at the clear yearning of the novice nuns who may well have been forced to enter the convent against their wishes.

Children ran about between the stalls, knocking over baskets and boxes, angering the traders who, if they caught them, boxed the ears of the young scamps and sent them on their way. Pretty young ladies, hanging on the arms of sailors or older gentlemen, swayed their hips and laughed gaily, hoping to persuade their admirers to buy them ribbons, trinkets or lace from the stalls or, there were others who just wanted drinks from the taverns. Eventually most of them became aware that an incident had occurred, and soon a crowd had congregated around the group of soldiers.

Having managed to calm the terrified horse, the soldier looking after him led him through the throng to a quiet corner where they could both catch their breath. It was then the soldier noticed blood trickling down the horse's right hind leg. On examination he discovered a cut, about an inch long high up on the animal's rump which he thought looked suspiciously like a stab wound and would account for why the horse had reared.

While Robin and Hugh decided to stay to guard the wagons and their cargo, Will and Arthur pushed their way through the crush of people to find Doctor ben Abadi already kneeling beside the serjeant.

Arthur ordered the soldiers to push the mob back to give them room. They seemed to be relieved that someone had taken control, and they swiftly moved into action forming a cordon. It was at that point that a monk from a nearby priory, accompanied by a young attendant, arrived and many of the crowd slipped away to everyone's relief. The monk looked at the Jewish doctor with disdain; it was clear he thought the non-Christian but well-educated man was his inferior.

Doctor ben Abadi looked up at Will and shook his head. 'There is nothing I can do. He is with his God now. The fall broke his neck.' He got to his feet and approached Will and Arthur. 'Sir William, I am delighted you took my advice and have been using the ginger root I gave you.'

'Yes, he has but it is a little strong though, doctor,' replied Arthur.

'I think we have more important things to discuss than the smell of ginger,' said Will, gravely and the doctor changed the subject.

'Come, my friends, we must remove the serjeant's body from here. Something tells me this was not an accident, and overhearing some of the whispered comments from within the crowd, it seems your serjeant had offended the people a little earlier.'

'What's happened?' Master Smith appeared at Will's side. On seeing the serjeant's body he quickly assessed the situation. 'We need to get him out of here and get this area clear before the situation becomes unpleasant.' He turned to Doctor ben Abadi. 'What do you suggest, Doctor? The *Somerset* is on the other side of the harbour and, remember, we still need to catch this morning's tide.'

'But we can't just leave him and sail away,' said Arthur.

'And we have to return to the Earl...' said a nearby soldier.

'And rather quickly judging by the mood of the townsfolk,' Doctor ben

Abadi added.

Having secured Ash to a rail, the soldier who had been tending him arrived. 'Doctor, this weren't no accident. The poor horse 'as bin wounded an' that'll be why 'e reared. 'E's got a nasty a cut on 'is 'ind quarters tha' I reckon needs lookin' at. Could yer come an' look at 'im, please?'

The doctor left with the soldier, leaving Will, Arthur and the master in the midst of the group of soldiers. One of them approached Arthur. 'Sir Arfur, we need ter get away from 'ere bu' 'ave no notion of wha' we should be doin'. We're used ter takin' orders and we don' 'ave no-one ter lead us.'

'What think you, Will?'

'I think the doctor is right. The first thing we need to do is remove the serjeant's body from here. He should be lifted onto one of the wagons then we can take him closer to the *Somerset*. Perhaps moving away from this crowd may be enough to soothe tempers.'

'But what if he's right and this was a deliberate act?' asked the master.

'Even if it was, I doubt that it was meant to kill him,' replied Arthur. 'I believe that was an…an…unfortunate result.'

'Bu' wha' about us, Sir Arfur,' the soldier asked again.

'We can think about that once we have cleared this area. For now, detail some of your company to carry the serjeant to one of the wagons and we will discuss what to do next once we are there.'

They were walking back to the wagons, when the doctor returned with the soldier who was once again leading Ash. He had a small pottery jar with a cork top in his hand, which he popped into one of the pouches hanging from his chain belt. 'It appears as though something sharp has been thrown at the animal, but it must have been light as it pierced the skin, drew blood but did not embed itself in the animal. I have cleaned the wound and have covered it in bee's honey which will soothe and prevent infection.' Will wondered what other *miracle* cures the doctor had in his pouches. 'Now let us join…'

He was interrupted by the monk, his black robe coated in dust from the knees to the hem from where he had been kneeling by the serjeant's body while he prayed over him. Looking directly at Will and Arthur and completely ignoring the doctor, the monk asked: 'Are you making any arrangements for returning this man to his family?'

A grey-haired and whiskered soldier stepped forward. 'I bin wi' the serjeant many a year an' 'e never mentioned no family ter me. Don' think 'e 'ad none.'

'In that case, may I ask if you will you be taking his body back to England?'

Arthur tilted his head to one side and fixed a keen stare at the monk. 'Why do you ask, brother...um?'

'Brother Julian,' said the monk. 'It's just that, I believe I heard you will be sailing soon and wondered if I could help with laying your officer's body to rest here. I am sure my Prior would agree to us giving him a respectful burial in our graveyard.'

Doctor ben Abadi, standing behind the monk, stayed silent but gave Will and Arthur a nod. The soldier saw it and said: 'That'd prob'ly be for the best.'

The others agreed and Brother Julian turned to his young companion. 'Go to the Prior. Tell him what has occurred and request two brothers and a stretcher to be brought to me here in all haste.' The boy ran off and disappeared down a narrow street at the far end of the market.

'You know, we have spent the last almost three weeks with this man and now he's dead and we have no idea what his name was,' said Will. He turned to the whiskered soldier. 'Can you tell us? We may have to leave his body here, but I would like to think his headstone had a name on it.'

''Twas Godwin Webster, Sir William an' I do believe 'e come from somewhere north o' Lunnon.'

'Godwin?' Arthur rubbed his chin. 'You know I would never have thought of him as a Godwin. Do you know anything else about him?'

'No, Sir Arthur. Bless yer, the serjeant kep 'isself' ter 'isself. Good officer 'e was bu' we never knew nothin' abou' 'im otherwise. Kep' isself ter isself, so 'e did.'

Doctor ben Abadi stroked his beard. He had been listening to the conversation and clearly had something on his mind. He addressed the soldier. 'You say you have been with him a long time. Can you tell us who has seen the longest service with this company and would be the two most likely men the serjeant himself would have appointed to take charge if he was incapacitated?'

'Incapa...what, your Honour?' The soldier looked from Arthur to Will and back. The long word was obviously unknown to him.

'I'm sorry...um...you did not give your name...'

'Allen,...iss Walter Allen, Doctor.'

'Thank you, Walter. Now let me rephrase that. If the serjeant, for one reason or another was unable to carry out his duties, which two men of your company would he ask to stand in for him?'

Walter scratched his almost bald head while he thought. 'Righ' I would say prob'ly John Packard and Gilbert Pritchett. They've both bin wi' us fer a long time an' they're pretty reliable. The serjeant used ter gi' 'em orders ter pass down ter the men an' 'e seemed ter trust 'em alrigh'.'

'What are you thinking, Doctor?' asked the master, who had only half paid heed to the conversation. His attention kept straying back to the *Somerset* which was now a hive of activity.

The *Somerset* being a ship of cog style, had a rounded hull and a single mast with one huge sail. Her rudder was at the stern and, if becalmed, or entering a narrow harbour mouth, she could be rowed. At the prow was a small deck with a regular pattern of spaces cut out of the parapet similar to that of the top of castle walls. The upper deck at the stern was much larger and styled in a similar fashion to that of the prow, but underneath was where the Master of the ship had his quarters. On both sides of the hull of overlapping planks, were two 'gates' which had been fashioned to allow for loading and unloading of cargo. These gates, on the side of the ship against the harbour wall, were open and had two wooden ramps, secured at one end to the deck and the other resting on the quayside. Robin and Hugh were already onboard to begin supervising the loading of the wagons onto the deck. The horses had been unharnessed from the shafts and were led up the ramps onto the deck two at a time.

Although most people on the quayside had gone there to visit the market, many were parading up and down just watching the activity on the ships. Some huddled in small groups curiously waiting to know what had happened to the serjeant, and whether the troops were going to arrest anyone for attacking his horse, or grimly relishing the sudden and exciting turn of events. Sailors about to join their ships for their next voyage were saying goodbye to sweethearts, or young ladies who perhaps they had only met the evening before. Groups of people were occupied in watching what the soldiers were doing, especially now there had been the dramatic death.

Aware that the master's mind was elsewhere and that time was passing quickly, the doctor continued. 'Well, one party will be heading to London once you reach Newhaven, the other, plus myself and my pigeons, will be travelling back to Poitiers, and both will need a senior officer, someone to take the place of the serjeant.'

'Oh aye. That's right,' said Walter.

The doctor turned to Arthur and Will. 'I suggest that we appoint these two responsible men to lead the two parties to their respective destinations. Are we agreed?'

'Whatever you are going to do, you must decide quickly, gentlemen, The tide will not wait while you dilly-dally.' The master was becoming impatient and he spun around at the sound of a shrill neighing and a shout coming from the *Somerset*. A soldier had been leading a horse up one of the ramps when it baulked, refused to go any further and tried to reverse back to the harbour. Another member of the crew ran up the ramp to push the horse from behind, but the strength of a terrified horse was not to be underestimated. It bucked sending the sailor behind him off balance, and he fell headlong into the sea beside the ship, just as a wave pushed the hull of the ship back towards the harbour wall.

The sailor, realising the danger he was in, tried to swim to the nearest steps on the harbour wall. Kelvin threw one end of a rope for him to grab, intending to haul him out of danger, but it missed and dropped into the water just out of reach. In desperation, the sailor tried to haul himself out of the water by grasping one of the thick rope fenders on the harbour wall but it was still wet from the high tide, and slippery with seaweed. He could not get a grip. His crew mates on the *Somerset* howled in despair as he slid back into the water. Families passing by realised what was about to happen and mothers grasped their children tightly turning their heads away; all of them aware there could only be one way this incident would end. From the quayside, Will saw the expression on Kelvin's face; nothing needed to be said.

The next wave shifted the ship closer to the harbour wall. The sailor ran out of time. Powerless to help but unable to look away, the observers on the harbour and the ship witnessed, as with his final agonised plea to God, the sailor was crushed between the wall and the hull of the ship. His cry told all those too far back to see what had happened. Kelvin, head hung low, let the end of the rope he was still holding fall, and turned away.

Many members of the crowd dropped to their knees and crossed themselves, joining with the crew to show respect for the victim as they prayed for their lost crew member. It had all happened so quickly, there was nothing that could have been done to save him, but many of the crew felt they had failed him.

This kind of accident was always possible when in harbour; being a sailor was to live a life of risk, they all knew that, but understanding tragic accidents could happen, did not lessen the grief or shock when they did. One slip, one moment of not concentrating, and your life was done.

It had all happened too quickly for Master Smith to get back to the ship. He stood, ashen-faced and overcome with the horror. 'My God! Another death!' I pray this voyage is not cursed.' He shook his head in disbelief. 'Now, for pity's sake, will you make your decisions and let us tarry no longer. I will attend to my ship, gentlemen. Make haste, please, before we lose anyone else. And Brother Julian, I for one will be content with whatever you decide in regard to the serjeant, but our crew member will be taken back to Newhaven to his family.'

The master marched up the ramp and detailed four men to retrieve the sailor's body. Watched by an increasingly large number of morbidly fascinated spectators, two sailors lowered themselves onto the wooden framework their dead crewmate had tried to reach, and eased themselves into the water, while crew members aboard the ship pushed the ship away from the wall with wooden poles. No-one would be crushed while trying to recover their dead shipmate. A third sailor slid into the water, wound the rope securely under the dead man's arms enabling the two above to haul him up to where two more waited to wrap his body in an oilcloth sail.

A few minutes later all five, one dripping wet, walked up onto the ship carrying the dead man onto the deck, where the entire crew stood to one side, respectfully removed their hats and bowed as their shipmate was laid gently in a storeroom for the voyage.

A few minutes later, Brother Julian's young attendant returned followed by two more monks carrying a folding stretcher between them. Brother Julian took them to where two soldiers guarded the body of the serjeant. They made the sign of the cross over the serjeant, lifted him gently onto the stretcher before pushing their way through the spectators to return to the Priory. Brother Julian nodded to the doctor, Will and

Arthur, then fell in line walking quickly behind the two stretchers bearers, with the boy following trying not to trip over his robe which was obviously meant for someone a year or two older.

Will, Arthur and the doctor made their way to the ship where they joined the escort soldiers on the quayside and sought out John Packard and Gilbert Pritchett. The two men agreed that someone needed to take the position of senior officer of the two groups. As luck would have it, John Packard had always expected to be amongst the party returning to Poitiers, and Gilbert Pritchett was one of the party heading back to England. Neither felt particularly eager to take on the responsibility of senior officer, but they understood that someone with experience had to take charge and the reasons why they had been selected so, although unenthusiastic about their new roles, they both reluctantly agreed.

The next thing to do was to get everything on board. It seemed incredible to Will that, with all that had happened since they had arrived in Honfleur, only half an hour or so had passed, but that meant they still had time to catch the tide if they hurried on with the loading.

Gilbert Pritchett divided his men into two groups, one to begin taking the horses on board while the remaining group waited with the horses still on the quayside. Some of the horses walked up the ramps and onto the deck without fuss, but some baulked. To speed things up, and to avoid any further accidents or incidents, Gilbert ordered them to be blindfolded. If they were unable to see where they were going, it was likely the risk of panic would be reduced.

While the last of the horses was taken onboard, and they were all settled in temporary stalls set up to prevent them from swaying around during the voyage, Will and Arthur joined Robin and Hugh in securing the three wagons. Once in place, a block of wood was wedged under the wheels and a rope, lashing each wagon to the next then tied securely to the mast would prevent any rolling of the wagons when at sea.

With the horses, wagons and, since the loss of Gwilim and the serjeant, now nineteen men, one of the ramps was pulled up and strapped down securely against the side of the hull.

Hearing the master now impatiently barking orders at his crew and clearly in a hurry to set sail while the tide was with them, Arthur hurried toward the remaining ramp, but Will took one last look around suddenly aware that the doctor was nowhere to be seen, and the troop returning to Poitiers were beginning to mount. Chewing a fresh piece of ginger, he had wanted to thank the doctor and say farewell, but there was no sign of him so, regretfully, he turned away. One of the crew had just bolted the gate behind him when a clattering sound on the cobbled street made him turn.

The doctor, sitting at the front of a cart being pulled by two mules, drew into the square and halted by the troop who would escort him back to the Earl. On the cart he had a number of earthenware jars which Will assumed would contain his healing potions and ingredients, a tied up bedroll, an oiled cover for the cart, and four cages of pigeons.

'Hello there, my friend,' he called to Will and waved. 'I am about to join these fine fellows and begin our journey to Poitiers,' he shouted loudly enough to be heard above the noises on the harbour.

Will smiled and shouted back. 'I am glad to see you, Doctor. I had hoped to see you again before we sailed. I wanted to say my farewells and to thank you. I am still chewing the ginger root and, hopefully, all will be well this time.'

'Good. It should work for you. At least the sea does not have much of a swell and the breeze is promising for a reasonable voyage. We may be saying our farewells but I do not believe this will be goodbye. I feel we shall meet again, so your God go with you, Sir William, and good fortune on your endeavours.'

'And to you, Doctor.'

John Packard, at the head of the column of soldiers, began to lead his men towards the narrow lane that led out of town and, as the line of soldiers parted in the middle, the doctor slipped his cart into the gap. This time the crowd stood back to allow them through; it was clear there was little liking for the soldiers and the townsfolk would be pleased to see the back of them.

Will waved farewell to the departing escort as they rode away on their journey back to Poitiers then turned away to join Arthur as the *Somerset* slowly headed out of port. He looked around at the tethered horses who had now calmed. 'Oh good, Ash is with us.' He pointed out the horse that had belonged to the serjeant. ' I wondered what had happened to him.'

'I like Narbonne, he suits me well, but I have a hankering to take Ash with us and give him a home somewhere peaceful,' said Arthur. 'I feel he has been through enough.'

'Well, if Gilbert Pritchett is agreeable to let us keep Ash, perhaps we could offer to buy him,' Will answered.

'Thank you, Will.' Arthur smiled widely. 'I hoped you would say that. In return, perhaps, during the voyage while there is nothing else for us to do, we can find ourselves a quiet place on this ship and begin your reading lessons.'

Chapter Thirteen

Master Walter Smith stood on the raised poop deck at the stern of the ship, watching his crew, as they extracted the long oars from the fastenings, and took their places ready to row the ship out of the harbour. Honfleur was not only a very active sea port, but it was also at the estuary of the River Seine which made the harbour busier than most. The constant stream of smaller boats arriving from the river side were potential hazards to the larger vessels moving in and out of the harbour.

But the crew needed no supervision, most had been with Master Smith for many years, were all experienced able seamen, and rowed in and out of Honfleur and other harbours, including Newhaven, regularly. They knew very well what was required of them; the tides, the currents, and likely hazards. Within the haven of the stone walls, although there was some movement of water caused by the tide and the wake of other vessels moving around the harbour, ships were sheltered and the water fairly calm.

The master gave the order for the anchor to be pulled up and two crewmen standing by the quayside mooring rings, one at the bow and another at the stern, waited for him to give the order to unfasten the ropes and take them on board. On hearing the command, they quickly unhooked the ropes and clambered up the remaining ramp onto the deck, hauling the ropes in after them. Once safely on board, two waiting crewmen pulled up the last ramp, secured it, then closed and bolted the gate. Having stacked the ropes under the prow deck safely out of the way, all four collected their long oars to take their places with their fellow crewmen, ready to row the *Somerset* out of the harbour.

Kelvin, the steersman, stood alone and sullen, glowered as he leaned on the tiller, a long wooden arm attached to the rudder, by which the ship was steered. The Somerset was a large ship and it could be an effort to steer her especially in rougher seas, and here Kelvin's massive strength was an asset.

Walter Smith, a widower since Kelvin was eight years old, was well aware of his son's failings in working well with others and maintaining an even temper. The crew disliked him and tolerated him only because he was their master's son. But Kelvin's temperament was not the only drawback in finding him a suitable job on board ship. His size and lack of agility prevented him from climbing ropes and rigging, so the master had given his son the job of Steersman where he could work alone.

Kelvin had made several attempts at finding other work on land before joining the ship; apprentice wheelwright for one, then apprentice blacksmith, but each time, some trivial incident had set off his ill-tempered nature, a fight ensued and he was dismissed.

The final straw came when, at sixteen years of age, he had tried his hand at farm labouring, but had skewered one of his fellow farm workers with a pitchfork following an argument over a girl Kelvin liked.

Walter and Kelvin had been forced to flee their home during the night to save Kelvin's life, as the family of the dead man had threatened to lynch him. It was then that Walter realised he would have to keep Kelvin close. If Kelvin could not control his temper, his father would have to do it for him. Fortunately, Kelvin had never turned on his father and Walter prayed he never would.

As the oars dipped and rose through the water, the wake created small white crested waves that rippled under small boats causing them to bob up and down, and larger boats to gently roll.

On the smaller raised deck at the prow, the Boatswain, who supervised the crew, stood looking out for any hazards such as small boats out for a day's fishing, or merchant ships making their way in or out of the harbour.

Looking over the side of the ship with Robin and Hugh, Will and Arthur watched shoals of small, brightly coloured fish as they swam between the hulls and around the stone jetties where the smaller boats were moored. A few fish skeletons that remained after a gull's meal, and discarded pieces of wood floated past, and they listened to the gentle rhythmic slapping of the water against the creaking hull of the ship.

Forgetting the tragedies that had occurred that morning for a moment, his hands still on the rail, Will stood back and inhaled the bracing sea air. He took a deep breath, filled his lungs and thanked God for the pleasant cool breeze, that gently billowed the sails of those ships that had not furled them away. He looked up, the October sun low on the horizon blinded him for a moment and he shaded his eyes with his hand. He was relieved they were indeed fortunate to have no clouds in the sky, no sign of rain, just clear blue sky as far as the eye could see. Blue sky...and gulls; they were everywhere, strutting around the quayside trying to snatch anything edible, and making an awful din with a call that very often sounded like laughter. Others sat or paraded up and down on the rail of the ship trying to peck at the deck hands who came anywhere near them, or perched atop the mast, waiting and watching for unwary fish to swim by. It was a rare moment when a gull dived into the sea and flew out empty-beaked. Disturbed by the crew as they began rowing towards the harbour mouth, the gulls flew off to bother a different crew or pester market visitors.

'Come, Will,' Arthur said, leading Will away from the rail. 'Your first reading lesson awaits in our wagon.' With the covers now taken off the wagons, folded and stowed away, Will and Arthur made themselves comfortable on the hay and Arthur drew a knife from its leather sheath attached to his belt.

Once beyond the rough, uneven waves just outside the harbour, some of the other crew members climbed the rigging to release the single square sail, then those on deck hauled on the ropes to raise it up, and made fast the ropes. Those who had been rowing, then raised the oars out of the water, heaved them, dripping, back onto the deck, fastened them by metal clips to the side of the hull where they were out of everyone's way, and secured against rolling around the deck in rough seas.

Seated on their wagon, Arthur explained that, from what his uncle had told him, the alphabet – the symbols of writing used – was invented by the Catholic Church and the first evidence of writing had been in Latin. But Arthur doubted that as he felt that written Latin must have been based on something that had existed before. During his travels he had spoken to sailors and wanderers who had seen other forms of writing that appeared to be much older than Latin. With his knife he gouged out letters, on the side of the wagon and asked Will if he recognised any of them.

'Yes. 'This one...and this one and these two...and this, and this and this one,' he said proudly.

'And do you know what they are?'

'Yes. They are the letters that spell my name...'W-i-ll-i-a-m.'

'Good. We have a start. We are not going to be at sea for long enough to be able to make much progress now, but while we are travelling to Winterne, we will have time to work on your reading on the journey. For now though...' he reached behind him for the leather bag he always kept close at hand, '...in here I have a piece of chalk which can be used for writing. I will write a few short words containing the letters of your name, and I would like you to see if you can select them.'

It was when they headed out to the open sea from the shelter of the harbour that the waves created by crosswinds, made the ship buck and toss a little more wildly. The criss-crossing waves crashed into the harbour wall and against the prow of the ship as she sliced her way over them and fine sea spray flew over the hull, soaking the crew and decks in a shower of cold sea water.

It was at that point the ship exited the harbour and sailed into the rougher water, rearing and dipping as it ploughed through the choppier waves. Having been fairly smooth up to that point Will had not realised how the crosswinds outside the harbour would affect the strength of the waves and the colour drained from his face as they soared and plunged with the turbulent sea.

'Are you feeling unwell?'

Will nodded.

Arthur appeared untroubled by the change in the condition of the sea and Will envied him his strong stomach. 'Perhaps we should leave the reading lesson and get you over to the rail again.'

Will need no encouragement. Fearing he was going to be sick, the sooner he reached the rail the better and, being unwell in the wagon was not an option. He jumped out of the wagon, headed in a hurried but lurching walk towards the side of the ship, and leaned against the rail trying hard to keep his breakfast down.

'Take in a deep breath through your nose,' said Master Smith as he walked by, heading to the upper deck at the stern, 'then breath out through your mouth, but turn your head away, please. I cannot abide the smell of ginger.' He winked at Arthur and patted Will heavily on the back, which Will could have done without. 'Do not worry lad. This bumpier bit will soon be done and you will feel better. But, if you are going to be sick, remember to face away from the wind or you'll be sorry when what you've brought up comes back at you.

He looked up to where Kelvin, sullen as ever, battled with the tiller, keeping the ship steady through the irregular peaks and troughs of the waves. 'I must go and join my son. Excuse me, gentlemen.'

Soon after passing through the rough water into calmer, smaller waves, the ship stopped bucking and the feeling of nausea began to ease. Will relaxed and a little colour returned to his ashen cheeks. He sent a silent thank you to Doctor ben Abadi. Thanks to the good doctor, it seemed there was a possibility that, even if he did not actually enjoy this sea trip, it might not make him suffer as badly as he had before.

When satisfied there were no hazards between themselves and the open sea, the master again left Kelvin in charge and returned to the main deck where he joined Robin and Hugh who leant against the rail, looking out to sea.

'It looks as though we shall have a good voyage, gentlemen.'

'It certainly does, Master Smith,' said Hugh. 'For myself, I would not mind the wind being a little stronger, but I do not believe that would suit our friend Will. He has been chewing that damned root since we arrived in Honfleur and, between us,' he wrinkled his nose, 'I prefer to be in the open air.'

Master Smith smiled, something they had not seen him do before, revealing several missing teeth. 'Ah. The ginger root. Yes, it does have a powerful odour, but there are two of my crew who always chew it during the first hour or two of each voyage since Doctor ben Abadi suggested it. They swear it helps,' he rolled his eyes, 'and I hope Sir William finds the same benefit, but I for one agree that to be out here in the open air is far preferable than being around the smell of it in a confined space.' He laughed and headed off towards the bow where they watched him climb the steps to the smaller deck where he joined Simson, the Boatswain, who they had previously seen supervising the rowers as they left Honfleur harbour.

Without being too obvious they were looking, Hugh and Robin watched as the Master unrolled a chart and laid it out on a wooden ledge. Simson pointed out something that seemed to be of significance and they began talking animatedly. The Master nodded, stroked his chin and considered the chart a little longer, nodded, rolled up the chart and handed it back to Simson.

Robin turned to Hugh. 'I hope we are not to expect some trouble.'

'It looks as if they're concerned about something, but…but look, just take a look out there.' Hugh took his right hand off the rail and pointed down to the sea then up towards the sky, 'There's nothing on the horizon, no French…no pirate ships to be seen, no storm clouds above and a short journey ahead of us. The crew are going about their tasks, none of them seem troubled about anything. Maybe we are worrying overmuch.'

'Then why does the master pucker his brow in a frown?'

'He's coming back…don't look. Why don't you ask him when he passes us?'

Robin glanced towards the prow deck. The master was indeed heading towards the steps and Robin saw him nod to one of the crew standing at the door under the poop deck where the master's cabin and lockers were situated. The crewman nodded back and entered the cabin area closing the door behind him. The master, seemingly satisfied then descended the steps to the main deck and proceeded along the deck toward where Robin and the others were trying not to show they had noticed anything amiss. From the look on the master's face, he certainly had something on his mind.

'Arthur, when Master Smith goes by why don't you ask him, what's wrong?' suggested Hugh as Will and Arthur walked up to join them.

'Something bothering you?' asked Will.

'Me? Why me?' chuckled Arthur. 'If you want to know what's wrong, be brave…just as you were on the battlefield, Hugh. If you can show that kind of courage, then surely something as simple as asking a question of the master won't be too difficult for you?' Arthur teased.

'Shh. He's almost here,' said Robin, in a hushed tone.

As Master Smith, preoccupied, approached the four young knights, they continued to look out to sea, seemingly having not a care in the world. It was not until he had gone passed them on his way to the stern, that Will turned.

'Master Smith, you have no idea how grateful I am that this voyage, so far, has been pleasurable.'

The master, stopped, turned to Will and his companions. 'I am delighted to hear that, Sir William.' He looked at the sky and up at the billowing sail that gave a loud slapping sound as it flapped in the wind. 'The wind remains favourable, the sky is still cloudless...hmm, um...yes, I believe we shall be at Newhaven before the light begins to fail.'

Looking around at his three friends, Will said: 'That's good news, is it not?' All three nodded, somewhat astonished that it was Will who had had the daring to speak up. 'But you seem deep in thought, Master Smith, is there a problem? Perhaps I and my friends could be of some service...?'

The master forced a smile and shrugged. 'No, nothing amiss...just the customary responsibilities of a Master Mariner under sail.'

But Will was not to be put off. 'Ah...it's just that when we saw you with Simson, a few moments ago, you both seemed to be concerned about something on a chart. We thought there might be something wrong?'

The master looked in turn from one anxious face to another as all four of the young battle-weary heroes, the Earl had placed in his care, awaited his response. 'Ah, I hoped you hadn't seen that.' He looked down at the deck and sighed, then looked up at Will. 'We are now in the area where we may encounter French warships. I hope you gentlemen will not be opposed to our sailing under the French flag, the Oriflamme.'

'But that's their battle flag!' Arthur protested. 'Why would you use that...that blasted red-orange rag with its blazing sun?'

'We have seen that flag too many times to want to ever see it again,' exclaimed Robin.

'They flaunt it as a forewarning that no quarter will be given to our wounded on the field,' said Hugh. 'In God's name, why? Why would you fly it?'

All five heads looked upward at the two flags the *Somerset* was currently flying, the red Cross of St George against a white background, and the quartered crest of the Earl of Salisbury with its three red lozenge shapes on a white background, and the three armoured flexed and conjoined legs of the Isle of Man, of which he also held the Lordship.

'Does the Earl know you do this?' Robin demanded an answer.

The master nodded. 'Oh, believe me, gentlemen. I understand your feelings, I really do, and yes, the Earl is aware. Many of our ships do the same thing. When Simson and I were looking at the chart, I knew the time had come and expected your reaction. I am sure your fellow soldiers will feel the same.'

Robin shook his head in disbelief. Hugh turned his back on the master and walked to the rail. Will looked down at his feet. Only Arthur waited, politely hiding his hostility to the plan. 'You see,' the master continued, 'we may be unfortunate enough to come across French warships in this area. We are no match for their speed or their number of fighting crew. So, to avoid confrontation as we sail further north, we will make ready to change to the French flags until we are in sight of the southern English coast, then we will change back. I ask for your understanding. We are not fast enough to outrun their warships of which, thankfully, there are few. Neither do we have the weaponry or men to defend ourselves, so we have to be cunning, show their flags and hope they will take us for a French privateer and leave us alone.'

The door under the stern deck opened and the crew member appeared carrying a large bundle draped across his arms. He approached the master. They recognised a folded Oriflamme and the blue Royal House of France with three gold fleur-de-lys.

Hugh spat overboard, in disgust. The master said nothing; he knew they were now resigned to accepting the necessity of flying these flag. 'Do not raise them yet but leave them where they can be reached in a hurry if need be,' he ordered the sailor.

'Aye aye, Master, I'll leave 'em on top o' the barrel by the door,' came the reply. 'Them'll be 'andy there.' He walked back towards the cabin door and laid the flags across the top of the barrel.

'Now, if you will excuse me, gentlemen,' said the master. 'I must be about my duties.' Aware that all four pairs of eyes were staring angrily after him, he had almost reached the steps leading to the upper deck when he turned and walked back to them. 'I do regret this. I bitterly regret having to use these foul rags,' he nodded over to where the French flags were laid. 'But it is my job to protect my crew, and the Earl's ship whenever, and wherever necessary, something for which I must use all my experience and cunning.' His eyes narrowed and his mouth set in a firm, thin line. 'I am truly sorry you do not approve of my action and...well, while I understand your feelings, you must understand I am master of this ship and I *will* do whatever I believe necessary to get us from one safe harbour to another, although sometimes it sticks in my craw to do it. Forgive me if you can. If you cannot, then look around this ship at the men under my command. I know them all and I know the families of those who have them. I will not put my men at more risk than they face each day with the shifting moods of a perilous sea, when I could have done something about it, whether I like it or not. Although we rarely see any of their warships, we do have to be prepared. Thank you, gentlemen.' He turned on his heel, walked straight to the steps and climbed up to the poop deck, where he leant against the back rail, looking out to sea.

Silent, and utterly mortified by Master Smith's reasoned reaction, and now more sympathetic to his way of thinking, all four realised the master had little choice. The *Somerset* was not a warship; it was not built to withstand a battle at sea, therefore, the master had made the right decision, no matter how hard it was for them to stomach.

Arthur looked around at his friends and saw acceptance in their eyes. 'He's right.'

Robin walked over to the barrel where the folded French flags lay. He looked down at the Oriflamme. 'I have never been so close to one of these. It always felt like an unholy symbol when we saw it on the battlefield, almost as though the Devil himself had put it there. I remember trembling each time I saw it.' He ran his hand over it and looked up to see Will, Hugh and Arthur watching him, pensive. 'I knew, each time I saw this...rag...that that was the day I would die. I fully expected it. In my prayers I said my farewells to my children, commended them into God's hands, and made my confession. But I am still here and, you know, it may sound strange but touching it seems to have taken some of the power out of it, diminished its terror. It's just a piece of gaudy material. It no longer has its unholy effect.'

Hugh gave a sad smile. Will nodded. Arthur lowered his head. Robin walked back to join them and, without any given signal, they all looked up at the Cross of St George blowing in the sea breeze above them.

They had been at sea for what they believed to be three hours or so, without seeing anything of interest, when two of the soldiers amongst those squatting on the other side of the deck, began singing a jolly song that none of the knights knew. Their song lifted the gloomy mood that had been created by the sight of the French flags. Another of the soldiers ran across to one of the wagons, reached over the side and pulled out a lute then ran back to join his companions. It only took him a few moments to pick up the tune and join in accompanying the singers.

Will and the others crossed the deck to join them, and Robin began drumming his hands on the top of a wooden barrel in time with the rhythm. Soon a few members of the crew began singing along while going about their routine tasks. Unexpectedly, one of the soldiers who had been sitting cross-legged on the deck tapping his feet in time to the music, pulled off his boots, jumped up, hauled his neighbour to his feet, and linking arms they danced around in bare feet, encouraging others to join them. Within the blink of an eye the sound of ten pairs of bare feet slapping against the deck blended with the jolly sound of singing, drumming, the lute and the occasional snort from a few of the horses.

Kelvin, on the poop deck, still at the tiller, did not look at all impressed, but Master Smith gave him a nudge, as if to encourage him to cheer up. He gave up when it failed to raise a smile.

A shout went up from one of the crew high up in the rigging. 'A ship!'

The singing ceased. The lute player, having been listening to the singing had not heard the shout, and continued playing for a few seconds longer until he became aware that something was happening by the sound of silence around him. The master called up, 'Where away, what direction, Silas? What colours are they flying?'

The seaman on the rigging pointed in the direction of the other ship and shouted down, 'Nor-nor-west and tis the French flag...and he's heading towards us.'

At that, without waiting for orders, members of the crew ran to the lockers and hauled out bows, arrows, long knives, pikes and swords with which to defend themselves if the need arose. The master barked out the order to lower the Cross of St George and the Earl of Salisbury's crest and raise the Fleur-de-Lys and Oriflamme, and hurried to the prow deck. The English flags were quickly lowered and the French flags hoisted. Would that be enough to foil the approaching French ship?

The soldiers, the four archer knights, all rushed to get their weapons. The next few minutes, while Silas kept watch from the rigging, were tense.

No-one spoke. A tense stillness spread across the ship, each man occupied with his own thoughts and preparing for battle. The only sounds to be heard were the, huffing and snorting of the horses, the creaking of the timbers, the rush of the sea and the flapping of the sail.

Will was not frightened, if anything, he felt saddened. At least that was the nearest description he could come to the way he felt. He had become a knight, had been released from active soldiering, he had been permitted, after so many years without the prospect of a future, to go home. He had been given an estate. He now had a life to look forward to, had allowed himself to dream of a future – even though he was unsure of his capability to succeed – but needed the opportunity to try, to prove himself. He now had hopes of giving his mother a decent home for her last years, he had thought, albeit briefly, about marrying and having his own family, something he had never given a thought about before as he fully expected to die on the battlefield. All these things had become possible and, well, now all that would come to nought if he lost his life in a sea battle. His mouth was dry, he tried to swallow, but his tongue stuck to the roof of his mouth. He glanced at Arthur, standing beside him, wondering what he was thinking. Robin and Hugh stood, grave-faced and statue-like on his other side, and he had a sudden realisation that they had the same dreams for the future; Robin being with his children again, Hugh will have visualised the time when he would ask for his Margaret's hand in marriage, even Arthur setting up home at Winterne, they all had something to get back to England for.

Will looked over at Chataigne. He had become very fond of her and now, like some of the other horses, she was snorting, her tail unhappily clamped to her hind quarters, her ears back. What would happen to her if he died? Evidently, the horses understood the change in atmosphere. That was when the other ship appeared on the horizon. Was this ship to be their death?

The master stood, braced, staring ahead waiting for the two-masted, two-sail vessel to close the gap between them. He guessed from its direction it had left one of the Normandy harbours but which one? With the additional sail, it travelled more speedily. One of the crew drew near to the knights.

'It will be on us within the half hour, Sir Arthur,' the crewman volunteered. 'She don' seem much bigger than us even though she've got two sails. She can go faster alrigh' but iss doubtful' she can ram us. It don't look ter me like a warship, an' anyway, wi' all them soldiers we got 'ere, it migh' be alrigh' 'cos we'd 'ave more fightin' men than she do.'

Will forced a smile. That gave him something to hope for.

The master turned to the crew with a massive smile. 'Rest easy, lads. It's the *Bertha*! My eyesight must be going or I'd have recognised her sooner. She's done the same thing we have. Probably seen us before we saw her and changed her flags. That's Master Stocke's ship and she'll have come out of Calais. There'll be no battle today. You can put your weapons down.'

Relieved the potential threat had proved to be a false alarm, smiles and laughter broke out around the ship, a cheer went up that startled the already skittish horses, the soldier with the lute dropped his pike on the deck beside him, sat down on the deck, picked up his instrument and began playing a merry tune.

Crewmen hurried to stash the weapons back in the lockers and took up their appointed duties again, while the escort soldiers and four knights placed their own weapons back in the wagons before checking on their horses. Will allowed himself to breathe again; his dream for the future, and his hopes for Robin, Hugh and Arthur, who he had come to think of as friends, were alive again.

A cheer went up, startling the horses again, several of them stamped their hooves and swished their tails but, Narbonne was more agitated and threw his head back trying to slip out of his tethers. Arthur went to him, stroked his neck and spoke in quiet tones to him until he relaxed and settled.

By the time Narbonne was soothed, the *Bertha* had drawn level with the *Somerset* and had slightly overtaken but the masters on both ships began a shouted conversation with each other across the narrow stretch of sea between them.

'Where are you bound, Samuel?' asked Master Smith. 'You had us worried for a while showing those flags.'

The master of the *Bertha* chuckled. 'Ah but you used the same ploy, Walter. We're heading for Dover this time. And you?'

'Newhaven. Seen any French warships?'

'No, not this time. So far anyways.'

'I see you have an unusual cargo this time. Don't usually see you carrying horses.'

'We are taking goods and their escort for my lords the Earl and the Prince, they will then be taken on to London.'

'Surely Dover would have been a shorter land journey to London, or even Gravesend.'

'Aye, mebbe, but we have passengers who are going to the west country. Newhaven's between the two, so mebbe that's why we're ordered to go there.'

Samuel pondered for a moment, clearly thinking about the logic of using Newhaven but the *Bertha* was still moving slightly ahead. They would soon be out of shouting range.

'I just do as I'm ordered, Samuel,' bellowed Walter. 'Tis the Earl's ship and I'm just one of his servants.'

'Aye, well, God speed, you Walter, and I pray the rest of your voyage remains peaceful and safe from them French warships.'

'And to you, Samuel. Fare thee well.'

He waved to the master of the *Bertha* and watched for a moment as she sailed on. Then turned towards where the four knights, who were now standing around the lute player, were vying with each other over which tune they would like him to play next and waiting to see whether he knew them. Will and Arthur, stood aside to let the master between them and Robin and Hugh.

'Well, sir knights, we now have approximately two hours left before we reach Newhaven. Sunset will be an hour or so after we arrive, and we must make the most of the remaining daylight to disembark the horses and wagons. Have you thought about what you will do when you arrive?'

'Well I plan to travel with the escort for a while as they take the road to London,' said Robin.

'And I shall stay with them until they reach London, then try to find a group of travellers heading towards the north,' added Hugh.

'Gilbert,' the master called. 'Could you join us for a moment, please?'

The acting serjeant had been sitting cross-legged on the deck with a few of the men in his company, playing knucklebones. He looked up to see the master beckoning him to join them. Handing the sheep's knucklebones over to one of his men, he walked over looking somewhat puzzled. 'Is there a problem?'

'No, nothing to worry about, Gilbert,' said the master. We've had enough accidents, incidents and worries for one day, have we not?'

Gilbert nodded. 'Then what can I help you with?'

'What are your plans for when we arrive at Newhaven? By the time we unload it will not be long until sunset. Do you intend to begin your journey immediately or will you wait until morning?'

Behind Gilbert, the group of soldiers he had just left were watching with curiosity, wondering what the ships master wanted with their new leader.

Gilbert lifted his cap, scratched his head and looked down at the deck. 'I s'pose I hadn't thought much about that yet. P'raps I should 'ave... but...well, up ter a few hours ago the serjeant would've bin mekkin' the decisions. T'would 'ave bin 'im that'd 'ave told us wha' we was goin' ter do, but now I don' know.'

'Can I suggest then, ' said the master, 'that you find somewhere to camp overnight and make a start in daylight tomorrow. The horses will still likely be uneasy after they leave the ship, and giving them a night to rest on land, get their land legs back and have a good feed, will get them back to rights in no time. They'll be ready to move on again in the morning.'

'Aye, that'd prob'ly be best. I'll tell the lads. Thanks, Master Smith.' And he left to join his men to let them know what had been decided.

'It would be better for you lads as well,' the master said to Will and his friends. 'My suggestion for you all would be to find rooms at a local Inn for the night. 'The Ship' or 'The Swan' are both fairly clean, the food is plain but good, the straw in the mattresses is changed every two weeks and the old stuff burnt, or so I'm told, so they don't have so many fleas and the beds don't stink.'

Arthur laughed. 'Thank you for the recommendation.'

'We'll certainly think on it,' said Hugh. I had thought to a stay in the wagon tonight but the idea of a warm fire, a hot meal and flagon of ale or two sounds more inviting, fleas or not. What say you, Robin, Will?'

'It would be better for us to stay overnight, Arthur', said Will. Any band of travellers heading our way are not likely to leave at night, and we are more likely to find company in the morning.'

'And that company is like to be at an inn,' said Master Smith. 'That's where travellers tend to be found while gathering together or resting overnight.'

'And Hugh and I have arranged to leave with the escort in the morning,' said Robin. 'As long as we rise early, I do not believe we need to camp with them and I agree with Hugh. It is the inn for me also.'

'Then I'll leave you for now, gentlemen,' said Master Smith as he turned to go, but then he stopped and turned back. 'Of the two inns, The Swan is the one I favour, I think the food is better, but The Ship will do almost as well, and The Swan may be the busier of the two.'

'Speaking of warm fires and hot meals,' said Robin, he shivered. 'I feel a chill in the air since the sun has lowered. 'I am going to get my cloak.' He walked away toward the wagon he and Hugh had been sharing. Robin called back; 'Hugh, I can bring your cloak if you want it.'

Hugh nodded his thanks and turned to Will and Arthur. 'I hope all will be well for Robin when he returns to his family,' he shook his head sadly, 'but I fear there will be heartbreak for him.'

'But he is looking forward to being with the children again...'

'Yes, and I am sure they will be happy to see him, but the little lad has never seen him and will take time to become accustomed to having his father at home again, but it is not that that concerns me too much.'

Will and Arthur exchanged puzzled glances.

Hugh continued. 'You see, during our talks I have come to realise just how much Robin loved his wife. He talks all the time about her. She is in all his memories of home, the farm, with the children...' he paused. 'Robin *sees* her everywhere...'

'I think I understand,' said Will. 'When he arrives back at the family...'

'...He will have to face the fact that she has really gone,' Arthur added. 'While he has been away that fact has not been a reality.'

'Exactly, but also his older children have grown up over these years and will no longer be the little ones he remembers them as being. He has these images in his head even though he knows...is fully aware...time has gone by.'

'He's coming back,' said Will.

'Then quickly before he returns,' said Hugh glancing behind him to see how far away Robin was. He lowered his voice. Arthur and Will moved closer. 'I am thinking of inviting myself to stay with him for a week, perhaps two. I can tell him I am in no rush to return home, and perhaps I could help with anything that needs doing around the farm. What think you?'

As luck would have it, Gilbert had waylaid Robin on his walk back and they walked over to where Robin and Hugh's horses were tethered. Hugh was able to continue talking to Will and Arthur.

'But what about your Margaret?' said Arthur. 'I thought you were in a hurry to talk to her father.'

'Another week or two probably will not make much difference. I know in my gut she will be waiting for me and I would rest easier if I knew Robin was settled.'

'I hope he realises what a friend he has in you,' said Will. Arthur nodded his agreement.

'Tell me something, said Will, 'and please do not take this amiss, it is meant well, Hugh. How do you know Margaret will still waiting for you? It has been a very long time since you saw her last. What will you do if she has wed another?'

Hugh looked down at the deck and sucked air between his teeth. 'Hmm. That is not something I would find easy to bear but, if I am too late, then so be it. It may be that by staying with Robin for a while, I am putting off having to face that reality. I have held Margaret in my heart and in my dreams throughout my time in the Prince's service. She said she would wait and, at this moment, I have hope.' He looked up to face Will. 'If, though, she has grown tired of waiting or her father forced her hand, then there is nothing I can do other than accept it and wait until someone fills her place in my heart. Now that I am a knight and a man of means, I have no need to make a marriage of convenience for land or money. I will not marry for anything other than love.'

'Her family live near your land, is that right?' asked Arthur.

'Yes, indeed. We have neighbouring farms.'

'Then how would you feel if you are neighbours and she has indeed married another?'

Hugh screwed up his forehead, deep lines furrowed his brow. 'I would need to think on it seriously but, at this moment, I feel that it would be better for me to sell my property and travel, perhaps settle elsewhere.'

'Well, if that does happen, you would always be welcome at Winterne,' said Will. Although the four young men had been barely aware of each other during their years in the war, during the journey from Poitiers their friendship had grown into something akin to brotherhood; they had become so close over the weeks, their parting would not be easy.

Hugh smiled and looked from Will to Arthur and back again. 'Thank you Will. That is indeed generous of you,' he laughed, 'but I think you may have enough to deal with taking Arthur here with you.'

'You may well be right,' Will said, smiling at Arthur's pained expression.

'But, if I do decide to leave Bliddorth,' Hugh continued, more seriously, 'I shall certainly come south to visit you and thank you for the invitation. You have my gratitude., but see, Robin is returning. It is time to be serious.'

Robin joined them and handed Hugh his cloak. 'You seem quite solemn,' Robin said, looking at all three but particularly at Hugh. 'Is something amiss?'

'A little,' Hugh replied. 'We were just discussing what I would do if Margaret has not waited for me.'

'Ah. Yes. I understand the long face now.'

'Excuse me for a moment,' said Arthur. Gilbert was talking with one of the soldiers appointed to take care of the horses and Arthur thought it would be as good as any to talk to him about Ash. 'I mean to have that horse, no matter what it costs.'

Just then a shout rang out from the high point on the rigging. Luke, the youngest and the most recent member of the crew, had replaced Silas on watch and had some news. 'Land in sight, Master!'

The soldiers, four knights and those of the sailors not involved in some duty, headed for the starboard side peering into the distance to see their first glimpse of land since they left Honfleur. Soon they would be home in England and ready for the next stage of their lives. Everyone was smiling, especially Will who could still not quite believe he had managed the voyage without being seasick, and once again wished he could thank Doctor ben Abadi.

Soon the white, chalk cliffs came into sight filling each of the travellers with relief that their time at sea was almost at an end, and had crossed the English Channel with no trouble from French warships. The master had told them that French ships were rarely seen so close to the English coast. Arthur suggested to the master that perhaps it was time to take down the Fleur-de-Lys and Oriflamme flags before any English warships came into view. Having forgotten the French flags were still flying, the master thanked him and issued the order to have them taken down without delay.

Facing away from the sea, elbows resting on the rail, Hugh and Robin watched the French flags being lowered and the English and Salisbury crest flags raised. One of the sailors folded the detested standards and carried them to their storage under the poop deck.

'Good riddance!' said Hugh. At his side, Robin nodded grimly.

Will, leaning against the rail on the other side of the deck watched the white peaked waves gather and fall until Arthur returned.

'He has agreed, Will. Ash is to be mine. Gilbert is happy to let me take him at no charge. He said has enough horses for their journey to London, and would rather not be burdened by having to care for more than they need. I believe he was quite relieved not to have to worry about looking after Ash as well.'

'So, now we have three horses to take to Winterne and he is very welcome. We could have the makings of a very nice stable...even if we don't have a roof over our heads,' Will laughed. 'To be honest, Arthur, I have no idea of what awaits us when we arrive. The Earl said the building needs renovating...let's hope it is no worse than that.'

'But he is sending you his Steward to make a list of your needs and provide the right people to get the work done. At least you won't have to cement in every stone yourself. He did not say the manor is falling down, simply that it has been neglected. Did he give you any cause to think otherwise?'

'No. I was given the impression that some of the house is in good condition, from what he told me. Well, we'll find out for ourselves in a few days and, whatever condition it is in, I look forward to getting there...to home.'

'Look, I can see harbour lights. Do you think that's Newhaven?' Arthur looked hopeful.

'I don't know. Why not ask one of the crew. They should know.'

'No, they're all busy, but it seems we're not far away.'

Just as that moment, the ship turned landwards as Kelvin steered a course for the harbour. Gilbert began issuing orders to his men to gather up their possessions and move away from the sides of the ship. Two teams of men, one on either side of the ship, ran to unfasten the oars and the riggers rushed to climb the rope mesh to obey the master's master shouted order to lower the sail and furl it.

Robin and Hugh, to stay out of the way of the rowers, went to stand in the middle of the ship by the wagons. Will and Arthur, having decided that they too might be in the way, went to join them and climbed up onto the seat of their respective wagons to wait. For now there was nothing they could do and it was better for them to stay out of the way of the crew until they moored up in Newhaven harbour.

Although not yet dark, the evening clouds began to gather and the sea had become an inky black but, whereas the others were all looking towards the harbour, Will had noticed the orange glow of sunset reflected on the deck and looked around. He gasped and one by one the other three turned to see what he was looking at. They too stood, open-mouthed gazing at the lowering sun. All four had seen spectacular sunsets before but never at sea, and never like this. The darkening sky was streaked in bold and brilliant shades of pink, purple, scarlet, orange and gold and the colours seemed to be shifting mirrors on the surface of the sea as the sun descended to meet it.

'I don't believe I have ever seen anything like this,' said Arthur. 'It is simply quite glorious and, my friends, I believe it is a good omen for us.'

'I hope you're right,' said Hugh, with a glance at Robin that Arthur saw but Robin did not. Arthur gave a slight nod in acknowledgement.

As they continued looking at the setting sun, their backs to the prow, they became aware that the walls of the harbour were now on both sides of them and the rowers were slowing down. They had arrived in England; they were almost home. The end of their respective journeys, their hopes for the future and their fates unknown, but now they were in sight and whatever lay ahead would be away from the horrors of the battlefields.

Chapter Fourteen

As the light drained from the sky, wicks in candles and oil lamps around the harbour flamed into life. On the ships in the harbour or moored outside it, oil lamps were carefully lit and hung on hooks on the masts and at points in the stern and the prow. In the harbour-side cottages and inns, candles on tables flickered in the breeze as people walked about or opened doors. Tongues of orange, red and yellow flames from indoor open fires danced, their reflections glowing on dusty, unwashed leaded windows.

Having disembarked, Will finally stood again on English soil but his legs still felt as though he were on board the *Somerset.* He sat on the harbour wall watching the bustle of activity of other ships loading and unloading, passengers disembarking, and crews, now free of their duties, darted off to the nearest tavern. Soon the feeling of swaying eased, but he noticed how differently those who worked on ships managed to walk steadily, whereas those unused to being at sea, including the escort soldiers and his friends, all took a little time to lose their 'sea legs'.

He stood, wrapped his heavy woollen cloak more tightly around him to keep out the gusts of cold air. The gentle breeze that had brought them safely home had grown stronger and, without the warmth of the autumn sun, had become almost wintry. He stared down at the narrow band of moonlight that gleamed on the perpetually shifting sea, and felt his throat tighten, his eyes tingled, and he batted away a tear with the palm of his hand. He had not cried since he was a child; what emotion was this for a grown man to yield to; a man who had seen and, he believed, been hardened by seeing so much horror for so long?

Arthur walked over to join him and laid his hand on Will's shoulder, jerking him out of his thoughts. 'Two of the crewmen are taking the body of the man who died at Honfleur off the ship and back his family. The master is going with them to pay his respects and give them his pay. He said he will also pay for a decent funeral. It's likely he would end up in pauper's grave otherwise, and Gilbert and his men have taken the wagons off the ship.' He looked out to sea, following Will's gaze. 'It's good to be home, isn't it?'

Unable to speak, Will nodded.

'Come, Will, they are taking the horses off and I want to be sure that Ash, Chataigne and Narbonne do not become caught up with the escort mounts. We will have to give them English names before we get to Winterne, I am sure their French names will be extremely unpopular here in England.'

As they walked back they found Robin and Hugh removing their own few belongings from the wagon in which they had travelled the long journey through France from Poitiers to Honfleur. Theirs had been the first wagon unloaded from the ship.

'I have not yet regained my land legs and feel as though I am still rolling with the ship,' said Arthur.

Will laughed. 'I am pleased I am not alone. The swaying is not quite as bad as it was, but...'

'We have spoken to the landlord of The Swan,' said Hugh, stepping down from the back of the wagon. 'They have vacant rooms so I have asked for two...and both rooms have two mattresses and, it seems you are both in luck. There is a party of travellers staying there that you can join. They are heading towards Salisbury, by way of Chichester and Portsmouth.'

'That will be good for us, will it not, Will? Arthur grinned. 'We will have company for more than half the journey.'

Hugh added: 'I understand they are joining a guided party that journeys as far as Bath. They are all meeting at the harbour tomorrow morning.'

Will was relieved. Being with others on the road, would lessen the risk of being robbed...or worse. 'If there are more travellers heading towards Bath or Bristol, it may be that we can be accompanied for the best part of the journey.'

Gilbert Pritchett approached them. 'Sir Arthur, Sir William, if you still want' them 'orses, I'd take 'em now. It'll not be long before we'll be 'itchin'

the teams up ter the wagons an' getting' ready ter find somewhere ter camp overnight.'

'Very well, thank you, Gilbert. Will, could you take our belongings out of the wagon while I fetch our horses?' He turned to Hugh. 'Does the inn have stables?'

'Yes, and there are still five more spaces. You are taking Ash as well, aren't you?'

Arthur nodded and hurried off with Gilbert towards the ship, pushing through the groups of people gathered on the dock watching the bustle of activity around the ships. But they had not gone far when the sound of feminine laughter made them turn towards the sound. Three pretty young women, one blonde, her hair plaited and tied in front of her ears, then up behind the ears and fastened with a ribbon approached them. Her companions, who wore their dark hair loose and long, were smiling at Arthur. The blonde said: 'You jes' come off tha' ship, din't ya, mister.' And with swaying hips she moved closer to Arthur. She ignored Gilbert.

Arthur stopped and smiled at her. 'That's right.'

'Well, if you ain't go' anythin' be'er ter do, why not buy us girls a nice warming cup o' mead.' She moved closer still and lowered the blue woollen shawl that covered her shoulders.

From where they stood by the harbour wall, Will, Robin and Hugh observed the encounter.

'Do you think he'll go with them?' Robin grinned.

'How much would you like to wager that he does?' said Hugh.

Will, on the other hand, knew how important Ash had become to Arthur and said: 'I'm not wagering. Arthur will not go with them when he is so eager to collect our horses.'

They watched as Arthur stopped and bowed to the young ladies and saw him speak to the girl with the fair hair. Had they been able to hear what he said, they would have heard Arthur apologise, saying he was in far too much of a hurry to spend time with them at that moment but, perhaps another time. He also suggested that perhaps they should be inside their homes keeping warm, instead of dallying around the dock where they would be likely to meet some unsavoury characters now that it was getting dark.

The two dark haired girls who stood behind her looked disappointed and began to look for other young men around the harbour, but the blonde replied, 'Sir, we forgi' yer, on condition you meet us tomorrer at The Ship an' 'ave a cup ' mead wi' us then.'

'My friends and I,' he pointed toward Will, Arthur and Robin, 'would be delighted to on the morrow. Perhaps you ladies would be so kind as to take supper with us as well.'

The blonde hurried back to her friends, shouting. 'Ere, we're ter get fed an' all.' The girls huddled together and giggled, clearly talking about the four young men, they smiled over at Will, Robin and Hugh, who bowed and smiled back.

'But we are leaving shortly after breaking our fast,' said Robin, with a disapproving scowl on his face. 'What is he doing?'

Don't worry' said Will. 'Arthur knows we are leaving. If I am right, he is simply having a little fun with those girls.' He laughed. 'There is nothing on his mind at this moment other than ensuring Ash will be coming to Winterne with us.'

'He's taken a real liking to that horse, has he not?' Hugh said.

Will gave a little smile. 'Arthur has a big heart and feels sorry for him. He thinks that after being around battles for so long then having the serjeant killed, the horse needs some peace and careful handling, and Winterne sounds as though it will be the perfect place.'

'What about Narbonne though?' said Robin. 'Is he leaving him behind?'

Will shook his head. 'No, he's taking him too. He thinks the three of them will be the start of our stables.'

Hugh laughed. 'Do you think that perhaps he will be big hearted enough to pay the landlord for our supper this evening?'

Chapter Fifteen

Chataigne and Narbonne, having had weeks to grow accustomed to each other, were settled together within the same large, straw-strewn stall at The Swan's rear courtyard stables. Ash was in a single stall next to them and, on the other side of him were the grey gelding, Thunder – gentle and biddable and nothing like as stormy as his name would imply – and Gypsy, a female chestnut with a black mane and tail, and a temperament that was not always trustworthy. She had been known to bite and kick on occasions but had recently been relatively docile. Will wondered whether the sea voyage had troubled her and dented her confidence. Both the escort horses were rounceys, smaller in size than the destriers and chargers but swift, brave and intelligent and popular as army mounts.

On their way to the stables in the walled courtyard at the rear of the inn, Will pointed out a high-sided wagon positioned in the far corner. A heavy link chain coiled from the handle of the door, through the spokes of the front wheel and back to the handle and was fastened by a large metal padlock.

'Whatever is in that wagon must be valuable,' said Robin. 'Look at how well it is secured.' 'They are obviously not taking risks,' agreed Arthur. 'Just look at the thickness of that chain…'

'…And the size of the padlock,' said Hugh.

Inside the stable block, six other seemingly well-cared for horses, of various colours and sizes, two of them heavy-set draught horses, were settled in pairs in their stalls. That left just two empty stalls in which several wing-flapping and squabbling red-brown chickens strutted, pecked and clucked while rooting around in the hay for anything tasty that was worth scratching out. None of the horses appeared to be particularly bothered by their feathered stable-mates, even when they flew across into the occupied stalls. Several times Chataigne calmly stepped out of the way when a chicken stalked a beetle under her, and even Narbonne appeared quite indifferent to the stall invader.

A clucking sound made Will and Arthur look up to find more chickens peering down their beaks at them from the roof beams. When he looked down again, it was then Will noticed eggs in the hay mangers on the partitions between the stall Chataigne and Narbonne shared, and the one next door, where Ash was housed for the night.

Two young stable boys, Will guessed no more than twelve years old, threw off the moth-eaten blankets wrapped round their shoulders, jumped up from their hay bale seats at the far end of the block, and rushed to assist. The sign of The Swan Inn displayed on their brown tabards proclaimed them as being employees of the establishment, but that was the only smart item of their clothing. Their patched and ragged dirty brown breeches, the thin shirts under the tabards and the cheap, thin oversized boots, stuffed with straw to fill them out and stop them coming off, drew sympathetic looks from all four men.

The boys offered to settle the horses; it was their job, but Will and his friends gently refused the offer; they had looked after their horses for weeks and that night would be no different. The lads looked a little disappointed and returned to their draft free corner of the stable block. When they were out of earshot Arthur whispered that guests at the inn would usually let the boys look after the horses, and slip them some coin to do so.

After removing the reins and saddles, brushing down their horses and making sure they were comfortable, Arthur called the boys over.

'There's a penny each for you,' he said, holding out two coins. 'Make sure our mounts are given fresh water and hay. If you look after them well and we are satisfied, there will be another penny for you in the morning.'

The boys looked at each other, wide-eyed and stunned. Two whole pennies…each! The taller of the boys, fair-headed and freckled spoke up.

'Yes master. We'll look arter 'em righ' well we will, won't we Dickon?' The other boy nodded enthusiastically but said nothing.

'Well you make sure you do,' said Arthur, trying hard to be formidable with the boys, as Will, Robin and Hugh joined him. 'And I would collect the eggs if you want your employer to have them for his guest's breakfasts.'

'Don' yer worry, sirs. Them'll be safe wi' us,' the older boy called after them as they headed for the rear door of the inn.

At the door, Hugh turned back. 'Who do the other horses belong to?' he asked.

'Them travellers inside. Thass who them belong ter, sir, and they ain't so gen'rous as you. Are they, Dickon?' The other boy shook his head, but still remained silent.

Hugh smiled, took a last glance at the boys holding their hands out to the meagre warmth of an oil lamp on the small wooden table between them, and sprinted off to catch up with the others who were waiting for him.

The air outside had turned very cold after the sun had slipped below the horizon, and the breeze had gathered strength. Boughs of nearby trees swayed and branches clunked against each other in the wind, loosening dying leaves, sending them spinning and dancing in the air until they fell to the ground and blew across the cobbled courtyard heaping in a corner of the wall, in a carpet of red-gold and brown.

As Arthur, in the lead, opened the door the warmth and the mouth-watering aromas of cooked meat, herbs and freshly baked bread were inviting and very welcoming. Ahead of them, in a stone hearth with a large open fireplace, tall red and yellow flames curled around three sizeable logs that threw out enough heat to extend throughout the bar room. A metal box to one side of the hearth held a further stack of logs and, suspended from the mantle, bunches of herbs dried out in the heat, adding their fragrance to the heady aromas filling the room.

In the middle of the room were two long wooden tables set longways to the fireplace. The benches could accommodate six people on each side but, on this night, there was just a quietly spoken middle aged couple who sat opposite each other, keeping warm by the fire while eating their supper.

Two comfortable booths on each side of the room, with a long wooden table and cushioned benches in each, separated by wooden partitioning, completed the rest of the bar room seating. As the two booths on their right were already taken, Arthur led the group to the one on the left that was nearest to the fire, and by the window where they could look out onto the street; at least they could after Arthur and Will, sitting opposite each other, wiped the grime off the window with their cuffs.

A young woman, her hair pulled back tightly off her forehead and enclosed in a white headdress, approached them with two flagons of foaming ale in each hand. She set them down on the table in front of the four knights, then smoothed down her apron. Will noticed her dress and apron were both spotted with smears of grease and she had smudges of dark rye flour on her brow and forearms. 'Have you been making the bread,' he asked her, with a smile.

'Yes, sir. Thass one o' my tasks each day. The other be ter serve trav'llers like yerself an' I been doin' it since sunrise an' we be busy, an' as yer can see, I ain't done yet. So I tek it yer'll all be wantin' the rabbit stew?'

Robin, Hugh and Will nodded. 'Yes. Thank you,' Arthur told her and she scuttled off to somewhere around the other side of the fireplace where they were unable to see her.

Later, basking in the warmth of the crackling open log fire of The Swan Inn, the four very ordinary looking knights, who appeared to be nothing more than typical travellers, seated in a booth around a solid oak table, dined by candlelight on a hearty rabbit stew flavoured with bacon, onions, barley, bay leaves, sliced purple carrots, mushrooms, thyme and parsley, and served in a bowl, with a basket of warm bread, and washed down with a flagon of ale.

Having finished his meal first, Hugh broke off a chunk of bread and wiped it around the bowl, popped it in his mouth, then sat back and loosened his belt. 'That was the best meal I have had in years.' He smiled contentedly. 'No more camp food for me.'

Arthur removed the kerchief he had tucked into the neck of his shirt – in case any food dripped down his front - setting it down on the table beside his now empty bowl. 'I agree. Will...whoever the cook is we need to take him with us to Winterne.'

Will chuckled. 'I doubt whether...'

He was interrupted by the landlord, who introduced himself as Henry Brewster. A kindly and ruddy-faced man, he clearly enjoyed his profession and seeing his customers were content. 'Can I get you anythin' else gentlemen? More ale? Bread and cheese?'

Will and Robin finished eating and pushed their bowls away.

'Thank you Master Brewster,' said Robin. 'That was indeed a fine supper and very welcome but, I for one, have eaten all I can. Please thank your cook for us.'

'You've jest done tha',' said the landlord. ''Tis me. I do all the meat cooking in my own inn. That way I can mek sure 'tis allus the same quality. Cooks come and go, an' o' course they allus cook diff'rent to each other, and' tha's not good fer the good name o' The Swan, so I do it meself.'

'But the young woman who served us makes the bread?'

'Aye. I can trust 'er ter do...'

He was interrupted by a loud noise out on the street; the sound of running footfalls over the cobbles, a shout went up. Will and Arthur peered out. In the glow of the street lamps, they saw one man being chased by another, followed by three young women, one blonde and two with long dark hair.

'The second man looks very like Kelvin?' said Will. 'And those were the girls we saw you talk to at the harbour, Arthur.'

'I thought so too,' replied Arthur. 'Come, let's see what's happening.' Robin slid along the bench to let him out.

'Why do you want to get involved?' Robin asked Arthur.

'Because Walter Smith was good to us and if his son is in trouble...'

'...Or causing trouble,' Will added.

Arthur looked at Will and nodded. 'Yes, or that, then I think we should help his father by stopping this getting any...worse.'

A woman's scream cut him off, and all four rushed out through the door into the street where they found Kelvin lying on the ground, a knife in his chest. The blonde girl with the plaited hair and the blue shawl was kneeling over him crying, her dress wet at the knees where the wool drew the dampness from the cobbles. Her two friends tried to pull her away but she resisted their efforts and remained staring down at Kelvin's body. A man was pleading with her...'Kate, Kate...'e come a' me wi' the knife. *Please*, I din't mean...I 'ad ter defend meself. Kate...*please*.' He struggled to release himself from the grip two other men had on him. '*Kaaate! Look a' me! Please!*' His voice had risen to a shriek. All eyes turned to look at him. His bottom lip bled from two nasty cuts, the skin on his right cheekbone was split and his right eyelid cut and swollen with the blue and black bruising more evident with each passing second. He had taken a brutal beating.

'In the Lord's name...*No! Not my boy!*'

Everyone turned to see Walter Smith, a horrified expression on his face as he gazed down at his son. Close behind came the constables, the Law enforcers, eager to apprehend someone.

Kate looked up at the man still being restrained with a look that mingled fear, pity and, Will thought, something else...love perhaps?

'Alfred...wha' 'ave yer done?'

Alfred stopped struggling. Through tears, he looked down at the girl he obviously adored. 'Kate. 'E wanted yer, bu' 'e never cared fer yer. Not like I does. I wanted ter tek care o' yer.' Kate stood up and walked towards him. Her friends huddled together, shaken by the incident. Kate stood in front of Alfred and held out her hands but, having both arms held tightly by his captors, he could not touch her. 'I'm sorry, Alfred. I jest thought to have a bit o' merriment. I never meant anythin' by it.' She looked down at her feet. 'I never thought 'e would be like tha. 'Onest I never.'

All the fight had gone out of Alfred. He said, in almost a whisper: 'When I seen 'im tek yer up tha' alley, I knew wha 'e were up ter, an' I weren't gonna let 'im get away wi' tha'.'

Walter Smith stumbled towards the body of his son, just as the constables took control of Alfred from his captors. A crowd had gathered in a circle around them; a dramatic incident such as this always drew an excited, inquisitive crowd.

Kate cried out: 'No! Don' tek 'im away. 'E was on'y tryin' ter look arter me. It weren't Alfred's fault.'

''Tis too late fer that, Kate. 'Alfred's goin' ter 'hang fer this.'

'Wait!' cried Walter. 'Did anyone actually see what happened here?'

'Master Smith.' The older of the two constables spoke up. 'Master Smith...Walter, Alfred's goin' before the Justice o' the Peace an'll likely hang, so justice'll be done fer the killin' o' Kelvin. Yer don' wanna ter stop us doin' our duty do yer?'

'Herbert Carter, you and I have known each other these many years and you know...knew my son. You know what he could be like.' He stopped, walked up to Alfred and took a long look at his face. 'Alfred, answer me true now. Do you have a knife?'

Alfred looked at him through his one good eye, the other was now completely closed. 'No, Master Smith, I don't.'

'Herbert. Search him,' ordered Walter.

'Yer wastin' yer time, Walter...an' ours.'

'Just do it, please.'

'Oh, very well.'

The younger constable went through Alfred's clothing and found nothing. 'No knife. Nuthin' but a few small coins.'

Walter turned to Kate. 'Now, Kate. Tell me true what happened.'

Kate turned to her friends, then back to Walter. 'T'was like I said. I jest wan'ed ter 'ave some fun and Kelvin said 'e was goin' ter buy me supper an' tha' 'e 'ad a present fer me. I din't think there'd be any 'arm innit'.' She looked at Alfred. 'I'm sorry, Alfred. I know you was jest tryin' to defend me now...arter wha' 'e tried to do.'

Walter walked over to Herbert. 'I think perhaps this was a case of self-defence. He was my son, but we all know how he could be and...I can tell you now that the knife in his chest belongs to him. It's Kelvin's own knife. He was armed and Alfred was not.'

'I don' know 'ow it appen'd, Master Smith,' sobbed Alfred. 'It were all so quick. One minute your Kelvin 'ad the knife in 'is 'and an' I were tryin' ter keep from bein' stabbed an' the next 'e were fallin' ter the ground...I dunno wha' appened. 'onest I don't.'

Kate's two friends walked away. Their heads down and silent. Their days of flirting and naively wanting a bit of fun were done forever; this was an experience they would not forget. Kate watched them leave in silence then looked hopefully at Herbert while he considered what to do about Alfred. There had been a death. It was his job to uphold the Law. On the other hand, if this was self-defence, then no murder had been committed and Alfred was unarmed. He made up his mind. If Walter felt that Kelvin had brought his death upon himself then who was he to argue. Walter was right, Kelvin could be difficult and was known for his unpredictable bad temper and getting into fights; he was also known for his rough handling of women.

'Alfred. You can go,' said Herbert.

A cheer went up from the crowd and Kate ran to Alfred to hug him, as the constables let him go. Walter nodded in acknowledgement. 'I am content with your decision. I cannot support the hanging of a man for defending a woman and himself, even if the victim is my own son. May he rest in peace now. I will send for some of my men to help me take his body back to the ship and we'll give him a burial at sea.'

Alfred led Kate over to where Walter Smith stood, head bowed, beside the body of his son. It took him a few moments before he became aware of them. 'I am so sorry, Master Smith. I don't mean no 'arm, 'onest I din't,' said Kate.

The expression of Walter's face was difficult to read but when he looked at her, he said: 'I know you meant no harm. Sadly, Kelvin did, and this was not the first time...but it has been the last.' He looked down at Kelvin's body again and drew a long sigh. He turned to Alfred and Kate. 'Go now and do not think of Kelvin or what happened here tonight again, Kate. I hope you will find happiness.'

The crowd thinned and began walking away. There was nothing more to see. As Kate and Alfred left Walter alone, Will approached the stricken man. 'We will help you take Kelvin back to the *Somerset*.'

Henry Brewster appeared carrying a folded stretcher under his arm. 'Here, yer can use this...but I wan' it back, mind.'

Walter watched silently as Arthur, Will, Robin and Hugh gently lifted Kelvin's body, the knife still embedded in his chest, onto the stretcher. They took a corner each and followed Walter, in silence, back to the harbour where, two of the crewmen on watch, realising what had happened, called to their crew-mates and ran down the ramps to assist. Will recognised Silas and Luke amongst them. He and his friends, stood back to let the crew members take the corners of the stretcher from them; it was right that they carried Kelvin's body on board the *Somerset*. Walter stumbled up the ramp without looking back at the young knights; he appeared to have forgotten them altogether. As he reached the deck he shouted an order for someone to bring him a flask of Aqua Vitae; a strong spirit distilled from wine, and ordered the stretcher-bearers to follow him into his cabin. He would keep Kelvin with him until his burial at sea.

'Poor Walter. Kelvin was a worry to him but he seems broken,' said Arthur.

Robin nodded. Hugh said: 'He does. No matter how difficult Kelvin was, he was his son. Come now, there is nothing more we can do here. Another cup of ale, a look in on the horses, and then perhaps it will be time we slept. We have an early start in the morning.'

That was the last time they saw Will Walter Smith or his crew. The *Somerset* sailed away at dawn the next morning.

Chapter Sixteen

Having paid for their rooms and meal before going to their shared rooms at the end of the corridor upstairs, the four were pleased with the cleanliness and, more importantly as it had become a cold autumn evening, that their rooms were either side of the warm chimney.

The following morning, after dressing, the first thing Arthur and Will wanted to do was the take a look at the horses. Taking all their belongings, including their long bows and arrow bags, they headed down the stairs, through the rear door, crossed the courtyard and entered the stables.

Chataigne and Narbonne looked over the door of their stall and gave a soft nickering sound, their ears flicked forward pointing towards Will and Arthur in a sign of welcome. It was clear that, not only were their horses comfortable, well fed and watered by the boys, who apparently slept in the stables, but eager to earn the second penny each, they had awoken early, cleaned the hooves of all five horses and given their coats and manes a good brush. Arthur was impressed and winked at Will. 'See what some people will do for a penny, Sir William.'

'Oh. You reelly a knight, sir?' asked the taller boy, who stared in fascination at the long bows.

Will laughed and ruffled the boy's hair. 'Yes, I really am and so is Sir Arthur here. His Lordship, the Black Prince knighted us himself.'

'Ere, d'you 'ear tha', Dickon?' Them's reel knights. Us don' get many o' them in 'ere, do us?'

Dickon shook his head.

'And what's your name?' Arthur asked the taller boy.

'Iss Bartley, Sir Arthur.'

'Well, Bartley, Dickon, Sir William and I are going for a cup of ale before we begin our journey, then we will return for our horses and you shall both have the other penny each we promised you. Thank you for taking care of them so well.'

They found Robin and Hugh sitting in the same booth they had occupied the previous evening. They already had their cups of ale. In a basket in the middle of the table was a selection of flatbreads and hunks of cheese.

'Henry prepared this before we arrived,' said Hugh. 'Although he is one who prefers to have his first meal of the day at noon, he provides food for his customers when they are travelling that day.'

'We have just been talking to those people over there,' Robin nodded towards the booth directly opposite where one woman and three men sat eating. Two of the men looked over and nodded in acknowledgement, the woman gave a shy smile.

'It seems they will be amongst the party heading for Salisbury this morning. You should introduce yourselves, as they will be your travelling companions.'

Henry arrived at the table with two more flagons of ale for Will and Arthur. 'G'mornin' gentlemen. I trust you slept well arter tha' ruckus las' nigh'. You knew the victim, then.'

'Not well,' said Will. 'He was the steersman on our ship.'

'And Walter's son, weren't 'e?' said Henry, with a scowl. 'Don' wan' ter speak ill o' the dead but tha' Kelvin'll not be missed aroun' 'ere, I can tell yer.'

'Except by Walter.'

'Aye bu' 'e was a wrong un, tha' lad,' Henry continued. 'Still, mebbe some good 'as come out o' it if young Kate'll learn 'er lesson and Alfred's got a good 'eart. She could do worse than settle wi' 'im. Righ' I'll let yer get on wi' yer food an' ale. Yer'll be wantin' ter get off afore long.'

'Henry, before you go. I have a question for you,' said Will.

'Was tha' then?' Henry sat on the end of the bench, Robin and Arthur slid up a little to give him room.

'Young Dickon, the stable lad. Does he speak?'

Henry shook his head. 'Not tha' I've 'eard. 'Im an' 'is brother, Bartley, come 'ere a few months ago. Found 'em sleepin' in the stables I did, skinny little mites, they was.'

Arthur asked: 'Do you know anything about them?'

'Not reelly, well, not much anyways.' Henry settled back, leant against the wooden partition. 'Young Bartley said they'd come from a village called Pydynghowe, jest outside Newhaven. Seems their father 'ad bin in the Earl of Warrenne and Surrey's enlisted men an' got isself killed in France. Their ma struggled on fer a while, then she died too leavin' the boys alone. Bartley thought it best ter come in ter the town an' I found 'em shelterin' in me stables durin' a storm and' I've let 'em stay 'ere ever since.'

'Trouble is they's got no education an' I can't gi' 'em none. All I can do is feed 'em an' put a roof over they's 'eads the best I can. An' no, in answer ter yer question, no I've never 'eard young Dickon speak. Bartley says 'e never 'as since their ma died.'

'Do you know how old they are?' asked Will.

'Never asked, but my guess is...' he put his elbow on the table and rested his chin in his hand, rubbed his beard. '...I would think young Bartley'll abou' eleven years, mebbe twelve an' Dickon prob'ly eight or nine.'

Arthur and Will looked at each other. Will's eyes asked the question Arthur had seen coming. He nodded.

'Henry, how would you feel if we offered to help the boys?' asked Will.

'In wha' way?'

'The four of us were knighted a few weeks ago on the battlefield at Poitiers...'

Henry frowned, sceptical.

'It's true and it can be verified,' said Arthur. 'Sir William, here, has been granted lands and a manor in Somerset and he and I are on our way to claim ownership of the estate. Sir Robert and Sir Hugh, sitting beside you, are also on their way to their lands.'

'Very well. Say I believe you. Wha' is it you wan' ter do fer them boys?'

Will snapped out his answer. 'Adopt them. Take them with us, become legally responsible for them. They will be given a home, cared for, clothed, educated, well fed and trained for a career to enable them to look after themselves for the rest of their lives. What do you say?'

Henry stared at Will open-mouthed. 'Well, I dunno. T'would be good fer the boys, thass true...but then I'd lose me stable 'ands.'

Arthur reached into the pouch suspended from his belt and pulled out some coins; four gold nobles. 'Here, that should help you to find someone to take on the job, Henry. That amount should be enough to pay someone for a year or two.'

Henry smiled widely, revealing two missing teeth, his upper eye tooth and one at the front of the lower jaw. 'Tha' should do nicely, Sir Arthur. Thankee.'

'It looks as though you have a growing family, Will,' said Robin. 'I hope you know what you're taking on.'

Will laughed. 'No, I have no idea and I don't think Arthur has either, but I believe we can manage, and what's the point of having this good fortune if we cannot do some good with it for someone else.'

As Henry removed the used cups and baskets from the table, Arthur looked up at their stubble-chinned landlord and said: 'Henry, do you know where we may be able to obtain a cart or covered wagon. If it was just us travelling, we could ride and wrap ourselves in our bedrolls at night if there are no inns available, but it's a long way to Somerset and the boys will need more comfort.'

'Aye. Tom Chandler at the end of the main street 'as some wagons an' should be able ter le' yer 'ave any other supplies yer migh' need, bu' the time is rushing by an' 'twill not be long afore the travellers'll want ter leave.'

Arthur looked at Will and nodded. 'Yes, we must be gone, Henry. We will collect the boys at the same time as the horses, and then visit the chandlery before heading to meet the travellers.'

Henry called for one of his serving girls to clear the rest of the table, and was just about to head to the kitchen when Will caught up with him. 'Here's another noble for your trouble, Henry.' Henry pocketed the coin before Will had the chance to change his mind. 'Do you want to be with us to explain to the boys that they will be coming with us? We thought you might want to say farewell, or should we just take our leave and go?'

'Aye. I'll come ter explain ter the boys. 'Twill be a new adventure fer 'em.'

While Will and Henry were talking, Robin and Hugh walked over to the door that led to the courtyard, but Arthur approached the booth where the Salisbury travellers were sitting, they had been watching and listening to the exchange between Henry, Arthur and William, with interest.

From their garments, especially the men's velvet doublets, the young woman's hair caul – a gold net on either side of her head that secured her flaxen plaits – and their fur trimmed cloaks, Arthur knew these people were reasonably wealthy; he supposed a merchant family.

The woman's deep blue eyes regarded Arthur with obvious admiration. 'Pardon my boldness in speaking before we have been introduced, Sir Arthur, but I could not help but overhear of your kindness in regard to those two young boys. It is a good deed you are doing.' She looked down again, lowering her eyes, modestly.

Arthur smiled. 'Madam, for my part there is nothing to pardon and with regard to the boys, I must confess it was Sir William's idea, but a good one I think. Could you tell me how long before the party will be leaving? As our circumstances have now changed, we have some items to buy we had not anticipated we would need.'

The older man, who Arthur took to be the woman's father looked at her with obvious affection. 'My daughter has been brought up to stand her ground against her brothers. She, therefore, occasionally shows a lack of modesty enjoyed by other fathers but, to my shame, I have to admit her lack of propriety is my own fault.' He chuckled. His daughter smiled revealing a top set of small, perfect teeth. Arthur looked over at her brothers, the younger of the two seemed to find the conversation amusing and smiled at his sister. The other brother, however, was not so polite. He scowled, turned his face away but Edgar shot him a look of exasperation at his lack of manners. Clearly only to obey his father, the sullen young man forced himself to look in Arthur's direction and acknowledge his presence with a slight nod of the head; he did not smile and looked away as Arthur gave him an exaggerated meaningful bow in return.

'I believe you have another hour yet, Sir Arthur,' the man continued. 'We will be leaving from the harbour and taking the Worthing then Chichester Road. If you have not joined us, we will leave at the appointed time together with the rest of the party, but will dawdle along at the rear of the group to enable you to catch up.'

'Thank you, Master…?'

'Coombs, Sir Arthur. Edgar Coombs, at your service, and this is my family, my sons, Roger…' It was Roger who had glowered. Dark Haired and dark disposition, thought Arthur. '…and Martin…,' Martin stood, bowed to

Arthur, and appeared quite amiable. '...and this is Matilda. We are returning to Salisbury where I am a wool merchant. We take our wool to Flanders to have it spun, dyed and made into good quality cloth there. We are returning with a quantity of bolts of cloth to sell in Salisbury.'

Overhearing the conversation from near the kitchen door, William thought that explained the good quality of their clothing.

'Then that is your wagon in the courtyard?'

Robin coughed, hoping to attract Arthur's attention. It was time for them to leave and he was growing a little impatient.

'Indeed it is, Sir Arthur. We keep it secured when we have merchandise.'

'Very wise, Master Coombs, very wise. You can't be too careful.' Arthur took a step back and then another, aware that time was pressing. But Master Coombs it seemed was in no hurry to let him go.

'What is your destination?' Master Coombs asked as Robin coughed again.

'We go on some way after Salisbury,' Arthur answered, politely. 'To Sir William's property close to the City of Wells in Somerset, so we look forward to developing our acquaintance on the journey, Master Coombs. But, now we must go. As you know, we still have some matters to attend to. Farewell. We shall meet again at the harbour.' As he turned to go, Will joined him and waved to the Coombs family.

The four young knights walked towards the stables together in silence, each with their own thoughts at this being their last moment together. Although Will and Arthur would be together for the foreseeable future, and Robin and Hugh would be travelling together for a while, over the weeks they had all spent together, a close connection had been forged between the four. Very soon two would go one way and two another, and it was unlikely they would meet again; that thought was subduing them all.

Will thought about the conversation he had with Robin at the riverbank, and knew how anxious he was about his return to his family, even though it was what he wanted more than anything. He thought of how eager Hugh was to see his Margaret, but there was the underlying fear that she may no longer want him. Many years had passed since they last saw each other.

Whatever the Fates had in store, with the distance between them all, Will knew he may never discover what the future held for two of his closest friends.

At the stables, Robin and Hugh, gently shooed chickens from their path as they saddled up Gypsy and Thunder, hooked their leather bags over the pommels and made ready to go. Standing in front of Arthur and Will, Robin said: 'It is time we left to join the escort.'

'It seems strange to be leaving without you both,' said Hugh, looking down at his feet.

The boys watched agog at four grown men as they went through a few awkward and tongue-tied moments trying not to demonstrate their affection for each other, before Hugh reached out to grasp Will's hand. But, Will was having none of that; it wasn't enough to show how much he would miss these two dear friends. Moving closer he stood in front of Robin and Hugh and put his arms around them both, breaking the emotional barrier of men not demonstrating how they are feeling. Robin and Hugh hugged Will and then it was Arthur's turn. Bartley and Dickon were shocked at seeing these adult men clearly displaying the bond that had grown between them, something they had never seen grown men do before.

'I am afraid we have to go or we may miss the escort,' said Robin, as he began to walk Gypsy towards the door. He stopped to let a mother hen and her parade of yellow fluffy chicks scurry into the refuge of one of the empty stalls where they would be safe from hooves. 'Perhaps we should have learned a lesson from Doctor ben Abadi and bought some messenger pigeons to help us keep in contact.'

'We may have to think about how we can find a way to send messages to each other,' said Arthur.

'Well, you know where to find us at Winterne Manor,' said Will. 'If you ever feel the need to visit pastures new, there will always be a welcome for you both there.'

Robin and Hugh mounted their horses and settled themselves into the saddles. 'And good luck to you both with your new plans,' said Hugh, with a quick glance towards the boys. 'Safe journey to you all, and God go with you.'

'And to you both,' Will and Arthur said together. Sadly, they watched as their two friends walked their horses onwards to the courtyard gate, where they turned back and waved before disappearing behind the wall and into the lane.

Arthur and Will looked at each other in silence for a moment, both solemnly understanding that it may be the last time they would see or hear of their close companions. But, time was moving on, and there were things to do that could not be put off.

Henry arrived, his usual blustering self, oblivious to Will and Arthur's cares, and their moment of reflecting over recent weeks was ended. A few minutes later Arthur stood with Henry and Will beside him, explaining to Bartley and Dickon about their plans. Will stood quietly watching the boys' faces as Arthur explained what they had in mind but, when the manor itself came into the discussion, it was Will's turn to speak.

'And so, although I cannot say at this moment, that the manor is as comfortable as we hope to make it,' he said, 'we understand that much of it is habitable...that is to say, can be lived in now. We will be working on making the entire building more comfortable though and there is a lake, woods and I believe stables.'

The boys looked from Arthur to Will, and back to Henry.

'Bu' Master Brewster, are we not ter stay 'ere?' asked Bartley. Dickon, moved behind his brother, puzzled by what was happening and Arthur thought that, understandably, he was perhaps a little frightened.

'Bartley, my boy, you an' Dickon 'ave bin 'ere wi' me fer a long time, but I can' offer yer any more than more o' this. Sir William an' Sir Arthur is offerin' yer a good 'ome an' you'll get some schooling an' the oppertooni'y fer a good future fer yer both. These kind gentlemen'll bring yer up righ' an' I can' see as there's anythin' fer yer to be scared abou'. Think on it, my boy, you lads'll be living in a big manor 'ouse thass warm. Winter's comin' an' blankets on the hay is all very well, but at the manor yer'll be sleepin' in yer own bed o' yer own wi' fur covers, or sat in front of big hearth with a warm welcoming fire an' smells o' bakin' and stews that are bein' made fer yer, an' yer'll not be livin' on wha'ever scraps I can gi' yer.'

Bartley looked around at his little brother and gave him a hug. 'Will yer trust me ter mek the righ' choice, Dickon?' Dickon nodded.

Bartley stood straight, pulled his shoulders back and regarded Arthur for a moment, then looked Will right in eye and boldly asked, 'Sir William, if we does wha' yer wan' an' come wi' yer, can Dickon 'ave a dog?'

All three men laughed at Bartley's daring. Will moved closer and hunkered down in front of the boys. 'Yes, Bartley, if you would like it, I'm sure we can find a dog for Dickon.' He was rewarded by seeing a smile light up the smaller boy's face. 'But is there anything you would like for yourself?'

'Nothin' I can think of, Sir William, thank you, bu' I'll let yer know if I think o' somethin' later.'

Will stood up. 'Fair enough. Now, do you have anything you want to take with you? Clothes or any personal possessions?'

'We on'y 'ave these old blankets an'...' he ran over to their corner and reached down behind the hay bale seating, pulled something that looked like a book out and ran back, 'an' this Sir William. It belonged ter our mother.' Bartley showed Will a gold embossed, brown leather-bound prayer book. 'Thass all we got of 'er now.'

Arthur took the prayer book from Will and carefully turned a few of the fragile pages. 'Where did she get this from, do you know?'

Bartley shook his head. 'No, she never said. I jest remember she allus 'ad it. Don' think she knew wha' it said, 'iss in that strange writin'...Latin I think she said it was, but she allus kep' it wi' 'er. Meant a lot to 'er, it did.'

Arthur handed it back to Will. He did not open it but looked at the fading gold writing on the front cover wishing he could read what it said, then handed it back to Bartley.

'Well, if there's nothing else then it's time we were on our way. Say your farewells to Master Brewster and you can both ride Chataigne to the Chandlery. Oh, and its best if you start calling her Chestnut, we're changing their names to English ones. I will need to remember that myself.'

'And you can think of an English name for Narbonne, if you would like to,' said Arthur. 'These horses came with us from France but, as we are at war with the French, we don't think those names will be popular here in England.'

Bartley thought about that for a moment and then said: 'Well you already got Chestnut an' Ash.' He looked up at Arthur. 'Yer goin' ter need another tree name, mister...sorry, I mean *Sir* Arthur.'

Arthur chuckled at that. 'He's right, Will. Another tree name...very well, Bartley. I will think on that. Now, it is time we took our leave of Master Brewster. Say thank you to him for looking after you both for so long, Bartley, and you, Dickon.'

'Thankee from us both, Master Brewster,' said Bartley. Dickon nodded vigorously and smiled.

Henry sniffed, blinked and turned away and made a great fuss of refolding a horse blanket that was lying over a stall door. Then he turned back and gruffly said: 'Now boys, yer mek sure yer pay these kind gen'lemen heed on wha' they tells yer ter do. Yer 'ear me?'

The boys nodded.

'An' I'll 'ave them tabards back, yer'll not need them no more.'

Dickon ran over to the hay bales to fetch the tabards and handed them to Henry. 'Righ' then, you'd best be off or yer'll be late ter meet them travellers at the harbour.'

'Come boys,' said Arthur and he lifted first Dickon onto the newly named Chestnut's back, settled him into the saddle, then sat Bartley behind his brother. 'Comfortable?'

'Yes, Sir Arthur,' said Bartley. As he slipped his arms around Dickon's waist, Will took hold of Chestnut's reins and led her out of the stables into the cobbled courtyard, passed the still locked wagon, and headed towards the open gates. Arthur followed leading Narbonne and Ash. Henry stood in front of him, blocking his way. 'Now I wan' yer oath yer'll look arter them boys. I've got used ter 'avin' them 'ere.'

'Have no concern, Henry. Bartley and Dickon will be given Will's name, it will be legal and we'll see to their upbringing.' Arthur was surprised at how much Henry was evidently going to miss the boys. 'If you are concerned, and I know it's a long way, but I am sure you would be very welcome to visit if you would like to see how they are.'

For a moment Henry's eyes lit up and looked as though he might take up the offer, but then he offhandedly cleared his throat, looked away to pat Ash on the neck and said: 'Tis too far an'…an'…why would I wanna see them again?' They all heard the catch in his voice. 'It'll be good ter get rid o' 'em, get 'em off me 'ands, an' yer welcome to 'em.'

'Well, yes, I suppose it will be too far.' Arthur hid his smile. 'I understand, Henry, but now I must go. If you should change your mind, head towards Wells and Glastonbury, the village of Winterne is on the road between, and you should be able to locate us easily. The invitation is open for any time to suit you.'

At the courtyard entrance Will and the boys were waiting for Arthur. Will gestured that they had to leave and Arthur began walking towards them.

'Hmm. Yes, well mebbe...but prob'ly not. Anyways, get goin' or yer'll be late ter join them travellers. Farewell, Sir Arthur. T'was good ter meet yer and Sir William an' the other two knights, an' I wish yer well.' He turned his back, went through the rear door of the inn and closed it behind him without a glance back.

On the way to the chandlery, they passed a stable-yard where a number of mules were for sale and decided to buy two to pull the wagon. Their own horses were unused to pulling carts and Arthur suggested it would take too long to get them used to being in the traces. Although mules could be contrary, the pair they chose, one grey, one brown, walked well and appeared relatively docile.

At the chandlery, they found a wagon with high sides and a tailboard of the same height as the sides, that could be unbolted at the top and lowered to make a ramp. The roof covering was made of thick oiled linen, Arthur said it was a little like the material the *Somerset* sail was made of, and the chandler assured them both that it would repel light rain, although he would not guarantee in a deluge. For that they would have to find shelter.

Eager to find a safe hiding place for the coins that were still in his saddlebag, Will told Arthur he wanted to examine the wagon for any faults, and reminded Arthur of the wagon that collapsed in France. He also suggested that, bearing in mind time was short, while he carried out a brief inspection, Arthur could help the boys find the warm winter clothing they would need. Arthur agreed, and took the boys over to the other side of the chandlery to look for warm, lined cloaks, boots and woollen hose and breeches for Bartley and Dickon, and for themselves.

Once they were out of the way, inside the wagon, Will hastily inspected the wooden sides. They, too, had a wool-filled cavity, but the gap appeared a little too narrow for stashing the pouches. Pressed for time, and aware that Arthur and the boys or Tom Chandler could reappear at any time, he had no time to lose. He sat on the wagon floor and looked around. The sides of the wagon were all exposed and there were no hiding places in the corners, the floor was built of a single layer of thick planks, so that was another setback. There appeared to be nowhere suitable for secreting anything away in the body of the wagon. He looked up at the roof covering but, of course, there was no place to hide anything.

'Will!' Arthur called him to join them. Cursing under his breath, Will had run out of time and headed to the front of the wagon to exit over the seat. The seat! The seat was a wide, strongly made, wooden, rectangular box that was open at the bottom. Will rolled over onto his back and pushed himself along until he could look up into it. In each corner, were cobweb covered metal brackets supporting the seat and ledges. Suspended above the ledges and held in place across double sets of hooks were an axe, three chisels of varying sizes, a small mallet, two saws and two different sized awls used for boring holes in wood. Those tools would be useful at some time but, bearing in mind the cobwebs and dead spiders, no-one could have used that seat in months. With a folded wool blanket to cover the entire seat, it was possible that, for the few days left of the journey, neither Arthur or the boys would be aware that there was anything under the seat, and he would not have to keep carrying his saddlebags with him every time he dismounted from Chestnut; he was certain that before long this would attract the curiosity of his fellow travellers. If he could just find a way to secure the coins to the ledges.

'Will!' Arthur called again. Will jumped down from the wagon and hurried over to join Arthur and the boys who were excited to show him what they had chosen. They had warm cloaks, leather boots, warm tunics and woollen hose, and fur covers to use as bedding – Will thought one of those would make a perfect seat cover, thick, warm and wide enough to cover the seat, so suggested they bought another two to be on the safe side. 'We can always put one on the seat of the wagon to make it more comfortable for you boys and whichever one of us is driving the mules. After all, we are in autumn and, even if the sun shines, the days are shorter and as the sun begins to go down the air becomes colder. When you move around you are warmer but when you sit still, you feel the cold more. A fur cover over the seat will help to keep you warm.'

Arthur nodded his agreement. 'Truly. Winter will be on us soon and any additional warm clothing and coverings will be welcome, especially in a building that has not seen occupants for some time. As yet we have no idea what awaits us at Winterne…'

'…After all, we do not know if the building even has a roof!' Will ,winked at Arthur, who grinned.

'No roof!' said Bartley and Dickon's face was a picture of disbelief.

'I speak in jest, boys.' Will laughed and ruffled their hair.

'But no-one has actually said there is a roof on the manor, have they, Will? Arthur teased.

Then it was time to pay for their purchases. In addition, to the wagons, mules, clothes and warm coverings, they bought breast-band harnesses for the mules, several bags of hay and oats to feed the animals when perhaps grazing land was not easily come by.

Lastly, they bought a copper cooking pot, a metal support for suspending it over a fire, flints, two jars of ale with cork stoppers, two jars of spiced mead with stoppers, a bakestone for flatbreads, rye flour, a truckle of cheese wrapped in a gauze-like cloth, knives, feedbags for the horses and mules, wooden bowls, spoons and cups for the humans to eat and drink from, and wooden buckets for the horses and mules, eggs, some salted herring, string of onions, red apples, some mushrooms, purple carrots and dried herbs, parsley, thyme and rosemary. Will had suggested that over the nine days or so before they reached Winterne, if they were unable to find an inn to stay at overnight and had to find their own food, it would be best to be prepared and, if they were not needed on the journey, those things would be useful when they reached the manor; nothing would be wasted.

With the mules now hitched to the wagon's shafts and all their purchases and belongings loaded on board, the boys sat either side of Arthur on the driving seat.

'Your legs aren't long enough to reach the toe-board, so just hold old to the end of the seat or the sides,' Arthur smiled at their small feet dangling freely above the toe board.

Will rode beside the wagon on the now re-named Chestnut, while Ash and the still-named Narbonne, tethered to the back of the wagon, tagged along calmly ignoring the busy street noises. Street food vendors trying to outdo each other as to how loud they could shout about their wares, vagabonds begged for alms, jugglers threw as many wooden hoops as they could keep in the air without dropping them, tumblers performed somersaults and other acrobatic acts hoping their audience would throw a few coins their way.

Children ran about making a nuisance of themselves, as adults out for a casual stroll to watch the performers or to examine the goods for sale, became increasingly exasperated with the youngsters running into them or almost tripping them up not looking where they were going. A stout middle-aged man called for the constables to control the children when his wife had her bottom slapped by one of the more impudent older boys as he ran by.

Horses and wagons clattered along on the cobbles and constables stalked around looking for someone to apprehend. Shop and tavern owners called out from their doorways attempting to entice passers-by into their hostelries for a cup of ale, a goblet of wine, fish or rabbit stew, a slice of beef and their finest bread. It was those who shouted the loudest, who usually got the custom.

At one point Will thought he caught a glimpse of Kate and Alfred looking around the stalls, but he lost sight of them when a crowd gathered around a street peddler selling carved leather pouches, belts and wristbands. He hoped the couple would be happy and that Kelvin's death could be put behind them; Alfred need not have that on his conscience when he had been defending first Kate and then himself.

They were almost at the harbour when the mules shied and baulked as three little boys ran directly in front of them trying to run away from the constables. Will reached out to grab the bridle of the nearest mule to stop him from rearing, just as Arthur heaved on the reins. Dickon, enthralled by all the goings on around him, had forgotten to hold on and was thrown forward. Shrieking, he pitched forward, head-first between the rear ends of the mules, clutched at anything to stop himself hurtling headlong onto the cobbles between their legs, and managed to grab the leather traces that tethered to mules to the shafts. Arthur thrust the reins into Bartley's hands and darted forward, grabbed Dickon by the seat of his breeches and hauled him back up to safety.

As Arthur clasped Dickon in his strong arms, the uninjured but shaken little boy tearfully buried his face in Arthur's leather jerkin, and whispered: 'Th...thankee, Sir Arfur,'

'Dickon spoke!' said Bartley. 'E ent done tha' fer mus' be a year or more.' Bartley's eyes filled with happy tears and he climbed across Arthur's lap to hug his brother. Will, who had been unable to hear over the street noise, stared at them dumbfounded. 'What is it?'

Over Dickon's head Arthur mouthed that the lad had spoken. Will shook his head in disbelief, his eyes wide. A miracle had happened and the future looked bright. But they had to move on, they were blocking the road and the constables now had the boys they had been chasing, and were leading them back along the street by their ears.

The mules having calmed, Arthur helped Bartley back onto his side of the seat, Dickon held on to Arthur's arm and Will rode in front of the mules trying to ensure nothing else would impede their progress to the harbour which lay just at the end of the street. Already Will could see a number of horses, and the Coombs family high-sided wagon they had seen at The Swan.

Arthur was busy talking to the boys, wanting to learn as much as he could from Bartley about their background. He tried asking Dickon about how he had liked living at the inn, but Dickon had gone quiet again. Arthur kept talking, Bartley kept answering and neither of them pushed Dickson to speak again; they just knew that he would when he was ready.

Will's head was full of thoughts about what they would find when they reached Winterne. This was the last stage of their journey and what awaited them was the unknown. He and Arthur had had little time for his reading and writing lessons, and he had hoped to at least be able to make a good job of signing his name and understanding the writing on the scroll proclaiming him a knight. Now there were two boys who he hoped would look up to him, and who he would not wish to know he could not read. He would have to talk to Arthur about that later, perhaps when the boys were asleep.

Arriving at the harbour they were delighted to see the Coombs family amongst a group of around fifteen people, most of them on horseback but there were several other wagons similar in style to their own and, in one of them was Matilda. Will turned away to hide his smile at seeing Arthur's eyes light up when he saw her sitting beside her brother, Roger, and missed her frown.

But Arthur saw it and, although he was pleased to see her, her reaction surprised him and left him feeling rather saddened; a slight feeling of disenchantment crept its way into his mind. He had felt a spark of attraction towards her, and thought he saw something of the same in her for him; her sweet smile had reached her eyes and he thought he saw a kind soul shining there in the deep blue, but had he been wrong?

Chapter Seventeen

Emerging from the busy, crowded street onto the harbour, the first thing Will and Arthur noticed, at exactly the same time, was that the *Somerset* had already left the harbour. Will was not only surprised she had sailed, he felt more despondent than he would have expected. In their room, during the previous night, they had planned to visit Walter Smith before leaving Newhaven to offer their condolences and wish him farewell. They had also wanted to find a way to talk to the Boatswain without Walter seeing, to ensure he would be looked after. But it was not to be.

He shifted in the saddle and leaned forward to stroke Chestnut's neck, her coat felt smooth and warm under his touch and it lifted his spirits. Briefly he wondered what Walter had decided to do with Kelvin's body, then he recalled Walter saying he would bury him at sea.

The cold wind had grown stronger, pounding the waves against the sea wall, sending spray up and over the harbour wall onto the quayside where it formed large puddles. The wind rippled the puddles mirroring in a smaller scale the waves in the harbour. Even within the shelter of the harbour walls the small boats bobbed wildly up and down and, the larger ships anchored beyond the harbour rolled with the waves. One ship's tender, a longboat, Will counted fifteen men aboard, rowed over the waves towards one of the larger ships. As the boat slid down between the waves, they were out of sight until they began to climb the next rolling wave. Watching them Will could feel the bile rising in his throat. He swallowed, took a deep breath and turned away. He had no intention of being seasick on dry land and he had no ginger root left. He pulled his cloak tighter and steered Chestnut back to their wagon.

Within the shelter of the building-lined street, the force of the wind had not been noticeable but, as soon as they cleared its protection, its strength flapped the wagon coverings, cloaks, ladies held on to their unruly veils, dead leaves gusted in the air and blew into heaps or into the sea.

Will stopped Chestnut alongside the wagon. 'So much for our hopes to see Walter this morning, Arthur. He must have been distraught at losing Kelvin.'

Arthur frowned but there was sympathy in his expression. 'Kelvin had a terrible temper and cared not how he treated people. It had been an ordeal for Walter constantly trying to protect his son from those who would take their revenge for his misdeeds. He must have spent each day wondering what Kelvin would do next and what the outcome would be. Now he has lost his son, but...' he inhaled through his teeth as he tried to find the right words, '...that...that constant worry has become a reality and, now it is done, he no longer has that fear hanging over his head. I suppose you get what you deserve, but I believe he was the only family Walter had.'

'You're right,' replied Will. 'I have no pity for Kelvin. Perhaps he would have been better joining the army. He could have vented his temper on the battlefield then, perhaps like us, he would have tired of fighting.'

'Mmm. You might be right...but I believe Walter wanted to keep him close. He probably thought he could keep him safe that way and persuaded the Earl he was needed on board.' Arthur moved the mules on. 'But come, we must join the others and get on our way.'

'I wonder if Robin and Hugh and the escort have left,' said Will.

Arthur looked up. 'Although the sun can only be seen through the clouds, from its position, I believe they will be long gone. I am sorry to see them go. I will miss them but I am glad they are together.'

Will gave a sad smile. 'I too will miss them and I pray their lives work out the way they hope, and it is comforting they are not going in different directions.' He gave Chestnut a gentle nudge with his feet and she walked on towards the waiting group of travellers.

Arthur drew their wagon up a little way behind that of the Coombs family. Matilda, sitting on the front seat peered around the side of their wagon a gave a little smile. Arthur, still somewhat puzzled by her earlier response was unsure how to react, but gave her a wave then purposely looked away, as though he was too busy with attending to something in the wagon.

At the head of the convoy, two men armed with swords, long knives and longbows strapped to their backs, rode on matching black coursers, as the convoy pulled out. In total there were five wheeled conveyances in the party, three covered wagons and two open carts, one of which was pulled by donkeys.

As they walked along, Will walked Chestnut a little faster to catch up with Master Coombs and his son, Martin, who were riding ahead of their family wagon. Master Coombs sat astride a large, dappled grey mount with a long, full white mane. Beside him, Martin rode on a slighter, smaller horse that to begin with, Will took to be another chestnut, but looking closer he noticed a base coat of black. Her eyes were large, with long black eyelashes, her nostrils were larger than any English breeds he had seen before, and she appeared to have a slight but noticeable bulge between her eyes. Her short back was also unusual and she proudly held her head high reminding him of some of the dignified ladies he had met. Will was fascinated with her. 'Good-day Master Coombs. Good-day, Martin. Forgive my curiosity but your mount, Martin, is unlike any I have seen before. Did you breed her?'

Martin reached forward and stroked the ears of his mare, who reacted by pointing her ears sideways and giving a fluttering sort of snort. 'No, Lady is of pure Arab stock.' Will could see Martin had a great affection for the mare. 'We brought her across from Flanders after seeing her being used as a cart horse and beaten. It was clear her owner had no idea of her intelligence or bloodline or how to care for her. I offered him a price that would allow him to buy a larger, stronger horse and...shall we say, encouraged him to believe that she was too small and weak for the kind of work he required her to do, and that it was unlikely she would last another year if he continued to work her in that way. He accepted my offer very willingly...'

'...Faster than a cat taking a fish from your hand,' Edgar Coombs broke in.

Martin smiled. 'Yes, he wasted no time in taking what was actually an offer well below her value. We followed him to a horse trader in the town and he found a sixteen hands, five year old male that suited him, and had been a working horse. I handed over the money and we untethered our girl here, and she has been mine ever since.' He patted her neck affectionately.

'Until recently I had scant experience with horses other than other people's at my father's smithy, but even I can see she is a beauty and clearly well looked after, Martin.'

They rode along in amicable conversation for a short while, but Will was aware of silent hostility from Roger. He could feel an intense glare from Roger's eyes burning into his back. While Martin and his father chatted easily to each other, and to Will, he noticed Roger did not speak to his sister and they travelled in silence. Neither did Roger speak to his father or brother, he just steered their horses along morosely. Will was at a loss to understand what if anything he had done to offend Roger, but refused to let it bother him. Roger, it seemed, had a personality rather like Kelvin's but, Will hoped, less violent.

After a few minutes Will bade Edgar and Martin goodbye, nodded to Matilda and slowed Chestnut to fall back to join Arthur and the boys. Dickon was still, but Arthur and Bartley appeared to be deep in conversation.

Will smiled at the sight of Arthur, his arms around both the boys as they cuddled into him, but still coping well at handling the reins. Dickon, nestled into Arthur and cosy under his cloak, appeared to be asleep, but Bartley was absorbed in all new sights on either side of the road; the occasional squirrel collecting food supplies for the winter, the drumming sound of a nearby woodpecker, rabbits scurrying through the undergrowth trying to find cover in the woodland on either side of the road.

'Would you like me to take a turn?' asked Will.

Arthur shook his head. 'No. I can continue until we make our first stop, then you can take over if you would like to. For the moment though, I would like the little one to sleep if he needs it. And Bartley and I have some news for you.'

Will laughed. 'You do? Have I grown another head or something?'

It was Bartley's turn to laugh. 'No, Sir William. Nought like tha'. Tis jest tha' I said wha' I thought Sir Arthur's 'orse should be named.'

'And what have name you chosen?'

'Well, you got Chestnut an' there's Ash an' so both of 'em's trees, so Narbonne needs ter be called after a tree, don' 'e?'

'Yes, I can see that, so what is the new name to be?'

'Yer can tell Sir William, Sir Arthur,' said Bartley.

'No, no, it is your choice and a good one, so speak up, my boy.' Arthur beamed at the lad who could hardly contain his excitement and sat champing at the bit, almost bursting with delight at being the one to re-name the horse.

'We're callin' 'im Rowan!' With shoulders back and chin up, Bartley seemed to be incredibly pleased with himself. Arthur looked at Will, waiting for his comment and saw a look of pride on his face.

'Well done, Bartley,' Will enthused. 'That is a marvellous name for him.'

'And I've told him it even contains four of the letters in Narbonne, said Arthur.

A sound above them distracted Bartley. 'Look!' he cried, pointing upward. 'What is it?'

Soaring above in circles was a large and beautiful bird of prey, the sun glistening on its white head feathers. Arthur explained it was a sea eagle, was also called an erne, and that they would probably see several of them while they were this close to the coastline, and within easy reach of treetops where they liked to build their nests. Bartley spent the next hour staring upwards waiting for another sighting but he was to be disappointed as no others came into view.

Chapter Eighteen

Although the wind was fairly strong, within the shelter of the trees they were afforded some respite from its force, but all around them the trees were being stripped of their dying leaves and, as far as the eye could see, the woodland floor was carpeted in withered leaves in glorious autumn colours that crunched when walked on.

After covering a good few miles and having skirted Worthing, they came upon an inn and the two men in front halted the party suggesting that it would be a good place to stop for dinner. The Sun Inn, provided a perpetual stew pot which was rarely emptied completely, but topped up with water or ale and ingredients as required. That meant there was always a hot meal available to travellers. The party enjoyed a hare stew with onions, leeks, mushrooms and herbs and hunks of dark rye bread, washed down with ale or wine for the wealthy. Of course, Will was wealthy, but was not about to produce the coins the prince had given him. That money was for the renovation of Winterne Manor. He was also aware that letting it be known he had that fortune, would be to invite theft and he was not about to do that, so continued to use his soldier's pay as did Arthur.

Before leaving the inn, several of the party, including Arthur, bought supplies of bread, cheese and ale in case they were unable to reach a suitable inn before they stopped for the night.

As the sky darkened and the evening chill crept into their bodies, they were still on the coast road. They passed through the centre of Suthewicke, a small village where people stopped to stare as they rode along the muddy main street, intending to look for an inn on the other side of the village. A soft drizzle had begun to fall bringing the temperature down even further and soon some members of the group were beginning to grumble, but the last inn was a few miles back and the Ryder brothers, leading the party, did not want to turn back.

After continuing for another six miles or so with the rain having become no heavier, they finally came across The Green Man Inn, and Edgar Coombs rode ahead to speak to Thomas Ryder to suggest it might be a good time stop for the night.

Thomas agreed halted, dismounted, and entered the inn to see how many people and horses could be accommodated for the night and soon returned with the good news that the inn had no other guests staying that night, and would welcome them warmly. Hot food was available inside and there were four long tables with benches in the bar area, a warm log fire was burning heartily in the grate, and the three rooms on the upper floor could be shared with four mattresses in each, and of course the ladies and children should take priority for these rooms.

With the door open, the inviting aroma of whatever was being cooked filtered out and invaded nostrils, making them feel hungry again. It was some hours since their last stop and the cold just added to their need for comfort eating.

In addition, for those who could be content with less comfortable lodgings for the night, the barn was full of hay and, if they had their own bedding, it would be a passable alternative. He had taken a look at the barn and assured them it was very reasonable. There was also a stable for the horses, mules and donkeys, and space at the back of the barn to leave the wagons overnight out of the rain. Will had hoped to be able to resume his reading lessons with Arthur once the boys were asleep but, with the number of people sleeping in the barn, it was not going to happen that night. Oh well, perhaps tomorrow.

At that point rain changed from a drizzle to a shower, and the decision was made for them. Those men who were amongst the travellers, helped by Simon Ryder and the two sons of the innkeeper, hurried to get the riding horses into the spacious stables at the far end of the front courtyard, while the ladies and children were sent inside to get warm.

Will and Arthur, together Thomas Ryder, Edgar, Roger and Martin Coombs plus some other men whose names they did not know, quickly tugged the animal teams towards the barn opposite the stables. Once outside, they uncoupled the animals from the wagons and carts, and handed them over to Simon and his group while they dealt with installing the vehicles in the barn, much to the displeasure of the resident chickens and geese that squawked, clucked, hissed and shed feathers as they scattered out of the way.

Bartley had objected at being sent inside with the children stating very firmly that he was no longer a child, but Arthur and Will, equally firmly insisted both boys went inside and told them to sit down and stay still until they returned from the barn.

Arthur and Will were laughing about Bartley's protestations as Thomas Ryder shuffled across the hay strewn floor towards them.

'Am I correct in thinking I am addressing Sir William Hallett and Sir Arthur Burnel?'

'You are correct,' said Arthur. Will thought he sounded quite haughty, which was unlike Arthur.

Thomas bowed and doffed his cap. 'I regret I have not introduced myself, Thomas Ryder, at your service, gentlemen. My brother, Simon – he is with the others attending to the animals in the stables - and myself have been hired to lead this party of travellers and act as protectors should the need arise.'

'Yes, we gathered something of the sort,' Arthur replied, waiting for Thomas to ask for money.

'This is undoubtedly large enough to lodge our menfolk overnight,' said Thomas, 'and the hay is piled high enough to make a comfortable mattress for us all.'

Arthur pointed out the wooden ladder that led to the loft. 'It looks as if there is plenty of room up there to spread out and, from what I can see there is more hay up there.'

'We should be comfortable enough here for one night. The barn is dry and there are no signs of leaks in the roof. I shall see you again inside, gentlemen.' And he turned away towards the large double doors, took a few steps, then turned back.

'My apologies. There is just one more thing.'

Here it comes, thought Arthur, this is where he asks for payment, but when Thomas continued, Arthur was pleasantly surprised.

'I have been told you were you were both at the Battle of Poitiers and have been soldiers in the Earl of Salisbury's force for some years?'

Will nodded. 'Yes, indeed. We were archers, but also trained in close fighting. Why do you ask?'

'We are a large party, Sir William, with many women and children and, of course a number of older men who are no longer fit enough to defend themselves, let alone defend others.' He looked around as if trying to ensure they could not be overheard. 'I would not want to offend any of the men in our party, but I am certain you understand my meaning.'

Will and Arthur both nodded and took a covert glance around at the men still in the barn. What Ryder was saying was true. Most of the men, other than Martin and Roger Coombs were older, some were overweight, and others did not have the weapons for defence. It was unlikely they would be of much use if the group was attacked.

'What did you have in mind, Thomas?'

'The roads are not as safe as they used to be but, with the number of good fighters away with the army...and many of the common people taxed into poverty to provide for our King's determination to regain his lands in France...and, please do not think this is a criticism...but, well...it has to be said, poverty is driving some people into crime and a rich party of travellers such as this, would be a perfect target on lonely roads. Can I rely on your assistance if the worst should happen?'

'Have you asked the Coombs brothers?' asked Arthur.

'Yes, and they have agreed. I understand they have no experience of combat, but they are young, strong and have had some training with the sword.'

'So that will make six of us...as you say, should the need arise,' said Will looking at Arthur. 'I believe we should agree. What think you Arthur?'

'You have my sword, Thomas.'

'Thank you, gentlemen. I mentioned to my brother that I would be speaking to you both and we hoped you would agree. Thank you again, but let us pray your assistance is not needed. I will take my leave and see you inside.'

There was no nearby back door giving a quick way into the inn and, once they had completed their tasks, Will and Arthur dashed through what was now a heavy downpour, across the large outer courtyard to the arched entrance of the smaller courtyard at the front of the inn, trying to avoid the many puddled potholes; their feet were wet enough as it was. In the porch, Will and Arthur removed their cloaks and shook off the worst of the rain before pushing open the wide wooden door.

Inside the bar room, the warmth from the open log fire and the number of bodies gathered in close proximity made the room feel stuffy and their damp clothing added to the humidity. As the door opened creating a draft, the yellow-orange flames of the fire and the flames on solid tallow candles flickered in the breeze casting moving shadows around the walls.

Looking through the confusion of people trying to get close to the fire or shouting orders for food or ale, Will and Arthur were unable to see the boys and began to push their way through the crush of people in the narrow bar room. As a man moved across in front of them, Arthur glimpsed the boys were in the company of a matronly lady who had clearly taken charge of them. She had already found them seats near the fire, a hunk of rye bread and cup of watered down ale. Bartley saw Will and pointed him out to her as they approached. The lady nodded to the boys, Will saw her say something to them, then she began to make her way towards Will and Arthur.

As she approached, weaving her way between the groups of wet and hungry travellers, Arthur noted her good quality clothing, a fitted gown worn underneath a black velvet fur-trimmed sleeveless surcote and, in keeping with the fashion, a spotless white gorget, a band of white linen wrapped under her throat and pinned on either side of her head concealing her hair. Over this she wore clean, white shoulder length veil and the overall impression was one of severity.

He whispered to Will, while she was still out of earshot, that she was likely to be very straight-laced and obviously a widow of some wealth. Will whispered back that perhaps Arthur should marry her. Arthur choked back a chuckle and maintained a straight face with difficulty.

With her occasional telling-off of anyone who would not move out of her way, and a forceful manner, the lady finally made her way through the overcrowded room to reach them and, Arthur was forced to think again about his first impression of the lady. Her radiant smile, extravagantly embroidered and jewelled belt, cuffs and belt-pouch revealed a more flamboyant personality than he had originally thought.

'Good evening, gentlemen. I am Mistress Edith Chapman. I believe I have the honour of addressing Sir William Hallett and Sir Arthur Burnel. Kindly assist me by informing which of you is which.'

Both men bowed to the lady and Arthur duly obliged by making the introductions.

'And which of you is the father of the two young gentlemen whose company I have had the pleasure of during your absence?'

Will stepped forward. 'That would...or rather, will be me. I shall be making the legal arrangements for the care of the boys once we reach our destination.'

'So they do not have a natural father.'

'No, sadly, their parents are both dead.' He went on to explain how the boys had come to be with them.

The lady waited for Will to finish and then said: 'And I believe you are journeying to Winterne?'

Puzzled by her enquiry, Arthur asked: 'Yes, that is correct but, may I...?

'Indeed, Sir Arthur, I should explain myself and my interest in your situation.' She sat down on a bench, smoothed down her skirt and gave them both a sweet smile that lit her warm brown eyes and took some years off her face. 'I shall be ending my journey at Shepton Mallet where is my home. It is only a few miles from Winterne and...well, to be honest with you I am looking for a position, possibly as housekeeper, and I understand from Bartley and Dickon that you will be renovating Winterne Manor. Are you in need of such a person?'

Arthur and Will looked at each other, neither of them really knew quite what to say and neither of them wanted to offend this seemingly very amiable lady who reminded Will of his grandmother. Will sat down on the bench beside her.

'Mistress Chapman, forgive me but I need to ask. Why are you looking for that type of position. Where is your husband?'

She looked down at the floor and Will was convinced she was about to cry but then she looked up and pushing her shoulders back, she looked Will in the eye and said: 'I am twice widowed, Sir William. My second husband died following an accident eighteen months ago.'

'I am sorry to hear that, Mistress Chapman.'

She gave a little chuckle which surprised Will and Arthur. 'I say accident but had he not been the worse for drink and chasing a young lady, it would not have happened. It was his own fault and at his age, he should have known better.'

'Do you have family or any kind of commitments?' asked Will.

'I have two daughters but they are both married and have moved away. I rarely see them or my grand-children. My son is employed at Sheen Palace in Richmond and I see him even less. My husband left me well provided for but I am...well, bored to tears to be honest with you. I have no need of employment, but I have nothing to do and would like to feel useful again.'

'I understand but, certainly, for the moment, I can do nothing to help,' said Will, sympathetically. 'You see, until we reach Winterne Manor I have no notion of how much work will be required to make the house habitable or whether any of the rooms can be used comfortably. I intend, when the renovations are complete, to move my mother and sister-in-law into the house.'

'Ah, I see, Sir William,' Mistress Chapman interrupted. 'I apologise for bothering you but I was under the impression you had no female support for the boys...or yourselves, and thought I could offer my services.'

'Indeed, I am sure Sir Arthur and I appreciate your offer and, as we still have a few days to journey, perhaps we can speak of this again. Are you travelling alone?'

'No. I have my retainer, Milo, with me. He was a servant of my first husband and has looked after me since his death. I have to say that my second husband was not too happy about having Milo with us, but I refused to let him go, and in the end my husband gave in.'

Will, although instantly full of admiration for the lady's strong, but caring and genial personality, thought it would probably have been unwise of the second husband to try and rid himself of Milo if the lady was determined to keep him. He wondered if the second husband ever won an argument with her.

While they were talking, Arthur became distracted and he sought out Matilda. He trembled with shock when his eyes found hers fixed directly on him. She smiled warmly, then gave a quick glance towards Roger, but he had his back to her and was still in conversation with Simon. Arthur knew they had to have a chance to talk and made up his mind to find a suitable time when Roger was not around.

Within an hour or so, the group had finished their supper and, with the window shutters closed, the room filled with the haze of wisps of steam rising from wet clothing, the smell of damp wool and sweat, ale, stew and more fresh bread baking. Many of the children, including Bartley and Dickon who were now sitting with Will and Arthur, were fed and warm and now beginning to nod off to sleep. Mistress Chapman suggested the boys could stay with her rather than sleeping in the barn, so without waking them, Will cradled Dickon and Arthur carried Bartley up the stairs, Mistress Chapman opened the door to the room she would be sharing with another lady, and the boys were gently laid on one of the mattresses.

The next morning, although the ground was awash with puddles, the rain had stopped but the air was cold. Will shivered as he awoke to find a chicken strutting, pecking at the barn floor just inches from his face. He nudged Arthur: 'Chicken to break your fast this morning, Arthur?'

Arthur opened one eye and looked at the hen. 'No. I think not. I am still full from last night's meal.' A movement near the door caught their attention.

Thomas Ryder, fully dressed and armed, stood at the open doorway holding an hourglass. 'Is everyone awake?' he called. Nudging a displeased brown hen off a large wooden crate near the door, he placed the hourglass on top, the sand was already running through to the lower chamber. 'I would ask you to be ready to leave when the bottom half of the glass is full, gentlemen. We have already awoken the ladies and children. I will leave you to make whatever ablutions you feel necessary and to prepare yourself for departure.' He left.

All around the barn and above, in the loft, the hay stirred as men began to wake to the sound of yawns, groans and snorts, threw off their bedding and pulled on their outer garments.

'Is it time to leave?' asked Martin Coombs, scratching his head with one hand as he descended the ladder, holding on with the other, from the loft. 'Good morning, Sir Arthur, Sir William. I trust you both slept well.'

Edgar Coombs followed Martin down the ladder and came to stand beside him. He nodded to Arthur and Will.

'Thank you. Better than I thought we would,' said Will. 'Come, Arthur and I will help you with your wagon and then you can help us with ours.'

Soon after with mules, donkeys and horses tethered to the shafts of the wagons and carts, and those riding upon them on board and ready to go,

Thomas and Simon made their final checks that everyone they should have was present, and they were leaving no-one behind. Arthur, tethered Chestnut and Ash to the back rail of the wagon, then mounted on the newly named Rowan, and prepared to move on.

Mistress Chapman came out of the inn with the two boys who had been in her care overnight. She greeted Will and Arthur, then helped Will to lift the boys aboard the wagon.

'I look forward to seeing you again when we stop for a rest.' Whether that had been addressed to the boys or to Arthur and William as well, none of them was quite sure. But it was of no consequence. They would find out later.

Will called out to thank her for looking after the boys. She waved but did not turn around as she hurried off to the front part of the column to join Milo. They did not see her again until the evening when they stopped for the night at Littlehampton. Thomas Ryder had gone along the line of travellers at mid-day to advise them, that as the weather was holding, after a short break to eat and stretch their legs, they would be continuing directly to Littlehampton which would give them good mileage for the day. He knew a very suitable hostelry a little outside the town where they intended to stop for the night.

Arthur had seen very little of Matilda that day, although he did catch a glimpse of her when she climbed aboard their wagon and gave him a brittle smile. Other than that, when he did see her it was only in the distance. For some reason Roger had moved their wagon further along the line, and they were now some way ahead.

Riding on Rowan, Arthur tried to contain his impatience to see Matilda again. Something was definitely wrong between her and Roger, and he was reluctant to make things any worse for her. All the same he wanted to find out just what the problem was. Perhaps Martin would be able to explain.

It was later that day he found the opportunity to talk to Martin. Edgar had gone forward to ride alongside their wagon, leaving Martin on his own. Arthur took advantage of the moment and urged Rowan on a little faster to catch up with Martin. Initially, he made polite conversation, discussing the improved weather and how well the column was progressing that day. Following those niceties, he asked about their trade and travels to and from Flanders. All of which Martin appeared only too happy to discuss with him, even inviting him and Will and the boys to visit them in Salisbury to stay for a few days and see for themselves show the wool trade operated.

Arthur thanked Martin for his invitation, but declined at this time as Will was keen to get to their journey's end to discover what had become of his mother and sister-in-law and his nephews. He also thought there was a possibility that the Earl's steward would be arriving at Winterne soon, and they had to ensure they were there when he arrived, but said they would be delighted to visit at another time. They rode on in amiable conversation for a while, then Arthur brought up the subject of Roger and why there appeared to be some animosity towards Will and himself.

Martin smiled. 'That's because of Matilda.'

'But why?' said Arthur. 'I have done nothing to offend her, I hope.'

'Oh no, no, Sir Arthur. You have done nothing but be pleasant and approachable and...in the case of the boys...charitable, and...well, Matilda and father were very impressed with the generosity you and Sir William have shown towards the boys. And, that's the problem.'

Arthur's frown expressed his puzzlement.

'Let me explain. Matilda has been brought up as well educated as Roger and myself and has been given the freedom to express her own thoughts. She is highly intelligent and can debate most topics with any man but...Roger has pressed father into agreeing a marriage for her with a friend of his, which will be a benefit to the business. Matilda has been put in a position where she has had little choice but to agree to this. Unfortunately, no matter what our father implies, our business is not doing too well...because of the war you understand...'

'...And this marriage will improve your situation.'

'Exactly,' said Martin. He stopped his horse. 'You have to understand, Sir Arthur, for the first time since the betrothal Matilda has shown interest in another man...yourself...'

'...And Roger sees me as a danger to your plans.'

'You understand now.'

'Indeed I do. The marriage proposal has been confirmed?'

'Yes. Matilda was officially betrothed to Guy Attaway before our last trip to Flanders. She will marry soon after our return to Salisbury.'

Arthur looked away, trying to hide his dejected expression. His stomach knotted and his feeling of desolation was more agonising than he could ever have imagined.

'I see this news has been difficult for you to hear, Sir Arthur. I regret to be the one to tell you. I had not realised you felt so strongly about our sister.'

'Neither had I. I thank you for telling me, Martin. It is better I know.' They rode in silence for a few moments, then Arthur said he was going back to join Will and the boys. As he turned away he saw Matilda looking back at him from the side of her wagon. She must have realised that he now knew the truth, and her sorrowful look back at him broke his heart.

Chapter Nineteen

Apart from becoming nodding acquaintances with many of the other travellers, each day became much like the one before as they skirted Littlehampton, then Portsmouth and on to Southampton, where the first small party of travellers left them.

Where Bartley and Dickon had been excited about setting out on the journey, together with the other children in the party, they were now bored with travelling and looked forward to the stops made along the way that broke up the tedious journey.

Martin and Edgar, kindly offered to take them on their horses for a while, and Mistress Chapman invited them to ride in her wagon several times, all of which helped to break the monotony for them a little. At other times, and in good weather only, the children were permitted to walk along together beside the convoy. Better still, during stops by the roadside, they were given time to play for a while under the watchful eyes of an appointed group of adults, while other adults prepared food, examined animals hooves or wagons for any potential breaks, or splintering of the wooden wheels.

It was during one of these stoppages, when Will had volunteered to be amongst those watching the children as they played, that Mistress Chapman approached him. She brushed off the dirt and dead leaves from the fallen tree trunk he was sitting on, and sat down beside him. She gave him a warm smile in greeting but did not speak for a few moments fascinated by the struggle Alice and Sybil Lister were having with eight-year-old Samuel Townsend. They had been playing hide and seek and had found him, but he refused to come out from his hiding place under a privet hedge until he was chased out by his ten-year-old sister, Amelia. Under a wide-trunked oak tree, on a pile of autumn leaves, the two most timid little girls amongst the younger ones in the group, Sarah and Maud Simkins, who Will estimated were about seven and five years old respectively, sat crossed-legged, playing with dolls and watching what the other children were doing. Will thought they would like to have joined in the fun, but were too shy to try.

'You see the power girls have, Sir William,' Mistress Chapman chuckled, pointing out Amelia's success. Will nodded, making no mention of the Simkins sisters. 'And we men think *we* are the masters.' He returned her smile. 'And how are you on this lovely morning?'

'Very well, thank you. A little chilly though, but I prefer this to rain and any morning would be good in comparison with all the wet weather we have had but, I hope you will excuse me making a personal observation...I wanted to ask you a question.' She looked over at where Bartley was trying to walk on borrowed wooden stilts, and Dickon was falling about laughing at his efforts.

'They are wonderful boys and I enjoy their company a great deal but, I understand you may feel this is none of my business, I have to ask though.'

Will wondered what was on her mind. Whatever it was she had obviously spent some time thinking about it.

'Sir William, you are a handsome young man, with that wonderful thick wavy head of red hair, a short beard that suits you well and those deep green eyes. You are...what...some twenty or so years?'

Will nodded. 'Yes. I will soon be one and twenty years old. Is that a problem?'

She chuckled. 'Not at all. Please understand, I do mean well. As I was saying you are a handsome young man...'

Will smiled,'...Thank you for the compliment, Mistress Chapman, please go on.'

'It is likely you will marry at some time in the next year or two and have a family of your own.' She looked over at Dickon and Bartley, the stilts cast to one side, and were now trying to catch Amelia Townsend who was a very fast runner and extremely agile, and continually swerved out of the way before she could be caught.

Will was beginning to understand what the lady was thinking but he let her continue.

'If you marry and have children of your own, what happens to Bartley and Dickon? Will they also be your heirs and treated equally or will they find themselves relegated to servant status?'

'I know you have become fond of the boys, Mistress Chapman, but believe me, so have I. I would not have taken on their care if I had not meant for them to be considered part of my family, and they will always have their share of my heart and my property. However, I was brought up in a working family and I have served as a soldier. My own life has not been easy and I have been given nothing until now. Before that I earned everything I had. So I very much appreciate what it is to have nothing, and how fortunate I am to have what I have now that I can share with whatever family I have in the future, and with Bartley and Dickon. Having said that, I would not have them grow up believing that life is easy. They must learn to earn their living just as any children of my own will.'

'But will your future wife feel the same?'

'I will not enter into a marriage contract with anyone who is unable to accept the boys as my sons. The formalities of that will be taken care of in Winterne.'

'Thank you for indulging me, Sir William. I hope I have not offended you by asking,'

'Not at all, Mistress Chapman...'

'...Oh, and I think we know each other well enough now for you to call me Edith,' she interrupted.

'Very well, thank you...Edith. In that case, please just call me Will. To be honest with you, still unused as I am to the title, I feel more comfortable without it, and I know you mean well in regard to the boys, so I take no offence...but I see Thomas is beckoning and I believe it is time we were on our way again.' He looked over at where the children were kicking up bundles of leaves and throwing handfuls at each other; their laughter rang around the tree-lined roadside. It was good to see them having fun but they had to move on.

'Come children, it is time to go.'

On returning to the wagon, Will found Arthur tethering the mules back in to the shafts of their wagon and huddled in conversation with Martin.

There was only one thing they could be discussing – Matilda. Will was not near enough to overhear their conversation, but it appeared Arthur was imploring Martin to do something, but Martin sadly shook his head and shrugged as if to show there was nothing he could do. Then it looked as though Martin changed his mind and he gave Arthur a huge smile before walking away. Will saw Arthur visibly heave a sigh of relief as he watched Martin head off to where the Coombs' wagon was located.

As Will and Edith walked back to the road with Bartley and Dickon following along behind with the other children, Edith said: 'I wonder if I can be of help to Sir Arthur.'

Will looked doubtful. 'In what way?'

Edith gave a little wry smile. 'I have become quite friendly with Matilda and...well perhaps I could invite her to ride with me for a while. Ladies often enjoy the company of other ladies, and she has had precious little female companionship with all those men in her family.'

Will could see what she was trying to achieve but wondered how it was to be managed. 'How will that help Arthur? I am sorry but I don't understand.'

Edith rolled her eyes. 'Oh, why are men are so blind!' Then she laughed. 'You see, if they could only find the chance to get together before they turn off to Salisbury later today, they will at least have the opportunity to talk discuss how they feel about each other...and what could be more natural – as far as Roger is concerned - than Matilda spending time with an old lady with whom she has become friends, before they have to bid each other farewell. Arthur and Matilda may not see each other again but, if they feel what I think they feel for each other, then...'

Will chuckled and shook his head. '...I have to admit you're a shrewd and devious lady and I admire you immensely. Now, how shall we go about it?'

'I will instruct Milo to pull our wagon out from the roadside slowly and allow Roger to go in front, possibly allow another of the wagons to go ahead of us as well. That way Roger will not have a good view of anything going on behind. Arthur should tether Rowan to the back of my wagon, climb in through the tailboard and close the cover behind him. That way he will be obscured from sight. I will invite Matilda to sit with me for a while, emphasising that it will do her good to have some female company.'

'But, what if Roger objects?'

'Then I shall speak to their father. Edgar and I are on very good terms...' Will noticed the hint of rosiness that stole across her cheeks. So, she has designs in that direction herself, he thought.

'Ahem, as I was saying, if Roger objects, I shall appeal to their father and insist that he allows dear Matilda to sit with me for an hour or two. Milo can continue driving the wagon. As far as anyone in her family is concerned, Matilda and I are in the wagon out of the wind but it will be Arthur and Matilda who can have some time together.'

'But where will you be?'

'Me? Oh, I shall sit on Rowan behind the wagon and no-one will be any the wiser.'

'But will you be comfortable astride a horse...'

'Oh my dear boy, I have been riding since well before you were born. I am an accomplished horsewoman and can ride side-saddle or astride... although I am perfectly aware it is not dignified for a lady to do so, but needs must as they say.'

'You are quite a lady, Mistress Chapman.'

'Yes, I know. I have been told that on many occasions.' She hesitated. 'I have just thought of something, Will. We must make sure Edgar and Martin are kept out of the way and I think you should ride forward, keep them in conversation at that end of the of the line. Now off you go and I'll let Milo know what is happening.'

But Will had qualms about her suggestion. 'That is all very well Edith, but you appear to have forgotten the boys in all this.'

'The boys?'

'Yes. If Milo is driving your team, you are riding on Rowan and I am with Edgar and Martin, who is to drive our mules? Bartley is far too young to take charge of a wagon, two mules and Ash.'

'Ah, yes. I see what you mean.' With knitted brows Edith contemplated the problem for a moment, then: 'Simple. I shall sit with the boys and lead your team.'

'This is becoming a complicated plan,' said Will. 'Are you sure you can control the boys and the team?'

'Tush! Of course I can, my boy. I grew up in Southwark where my father was a vintner. When I grew old enough he let me drive a team of four and wagons when he was making deliveries. I was just a young maid then and younger than you are now. So, yes, I can control a team and the boys will give me no trouble. Now let's go and get those two together. We only have three or four hours before it's too late and they turn off for Salisbury.'

Chapter Twenty

By the time the Coombs family left the party for their home in Salisbury, Matilda was a much happier woman. But, things had not turned out as simply as Edith had planned.

While Matilda and Arthur had been able to spend some time together and now understood that they both felt the same way about each other, she was still obliged to marry. Unless her betrothed, Guy Attaway, died before the marriage there was nothing she could do other than go ahead with the plans that had been made for her. She felt compelled to help the family business survive with the investment Guy would be making as a partner.

What none of the family knew was that Guy had decided to ride out to meet his future bride and her family. Thankfully, he and his brother, Adam, met the column shortly after Matilda had returned from her 'visit with Edith'. Had they arrived just twenty minutes before, things could have been very different – Guy would have been within his rights to issue a challenge to Arthur – and, with her heart in her mouth at the thought of how close they were to having been caught, Matilda heaved a sigh of relief, as did Edith. The notion of Guy coming to meet them on the road, had never occurred to either woman, and Edith's heart beat much faster at the knowledge that her scheming may have caused the death of one of the two men, and disgrace to Matilda. It would also have put paid to the plans she had for a future with Edgar. He could never marry a woman who had helped his daughter go against his wishes. God had clearly been on her side.

Arthur had watched Matilda leave to join her family with a heavy heart knowing that, although she loved him, it was almost impossible that they could ever be together. Was it enough to know how much she cared? In one way it was a comfort but, on the other hand, the ache to have her as his wife was more painful than ever. Sitting astride Rowan, Arthur had a strong urge to ride after Matilda, scoop her up onto his saddle and ride off with her, but two things stopped him. One was the sure knowledge that she would never forgive herself – or him – if her father lost his business because of her disloyalty.

The other was seeing two, very well dressed riders, approach the Coombs' wagon and Edgar greet the older man warmly. Peering around the side of their own wagon, Arthur observed the friendly welcome the newcomers received from both Edgar and Roger, but Martin seemed more reserved and Matilda appeared to be courteous rather than enthusiastic in receiving them.

As the strangers made ready to dismount, one of them did so with ease but the other remained on his horse until his companion, walked around to join him, detached a walking stick from the saddle and assisted him down; there was a clear age gap between the two and Arthur wondered which Matilda was expected to marry. The first man then held the reins of both horses, while the older one of the two, grey-haired and with a pronounced limp hobbled alongside Edgar and Roger around to the side of the wagon.

Arthur urged Rowan towards the side of the road and under cover of the bushes, they moved nearer to where the three men were deep in conversation. Speaking in low voices, Arthur found it difficult to hear what they were saying, but he needed to know. He dismounted, looped Rowan's reins around a branch and dropped to the ground, slithering through the undergrowth on his belly like a snake until he was within earshot, giving no thought to the mud that would cling to his clothes or twigs and stones that dug into his breeches as he crawled along.

'I suggest,' said Roger, an urgent expression on his face, 'that we ask Guy's brother, the Prior at Ivychurch, to conduct the marriage with all haste. I assume, Guy, that this is what you want also?'

Arthur was horrified. Edgar had promised this old man Matilda's hand in marriage. It was outrageous! How could he? Did the man have no shame? Tears of rage sprang to his eyes. He batted them away with the heel of his hand, pulled himself up to his full height, took a moment to calm his rage and stepped forward then...felt a hand on his shoulder.

'This is not the way, Arthur.' Will stood behind him. 'Edgar has authority over Matilda whether you like it or not, and if you go charging in the only thing you will do is cause trouble for her.'

'But it...it's so unfair, unjust, I cannot stand by and watch this happen. You understand don't you?'

'You know I do, but you can change nothing. Edgar needs this marriage to go ahead if he is to save his business. For now, at least, you must put Matilda from your mind and cling to the fact that she cares for you.' With his hand on Arthur's shoulder Will gently steered his friend back through the bushes. 'One thing you have in your favour, apart from the fact that she loves you, is that her betrothed is old and appears weak. Matilda is young, healthy, strong in body and equally strong in spirit. You may have to wait but, looking at him, it cannot be long before he quits this life and then she is free to marry who she pleases. Patience, my friend.'

Arthur gave a sad smile. 'That may well be, but how will I know when the time comes. We will be nowhere near.'

Will gave a little chuckle. 'Ah, now I think I know someone who can help you there.'

'Who?' The hopeful look on Arthur's face almost broke Will's heart.

'Edith. The lady is determined to help you both and she has her own plans for herself and Edgar, and is likely to be visiting the Coombs' household on regular occasions. She will be your ally.'

'Edith is a kind and...I would say, formidable lady. That hour she arranged for Matilda and me to spend together I will never forget.' Arthur stared into the distance, lost in thought until Will touched his arm, bringing him back to the moment. He smiled, sadly. 'Did you know that Matilda is eighteen years of age and her eyes are the bluest I ever saw.' His eyes glowed as he tried to find the exact words to describe the colour of her eyes. 'You know when the sun shines on the sea, around the rock pools and it's a crystal clear blue-green. Is it aqua they call it or azure? I'm not sure...but...but I have never seen anything like that colour. And...and her hair, it is the colour of ripened corn and it shines like the sun...' He glanced at Will and found him, head tilted to one side and a beaming, kindly smile on his face. 'Hmm. I am talking about the lady overmuch, am I not? But one last thing I will say, Will. You and I have both been at war for years. We have both received wounds and scars but I tell you in all sincerity, I have never felt the pain, such an ache as I feel right now. I would not wish this on anyone...except, perhaps, Roger. I hope one day he experiences what Matilda and I are going through, then perhaps he will understand what he has done.'

As they walked back to where Edith was watching the boys in their absence, Arthur also admitted. 'Matilda kissed me, you know,' he looked like a shy little boy. 'She kissed me then apologised for being forward.'

'I suppose under normal circumstances it could be considered as being forward,' said Will. 'But, bearing in mind how little time you had together, and that it is be unlikely you will meet again for some time, it is understandable. At least you will have that kiss to remember.'

Arthur sighed. 'It will be an agonising memory...but a cherished one. Does that make sense?'

A short while later, Martin and Edgar trotted up to Will and Arthur to bid them farewell; Matilda was nowhere in sight. After saying their goodbyes, Will saw Edgar proceed directly to Edith's wagon. After talking to her for a short while, he kissed her hand and held it a little longer than was necessary, before steering his horse towards where Martin waited for him. Edgar turned back, waved to Edith and a few moments later their wagon, separated from the column. With the four mounted men as escorts, Edgar and Martin on one side and Guy and his brother on the other side of the wagon, they took the road to Salisbury. They were just about to turn a bend when Matilda, clearly not caring whether she was seen or not, peered around the side of the wagon and looked back longingly at Arthur until she jerked back out of view. Arthur supposed Roger had noticed and tugged her back. Helplessly, he watched until their wagon turned a bend and went out of sight.

Arthur chose to drive the wagon. Having the boys, with Bartley's constant chatter, for company, would distract him from his melancholy. Will, on the other hand, decided to pay Edith a visit and cantered along to her wagon, where she sat beside Milo, her eyes closed against the low autumn sun. Milo nudged her as Will drew alongside and she greeted him with a wide smile.

'How is Arthur?'

'Not doing too well, Edith, but I wondered if we could talk about something that has been troubling me about all this.'

'Yes, indeed we can but the sun is in my eyes. I will go into the back where I can make myself comfortable and get in the shade. I know with winter coming soon I should not complain about the sun but, being so low in the sky and with it shining directly on us, it has actually made my head ache. It will do me good to get some relief from it.' In an unladylike manner she swung her legs around the seat and clambered under the canopy to meet Will at the back of the wagon, where she could talk to him as he rode along behind.

'Now, what troubles you, my dear?'

'Why is Roger so keen on this marriage? I thought Edgar had brought Matilda up to be an equal to her brothers but, even though I understand Edgar is going along with this to protect his business, I have the impression that, if Matilda refused, surely he would not have forced her.'

'Yes, I believe that as well. You know Roger is the first born I suppose?'

'Yes...well, yes I thought he was.'

'But did you know that Matilda and Martin are twins?'

'No, that I didn't know. They are similar in looks but as brother and sister that is not unusual. I had not thought they were so close in looks as to be twins though.'

'As the older child, when Edgar dies, his business and any other property...unless he remarries of course...will go to Roger. Martin will have to find some way to provide for himself, unless...of course...Roger allows him to continue in the business.'

'Do you doubt that?'

She nodded. 'Yes, I do. I believe Roger is determined to gain everything he can which is why he has instigated this marriage. If Edgar's business fails, he will inherit nothing.'

'But what about Edgar's home and other property...there's property in Flanders.'

'Well, it seems Edgar is deeply in debt which means he could lose everything if the business fails and he cannot pay his creditors. My guess is that he hopes Edgar and Guy will die soon...Guy certainly does not look the picture of health...'

'...I thought Roger and Guy were friends though.'

'Hmm,' Edith pressed her lips together. 'I don't believe Roger is genuinely friends with anyone. What I do believe is that Roger will make friends where there is gain in it for him.'

'I found him very ill-mannered.'

'Why should he be pleasant to you when there is nothing to be gained from it, and you...or rather *your* friend could be a potential threat to his plans.'

'But surely, if Matilda marries Guy and he dies, then his property becomes hers.'

'Ah. Yes, you're right but something tells me that Matilda's life may be in jeopardy not long after Guy dies...an accident, a sudden illness. If Matilda has no children then whatever she inherited from Guy will pass to her family...Roger.'

'But what about Martin?'

'And how long do you think Martin will be allowed to live?'

Will shook his head in disbelief. 'Are you serious about all this? It's a terrible situation that Matilda and Arthur are to be kept apart, but this is unbelievable. Wait! What about Adam? As Guy's brother surely he would...'

'No. He inherits nothing from Guy. I wheedled this information out of Edgar. It seems Guy made out his Will on the day of the betrothal and, once they are wed, everything goes to Matilda. Adam, it seems, has his own fortune having married well. Unfortunately, Edgar trusts all his children have the same nature and that Roger is as true to him as Matilda and Martin.'

'This is awful. Far worse than I had imagined. Is there anything we can do?'

'You and Arthur cannot. But I can. My relationship with Edgar has developed and I am invited to visit but I shall not go alone. Milo will accompany me and will be by my side...as my escort and guardian. He will chaperone me at all times and, being wary of Roger's intentions, I will be on my guard.'

'But surely you will be as much of a threat to Roger's plans as Arthur is?'

'Yes, that may well be true but, if Edgar is as fond of me as I believe him to be, I may be able to influence him in certain ways. I can certainly look after him, and do everything I can to protect Matilda. It is my intention to have that young lady happy and I believe that is what she will be with Arthur.'

'But you will be in Shepton Mallet most of the time.'

'I have been invited to the wedding which takes place in three weeks, and Matilda has asked me to assist her with the planning as she has no mother or sister to help her with the wedding preparations. I shall arrive a week before and stay...well...as long as I feel necessary afterwards. Milo is also very good at not being very...visible. Servants can often go to places without being noticed where we cannot. He is also very good at listening to servants gossip and you would be surprised at what truths can be learned from that source. Just leave it to me. I will ensure messages are sent to you when I have some news.'

'You will be at home in two days and there is but a short distance of some seven or eight miles between your home and Winterne Manor,' said Will. 'While we were in Honfleur I met a doctor who had pigeons that carried messages for him tied to their legs. They came from his home and would somehow find their way back from anywhere they were taken to. To keep in contact with me, perhaps I should find some pigeons at the manor or nearby and bring them to you.'

'I have heard of that before and it would certainly be a very good idea. I can take some with me when I go to Salisbury. I will tell Edgar that they are for sending messages to my housekeeper, that should be believable.'

'I will not tell Arthur of this discussion. He is desolate enough and I would not have him in fear for Matilda's safety as well, at least not until it may be necessary.'

'Then it is time you returned to him and the boys. I will see you when we stop at the next inn.'

Will turned Chestnut and rode back to their wagon and was pleased to see Arthur talking to Bartley and Dickon about archery, and smiling.

'Ah, but Sir William here saved the life of the Black Prince,' said Arthur, as Bartley looked at Will in admiration, as if seeing him for the first time. 'Sir William is an expert with the bow and, if you behave yourselves well, I am certain he will give you some lessons once we are settled.' As Arthur looked up at Will he gave a sad smile and Will understood, no matter how wretched he felt, and he did look as if his world had just come to an end, he was simply putting on a brave face for the boys.

Chapter Twenty One

Over the next two days, Will, Arthur and the boys spent most of their time with Edith and Milo. Where the road was wide enough the two wagons lumbered along beside each other. Sometimes, the boys chose to ride in Edith's wagon and listened intently as she told them stories her mother had told her. From Will's point of view, apart from taking the boys into his care and the great comradeship he felt for Arthur, meeting Edith had been the best thing about the entire journey. To him, Edith's maternal devotion to them all was evident, almost like that of a favoured great aunt. He had become very fond of her, and he realised that this astonishing lady would leave a big gap in their lives once they reached Shepton Mallet.

Due to Edith's kind and genial nature, she had also become a great favourite of Thomas and Simon Ryder who were regularly to be found trotting alongside her wagon engaged in lively conversation.

Bartley and Dickon also got on very well with Thomas and Simon, and Arthur briefly mentioned in passing to Will one day, that perhaps the boys might actually find life boring at Winterne. After the excitement of having so many people around them, and making friends with the other children, life at the manor would probably seem a little dull.

Later that afternoon, when Will remembered Arthur's casual comment, he made up his mind to get the boys involved with the renovations of the manor, and let them choose the furnishings for their room. He would have them involved with making sure the stables were fit for use – and, more importantly - he would hire a tutor for them as soon as he could find the right one. He would keep them too busy to be bored.

If anything, although they were all aware time was passing, they were unprepared for how quickly the last night before Edith was due to leave the group for Shepton Mallet arrived.

On that last morning, clearly feeling she wanted to make a lasting impression on her fellow travellers, Edith had dressed in a black long-sleeved kirtle with a purple sleeveless surcote trimmed at the neck and the long sides with black fur. Her hair, enclosed within a crespine, an elaborate hairnet in filigree gold and white silk and embossed with more delicate gold tracery, topped by a short white gauze veil, gave the impression of a lady younger, and taller than she actually was. These were not her usual travelling clothes. She had obviously kept them specifically for her return to Shepton Mallet.

With her head held high and her shoulders back, Edith was an magnificent sight as she approached Will and Arthur's wagon to say her farewells.

'The lady is quite a vision,' Arthur whispered from the side of his mouth.

Will agreed. 'She certainly is. See how many heads are turning as she passes by.' He climbed down from the wagon and walked toward Edith, linking arms as he turned to escort her to where Arthur and the boys were waiting.

'You look magnificent, my lady,' said Arthur, looping the reins around the seat, he clambered down, took her right hand in his and kissed it.

'Thank you, Sir Arthur.' Edith gave him a sly grin. 'Look at them.' With a quick nod of her head, she indicated the other travellers who were still watching her. 'I thought I would give them something to look at before we take our leave and I have no intention of arriving in Shepton looking as though I have been travelling for days, even though I have. I have my reputation to uphold, after all.'

Bartley and Dickon jumped down from the wagon and ran to hug her.

'Will, Arthur, you know, you and the boys would be very welcome to stay at my house overnight, if you would like to, that is.'

Much to the boys' disappointment, Will and Arthur, spontaneously but graciously, turned her down explaining that with just a few miles to go before they reached Winterne, by travelling on they could arrive at the village of Winterne early the next morning and get a good start on the day, but they promised the boys they would see Edith and Milo again soon.

Soon after, Edith paid the escort fee to Thomas, said her farewells to new friends, then without bothering to be ladylike about it, she clambered down from her wagon and rushed over to give Bartley and Dickon a smothering hug. With tears in her eyes she reached into the pouch suspended from her belt and, to their delight, handed them two pennies each. 'Now, that's the beginning of your fortunes. Don't waste it, my precious boys. And another thing, remember to do as Sir William and Sir Arthur tell you, learn your lessons, pay attention and be polite. If you do all those things, you will grow up to be charming young men who all the ladies will swoon over.'

Dickon pulled a face reflecting what he thought about the idea of having young ladies swooning over him, but Bartley giggled.

'Now, my dears, I really must be gone...Sir William...Will, don't forget about the pigeons, and I hope you find your mother, and your sister-in-law and her family well.' She hugged Arthur and Will then turned and without looking back, climbed back aboard her wagon with a helping hand from Milo. Picking up the reins again, Milo urged their horses onward and, with Edith's shoulders shaking and a good bit of eye dabbling with her kerchief, they rode off along the Shepton Mallet Road, with four pairs of eyes sadly watching them until they were out of sight.

'Come boys,' said Will, shepherding Bartley and Dickon back to the wagon, 'it is time we were on our way as well.' He nudged Arthur. 'Look, look over there, beyond the trees. See Bartley, Dickon, do you all see those hills...they are the Mendips and we are close to my home. I have not been to Winterne but I understand it nestles within their valley, as does my home village of Westbury.'

'They are a splendid sight, Will and I must admit, I will be glad to reach the end of this journey. We seem to have been travelling forever.'

'Indeed, I will pay Thomas then we can be off,' said Will. As he rode back down the ever-decreasing line of travellers, Will suddenly felt empty. First the Coombs family – most of whom they were able to get on with - then Edith, now all gone, and although he spoke in jest earlier about perhaps not having a roof on the manor, he really did have no idea what they were going to be faced with.

After travelling a further three miles, with the sun going down, Arthur and Will decided to camp in the woods outside Winterne for the night. After lighting a fire, hobbling and feeding the mules and horses, they made a serviceable meal of cheese, salted herring, bread, apples and some hazelnuts and blackberries the boys had picked on the way. Soon after sunset, it was obvious the boys were tired and, having made up beds for them in the wagon, Will and Arthur sat around the fire for another hour or so over cups of ale while talking about Matilda and the situation with Roger.

Will avoided telling Arthur what he had heard from Edith. If there were dangers for Matilda, they would come later, but she would be safe for the next few weeks until after the wedding, and Edith would keep them informed of that situation. There was no need to add to Arthur's unhappiness until they knew what they were dealing with. Will mentioned the conversation he had with Edith about obtaining some messenger pigeons. Arthur laughed and asked where they were going to find them.

Will frowned. 'Hmm. I was wondering that as well.'

Eventually they decided it was time to bed down for the night, and after ensuring the animals were hobbled securely and the boys were warm and comfortable, they settled down under two trees, close to the wagon and were asleep almost as soon as they shut their eyes.

At the sound of the birds singing their dawn chorus from the trees, Will awoke to find Rowan missing. He sat up, spun around. Arthur too was gone! His stomach turned over as an awful thought crept into his sleep-fuddled brain. Struggling not to believe what he was thinking, he got to his feet, heart thumping rapidly in his chest, and stared at the wagon. Forcing one foot in front of the other he took a deep breath and climbed carefully onto the seat before silently creeping inside. The boys were still sleeping soundly. Trying not to disturb them he lay on his back and pushed himself along until...

'Will,' Arthur called his name softly. 'Come out of there. Your coins are safe.'

When a shamefaced Will emerged from the wagon, he saw Rowan hobbled again and standing with Chestnut and Ash, and Arthur, hunkered down beside the cold embers from the previous night, adding new kindling to restart the fire. Arthur's rigid posture and his turned back told Will all he needed to know about Arthur's reaction to his suspicions at finding him gone. Will had instantly thought the worst of him.

'Did you think I would steal them from you?' Arthur said without looking around. 'Here!' He threw a linen bag at Will's feet. 'In the time we have been together, Will, have you not learned to trust me?'

Will picked up the bulky bag and walked around to face Arthur. He dropped to the ground and sat cross-legged in front of the man he had so clearly wounded with his instant mistrust. Will had no idea how to apologise for his behaviour and the deep hurt it had caused. Could they ever regain the bond they had until that moment? Or would his lack of faith have caused permanent damage? Arthur did not look at him: in fact, he looked anywhere but at Will while he fiddled with the brushwood and sticks and struck the flint with his knife to create a spark. A heavy silence hung over the pair broken only by the snuffling of the horses and the increasingly loud dawn chorus from the canopy of branches above them. The cheerfulness of the birds as they welcomed the morning sun was a stark contrast to the atmosphere below.

Will shook his head. Why was his first instinct to panic, to believe Arthur was a thief? Nothing, in all the time they had been together had given him any reason to think badly of Arthur, and now he destroyed the closest friendship he had ever known.

'Arthur. I am so sorry. I cannot begin to apologise. My only defence, and I know it does not excuse me, is that I have spent so long trying to ensure the Prince's funds were kept safe that I acted on impulse without really thinking. But...where were you? Where did you go?'

Arthur looked up at Will with a cold, detached expression. 'I went back to that farm we passed shortly before making camp last night. I thought to get the boys fresh food to break our fast. There's ale in the costrel.' Arthur seemed more disappointed than angry which made Will feel more guilt-ridden than ever. Perhaps it would have been easier to cope with Arthur's anger.

The fire took hold and Arthur laid the bakestone over the top of it.

Will opened the bag to find a leather drink bottle - a costrel that looked a little like a small barrel with a short cord handle - a fresh and still warm loaf of dark rye cheese bread, with an appetising aroma of herbs, some chunks of salted bacon and a hunk of cheese.

'I knew about the coins. I always knew,' said Arthur, sitting back against the tree trunk and looking directly, and sternly, at Will.

At least he was talking, thought Will. 'But how? The Prince told me to stay silent, never to mention I them to anyone.'

'The Earl told me while you and the Prince went off on your own. He did not tell me how much you would be given, but said that the Prince was going to give you generous funds, in gold coin, towards the work that needed to be done at Winterne, and you would need a guard, but I was to stay silent and not even to tell you that I was aware of it.'

Will took a long stick and poked the fire to let a little more air under the wood. Two larger flames spiralled into life. 'Perhaps if neither of us had obeyed their insistence on silence, this would not have happened. I would have trusted you with my life...' he looked up at Arthur and their eyes met, '...I still do. I ask your forgiveness, Arthur. You have been the closest friend I have ever known and I feel mortified to have acted the way I did.'

Arthur gave a sad little smile and shrugged. 'Who knows, Will. Perhaps had I been in your position, I would have reacted in the same way. It is possible I would have...but understand this...' he raised his right hand and balled his right fist, pointed his index finger towards Will to emphasise what he was going to say, 'I will never, I repeat, never betray you or the boys. We have a brotherhood. You and I understand each other. You have offered me a home and now, with the boys, a family. I trust you not to betray me and I shall be by your side as long as you need me. That is my oath.'

A shuffling noise came from the wagon. The boys were awake and were about to join them but they were not doing so quietly. Bartley was shouting at Dickon about something.

'Well before we deal with whatever is happening in the wagon, Arthur, I shall say this. Thank you for your forgiveness. I am indebted to you for many things and now this. Thank you for your oath and you shall have mine. I shall not betray you and I bitterly regret having had momentary doubts. It shall not happen again, my friend and from now on...no secrets.'

'Agreed.'

The atmosphere immediately improved but Will had just one more thing to say before the boys reached them. 'And you still have to teach me to read!' he said, with a smile.

'Indeed, Sir William.' Arthur inclined his head. 'Once we are settled, it is something we can work on when the boys are abed during the long winter nights. But, for now it would seem that we have a dispute to settle.'

At that moment, the boys bounced out of the wagon spurred by the sizzling aroma from the chunks of bacon on the bakestone and the smell of warm, fresh bread, but Bartley was still upset about something.

'Yer bein' daft, Dickon. There weren't no-one there, I tell yer.'

Dickon nodded his head. 'There were,' he muttered a protest. 'I see'd 'em. I did. There was two o' 'em an' they run orf in ter the woods when you shouted at me.'

'Bartley, Dickon, what is all this? Why all the shouting?' said Arthur.

'We get this sorted out or there's no food until we do,' said Will.

'Well Dickon says 'e see'd two small men sittin' on the tailgate o' the wagon afore I woke. I never see'd 'em an' I don' believe 'im,' said Bartley.

Looking down at the whey-faced little lad, Will asked: 'Dickon, did you have a dream? Are you sure you were awake?'

Dickon nodded his head vigorously.

'You are sure you were awake?'

Again Dickon nodded.

'Did they speak to you?' asked Arthur.

Dickon smiled and nodded for a fourth time.

'Can you tell us what they said?' Arthur asked.

This time Dickon shook his head.

'Why not? Is it a secret?' asked Will.

Dickon hesitated, he seemed to be trying to find the right words. 'Spoke diff'rent,' he whispered.

'That can't be righ',' said Bartley. 'We all speaks the same, don't we?'

'Well, no, Bartley. We don't all speak the same. You'll find that people from other countries speak differently and even people from other places in England speak differently to each other.'

Bartley looked puzzled. It was clear he found that hard to understand.

'Dickon, show us where these men went, will you?' Arthur took the boy by the hand and Dickon led him, with Will and Bartley following, to a small thicket of fern fronds within the trees close to the back of the wagon. He pointed to a small gap in the undergrowth.

'They went in there?' asked Arthur.

Dickon nodded.

'Did they frighten you?' asked Will. 'What did they look like?'

Dickson shook his head and smiled, then taking the tips of his ears between his thumbs and forefingers he tried to stretch his ears upward.

Arthur frowned. Will scratched his head and stared at Dickon. Bartley laughed.

Without searching the thicket, Arthur and Will gave a cursory look around. 'Well there's no sign of anyone now. Come on, let's eat,' said Will.

But when they returned to the fire, half of the loaf of rye bread and the costrel of ale had gone.

'It would seem we have been robbed, Will,' said Arthur. 'Which means that Dickon's story about two small men being here was likely to be true.'

Dickon grinned and poked his tongue out at Bartley.

'Well being robbed does not seem to be a good introduction to Winterne,' said Will. 'Let us pray that things improve.'

Chapter Twenty Two

At the edge of the woods, the two men and two boys stopped to look down on the village of Winterne, nestled in a fertile valley surrounded by woodland. The dawn sky, layered with streaks of pink and lilac, and strewn with ribbons of fluffy white clouds, was a canvas painted by the gold-orange early morning sun. It spread a purple-blue shadow across the early morning mist as it clung to the land, and drifted between the trees and over the fields already blackened by the post-harvest burning of stalk stubble. The acrid smell of scorched earth still hung in the air. The scene took Will's breath away.

Bartley and Dickon, now friends again and having forgotten their earlier squabble, searched for a sight of the manor. They excitedly pointed out the lake but were disappointed the manor was hidden from view by the trees.

Arthur pointed to the church. 'It seems your village is coming to life, Will.' He smiled and bowed. The earlier discord between himself and Will, had vanished just as that of the boys, and was now a thing of the past where they both wanted it to remain. 'I believe it is time we ended our journey and you began your new life as a man of property.'

Will shifted in his saddle. 'Very well, *Sir* Arthur. Let's go down and meet the folk of Winterne. I hope they will accept me.' He seemed nervous.

The tree-lined dirt lane wound downwards and from time to time they lost sight of the village due to the mass the trees, then they would catch a glimpse of the church tower or what they took to be an inn. Soon they were at the outskirts of the village. Tall hedges lined either side of the road, that had once been paved but now many of the stones were missing or raised, and the wheels of the wagon became stuck several times in the uneven surface. Thankfully, as they approached *The Black Bull* Inn, the road was improved by a top layer of cinders that filled in the hollows and appeared to have only recently been put down.

To Arthur's great relief the courtyard of inn was an improvement on the road, and laid with slabs of stone making it considerably easier to keep the wagon rolling.

As he climbed down from the seat, he told Will: 'That is a road I would rather not travel again.' He lifted Dickon from the seat and held out his hand to help Bartley down, but Bartley grinned, refused his help and jumped down landing easily, before looking up at Arthur smugly. 'I don' no need 'elp, Sir Arthur, thankee.' Tethered to a rail at the far end of the courtyard, a tall grey horse with a long white mane, stood quietly swishing flies away with its long tail. Bartley started to walk towards it but Will called him back.

'Bartley, never approach an unknown horse from behind,' he warned. 'It might kick out at you…and it *will* hurt if it does.'

'Yes, Sir William. But I wonder who 'e belongs ter. 'E's righ' 'andsome ent 'e?'

Arthur put his arm around Bartley's shoulder and pulled him away. 'He certainly is h-handsome and its likely he'll belong to one of the guests inside. Come, let's go in.'

Before entering, Will and Arthur paused at the front of the inn for a moment. It appeared welcoming enough with its honey-coloured Cotswold stone swathed in trails of green ivy reaching up to the thatched roof. Now the early-morning haze had lifted, the warmth of the autumn sun broke through and bees hovered in and out of late flowering plants and butterflies rested, their wings closed, taking advantage of the sun before the days cooled.

On entering the inn, Will thought it looked very much like The Swan with the usual booth style seating on both sides of the room but, being a little smaller, it had just one long table in the middle. At the seat nearest to the roaring fire, at the end of the long table, sat a thin man completely dressed in black, with his back to the door, perusing some papers. Clearly absorbed in whatever business occupied him, he appeared not to be aware of the newcomers. A young couple, sitting either side of the table in their booth, reached forward to hold hands, their heads almost touching and were engaged in a whispered conversation. They stopped talking, looked up anxiously and gave Will, Arthur and the boys a nervous, cursory look, then looked away, relief written on both their faces. They were clearly hiding from someone. Will wondered if perhaps the time would come when they would need his help, but for now they were none of his business. There was just one other booth taken by two men who appeared, by their clothing to be farm workers.

The innkeeper, dried his hands on his apron as he headed towards Will and his party, a huge welcoming smile on his ruddy-cheeked face.

'Welcome sirs an' the young masters. What can Oi get fer ye?'

The man in black, suddenly aware there were new customers, turned towards them, looked up and gave a thin smile. He folded his papers and stood up. 'Edric, I believe these are the gentlemen for whom we have been waiting. Please, a cup of ale for us all.' He brushed passed the innkeeper and approached Will, but did not speak until he had stared at Will's face for what seemed to Will like an unnecessary amount of time. Then, 'I believe I am addressing Sir William Hallett?'

Several heads turned to pay attention to the conversation.

Taken aback, Will hesitated, looked at Arthur, then back to the man in front of him. 'Yes. I am he.' He became aware they had attracted the attention of the other inn guests and two young girls from the kitchen peered around the door but were chased, giggling and trying to catch a last glimpse of Will and Arthur, back to the kitchen by the innkeeper.

The man then seemed to notice Arthur. 'And you must be Sir Arthur Burnel?'

Arthur nodded. 'And you are?'

'Yes, of course, my apologies. I am Edwin Cheeseman.'

Will knew he had heard the name before but was puzzled. For a moment he could not recall where he had heard it. Then it came to him.

'Ah, yes of course, you are the Earl of Salisbury's steward, are you not?' said Will.

'Yes, indeed, Sir William. Pray, come and join me by the fire, although the sun shines outside, it has not permeated the inn as yet and inside it is still chill. You must be tired from your long journey all the way from Poitiers. And I see you have company.' He looked down at the boys.

'These lads are to become my adoptive sons and I will require some legal counsel for that I understand.' They took their seats at the table and Edwin offered them food but, after breaking their fast just a short while before, they declined to his obvious disappointment.

'Indeed you will require advice, but I am sure we can assist with that if it is something you are determined to do.' The boys stared at him, wide-eyed and silent. He turned back to Will seemingly somewhat unnerved by the boys' continual stare.

'Now back to business, Sir William.' He stopped while one of the serving maids set out a plate of hazelnuts, small pieces of cheese, hunks of white bread – which the boys had never seen before, and Bartley asked Arthur in a whisper what it was - wild raspberries and blackcurrants, before setting down the five cups of ale, two of them watered down. When she had gone, Edwin continued.

'Firstly I have something to show you.' He rifled through the papers until he came to one that, from where Will sat opposite, appeared to be a drawing of some kind. 'I have been asked by the Earl to give you this, it is an impression of the crest you asked for. I hope it meets with your approval.'

Will found it hard to comprehend that as an ordinary archer, his life has changed to such an extent that he now had his own family crest; it was exactly as he had imagined it. His mother, if she was still alive would be so proud of him.

'Yes. This is perfect, Edwin. Simple and perfect. Thank you.'

'May I suggest that you have it emblazoned on both sides of the front gates when they are mended, on the gates of the courtyard, on the front door, woven onto banners to be placed inside the hall, and to fly from the roof, and...and this is most important, that you have rings made with the insignia. As the Earl always says, if you have a crest, it should be seen.

'And I hope you don't think me presumptuous, Sir William, but while I have been waiting for you to arrive...' He managed to make that sound like a reprimand. 'I thought I would keep myself occupied with making some early arrangements for your comfort at Winterne Manor. All in all the property is not in as bad a condition as it might have been, bearing in mind it has been abandoned for a number of years.'

'Well, that is good news, Master Cheeseman. I had not realised it had been empty for so long.'

The steward continued. 'I have been here long enough to have had the chimneys swept, as I assumed you would want to have fires in the habitable rooms. In addition, I hired a group of women to begin the cleaning. They have been working at the manor for two days now and on inspection earlier this morning, I can confirm the building will be more welcoming than it was when I first saw it three days ago on my arrival. I have also taken the liberty of hiring a cook who, until we can add to your staff, is happy to act as housekeeper, there is a scullery maid to assist the cook, two house maids and a stable hand. You will also require a steward of your own and, to that end, I have selected two men who, from my own experience I believe to be suitable. They will be at the manor in the morning to meet you both and myself. I hope that will help ease your settling in to the manor.

'In time you will require other staff but I believe these will be a good start for you. For the moment, I would suggest that the hall, four of the seven bedrooms and the kitchen are all in reasonable condition. The solar...your private living room, the stables, the library, chapel and dining room could do with some work but you can live quite comfortably in the other rooms until the builders...oh yes, they too have been hired.'

Will and Arthur looked at each other in disbelief. 'We had no idea you would be here before us, Edwin, and we are certainly grateful for your efficiency in having so much in place before our arrival. Arthur and I thank you for everything you have done,' Will said, clearly delighted with the way this ratty-looking little man, with his small eyes, thin moustache and his black garments that seemed to drain any colour from his face leaving him pasty-faced, and who Will had not liked on sight, had turned out to be such a Godsend.

'It is my pleasure to assist you and, as for efficiency, it is merely experience. I have been in the Earl's service for many years and have learned how to look for what requires my attention. I remember how Winterne Manor looked before and it was a jewel amongst the properties owned by the Earl. I am delighted to be instrumental in returning it to its former glory. Now, when you have finished, perhaps we should make our way to the manor. I am sure you will want to finish your journey and I think the manor will have one or two surprises for you.'

Bartley and Dickon, red splodges of raspberry juice around their mouths, nodded enthusiastically; they were ready to go. All three men laughed and stood up ready to leave, but the innkeeper met them at the door. 'Sir William, Sir Arthur. I am Edric Lightfoot an' Oi been innkeeper yer for nigh on twenny year. It's roight pleased Oi am ter make yer acquaintance. If Oi kin be of enny 'elp enny time, then you jes' let me know.'

Before Will could answer, the door opened and a man carrying a closed basket dangling over his arm walked in. Bartley's nose wrinkled as the sour smell of strong body odour reached them. Dickon scuttled to hide behind Arthur. Everyone stared as the newcomer approached the first booth where the young couple sat; the woman slid away from him along the bench towards the wall. Her husband, if that's what he was, stood up, his body language making it very clear he was blocking the stranger from getting any closer.

Bartley nudged Will. 'Look, tha' basket's movin'. There's somethin' alive in there.' The basket was definitely juddering.

Will, bracing himself, approached the man, ignoring the stench emanating from his stained and worn tunic, made from two pieces of undyed wool material and sewn together leaving a hole for the head. It reached to his knees and was tied by a brown-stained frayed knotted wool belt. Will had no interest in finding out what had made those stains. The newcomer's tattered breeches ended at his ankles revealing dirt-ingrained legs, his thin leather boots were old and would not see him through another winter; the sole of the left one was already beginning to come away from the upper.

Edric called out from the table he was clearing. 'Wha' yer got there?'

'Oi got pups, them's fer sale.'

'Well yer kin jest be on yer way. There'll be no sellin' them pups in yer.'

At the word 'pups' Dickon had come out of hiding behind Arthur and looked up at him hopefully. His eyes pleaded to be allowed to see them. Arthur nodded and Dickon ran to the basket followed closely by Bartley.

'Now then, innkeeper,' said the man, 'don' be so 'asty. One of yer customers moight wan' one of 'em.' He lifted the lid to reveal two very young deerhound pups, that peered nervously into the light.

'How old are they?' Will asked.

'Oh Oi dunno. Mebbe six weeks. They be weaned.'

'You're a liar. They're no more than three or four weeks old, and where's their mother?'

'Now there's no need fer tha', master. No call ter say Oi'm a liar.' But, his nervousness evident he began backing towards the door. Arthur got there before him.

'My friend, Sir William Hallett, Lord of Winterne Manor, asked you where the mother was?'

With the young husband moving closer, Will, Arthur, Edwin and the innkeeper all hemming him in, the man put the basket down on the table and raised his hands in submission.

'The mother's out by me cart.'

Dickon and Bartley ran over to stroke the pretty, grey-coloured puppies while Arthur went outside. He came back a few moments later carrying the suffering mother in his arms, his eyes glistened, blazed in fury.

'In God's name, man! Look what you've done to her!' Arthur raged. 'She's feeding babes and she's starving. Look at her, man! You should be horse-whipped for this.'

The man flinched and cowered away from Arthur's anger. 'Oi got a righ' ter make a livin' ain' Oi?'

'Not when cruelty is involved, no. How many times have you bred this poor hound?'

He looked down at the tiled floor not wanting to meet Arthur's furious glare. 'Oi dunno. Six, mebbe seven...' Then with an attempt at bravado. 'But look a' 'er. The size of 'er, she's a strong un an' there's nothin' wrong in breedin' hounds.'

'You say she's strong! Look at her, man!' Arthur walked towards him, holding the hound out for him to look at but he turned away. 'She doesn't look to me as if she's been fed in days. Here, look at her ribs! See how thin her legs are. She's exhausted. When did you feed her last?'

'I think t'were las' noight.'

'You think? I said look at her...and...you think you fed her last night? You scum!' He turned away and took her to where Will was standing. 'Look at this poor girl. It makes my heart ache to see her like this. Edric, would you have one of your maids bring this poor hound some water please.' Will looked down at what had clearly been a beautiful hound and reached out to stroke her head. She whimpered under his touch. 'Well?' Will nodded.

Arthur turned to face her tormentor. 'You'll get no more pups from her. What say you, Will?'

Will looked over at the basket to see two pairs of big blue eyes looking back at him. Two more pairs of eyes were watching him closely waiting for his response. He smiled at the boys. 'Yes, we'll take them home.'

Dickon ran to him and hugged his legs. Will picked him up. 'Fank you so much, Sir Willyum,' whispered Dickon.

'You're going to have to think of names for them.' Dickon nodded vigorously.

Bartley grinned from ear to ear. 'Thass good, innit, Dickon. We on'y wan'ed one dog an' now we got three.'

'Yer'll pay for 'em o' course,' said the man, uncertainly.

Arthur ignored him. 'Will, this poor girl was tied to the cart by a short cord. She's worn out and was trying to lay down but her neck was being stretched. Look you can see where the cord has rubbed some of the hair away from her neck and her skin is raw. Do we pay him? Ah, here's her water. Thank you,' he told the girl who had brought it. She curtseyed and ran back to the kitchen, blushing. He put the bowl on the table and lay the poor dog down beside it. Edric frowned. The poor animal drank as though she had never seen water before.

'Wai' jest a minute,' said the man, head up and shoulders back. 'An' who are you ter tell me wha' Oi can and can't do?'

Edwin moved forward to stand by Will. 'Sir Arthur Burnel has already told you that Sir William is lord of Winterne Manor. You should understand that the village and the entire estate belongs to him by the order of the Earl of Salisbury and his Lordship, the Prince of Wales. Sir William is the Law here and holds the authority to *tell* you what you can and cannot do.'

The man appeared crestfallen.

Will looked around the inn at the other customers, Edwin, the innkeeper, the serving girls, even those who washed the pots had emerged from the kitchen. 'My first judgement in Winterne shall be by vote. What say you all, should this man receive payment for these poorly treated animals, or should he be sent on his way?'

Trying to bluff it out and justify his actions, the man began shouting about how he had looked after the hounds well, how the mother loved being with him, but no-one was listening. The vote went against him.

Edric moved to Will's side. 'Sir William, I take it you'd loike me ter throw this man ou' of me 'ostelry.' A cheer rang out from around the inn.

Will nodded. 'Before you do, Edric,' he said, turning to face the villain. 'I do not want to see you in this village or the surrounding area again. If I do you, be sure, you *will* face punishment. Do you understand?'

'Yes, me lord.' He bowed and began backing away towards the door.

'Think yourself fortunate you have been allowed to leave,' said Arthur as he cradled the mother hound in his arms.

At the door, the man turned and fled. They never did see him again.

Will picked up the basket of pups then hunkered down to eye level with the boys. 'I believe in telling you the truth and, although I think the little ones will grow strong and healthy if we care for them correctly, you must understand that may not be the same for their mother. We will do what we can to make her well again, but she has been through a great deal. She is exhausted and under fed. Much as it pains me to say it, you must understand that she may not be strong enough to live much longer. If that is the case we will attempt to find another nursing hound in the area who may be able to feed the pups in addition to her own litter to make sure they survive. But I cannot promise you she will. Do you understand?'

Both boys nodded. Dickon looked as though he was about to cry.

Having been so preoccupied with the hounds, neither Will or Arthur had noticed that Edwin was no longer in the room and were surprised at his absence. He had been there just a few minutes before.

'Edric, do you know where Edwin went?' Arthur asked, still holding the hound. As long and tall as she was, she was so thin she weighed very little in comparison with a healthy dog of her size, and he found it no burden to continue supporting her. She seemed comforted to be in his arms; somehow knew she was now in safe hands, and he could have sworn he heard her give a sigh of relief as her former owner ran out of the door.

''E were 'ere a minute or two ago?' said Edric, looking around the room.

'Are you looking for me?' Edwin entered the room from the rear courtyard. 'I have sent a rider to the manor to inform them you are here and they are to make ready to greet you.' He looked at the boys who were still stroking the puppies and smiled. 'To be perfectly honest, Sir William, we expected yourself and Sir Arthur, but not your...new found family and I wanted to give the staff time to prepare rooms for you all.'

'Thank you, Edwin, that was good of you. We do appreciate the efforts you have gone to on our behalf and, how long will you be staying with us?'

Edwin seemed a little taken aback by that question and hesitated. 'Have I not performed my duties to your satisfaction, Sir William?'

'Oh, Edwin, indeed you have, you have no cause to feel we do not appreciate everything you have done, does he Arthur?'

Arthur gave a smile and nodded, 'No cause for complaint as far as I am concerned, Edwin.'

'Then why...?'

'I was just wondering how long the Earl is going to let us keep you here?' said Will.

'Ahh. I see. Let's just say that with the Earl away in France still my duties are far fewer than they will be when he returns. I have assistants to carry out many of my tasks while I obey the Earl's wishes to aid you here. So, for the moment, there is no hurry for me to return to Donyatt. I believe there will be a message sent when they have need of my return.'

'Come then, it is time we went to our new home,' said Will. He turned to the innkeeper. 'Thank you, Edric. We shall meet again soon. I plan to have a gathering to meet the villagers once we have a home fit for visitors and, thanks to Edwin here, I don't think that will be too long away. Come boys, let us go. Bartley, do you think you are strong enough to carry the basket?'

'Oh, yes, Sir William. I can do tha'. Come Dickon, we're goin' 'ome.'

Back on the cinder-packed road, the wagon swayed as it trundled along over the rough, rutted surface and Arthur, driving, was relieved when they arrived at the heavy wooden gates, one of which needed the top hinge replaced and it hung askew joined only to the gatepost by the bottom hinge.

Edwin and Will rode a little ahead of the wagon and, as they walked the horses up the long tree-lined and leaf-carpeted lane that led to the manor, Edwin moved his horse a little closer to Will.

'I am pleased that we have had the opportunity to talk alone, Sir William...'

'Is something wrong?'

'No...just...um...extraordinary. I did not want to mention it in front of the boys, as I was unsure whether you would want them to know about something we have found.'

'I am intrigued, Edwin. Do go on.'

'We have had the most startling discovery of a secret passage in one of the bedrooms on the first floor.'

Will's eyebrows shot upward. 'A secret passage? Where does it lead? And, more importantly if no-one knew it was there, how was it found?'

'Oh, completely by accident. A maid was cleaning in the room, she tripped on a hole in one of the old rugs and leant against a device of some kind and a door beside the hearth slowly swung open. At the time I was working in the kitchen and Mistress Spinner came to find me.'

'Do you know where it leads?

'Oh, yes. None of the female staff wanted to investigate, so Josiah, who works in the stables, came with me. We took an oil lamp each, walked along a cobweb and dust covered tunnel until we found ourselves at the top of a staircase. At the bottom was another tunnel which, if my calculations are correct, I believe runs along the fireplace wall of the kitchen. From there we descended a spiral staircase and found ourselves in what appeared to be a wide, empty cellar. There is no way out of this room, so I can only believe it was used for storage.'

'But that would not explain the secretive nature of the room. Why keep a store room a secret?'

'My feeling is that we shall never know unless something is revealed on the documents regarding the manor which I have in my possession for you. I shall hand those over to you at supper this evening.'

'Obviously, the staff know about it and I will mention it to Arthur later, but I agree the boys should not know, not yet anyway. I don't want them exploring on their own.'

'Indeed, Sir William. My concern was for the boys also. The stairs are not in the best condition and I would not like an accident to occur.'

'I appreciate that, and thank you, Edwin. Perhaps you can show us tomorrow but I can see the surrounding wall ahead, so we shall speak no more of it until the boys are settled abed.'

'I would be happy to, Sir William. Oh, and the repair of the main gate is on my list of work that needs attending to.'

Sheltered by the canopy of tree branches above them, the sun rarely broke through enough to dry out the little-used puddled and rutted lane, and several times the wheels of the wagon stuck, but Edwin had already prepared for that. At intervals along the lane he had left a number of long, rough sacking bags which, when placed under the wheels gave them something to grip onto allowing them to be freed from the sticky mud.

It was now late morning. The mist had completely vanished, and the sun was high in the sky sending beams of rainbow colours through the spaces between cover of branches and remaining leaves, casting dappled shadows on the ground. Bartley and Dickon paid no attention to the scenery, they were far too busy playing with the pups.

'What are you going to call them? Arthur asked as he flicked the reins to spur on the mules.

'We thought River and Lake,' volunteered Dickon, to Arthur's great surprise, but he did not show it. 'And what about their mother?' He looked back into the wagon where the mother lay resting on one half of a woollen blanket, the other half was wrapped around her. 'She deserves a name.'

Bartley thought about that. 'Can we keep ter the same kind o' names as fer the 'orses?'

'You can choose whatever type of name you like, this is for you two to decide.'

'The boys huddled together in a whispered conversation. Then Bartley turned to Arthur and proudly said, 'Hazel.'

Arthur chuckled. 'That's a good name and perhaps, if we can make her stronger, she'll like having that name. Giving her a name shows you care about her. Look, we're here!'

They turned a corner and rode through an archway with twin barbicans on either side.

'The archway above has been well built,' Edwin began. 'It is slate roofed and, as you see there are shutters on the window apertures, but there is no glass in them. The windows in the barbicans do have glass in them as they are dwelling places although unused at present, and the arch above links them both. The heavy wooden gates, which are in good condition, can be locked and barred. I believe the previous occupant did have a gate keeper who lived in the gatehouse on the right. When, and if you wish, you can restore that practice if you feel there is need.'

Once through into the courtyard, Will pulled Chestnut to a halt. He wanted to take time to absorb the magnificent residence that was to be his home. His head spun, thoughts swirling; if this was neglected, how impressive it would be when it was renovated, and he wondered how the Earl could ever have thought him worthy of such a prize like it. If the Earl preferred another dwelling then how splendid that must be?

Built of honey-coloured Cotswold stone, the manor gleamed in the mid-day sunshine that reflected on the four three-panelled, lead-lined glass windows on all three floors. Will noted that the windows decreased in height and size on the upper floors. He was utterly astounded at the thought of owning, and being responsible for, anything so grand.

At that moment, the wide wooden door opened and a stream of people rushed out to stand, in two lines, one on either side of the porch, while they waited to meet their new master.

Edwin dismounted from his horse with a frown, and strode up to the woman Will assumed was the cook. 'You were supposed to be ready,' Edwin said in hushed tones that could still be heard by Will and Arthur. Will dismounted and stood back, politely giving time for the welcoming party to be ready for introductions.

'Where's the welcome cup?' said Edwin. The cook said something to the girl standing beside her, who rushed back inside and there followed an awkward few moments while they waited for her to return.

'Please do not concern yourself, Edwin, and do not reproach these ladies. I am certain they have been busy preparing the rooms for our arrival, and I am grateful for their help. Would you make the introductions please.'

Arthur and the boys, Bartley still clutching the basket of puppies, approached the front steps to be introduced, just as the maid hurriedly walked back gingerly carrying a tray with goblets of wine and stood to one side until told when to serve.

'Sir William Hallett, Sir Arthur Burnel, Bartley and Dickon, who will soon have the name of Hallett, I would like to introduce Mistress Spinner, who is your cook and acting housekeeper. These ladies are Jane and Emma Rose, your housemaids, Mabel Norton, your scullery maid and Josiah Knapp who will look after the mules and horses.' said Edwin. 'If it pleases you, Sir William, Josiah can walk the horses and team in pairs, to the stables along the bridal path that leads off from the top of the lane or, if you would like to see where your mounts are to be bedded, we can remove your belongings from the wagon, bring them into the house and then go together to the stables.'

'Where does Josiah live?' asked Will.

'He lives with his mother in the village but, if the need arises there is a small room over the stables where he can sleep on a straw mattress overnight. He has experience of foaling, shoeing and minor ailments, and is a very useful young man to have in your employ.'

'I will think on that. Perhaps we can arrange for something more comfortable for Josiah during the renovations, if he wishes to live in the grounds, that is.' He looked behind him at the barbicans. 'In the meantime, perhaps Josiah would be good enough to take the horses and mule team to the stables to get them settled. He can tether our horses to the wagon, then drive them to the stable yard and settle them for the night, but we can take our belongings off now.' Will turned to Josiah. 'Are you able to manage all the animals on your own, Josiah, or is there one of these young ladies who is able and willing to help?'

'Oi can do tha', Sir William,' said one of the Rose girls, Will was not sure which. 'Oi've 'elped me Pa, wi our 'osses.'

Josiah beamed, seemingly pleased to have her help. They climbed up onto the seat, waited until Will and Arthur had taken everything they wanted from the back of the wagon, including the newly-named, Hazel. Arthur and Will tethered Chestnut, Rowan and Ash to the tailgate, then Josiah and Emma drove the wagon away through the archway and turned off down the track.

Will decided they could wait until nightfall before visiting the horses and mules to ensure the animals were comfortable, but then he and Arthur could slip into the barn and retrieve the coins from under the seat of the wagon. Before that though, he would choose a room to suit him, and find somewhere secure to hide the coins.

Although Arthur was eager to see where Rowan and Ash would be stabled, he agreed with Will's plan to wait until after dark, when Josiah had left for the night.

'You may recall I did mention that some of the stabling was not in good condition,' said Edwin, 'but one of the blocks is quite reasonable and that is where Josiah will settle your mounts. There is room there for them all. It will not take long to make the other block sound once the builders arrive in a day or two. We have a good supply of hay and oats...'

'We also have hay and oats in the wagon. We purchased a plentiful supply to feed the horses and mules while travelling from Newhaven,' said Will.

'How far away is the stable block?' asked Arthur.

'At the rear of the house there is a large walled garden with a padlocked wrought iron gate – I shall take you to all areas of the house and grounds after dinner, if you wish, and the extended property tomorrow if that is in accordance with your wishes. But to return to the garden...beyond it is a field that borders the wood, and the stables are a little further on. There are two barns, perfectly sound, both of them, and a good place to keep the wagon until you require it. There are a number of chickens and geese in the barn, that have somehow survived foxes, weasels and the like, even though they had no protection during the time the house was unoccupied.

'Unfortunately, the local people, have been helping themselves to some of the flock as there has been no-one to stop them, but they have been told that will cease now that you are here.'

'And do you know what is being served for dinner, Edwin?' asked Arthur.

'Yes, indeed, Sir Arthur. Edric supplied us with a leg of lamb which Mistress Spinner has roasted on the spit. She has also made a custard tart to follow.'

Will called the boys over to stand beside him. He hunkered down to look them in the eye to speak to them. 'What do you think of your new home?'

Bartley asked if he and Dickon could still share a room.

'For as long as you want to. There are more bedrooms than we know what to do with and, when you're ready you can have rooms of your own, but that can come when you are older and more settled.'

That seemed to satisfy them both but Bartley had one more question. 'Where are the dogs going to sleep, Sir William?'

Will laughed. 'Do you want them with you?'

Both boys nodded vigorously.

'They you can...but you have to clean up after them.'

'But their mother needs to stay with them too, so they can feed.' They turned as Arthur walked up to join them. He was carrying Hazel who seemed perfectly relaxed in his arms and, if anything appeared to be a little brighter than she had earlier. 'We'll get some of that lamb into her, give her milk and eggs, and plenty of water to drink which will help her make milk for her pups. Once she's put on some weight and gained her strength, I think she will do well. I don't believe she is very old, even if she has had all those litters of pups, so with good feeding, youth on her side, exercise and nursing, we may see her live into old age yet,' said Arthur.

'Well, Edwin, lead the way if you will,' said Will. 'Come boys, come Sir Arthur, let us dine for the first time in our new home.'

A flock of birds flew from the roof towards the trees. Will and Arthur, having stood back to let everyone else enter the manor before them, looked up.

'Arthur, we have pigeons.' Will grinned, 'I wonder if we can train them.'

Epilogue

Sir Will Hallett

By early December 1356, the renovations to Winterne Manor were complete and the manor became a comfortable home for Will, the boys, Arthur and the household members, that included new staff, Edward Shaw, the Steward, John Palmer, Tutor to Bartley and Dickon, Margaret Bell, the Housekeeper and Jane Rose was promoted to Lady's Maid to care for Will's mother, Mary, who he had found alive and well.

Also, by the time renovations were finished, thanks to Arthur's help, Will had become an accomplished reader. With the sun setting earlier as the autumn days turned more wintry, once the boys were settled in their beds at night, and the light was too poor to continue with any work on the building safely, Arthur and Will settled down by the fire in the smaller, and more comfortable, winter drawing room to concentrate on Will's reading and writing. Lying on the hearth rug, at Arthur's feet, was Hazel, who had recovered strength and had become his shadow. Beside her on the rug, but at Will's feet, was a stray red-brindled greyhound they had found skulking around the garden at the rear of the manor a few days after they arrived. The dog immediately took to Will, and the family quickly acquired another canine member who Will named Eden. River and Lake, the deerhound pups, continued to spend their nights in the room shared by Bartley and Dickon, until the boys were given their own rooms. Then River chose to stay with Bartley.

Some funds remained following the completion of the renovations and this, together with tenant farmer rents, profits from Winterne Manor farm produce, plus the returns from an investment Will made into Edric's inn, gave Will and his family a healthy income over the years.

Agnes, Will's sister-in-law had re-married and was content in her new life with three children by Albert, and two further children by her new husband. Although she was delighted to see William had survived and done well for himself, she had no need of his help. Will was overjoyed to renew his relationship with his nephews and niece and saw them regularly.

Soon after, Will took possession of six rings showing his crest; one for himself, one for his mother and one each for Bartley and Dickon. The other two were for his future wife and their first born child. Will also followed Edwin Cheeseman's advice and had the crest displayed on gates, doors and banners around his property.

Over the next four years, Chestnut and Rowan provided Will with three healthy foals and, by purchasing two of Martin's Arab foals, soon the stables were full of prized horses and Arthur began his own string of horses with some of these foals.

In March 1357, Will became legally responsible for Bartley and Dickon and they took his surname. To all intents and purposes they became his legal sons.

In July 1358 William married Catherine, the eighteen year-old daughter of extremely wealthy goldsmith, Stephen Townsend. Catherine adored Bartley and Dickon and loved them as her sons. In May of 1359, they had a healthy daughter they named Isabelle. The following year their son, Albert was born. Both children were brought up to think of Bartley and Dickon as older brothers. Four years later, Catherine died in childbirth with their third child, another son who was hurriedly christened William. He lived for just four days. Both Isabelle and Albert thought of Bartley and Dickon as their older brothers. In memory of Catherine, William commissioned a tall stained glass window, which was situated on the half-landing of the main staircase. The image was of Catherine, dressed in a white flowing gown, her pale blonde hair loose and flowing and encircled by flowers. On the first finger of her right hand, she wore the ring with the family crest, and beside her stood a white unicorn. William never married again.

In September 1360, Mary, William's mother died at the age of fifty-five years having led a comfortable and happy life in her later years.

Isabelle and Albert grew strong and healthy but a riding accident left Albert unable to walk and he never recovered his strength. He died of a fever at the age of fifteen years old.

In 1377, Isabelle married Sir Gregory Maitland and they lived at Winterne Manor. They had five children, all healthy and all lived into middle to old age. William, Stephen, Catherine, Benedict and Eleanor.

Sir William Hallett, much loved and respected within Winterne and the surrounding area and great friend of William Montacute, the second Earl of Salisbury, died in 1390 at the age of fifty four years, surrounded by his family and his great friend of many years, Sir Arthur Burnel.

Sir Arthur Burnel

In 1359, on the death of Sir Reginald Fairley, the sole owner of Coxley Manor, near Wells, Arthur bought the extensive and comfortable property. He married Matilda Coombs had a family of four children, all of whom grew into adulthood. Isabel, Edith, Martin and William.

Arthur's interest in and love of horses created a profitable and gratifying business that began while he was still at Winterne Manor. Later, when he moved to Coxley Manor, he took Ash, his own preferred mount, two Arab yearlings and two of Chestnut and Rowan's two-year-olds. Having learnt a great deal about breeding horses, he soon gained a well-deserved reputation for breeding strong, healthy horses for various tasks, i.e. war horses, hunters and gentle palfreys suitable for ladies leisurely riding, and docile ponies appropriate for children learning to ride.

Their two sons, Martin and William, continued the family business, their daughter, Edith, married Bartley Hallett, but their daughter, Isabel, chose instead to take her vows and joined the order of Augustinian Canonesses at Ilchester Nunnery. On the death of Matilda after twenty-seven years of happy marriage, Sir Arthur renounced his wealth and property in favour of Martin, left portions of his estate to William and Edith and donated a portion of his wealth to Ilchester Nunnery and the Benedictine Monks of The Abbey Church of Saint Mary in Glastonbury and joined their order. He and Sir William maintained their friendship until William died. Sir Arthur lived a long and serene life as Almoner of the Abbey and died in 1408 aged seventy-four years.

Sir Robert Swinford

On returning home, Robin found his children, Edward now thirteen, and Cecilia, twelve, had changed a great deal. The image he always carried in his head was far different from the people they had grown into. Little Stephen though, was exactly as he imagined him to be, but it was clear that the boy was frightened of this stranger who claimed to be his father. Stephen seemed to spend all his time hiding behind one of his siblings or his grandmother, even though she clearly had no qualms about welcoming Robin home.

For the first few days following Robin's arrival, accompanied by Sir Hugh Armstrong, the distance that had grown between the children and their absent father had seemed insurmountable, but Robin persevered, convinced that the years he had spent with his children before being called to war, would have set a good foundation. He believed that given time they would remember how much love there had been between them. And he was right.

Just three weeks later, while Robin and Hugh attended to their horses in the stables, both older children entered. Cecilia began the conversation by apologising for their lack of welcome on his arrival and asked why he had left them for so long. It was at that point that his mother-in-law, with Stephen holding her hand, joined them. Robin explained that, like Sir Hugh, he had been forced to join the army to serve his liege lord, but had always longed for the time he could come home to them.

Cecilia explained they had never expected to see him again, assuming he was dead. It was then that she burst into tears and ran to hug him. Robin opened his arms and Cecilia was followed into them by an embarrassed Edward, who had thought himself too grown up for such displays of emotion. Stephen clung to his grandmother, who through happy tears gently pushed him forward to join his father and siblings in their embrace.

Standing behind Robin, Hugh watched as, at first Stephen tried to cling to his grandmother, but when Cecilia turned and beckoned to him, the little boy ran forward and hugged his father's knees. The ice had broken, and Hugh understood the time was right for him to take his leave and return to Blidworth.

All three children were encouraged with their schooling. The farm prospered under Robin's leadership, Edward showed great skill at making efficient and accurate bows and arrows, and became an expert fletcher.

Cecilia, who enjoyed sewing became a seamstress to the wives of wealthy merchants, and Stephen grew up to take over the farm management from his father when Robin became too old. Sir Robin Swinford died following a riding accident while out hunting in 1405 at the very ripe old age of eighty-one years.

Sir Hugh Armstrong

On leaving Robin's home in Ashford, Hugh joined a group of travellers heading towards London where he spent a few days looking around the city, putting off the day when he would discover whether his future was indeed with Margaret. Eventually he found an inn where a group of merchants were travelling north and joined them. After spending a few days travelling through the cities of St Albans, Buckingham and Bedford, Hugh began to feel anxious on the approach to Leicester. Nottinghamshire was the next county, and he was quickly approaching the time when he would find out what his future held. Was Margaret still alive? Had she married another? If not, would she still want him? What would he do if his hopes died?

On approaching his home just beyond the woodland surrounding the village of Blidworth, Hugh was surprised to see smoke rising from the chimney and healthy looking sheep and cows in the fields. Two young men were working in the fields, ploughing furrows following the harvest, and life seemed to be continuing as usual. Hugh assumed his father was still alive and running the farm.

As he tied Thunder to the fence outside the farmhouse, the door opened and Margaret, an empty egg basket looped across her arm, came into view. On seeing each other, they stopped in their tracks and stared – both shocked to see the other. Margaret took a few moments to recognise Hugh through the long hair and beard, then thought she was seeing a ghost. On realising the man in front of her was very much alive, Margaret dropped the basket and ran to him. They hugged. The years had changed nothing for either of them.

Margaret explained that both Hugh's father and her own had died and, with her brother inheriting her family farm, and Hugh being an only child, she had taken charge of his farm rather than see it neglected, and moved into the house insisting that, as they were betrothed, it was her right.

Hugh and Margaret were married within the month and had two sons, Matthew and Simon. After eighteen years of happy marriage, Hugh died in 1374, and Margaret followed two years later. Hugh's knighthood passed to their first born son, Matthew. When Margaret died, her brother, Thomas, helped Sir Matthew and Simon purchase additional land to increase their farm and supervised them on the running of it until they were experienced enough to take over their own separate areas of the farm. Later the farm was split into two separate properties both of which prospered.

Bartley Hallett

Will hired a tutor for the boys, John Palmer, who taught them reading, writing, Latin, measurements, addition and subtraction and logic – basically the art of arguing their point. Sir William also arranged for a fencing master, riding lessons and, at the suggestion of Sir Arthur, and much to the boys' disgust, a dancing master.

As he grew into his teens Bartley became close to Sir William's father-in-law, and was delighted to be taken on by him as an apprentice goldsmith.

In 1366, Bartley married, Edith, daughter of Sir Arthur Burnel. William gave them a large cottage in the grounds of Winterne Manor and they had two children, William and Eleanor.

Later he set up a business in London making gold jewellery, cups and crucifixes encrusted with precious gems and pearls, Bartley took on a number of apprentices and he too prospered in that trade.

At the age of forty-five, Bartley retired from any active part of the business and spent more time at home with his family. His assistant, Richard Smith, took over the business but continued to pay Bartley a share of the income for the rest of his life.

Dickon Hallett

During their journey to Winterne, Dickon and Bartley understood their lives had changed forever, that Will meant everything he said, and would care enough about them to become their legal father. Neither Will or Arthur pressed Dickon to speak again knowing, from the occasional times when he did speak, he would when he was ready.

With the stable filling with well-looked after horses, the stubborn but amusing mules, and the three dogs, Dickon settled into a new and happy life, became more confident and, following the rare times when he did speak, within six months he was fully conversational.

Their only concern then was that he had a habit of running off into the woods, 'to talk to the small people'. Most people thought he was a little mad but there was no harm in him, and so many folk locally believed in the 'little people' that they gave him the benefit of the doubt and left him to his illusions.

Of course, no-one admitted they believed him, but there were so many stories from local folk of sightings and strange happenings, that William, Arthur and the rest of the family humoured him.

But there was also a serious side to Dickon, and during the time the builders were working on the manor, whenever he was allowed, Dickon watched the renovations taking place, fascinated by the processes. Soon he was helping the builders, and it became obvious this would be his career. In time Dickon became a master builder and architect.

In 1381 the peasants revolt began in London, and extended to other parts of the country, including Bridgewater in June. Initially Dickon was not too concerned about the troubles but when it reached Ilchester, a little over twenty miles away, he began to think again. News reached Winterne of an attack by a large mob on a local Augustinian Monastery where they demanded a ransom before leaving. Excited by the success of their demand, they raided the manor house of John Sydenham, a local merchant, and killed one of his men, before storming Ilchester gaol and killing a man they had a grievance against. Thankfully, this was the end of the uprising in Somerset.

However, it prompted Dickon into planning an escape route from the manor in case of future need. Using the secret staircases and cellar, Dickon and his team dug out a tunnel that led from the cellar through the hillside and into the woods. Two men died during the construction of the tunnel and, as Dickon grew older and the tunnel was never used, he wondered if their sacrifice had been worth it.

Dickon never married but continued to live at Winterne Manor, was a favourite uncle to Bartley and Isabelle's children, and was immensely popular within the Winterne and Wells area.

Edith Chapman

True to her word, Edith kept in close touch with Will and Arthur. Shortly after her first visit to the Coombs' home in Salisbury, she sent Arthur this message strapped to the leg of one of their homing pigeons.

'Wedding did not happen. Guy suffered apoplexy but alive. M still betrothed. Returned from S'bury. Visit you - two days. More news.'

Once at Winterne Manor, Edith explained that, although Guy was desperately ill and would never recover what little strength he previously had, until he died Matilda was still contracted to him, and therefore not free to marry Arthur. However, with Roger's plan having been put paid to by these events, and Edith and Edgar's relationship developing into something more than friendship, when Edgar proposed marriage to her, Edith offered to invest some of her own wealth into the business, whereupon Edgar insisted on her becoming an equal partner and that, once they were wed, if he died before her, his shares would go to her.

Thwarted, this infuriated Roger to such an extent that, in his rage during an argument, he declared that it would have been better if Edgar had already died. This caused Edgar and Martin to question some of Roger's actions in the past, and they now realised just how devious and avaricious he was. Called upon to attend a formal meeting of the partners, Roger protested loudly when Edgar, Matilda and Martin signed the contract giving Edith an equal share in the business. Edgar dismissed Roger from the business by forcibly buying him out and declaring that he no longer wished to have Roger under his roof. Roger took the payment and stormed out. Martin had taken on the tasks that Roger had previously carried out and with greater efficiency.

Of course Edgar was deeply upset that Roger had turned out to be so self-seeking, but having his other two children, who were true to him, and Edith who had come to love him, by his side, he put Roger from his mind. They never saw him again. Later they heard he had left for London where he took up gambling. His body was found on the muddy shore of the Thames at low tide one evening. It was thought that he had failed to pay his debts and his death was an act of reprisal.

It was a little over eighteen months later that Guy died leaving Matilda free to marry Arthur.

Edith took Milo, her trusted servant, with her to Salisbury. When he became too infirm to continue his duties, Edith and Edgar looked after him in their home until his death.

Edith and Edgar were regular visitors to Winterne and much adored by all. They both lived well into their seventies and died within one week of each other.

Part Two

1510
In the time of Henry VIII
The First Earl

Chapter Twenty Three

In March 1510, the young King Henry VIII, was bored with life in the court and looking for some excitement. He and his new wife, Catherine of Aragon, were happy and in love, and Henry decided to take her on visit around a part of England she had not visited before, the South West.

Although still very young, Henry was a very attractive young man, already well known for his carousing, womanising and merry-making, and he had a large group of friends who vied with each other for the privilege of sharing that side of his life. None of these 'friends' wanted to be left behind, staying in favour with the King and not allowing anyone else to become the *preferred* companion was a vital part of ensuring your continued position at court, your fortune and, in some cases, your head. Therefore, each of these so-called friends were eager to accompany the royal couple on the trip. But Henry decided to only take his closest friends on this somewhat informal tour that was primarily meant as a pleasurable relaxation for Catherine. Even though Catherine had been in England since October 1501, she had not visited that part of the country, and Henry had been so effusive over the beauty of the region that he insisted Catherine would enjoy it.

Travelling with wagons of tents, escort soldiers, favoured courtiers and servants, on their way from Richmond Palace, Henry refused to become embroiled in the political mischief of the senior nobles who, underhandedly, competed with each other for preferential positions close to the king. Visits were made to members of the aristocracy at Slough,

Reading, Basingstoke, Winchester, Salisbury, Shaftesbury, Wincanton, the Abbey at Glastonbury where they prayed before the Holy Thorn tree, Wells and finally on to Bath.

At Wells, the Bishop of Bath and Wells had felt obliged to invite the royal couple to stay at his moated palace and, to his deep great regret, they had accepted. The cost of feeding, entertaining and finding accommodation for the King, Queen, a large party of noblemen and all the retainers would be outrageous but, having made the offer, he was now compelled to go ahead with it. He also understood the local gentry would see it as a great honour to have their King, and his new Queen, visit their small city and pray at their magnificent Cathedral.

On the second night of their stay, the Bishop held a banquet in honour of the royal couple, and one of the guests honoured by being given a seat at the top table, near the King and Queen, was Sir Charles Maitland of Winterne Manor.

Henry had arranged for his Head Steward to carry out some research on the people he would be meeting and, armed with the results of that investigation, had discovered Sir Charles had a keen interest in hawking and falconry and had acquired some prize birds. In addition, having a slightly paler shade of red-gold hair, and being a little under six feet tall, only two inches shorter than the king, Sir Charles could have been mistaken for a close Tudor relative. Henry found this very amusing and, suggested to Queen Catherine that she could take advantage of his absence the next morning to lay abed, while he invited himself and a select group of favoured courtiers, to visit Winterne Manor the following morning.

Being a somewhat solemn and intellectual person, not given overmuch to being particularly conversational, Sir Charles would not usually have been of interest to the sporting and active monarch, who enjoyed Real Tennis, wrestling, jousting and other physical pursuits. However, their shared appreciation of birds of prey prompted an enjoyable exchange of information, and Henry spent considerably more time with Sir Charles than was expected, upsetting many other of the guests who had their noses put out of joint.

Sir Charles, born in the same year as the King, was not known to be the type for gatherings and revelry, but had been unable to refuse the invitation to meet the King and Queen. Serious-minded, and studious, he preferred to spend his time in study, reading, and his favourite pastime, falconry. Unaccustomed to receiving such high-ranking guests at Winterne, Sir Charles was numb with fear at the prospect.

Fortunately, his steward, Edward Brakesby, had experience of just such an occasion at his previous employment, during the time of the previous king, Henry VII. Brakesby took control. On rising early that morning, he informed the household servants of the King's impending visit, and instructed individuals to carry out specific jobs to ensure the manor was thoroughly cleaned, and a good dinner was prepared. He appealed to their sense of pride in the manor and their love for their master, either of which were enough incentives for them to set to their tasks with a will. A little before mid-day, when the King and his party were due to arrive, the manor gleamed, and the kitchen staff had prepared a sumptuous meal. Sir Charles relaxed.

When the King and his companions arrived, they were delighted with the preparations, the catering and, from the King's point of view, the health and skill of the collection of peregrines, merlins, gyrfalcons – the largest of the falcon species - goshawks, sparrowhawks and lanners, was so impressive, he had a message sent to the Queen to tell her they would be staying at Winterne for the next two days, much to the dismay of Sir Charles.

However Charles need not have been so concerned. He just needed to have faith in his loyal steward as again Brakesby took control and ensured that everything ran smoothly for his Master and, when the King and his companions left, they were enchanted by their visit.

The peace and quiet of Winterne Manor, the trout in the lake, the excellence and condition of the books in the library, the quality of the stabled horses and the hawking, so captivated the King that he spent a great deal of time with Sir Charles. Finding Charles intellectual, cultured and, when not appallingly nervous, an erudite conversationalist, was a great surprise to Henry.

Even allowing for the amusement of finding their physical similarities, Henry had not formed a particularly good impression of Charles at first, but the longer they were together the more they discovered they had a great many interests in common, and a friendship developed. But, what Henry appreciated most about Charles was his complete lack of political ambition. Everyone else continually asked Henry for favours but, with Charles this was not the case. There was nothing Charles wanted other than to continue his life at Winterne and to marry Elizabeth Fairley in August; this had been arranged many years before, while they were still children, but they were fond of each other and happy with the arrangement.

When Henry found out Sir Charles was to be wed ten weeks later, he immediately invited himself and the Queen to attend the wedding. Elizabeth and Charles had already agreed on a small and intimate ceremony attended only by their families and closest friends and now he was in a quandary. If the king wanted to attend, how could Charles refuse, even though it meant there would be hordes of retainers? One did not decline the honour of having the monarch attend your wedding, not without causing great offence and Charles admitted to Elizabeth that he did not have that kind of courage. Elizabeth agreed that if, as it seemed, the king found favour with Charles, they would have to endure this unexpected mark of distinction.

Luck must have been with Charles, because a month before the wedding he received a message from Henry informing him that he and Queen Catherine would be unable to attend as, due to the queen being with child again, their doctors had recommended she should not undertake any long journeys, they would therefore be unable to attend, and he was sure Charles and Elizabeth would understand.

However, Henry did not forget. On the morning of the wedding, a messenger arrived from Richmond Palace with a rolled piece of parchment, sealed with the King's insignia having been pressed into the hot wax. Charles broke the seal and unrolled the scroll.

King Henry VIII had elevated Sir Charles Maitland to Earl of Winterne; the title was to continue through the male side of his family line. The messenger then handed Charles another short letter from the King explaining that this elevation was by way of a wedding gift, and that he and Catherine very much regretted they could not be there.

There was also an invitation for Charles and Elizabeth to visit Richmond

Palace during the following Spring, and Henry made it quite clear he wanted Charles's advice on the breeding of his hawks and falcons.

On entering the room where the wedding was to take place, he silently handed the scroll to Elizabeth, who had now become a countess. The new Earl was made speechless by the gift, and it fell to Brakesby to read the contents of the scroll to the assembled guests.

When the ceremony was over, Charles left Elizabeth and his guests for a few moments, climbed the wide wooden staircase and stopped on the half-landing. He looked up at the stained glass window of the maiden and the unicorn. Since childhood he had always believed that Lady Catherine Hallett was watching over him, and he now sent her a silent prayer of thanks.

Soon after the wedding, the Earl contracted builders to begin working on a new wing of the manor, this time in the Tudor style of white with black timbering. If his king was going to be visiting, they would need more fitting accommodation than he had been able to provide before, although King Henry had made no complaints about the quarters provided in the manor.

Epilogue

The invitations from the King became an annual event until Henry's jousting accident in 1536 when he became increasingly irrational, and the invitations ceased. By that time, Charles and Elizabeth had a family of three sons and one daughter, and found the visits to London and Hampton Court tedious and invasive. They were delighted when they were no longer required to attend.

The Earl, not being the type of person to enjoy court intrigue, and Elizabeth who had become increasingly annoyed by the constant and distressing flirting of the male courtiers towards her, were relieved not to have to continue making the long journeys to London. They continued to live quietly at Winterne watching their children and grandchildren grow into adulthood.

Part Three

1587
In the time of Elizabeth 1
The Monk

Chapter Twenty Four

The news of the Babington Plot spread to the four corners of England enraging those loyal to Queen Elizabeth but, in some areas her devoted subjects were slower to react than in others. Winterne was one of those places.

Members of the faction had plotted to kill Queen Elizabeth and have Mary Stuart, Queen of Scots, freed from her imprisonment and placed on the throne of England. Sir Francis Walsingham, personal secretary and Spymaster to Queen Elizabeth, by infiltrating Mary's circle of servants and associates, had, in fact, discovered two Catholic plots against his Queen. The Babington Plot – named after conspirator Anthony Babington – came to light due to the efforts of Walsingham's double agents and code experts. They discovered Mary's own agents had provided her with a way of communicating with her supporters by hiding coded letters inside a beer barrel. Once decoded, these letters from Mary, not only revealed her involvement in trying to depose Elizabeth, but confirmed her approval to have Elizabeth assassinated.

This led to Mary being tried before three hundred peers. At her trial, she was not allowed to speak and had no one appointed to defend her. Even so, she had signed a document agreeing to the scheme and was therefore, found guilty and executed at Fotheringay Castle; the order unenthusiastically given by Queen Elizabeth.

Anthony Babington and accomplices John Ballard, Chidiock Tichborne, Thomas Salisbury, Henry Donn, Robert Barnewell and John Savage were arrested, tortured, found guilty and executed by being hanged, drawn and quartered. Further executions were carried out but, following public protests, were not quite so brutal.

Catholic monks were banned from the country and all signs of Catholic faith had to be hidden. Many Catholic monks were smuggled into England from France and covert services were held. When this was discovered, having been tolerant of the Catholic religion up to that point, feeling betrayed and persuaded by her advisers that her life was at risk, Elizabeth's patience ran out.

Throughout England, protestants – many of whom were against the Catholic religion and loyal to Elizabeth - were incensed by the possibility of England coming under Catholic rule again, and used the situation to fuel hatred and mob-rule.

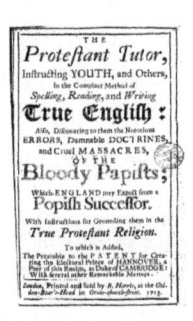

Chapter Twenty Five

With the autumn colours of daylight fading into the dark blue and purple of dusk, a mob of some forty men and older boys, armed with scythes, sticks, hammers, ropes, and cudgels, gathered together at the edge of Winterne village, together with a pack of overexcited hounds who howled and bayed frenziedly, aroused by the angry atmosphere around them. Blind religious intolerance had overcome common sense, and these ruffians wanted blood.

Tom Cooper, the wheelwright, and local blacksmith, his knuckles white with tension as he gripped his hammer tightly in his fist. He looked across at William Hunter, his co-conspirator, and wondered how William had drawn him into all this madness. Now it was too late to back down without losing face.

Knowing Tom had always had a strong devotion to their Queen, William had used that loyalty, persuasively convincing Tom into joining him make a stand against the Catholics, specifically the Maitland family, headed by Richard, Earl of Winterne.

Tom thought back to the night of that meeting. William had worked himself up into a real temper. 'We'll 'it 'em where it'll do them 'arm,' he spat, viciously. 'We'll get tha' fat monk o' theirs. 'Im wha' forgives 'em their sins when they do confess and tells 'em it don' matter wha' they do, 'cos God'll see 'em in 'Eaven!'

Tom was well respected and popular, and William knew he would need his support to influence others to join them. One by one William had aroused the anti-Catholic mood to inflame them into taking violent action against what many people called Papists.

With boastful arrogance their first, and an easy victim, was to be the Franciscan Friar, confessor and tutor to the Maitland family at Winterne Manor, Brother Matthew. Although he had been invited to live within the manor, Brother Matthew had refused the offer, preferring to live a solitary life in a small, but comfortable, wooden hut in Winterne woods, close to the manor.

The hot-tempered horde were determined to capture Brother Matthew as he said his evening prayers. He would be alone and easy to seize, unaware of what was to come. They had planned their attack knowing he would be defenceless in his single-roomed thatched hut. With the dogs making so much noise, Tom ordered their handlers to stay behind. He would send for them if they were needed. To take the monk by surprise, they needed silence, stealth.

As the men headed into the woods, the dogs whined and tugged at their leashes eager to join in the pursuit, but were restrained until their handlers received word they were needed. Tom and his accomplices vanished into the gloom with just the occasional shaft of moonlight to guide them. For a while they were still within earshot of the dogs, but the sound diminished as they ventured further into the thick woodland, and the density of the trees muffled the barking. However, it was not just the barking that was muted. Following Tom's instruction, there were parts of the woodland where, apart from the odd beam of moonlight that broke through the canopy of autumn-coloured leaves, some of the group found themselves enveloped in total smothering darkness. Fear overcame the need for stealth, and the odd hushed call of someone's name was risked as they attempted to keep in touch with each other. It would have been easy to become lost and Winterne Woods had a reputation for strange things happening, some said they had heard that people had even disappeared. Whether that was true or not was not important, when folk were superstitious, they were prepared to believe any scary or mystifying tale. There was no-one among these *heroic* grown men who had not heard yarns of people disappearing, and ghostly apparitions being seen. However, keeping their voices low was not such a good idea when it came to staying close together in an densely packed and darkened wood.

A few, on the edge of the group, began straying without realising the gap between them and the main body was widening, and before long they were completely lost.

After what seemed to William Hunter that they had been walking for far too long, he said: 'We should 'ave bin there by now. 'Ow much longer afore we gets there an' gives tha' monk o' them Maitland's a doin'. Oi bloody 'ates tha' fam'ly.'

'It en't the fam'ly we be arter. 'Tis tha' monk. I know yer en't fond o' the fam'ly but ferget them fer now. 'Tis jest the monk we'm goin' fer.' Tom chuckled. 'An' wi' tha' red 'air o' yourn, yer could be tekken fer one o' the fam'ly anyways.'

'Don' yer say tha'!' With a sudden fury, William flew at him and wrapped his hands around Tom's throat, forcing him back against the wide trunk of an oak tree. 'Don' yer ever say tha agen!'

Tom tried to speak. Tried to breathe. Tried to prise William's hands open, but William was too strong and he pressed harder, harder. Tom could feel his strength slipping away, the blood pounded in his temples, his legs buckled as the pressure tightened around his throat. His world turned black. Then voices. He felt William move back, his hands released Tom's neck, and the air began to flow into his lungs again. He coughed, choked, tried to speak but could only utter a hoarse croak. He opened his eyes.

William was held back by two of the men Tom had seen in the inn earlier that evening but he did not know their names.

'Oi'm…Oi'm obliged ter yer,' he wheezed.

William, still tightly held by the arms, struggled furiously to get free as Tom, his face as pale as the watery moon above, approached him. 'Oi dunno wha' possessed yer ter do tha' William, but 'tis not me yer wanna do 'arm ter. Iss them Maitlands. Yer allus did 'ate the Maitland fam'ly, Oi don' know why, an' Oi don' care. D'you understand me?'

William, lips pressed tightly together and breathing hard tried to wrest himself free from the strong hands that held him, clearly still furious at Tom. Tom was certain that he would be a dead man if William managed to get free.

'Yer 'ave a choice, William. Yer can calm yersel' an come wi' us, or yer can get taken 'ome. 'Wass it ter be? Yer wanna ge' tha' monk an' so do we all, an' that'll be enuff fer this noight. D'you understan' me?' William ceased struggling. His jaw clamped, eyes narrowed, breathing deeply, angrily. Slowly, his face relaxed. He nodded.

'Oi'm no' yer enemy, William. You jest remember tha',' he said. He walked away rubbing his sore neck.

William pulled his arms free and glared at his captors. He was not in a forgiving mood but his blind rage against Tom had surprised even him. One day he would make the Maitlands pay. Maybe not on this night...but one day.

The moon cast shadows over the trees, dark clouds formed into strange shapes that scudded across the sky. Joshua Baker stood stock still and grabbed the arm of his brother, Samuel, and pointed upward. 'Look up there. That cloud don't look roight ter me.'

From the beginning, Joshua and Samuel had been reluctant participants in William and Tom's plan to persecute the monk, their hearts were never in it and their consciences told them it was not God's work. Even the widespread religious hostility towards Catholics by Protestants in the wake of the Babington Plot, did not spur them into violence as it had many others. It was bad enough when Tom had started carping on about, *'them Catholics trying to kill our Queen, God Bless our Bess,'* but, when William had joined him, together they bullied the other men into mob rule, calling them cowards and 'Pape-lovers' if they tried to resist. Joshua was convinced some of the others following Tom and William were only there because they had been strong-armed, especially by William, into taking part, and threatened with punishments if they didn't, and not because they had any great sympathy with the 'cause'.

Even within the pale light of the moon, Joshua could see the terrified look in his brother's eyes. 'Tha' don't look like nothin' Oi saw afore. Tha' cloud shape looks loike a witch ter me. Yer roigh'. No matter what Tom sez, wha' they be doin' en't God's work,' said Samuel.'

'Yer roigh', Sam.'

'Well, they en't goin' ter see us from 'ere...and Oi'm' goin' 'ome. What say you, Sam?'

'Well, Oi'm roigh' behin' yer bu' wha' if Tom sees we'm gone? What'll 'appen then?'

'Oi don' think 'im'll notice. There'll be tha' much goin' on an' who knows, mebbe summat'll 'appen to 'e if things don' go roigh'. Come on, let's go 'ome afore they notice us 'ave gone.'

Shortly after, a little ahead of the rest, Tom grabbed William's arm and pulled him down to the ground as he pointed out the outline of the hut situated close to the riverbank. 'See. Oi said we was goin' the roigh' way. There 'tis,' he said to William.

They crouched down and looked through the undergrowth for any sign of movement at the hut while waiting for the others to catch up with them.

'There's no lamp burning. 'E must be asleep by now,' said Tom.

'What d'yer wanna do wi' 'im, when we gets 'im, Tom?' William asked, moving his hammer from one hand to the other; he was nervous. What they were doing was clearly getting the better of him, and it showed.

'Prob'bly drown 'im,' answered Tom. 'Could've bin an accident then.'

William nodded.

The others in the mob emerged in twos and threes out of the cover of the trees to join them, a few carried unlit torches, under strict orders not to light them before they reached the hut.

'Roigh', let's go,' ordered Tom. 'Quiet, now.'

Step by step, and careful about where they placed their feet, they advanced towards the hut. The lack of rain during the unusually warm late summer into early October, and the balmy breezes, had filtered through the leafy canopy leaving the woodland floor dry as a bone. Even much of the bracken was brittle and brown, and Tom worried that the sound of rustling dead leaves and the snapping of tinder-dry twigs, could give them away in the stillness of the wood.

A few minutes later, they arrived at the hut and waited until group of eight had gathered together before Tom and William tiptoed to stand on either side of the door. William reached out to push the door and swore as it swung open with ease. The hut was empty!

'Damn!' exclaimed William. "E's gone! Someone must've warned 'im! Get them torches lit. Who's go' the flints? We'll 'ave ter search the woods. The fat ol' lump can't 'ave got far.'

'I got the flints. Gimme them torches 'ere.' Walter appeared from the midst of the group.

Sparks from the flints caught the tallow wadding on the first torch and its flame was used to light the others.

'Jack! Where's Jack?' Tom called, his voice still low.

'I'm 'ere. What d'yer want?'

'Get back an' bring them dogs. We're gonna need them after all. An' be quick.' Their plan having been foiled, the dogs would be needed to pick up the monk's trail.

"Then you wai' yer. Oi'm not chasin' abou' arter yer.' Jack sloped off the way they had come.

Chapter Twenty Six

Just a little over an hour before, Kat, a kitchen maid at Winterne Manor, scurried up the back stairs to the rooms occupied by Richard Maitland, the Earl of Winterne, and his wife, Elizabeth. Kitchen staff were never allowed in these rooms; their place was below stairs, out of sight. But Kat had seen the Earl being kind to other servants and she just had to give him a warning.

'Where d'you think you're going, my girl?' Mistress Harper, the housekeeper had spotted her just as she reached the landing.

'Sorry, Missus 'Arper,' said Kat. 'Oi jest thought Oi see'd a rat and thought Oi'd better ketch it,' she quickly answered. Mistress Harper hated rats.

Mistress Harper went pale and took a few steps back. She looked this way and that and held her skirts tighter about her stocky legs. 'Very well but be quick and make sure the Earl don't see you.'

Kat curtseyed. 'Yes, Mam. Oi'll be quick, Mam.'

Just as Kat knew she would, Mistress Harper darted back down the stairs, only too keen to get away from the unseen rat and a few seconds later Kat knocked timidly on the main door leading to the chambers used by the Earl and Countess. Countess Elizabeth's personal maid, Jane, answered. 'You shouldn't be here. Get away with you.'

'Oi got ter speak ter 'Is lordship.' Kat darted under Jane's arm and ran directly to the Earl. Jane shouted for her to get out, but the Earl, sitting at a large wooden desk by the window writing something in a heavy red leather-bound book, heard the commotion and looked up, just as his wife appeared at the door of the adjoining room. She had been preparing for bed and her long, chestnut-coloured hair was loose, hanging down to her waist. Kat had never seen the Countess without a headdress and for a moment she stared, completely forgetting that she should curtsey.

'Well, child,' Elizabeth said, her voice kind and warm. 'What is it that is so urgent, you needed to speak to his lordship personally.'

Kat remembered why she was there. 'Me lord, me lady,' Oi come ter warn ye.' Kat dropped to her knees at the Earl's feet. 'Oi ask yer forgiveness, but 'tis important Oi do speak to yer.'

Richard Maitland frowned, astonished by the girl's brazen behaviour. 'Stand, child,' he commanded. 'You want to warn me...about what, pray?'

Kat stood and lifted her eyes to look into a pair of kindly brown eyes. 'Sir, Oi over'eard some o' the men in the village, talking they was about...well, about you, an' wot they was gonna do ter you an' other people in...well, you know, me lord...you Papists. They hate Catholics, so they do, an' wi' you and your lady bein' Papists they wants to raid the manor and do you some 'arm. Oi 'eard summat about them getting' rid o' Bruvver Matthew too...'

A gasp made Richard turn; Elizabeth ran to his side, she was ghostly white. 'Richard, if this is true...'

'I know, my love.' He tried to hide his concern for her sake, but Elizabeth knew him well enough to understand how worried he was.

'Child...it's Kat, isn't it?' the Earl asked, gently.

Kat nodded. She was shaking with fear and looked from the Earl to his wife and back to Jane.

'And you're certain of this?'

'Yes, me lord. Oi'd not lie ter yer. I swear's ter God an' on me ma's life, Oi wouldn't.'

'I believe you, Kat. Thank you for telling me.' Richard's stomach churned. 'Did you hear when this is to happen?'

'Kat nodded, 'Ternight, my lord. Iss ternight iss goin' ter 'appen an' when Oi 'eard tha', Oi run 'ere quick as me legs would go.'

'Very well, child. Thank you for letting me know. I am indebted to you for this information and now we must make plans. Jane, take Kat to the kitchens and tell Mistress Harper to give her some provisions to take to her family, then she must go home where she has a better chance of being safe. When you get downstairs, send Harris up to me and then find my brothers, Master James and Master John, wherever they are. Tell them it's important they hurry. I have work for them.'

Kat and Jane both curtseyed to the Earl and Countess and left the room.

'But Richard, James is not here,' said Elizabeth, she walked towards him and leaned against his strong shoulder.

'Damn! I had forgotten. He was visiting Alice and her father this afternoon, wasn't he?'

'That's right. They were going to discuss the final wedding plans.'

Richard eased himself away from her grip on his arm and stared into the empty fireplace, silent and brooding. Elizabeth said nothing. Richard was not only trying to work out a defence strategy, with James being away from the manor, he could be in danger if the mob came across him. Walking over to the fireside armchair, she sat down but said nothing giving Richard time to think. The best thing she could do for him now was to be quietly supportive, allow him time to plan what he was going to do. She had to be strong now for him, and for their children.

The sound of footsteps running up the stone stairs reached them. Richard turned to Elizabeth. 'Although I could do with every man I can gather around us, part of me hopes that James will decide not to return home tonight. With his marriage just fourteen days away I would not have him put himself at risk,' said Richard. He walked towards her, his arms outstretched and reached for her hands. 'Elizabeth, my dearest. I want to you take Edward and Catherine...and Mistress Morland...they will need you and their governess...'

'Need us where, Richard? I am not going anywhere. Do you honestly think I will leave you at a time like this?'

'Please do not argue with me, Elizabeth. You and the children must leave within the half hour. I will have more to worry about if the safety of my wife and children is at risk. I want you to go to your father's house and remain there until I send for you.'

Elizabeth tried to protest but Richard affectionately closed her mouth with his fingertips. 'Hush. No argument I said. I look to you to keep our children safe. I will not have them in danger here, and they will need you. Now leave me, pack only what you need to take.'

Just then there was a knock at the door and Harris, the Steward, entered unbidden as the Countess was leaving the room. Harris bowed to her as she walked by him, then turned to the Earl. 'You wanted to see me, my lord.'

'Ah, Harris. Thank you for coming so quickly. It seems we are about to have some uninvited visitors. I have had word that a mob is on the way to attack us. It seems they do not like our religion.'

'I did wonder if that would happen in the aftermath of the Babington Plot,' said Harris, 'and I believe it has happened elsewhere, my lord.'

'As did I.' Richard clasped his hands together, a habit used at time of worry. 'A discovered plot to assassinate our monarch was always going to have consequences. I had hoped that here, in Somerset, we would be far enough away to be left alone, but it seems that is not to be the case and now we have little time to prepare,' said Richard.

'Lady Winterne, the children, and Miss Morland will be leaving presently to visit her father in Wells. Instruct Roberts to make ready our fastest carriage and I think four should do, yes, four of our strongest, swiftest horses. Roberts will choose four of our housecarls to ride alongside them as their escort, their skill with weapons will keep Lady Winterne and the children safe on the road to Wells. I want this done now. They *must* leave within the half hour and, between us both, Harris, the sooner they are away from here better.

'Also inform Mistress Harper to send someone to secure the other horses, and she should instruct Cook to ensure we have adequate supplies of food and other necessities to last for two or three days if necessary, without having to leave the house. If anything needs to be brought in from the outside stores, have it done now, please.'

'Yes, my lord,' Harris replied and turned towards the door. 'Once I have relayed your orders, shall I return to see what more you would have me do?'

'Thank you, Harris. I have never had to ask before, but how good are you with weapons?'

Harris frowned. 'I dare say I can hold my own with a quarterstaff, if required, my lord.'

Richard's eyes opened wide. 'Good. I had no idea you were familiar with that weapon. We may have use for your skill later.'

'I have not always been a steward, my lord,' Harris gave a knowing smile.

Richard returned the smile. 'Thank you, Harris. There is more to you than meets the eye and, if we survive this night, I would hear more.'

Harris bowed and walked towards the door. 'Yes, my lord. I shall return shortly.' He held the door open as Richard's youngest brother, John, arrived out of breath from running up the many stairs to the upper rooms.

'You wanted me, Richard,' said John, brushing passed Harris on his way out.

Before he answered his brother, Richard remembered something. 'Oh, and Harris, before you go.' Richard took a few steps towards the door just as the steward reappeared.

'Yes, my lord?'

Richard leaned closely and said, in almost a whisper: 'Tell the four housecarls you select to go with Lady Winterne and the children, to stay concealed until the children are settled in the carriage. I do not want them worried by knowing they have additional guards. They will expect two men in the front, but they have no need to know that a further two will sit at the rear. The Viscount is a clever boy and may realise that, on a simple journey to his grandfather's they have more protection than they would usually have. The men can climb on board just as the carriage pulls out of the courtyard.'

'I understand, my lord.'

'Thank you, Harris.' Richard walked over to where John was warming his hands in front of the embers of a fire that had been left to die down for the night.

'Yes. I did want to see you.' Richard placed his hands on his youngest brother's shoulders. 'Now I want you to be brave,' he began. The rosy cheeks that glowed in John's face after running up the stairs, drained to an ashen pink. Richard continued. 'You may have noticed there is a little more activity than usual at this time of night. It seems we are to be attacked this evening by a protestant mob from the village. James, I hope, will be staying at Squire Attwood's home, in which case he will be safe. It worries me to think he may ride into the mob and...'

'...But surely, he would hear them and steer Wessex away,' said John.

Richard smiled down at his little brother. 'Yes, you know you're right. I'm worrying unduly. It's unlikely a mob would not be seen approaching...or heard, so he should have plenty of warning and head for the back courtyard. Now, I need you to do something for me...'

'Anything Richard, anything I can do to help.'

'Elizabeth and the children are leaving very soon and taking Miss Morland with them, they are packing to leave now. Four housecarls will accompany them, but I want you to assemble the other six, go with them to the armoury and collect as many muskets, swords, daggers, I want all our weaponry in one place easily available for us to defend the manor...'

'Yes, Richard,' John answered quickly, then turned to go.

'Just one moment, young man. I had not finished.'

'Sorry. I thought you had.'

'Tell two of the housecarls, maybe the Yeo brothers, to station themselves at two of the front upstairs windows with bows and bags of arrows. They are both skilled with the bow and can defend the manor from a higher vantage point.'

John stood still frowning up into his brother's face.

'What are you waiting for?'

'Sorry, I thought you might have something else to say. Is that all you need me to do?'

'Yes. For the moment. Now go!'

'Yes, Richard. Leave it to me.' It was clear that giving John something important to do was the best thing for him; it would take his mind off his fear. Richard couldn't help but smile as his much-loved little brother darted out of the door, his footsteps echoing down the first flight of the stairs. But a moment later Richard heard him running back up. John's face appeared around the doorway.

'Richard, have you thought about Brother Matthew? What are we going to do about him?'

'Oh Lord! I'd forgotten about him! Thank you for reminding me, but you get on with your duties and I'll think about Brother Matthew.' He turned away towards the window, pondering on this new and very worrying problem.

Brother Matthew had been with the family for almost fourteen years and, although he was not an amiable man, he had carried out family religious services, been involved in the education of the younger boys and Richard's children, heard the family confessions and buried their dead; Richard could not let him down. Now Richard wished he had not allowed

Brother Matthew to live outside of the safety of the manor. But the monk had been adamant that the hut suited him, the better to observe, as he said, "his obligations to God."

Richard now felt he should have insisted but, in hindsight...well? At the time, there was no reason to think...or was there? There had been the discovery of the Ridolfi Plot just the year before Brother Matthew had joined their household. The scheme to assassinate Elizabeth and put Mary Stuart on the throne, had involved such high-ranking people as the King of Spain, Pope Pius V and the Duke of Norfolk. Roberto Ridolfi, an Italian banker, had been able to travel freely and without suspicion for a while passing messages between all the conspirators. Eventually William Cecil, one of Queen Elizabeth's closest had discovered the plot. The Duke of Norfolk, a Catholic, who had hoped to marry Mary Stuart once she had Elizabeth's throne, and restore Catholicism in England, eventually confessed and was executed.

Although a Catholic himself, Richard Maitland and his family lived a quiet life away from the politics of London, and Elizabeth's tolerance of Catholic services suited them well. They kept themselves to themselves, and Richard had no great wish to go through religious upheaval again and had been quite content to continue with Queen Elizabeth as his monarch. Now, with this second plot in Mary's name causing so much antagonism towards Catholics, and the earlier warning from Kat, Richard finally understood that even though they were far away from Westminster Palace or Whitehall, they were no longer safe from the animosity towards anything involving the Catholic Spanish King or the Pope.

Pacing the room, being watched by his adoring deerhound, Jassy, Richard pondered further. He knew precious little more about Brother Matthew than he did on the day the monk arrived. You just could not get close to the man! Just recently, Richard had re-issued the invitation to live within the grounds of the manor after Anthony Babington and his fellow conspirators had been caught and imprisoned. Richard had not really expected reprisals then...nor had he since...although he recalled explaining that there may be some...unpleasantness, yes, that was the word he had used to Brother Matthew, but the obstinate monk still chose to stay outside of the protection of the manor. Now Richard realised he should have insisted Brother Matthew stay within the manor, but had given the monk his way. Now he wished dearly he had forced the issue and had him brought within the manor. It would have meant one less thing...person...to worry about.

But what could he do now for the monk? It was his duty to defend the residents of the manor. The servants, most of them having been with the family for years were in need of his protection. And, indeed, the manor itself would need to be defended. It had been the family home through the last two centuries and it now fell to him, as protector, to ensure it remained intact for the generations to come.

Elizabeth and the children would be safely away soon, but there was John and, if he returned in time, James, to protect. He came to the conclusion he could not ask anyone to put themselves at risk by leaving the safety of the manor walls, to help someone who had been so unconcerned for his own safety. Momentarily he wondered if he should go, but that would be abandoning - albeit temporarily - everyone in the manor.

While contemplating what his next actions should be, Richard became aware of the sounds of activity from the floor below; running footsteps, shouts and the clattering of metal; that would be the swords, arrowheads, muskets and the crossbows all being retrieved from the armoury. Then there were footsteps running up the stairs fast approaching his door. Harris, very out of breath, appeared in the doorway.

'Forgive me not knocking my lord, but Lady Winterne and the children are ready to leave. She has taken the children and Miss Morland to the courtyard door and asks if you would come down to bid them farewell.'

All thoughts of Brother Matthew at once forgotten, Richard nodded. 'Yes, of course I will,' said Richard, quickly heading towards the door. As he and Harris walked down the stairs together, he asked: 'How are the children, Harris? Are they frightened?'

'They are quiet, my lord. Quieter than normal I would say, but there are no real signs to indicate they are afraid, and I believe that Lady Winterne has told them this is a surprise visit to their grandfather's house.'

Richard smiled. 'And all the disturbance hasn't upset them?'

'Again, it seems that Lady Winterne has simply told them that this is nothing more than another of the defence practice drills we carry out from time to time, and it appears they are unaware of any real danger.'

Richard smiled. 'That is what I would expect of her, Harris. My wife is always at her best when times are difficult. She is far stronger than she looks.'

At the door, Richard slipped his cloak around his shoulders, put on a smile and went out to see his waiting family. Seven-year-old Edward, with the same shade of green eyes and red hair, a smaller version of his father, ran over excitedly and grasped Richard's hand as they walked back to where Elizabeth and five-year-old Catherine were waiting. Elizabeth's mouth showed a cheery smile that was not mirrored in her eyes; her firmly set jaw betrayed her tension, but only Richard noticed. Her light-hearted smile and excited manner hid it from their children.

'Father, we are going to see Grandfather,' said Catherine, happily.

'I know, my dear.' Richard hunkered down to look at Catherine face to face. 'Are you looking forward to see him?'

'Yes, but I am not looking forward to the journey.'

'Why ever not?'

'Because the carriage shakes and its bumpy riding in it and I always get bruises.'

Richard laughed. 'Then it's a good thing the journey is not too long, but I'm sure your mother will take care of those bruises once you arrive.'

Catherine pouted. 'Yes, I know, but I'd rather not have them at all.' She turned to Elizabeth who, amused by their daughter's complaints, seemed a little more relaxed. 'Mother, could I not fold my cloak and sit on it, then maybe I wouldn't get bruises?'

'Yes, Catherine. Of course you can. You sit on your cloak and I'll keep you warm by wrapping mine around you.'

'But what about me?' grumbled Edward, not wanting to be left out. 'I get bruises too, you know.'

Richard stood up and ruffled his son's hair. 'I'm sure your mother's cloak has room for you both to...'

'Father,' interrupted Edward, earning him a swift cuff around the hear from Miss Morland.

'Edward Maitland! You may be a viscount but you know it is very rude to interrupt your father when he is speaking. Those are not the manners I taught you.'

'Ow!' Edward rubbed his ear and glared at his governess. 'I'll wager that's another bruise,' he whined.

'Yes, you're quite right, Miss Morland,' said the Earl, ruffling his son's hair, 'and any other time I would agree with you but, the children are going away for a while and they are quite justifiably excited, so I think we can excuse Edward, just this once.'

'I'm sorry, my lord, I was only doing what I thought was right,' said Miss Morland, clearly vexed at the Earl's lack of discipline, but not in a position to contradict him.

'But Miss Morland is correct, Edward, you should not interrupt when an adult is talking and...' he wagged his finger at his sulking son, 'and we'll have no more talking of wagering, if you please.'

Edward looked up at Miss Morland rebelliously but did not apologise.

'But, come, you must be off. What was it you wanted, Edward?'

'Father, why is there so much noise in the house and so much rushing around?'

Knowing Harris assumed the children would think it a training exercise but wanting something more exciting, unusual, Richard had to think quickly. 'Here, come walk with me a moment.' Richard led his son a short distance from where his wife and daughter waited patiently. 'Can you keep a secret, Edward?'

'Oh, indeed I can, Father.' Edward leaned closer and Richard put his arm around his son's shoulder drawing him closer.

'Your mother's brother, Uncle Charles, has sent a message to say he is visiting us in a few days, and we are preparing for his visit.'

'But why is this a secret when mother can see what is happening in the house?'

'But you know how much your sister loves Uncle Charles, don't you?'

'Yes, but...'

'The secret is not being kept from your mother, it's being kept from Catherine. When Uncle Charles arrives it will be a wonderful surprise for her.'

One of the horses in the carriage traces snorted impatiently. Another stamped a hoof.

'Oh. I see...no I don't. If Uncle Charles is coming, why we are going to Grandfather's for a few days?'

'Ah, well you see, Uncle Charles is bringing a number of people with him, and that means we have to make rooms available for them and we do not have a lot of time, which is why preparations have already begun.' Richard stood up and gently guided Edward back to where Elizabeth and Catherine waited. 'So you understand now, Edward, that I am trusting you to keep the secret from your sister and, judging by how our horses are behaving, they are ready to be off.'

'Yes, Father. I understand.' Edward felt very honoured that his father had shared this confidence and, with his head high he almost strutted to the carriage.

Once the door of the carriage closed behind Edward, two housecarls slipped from the shadows and carefully climbed onto the foot board at the back, and gripped the handles tightly.

As the carriage pulled out of the courtyard, Richard's heart skipped a beat. Would he ever see his wife and children again?

Walking back into the house, his feet seemed to have a mind of their own and he found himself standing on the half-landing of the main staircase, staring up at the stained glass window depicting the maiden and the unicorn. It was a beautiful piece of art but, it was more than that. Lady Catherine had been there watching over the family all his life; she was a constant reminder of the durability of the Maitlands.

'My lady, I beseech you to pray for us this night. Send us your blessing, and your protection. If I am to die, please care for my family.'

Chapter Twenty Seven

One and a half miles away, at Squire Attwood's rambling thatched and honey-coloured Ham Stone house, nineteen-year-old James had just said goodbye to his betrothed, Squire Parker's daughter, Alice. The final plans for their wedding had been made, the musicians and food arranged, invitations sent to the main guests and the villagers of Winterne and the surrounding area had been invited to join in the festivities. The happy couple would celebrate with them for an hour or so at a hog-roast enjoying free ale, cider and mead and dancing on the green outside the church. All was prepared for the wedding in a few weeks.

As Alice blew a kiss, James mounted his favourite palfrey, Wessex. Showing off his horsemanship, James turned Wessex, doffed his feathered, green velvet hat, and headed up the lane towards home. The sun was setting, and James' stomach rumbled with hunger. He had been invited to stay for supper with Alice's family but politely refused, saying that Richard and Elizabeth were expecting him to sup with them, but that he would return tomorrow and, if the invitation was still open, he would be delighted to stay for supper then.

The way home took James through Winterne Woods and he would pass close by Brother Matthew's hut. James hoped that Brother Matthew would be inside having his own supper and would not see him go by. He had no real liking for the monk, and the least amount of time he had to spend with him, the better. But, as the sun was setting behind the Mendip Hills, it was not just the thought of seeing the monk that made James shudder. There was a strange atmosphere about the woods on this late afternoon that made the hair on his neck stand up.

Wessex shook his head and snorted, usually a sign he was tense or worried; so he too felt something was not right. James tried to urge him on, but Wessex reared, almost throwing James off his back. Only his riding skill kept James in his saddle, but the sooner they reached the manor, the happier they would both be.

And it was so quiet. Any other day the birds, especially the crows, would be heard cawing to each other as they headed for their nests high in the trees; tonight all was silent, it was unnerving.

James tried to convince himself he was imagining things, but then Wessex snorted and whinnied again, and all hope of trying to be sensible vanished with the sound. Winterne Woods was known for having a rather disturbing atmosphere at times, but there was never anything found that could possibly have caused the unease it created. Most local people avoided the woods during the darker hours, but those brave enough to risk a bit of poaching – for rabbits, partridges or even salmon from the River Axe that flowed through the far end of the woods – would tell themselves that it was only those who were superstitious who would believe in such nonsense; but some poachers vowed never to go back.

Wessex made a snickering sound and shook his head, clearly disturbed by something and a moment later, James heard it too. Coming from the village side of the woods, the sound of twigs being snapped underfoot, and James heard whispered voices. So that was what had made Wessex nervous! At least it was something normal and not ghostlike; as long as James could rationalise it, he wouldn't worry overmuch, but it sounded as though there were quite a lot of them heading his way and that was puzzling. Were they heading towards the manor? If so, then why?

Dismounting, he walked Wessex nearer to the sound, but stayed within the refuge of the trees. Until he knew more about this group, he did not want to be seen. Furtive figures, James estimated more than thirty of them were heading as silently as they could through the woods. There were far too many of them to be poachers, and if their gathering was innocent, why were they trying to be quiet. There was no-one to hear them except… James felt a chill run through his body as he realised that the only person who lived nearby was Brother Matthew. He knew a little about the Babington Plot and that Mary Stuart had been executed, but even with the limited interest he had taken in it all, he knew this was not a good time to be a Catholic and monks, in particular, were at risk. He had to get closer.

Tying Wessex to a nearby branch, James crept nearer to the approaching horde and was horrified to see they were carrying cudgels, hammers and halberds. Amongst them, to his surprise, he recognised Tom Cooper, normally a peaceable man, not given to violence at all; this was a different Tom to the man James knew. Then he saw William Hunter. That definitely meant trouble.

As if to confirm their purpose, James heard William say, 'Another few minutes and we'll 'ave 'im. Time'll come when there'll be no more o' them black 'n' brown robed monks 'n' good riddance, I say.'

James had heard all he needed to. He might not like Brother Matthew himself, but he would not wish any harm to befall him. Staying low, he headed back to where Wessex was waiting silently for him, mounted and walked him as quietly as he could away from their hiding place. He had to get Brother Matthew away to the safety of the manor.

But, when he arrived and explained to Brother Matthew what was about to happen, the monk stubbornly refused to be rescued, and James lost patience with him.

'Are you telling me that these villagers, who I have known for many years, would harm me? I don't believe it!'

'Indeed, Brother Matthew, I fear that if you don't come with me your very life may be in danger. What I overheard certainly gave me the impression that these men were not on their way to *talk* to you!'

'And anyway, why are you in the woods this late, surely you should be at supper with Earl Richard?'

James groaned. 'We are running out of time, Brother. Just *please* gather a few of your belongings that you cannot do without and let's go. They will be here soon!'

'Just answer my question!'

Frustrated with the waste of precious time, James said: 'I had just been to Alice's home...'

'...Aah, so that's it. Rescue the monk and be the hero of the hour!'

'Ooh...for pity's sake, Brother. This is nonsense. I am trying to save your life and...'

It was at that point they heard voices, a little louder now, and from somewhere far off James heard the sound of hounds barking and baying.

Brother Matthew heard it too and looked at James. The realisation that James was telling the truth shook him to the core. He grabbed his Bible and red silk ceremonial stole and rushed out of the hut before James.

'And I suppose you expect me to ride that?' said Brother Matthew pointing at Wessex.

James had not thought beyond getting Brother Matthew out of his hut and on the way to the manor, but now he realised that with the monk being as large as he was, Wessex would not be able to carry them both. If he let Wessex free, he knew he would run home to his stable.

'No. That is not going to be possible, we will have to move quickly...on foot.' He loosened Wessex's reins and folded them back across his neck to ensure they did not get caught on anything, then gave the horse a light slap on the rump prompting him to run on.

'Now, we move, Brother Matthew, before it's too late.'

James had had no thought of being a hero until Brother Matthew mentioned it but, with youthful exuberance he suddenly realised that that was exactly what he would be if he managed to get the monk to safety. It would be an adventure, he could be courageous and daring in saving the life of the family's confessor. He saw himself as the dashing hero, but he had no idea of what lay before them.

Behind, they could hear the mob coming closer and moving the slow, overweight monk along was a nightmare. It was not until James heard the thunder of hooves nearby that he looked around to see a herd of terrified deer fleeing from the noise and flames. Flames!

The flickering orange and red glow and the shouts from the horde, was evidence enough that Brother Matthew's single-roomed thatched hut was now ablaze. They had escaped with minutes to spare, but the mob would know the monk was no longer there and would soon begin looking for him.

Crows flew from their treetop nests, cawing loudly and it seemed that all the woodland wildlife that could not find a safe refuge in tunnels, was running away in fear of their lives.

'Brother Matthew, your home is destroyed. Do you not now see the urgency? Please hurry,' begged a terrified James.

Their pursuers would be on the move again very soon, following the dogs who, hopefully they would keep restrained. If they set the dogs free to run, with the monk being so slow, the gap between them and the pack would close quickly. James calculated, if the men kept the dogs with them, they still had a good ten minutes head start which would give him enough time to get Brother Matthew to the safety of the tunnel, if he would just make haste!

Half dragging, half pulling the monk whose life he was trying to save, James struggled to rush him along. But not being used to moving at any pace faster than a relaxed walk for years, and being far too fond of food and wine, Brother Matthew, panted, huffed and moaned incessantly as he tripped, stumbled over his long brown robe, and skinned his toes as his open rope sandals snagged on any bump, or upraised tree root on the uneven woodland floor.

It was now fully dark but, as the full moon emerged from behind a lonely purple cloud, James could see they were almost at the tunnel, the ivy-covered hill was in sight. Not much further to go. Brother Matthew suddenly doubled-up and clutched his right side.

'I have to stop. Please let me stop. I have a pain in my side. It's...it's agonising. I cannot go on! Please James, thank you for what you are trying to do...but let me stop,' he panted. 'Leave me here,' he begged and flopped onto a fallen tree trunk.

'I cannot,' James shook his head. 'If I leave you here, you *will* die, and I cannot live with that on my conscience.' He tried to lift the monk, but his weight made it impossible. 'Take two minutes to get your breath and then we must go on. It is not far now. We are almost at the door. Once inside, we will be safe. I will not leave you here.' He could smell the smoke from the blazing hut and wondered how much of the woodland would burn that night.

Brother Matthew looked up at his young rescuer, sweat gathering in beads on his temples and bald pate. 'You always were a good boy, James, but I am old, and my time is almost done.' The sweat began to trickle down the side of his face. 'You must leave me here. I cannot go on. If you stay with me, I will slow you down, your life may be forfeit and God will not allow them to mistreat a monk. I will be safe.' Without thinking what he was doing Brother Matthew used the silk stole to wipe the perspiration away from his eyes.

The baying hounds were closer now. James could just make out the dark shapes of the men and the light of the fiery torches through the smoke as it wafted towards them between the trees. They were *too* close!

'That may well have been true when we had one religion to follow, Brother Matthew, but now we have two, and followers of each believe God is on their side. These men are *not* on your side and will not listen to you.'

James hauled the exhausted monk to his feet, took his arm and placed it around his shoulder. 'Lean on me, Brother Matthew. We have about two minutes before we reach the tunnel and I know I can get you there in time. Come,' James urged. 'You *can* go on and by my oath you will not die here. I will get you to safety, whatever it takes.'

Chapter Twenty Eight

Downstairs in the manor, panicked servants rushed about carrying out the tasks assigned to them. John, having had a fascination with weaponry since he was eight-years old, had become skilled in the use of muskets and matchlock pistols. Having also been well trained in the care of them, he examined each one of the firearms set out on the great table in the hall closely. Satisfied which were in working order and clean inside, he loaded each one with black gunpowder, a wad of paper and a small metal ball.

At the other end of the table, two of the ten housecarls – trained fighting men employed by Richard for protection of the family – were testing the blades of daggers and swords to see if they needed sharpening. If they cut their thumbs, they were sharp enough!

Harris entered the room barking orders to the two accompanying footmen. 'Open those windows, close the outside wooden shutters and bolt them, then make sure the windows are secured again. When you have finished in here, go to all the other rooms and do the same.'

He approached John and looked at the weaponry being stacked on the table. 'I'll send someone to the upstairs storeroom, Master John. I believe there are some more crossbows left there by your father. I don't know how many bolts there might be though.'

'No matter. It only takes one bolt to stop a man,' John answered, gravely. Harris looked at what had been a cheeky and untroubled boy just a short while ago, but, within the last hour, he had grown into a responsible young man. 'And one less raider is good for us,' John continued, 'but anything we can lay our hands on is welcome. Some of these pistols have been neglected and are useless but, if the mob is not too large, we may have enough to hold the manor, and I doubt the mob has much more than sticks and cudgels.'

Harris doubted that. These were workmen and farm labourers who would be likely to have more dangerous weapons axes, knives, rakes, scythes; sticks and cudgels alone was more than the defenders of the manor could hope for.

'Master John, sir.' Robert Hallett, one of the housecarls, walked along the side of the table to stand in front of John and Harris. 'We are reduced to six men with four having just left to guard Lady Winterne and the children...'

'Is there a problem, Hallett?' Richard appeared in the doorway.

'Ah, my lord, I was just wondering how you wanted to distribute us around the house. With just six of us here, I was going to suggest maybe Robinson and Digby should be stationed on the roof. They are skilled archers and, like all good bowmen have made ready a good stock of arrows when they have not been on duty. Between them they could do a great deal of damage to any mob from up there.'

'I think that would be wise, Hallett,' said Richard. 'The Yeo brothers are at their positions on the first floor, already on watch for the mob. They are prepared with bows and bags of arrows and, once we have finished inspecting the weapons, John will take them muskets and ammunition.' He forced a tight smile. 'Having reinforcements on the roof is a good idea.'

'Now, John,' he turned to his youngest brother. At just fourteen years old, this would be the first time John was to experience violence. Richard had considered making him leave with the Countess but knew John would feel humiliated at being sent away with the women and children. 'You heard that, I take it.'

John nodded.

'What is the situation here?' He pointed to three muskets at the far end of the table. 'Are these of use?'

'No. This one has a split muzzle, this has no trigger pin,' he lifted the last one, 'and this...take a look at the firing mechanism.' He handed it to Richard who slid back the breech. 'I don't think this one has been used in years, it's so badly blocked, but no worry, the others all seem to be in good working order.'

Richard walked to the other end of the table, picked up a pistol from the stack, opened the breech, checked the movement of the trigger and ran a ramrod through the barrel. Satisfied, he turned to John. 'If you have done as good a job on the others as you have on this one, we will be well armed. What have we in the way of ammunition?'

John took his brother to the other side of the table where wooden crates of pistol shot and musket balls had been prepared. 'Each person with either weapon can supply themselves with ammunition.'

Beside the crates were bags of primer powder, ramrods and soft cleaning cloths. 'We also have crossbows and bolts, and there...' John pointed to a dark corner of the room, '...we have halberds, swords and daggers, enough for a small army I would have thought and each person with a pistol or musket will have at least one of these.'

Richard nodded. They *were* going to need a small army. He remembered something he had meant to take care of and looked around for his steward. 'Harris, how many children of the staff, under the age of twelve years do we in the household?'

'Eight or nine, my lord.'

'Eight or nine, eh?' Richard looked thoughtfully at John, then back to Harris. 'Have the new footman...what's his name, Simkins, is it?'

'Simson, my lord,' Harris corrected.

'Right, Yes, Simson. Well, have him round up the young ones. He's to take them to Doctor Browne. Tell him to inform the good doctor that I sent them, and he is to look after them for tonight. I do not want them here when trouble strikes. All being well, I will send for them tomorrow. Then Simson is to return here with all haste.'

Harris nodded. 'Yes, my lord. We will have the children away shortly.' He left the room.

Walking quickly from room to room, Richard became more confident that all he had ordered had been accomplished.

In the kitchen, the servants stood nervously quiet but appeared to be ready for whatever was coming. Two footmen stood by the door that led to the garden, one had a hammer, the other held a meat cleaver and a heavy poker. The two young scullery maids sat on wooden stools, huddled in a corner of the room, both deathly white with terror. Richard was surprised to see Kat perched on the edge of a stool staring into the fire. He thought she had already gone home to her family. She did not look up but clasped her trembling hands together to keep them still.

The cook, a sharpened butcher's knife in one hand and a heavy metal soup ladle in the other, edged up to him and whispered that Kat had refused to leave. His heart went out to the brave little maid. She had chosen to stay with them, even though she knew she would pay for it with her life if the mob ever discovered she had given the warning.

Harris was there, tight-lipped and tense as he gripped his six-foot quarterstaff in his right hand so tightly his knuckles were white. They all looked to Richard, silently.

'Have the household children left yet?' he asked Harris.

Harris nodded. 'Yes, my Lord. Simson gathered them together and they slipped out of the back garden gate a few minutes ago...ahem...my lord, I have also taken the liberty of sending Mistress Harper and the house-maids to Minister Haywood at St Benedict's Church.'

'Good. That's good. Thank...' His brow creased. 'Was the gate locked after they left?'

'Yes, my lord. I locked it and I have brought the key back.' He pointed to a wooden board hanging on the wall by the back door with bunches of keys in various sizes handing on hooks. 'I will keep a watch for Simson returning and let him in if it is safe to do so. However, if the mob are too close he has my instruction to hide until it is safe to return.'

'Yes, I understand, Harris. That was well thought out. We would not want them to burst through while the gate is opened for Simson, nor would it be safe for him to be seen.'

Richard's frown eased. Through the open door he saw the two housecarls, Digby and Robinson, taking another full bag of arrows up the small staircase heading to the first floor for the Yeo brothers, and return for a second trip to take their own weapons to the roof.

'Whatever happens in these next hours, I want to thank you for your loyalty,' he told those gathered around him. 'And if you need me at all, you will find me in the great hall.' He gave a warm smile, hoping it would hearten these supportive and loyal members of his household. His smile slipped as he turned away to wait in the hall.

'God bless you, my lord,' Cook called after him. Richard turned back to give her a warm smile, 'And God bless you all,' he replied.

Richard looked at the candle clock on the hall table. Almost an hour had passed since Kat had burst into their chamber. At least Elizabeth and the children would be safe. He took a deep breath. Had he done enough to protect everyone in his care? A horrible thought occurred to him and he ran back to the kitchen.

'Nell!' The cook had her arms around one of the scullery maids who was sobbing and trembling with fear. 'Yes, my lord?' She was taken aback that he knew her name. In all the time she had been employed at Winterne Manor, the family had only ever called her, 'Cook' which was customary in big houses such as this.

'Sorry, Nell, but you'll have to put that fire out. We can't give the mob anything to set light to the house with.'

'My lord,' Harris had followed Richard and overheard the conversation. 'The mob is approaching, and Digby has just informed me they have torches. They are bringing fire with them.'

'Then we need buckets of water ready. Quickly Nell, smother that fire! He pointed to their own large and welcoming hearth. 'Harris, have some of the men fill as many buckets as they can find and set them in the hall. We can douse the torches if they get through the door.'

Outside, they could hear the sound of the mob who were approaching faster than Richard had expected. Harris came to stand beside his lord, John ran by, gave a reassuring smile to Richard, before darting up the stairs. Hallett and Jones, satisfied with their own checks on the weaponry, joined Richard and Harris in the main hall ready to defend the main door. Each man had now strapped sheathed swords and daggers to their belts. Approaching footsteps echoed on the flagstone floor and Richard reached out a hand to welcome Nell who had come to join them in silent understanding that, when the mob attacked, the main door would be their target and they would be the first in the line of battle.

A stillness fell inside the manor. Standing within an arm's length of each other, the Earl and his small band could barely see each other in the gloom. A pale light cast from a few lamps still burning in the enclosed courtyard glowed through the hall windows, and the narrow bands of flickering moonlight glimpsed through thin gaps in the shutters, were all the light they had.

Each person, occupied with their own thoughts, waited for the onslaught to begin. Richard thought he should pray but could not think of anything suitable, words muddled in his mind. Whatever happened would not be arranged by God. It was up to them to defend themselves and the manor. He was afraid, but as Lord of the Manor, he could not show his fear. His staff were looking to him to lead them. If he showed a lack of courage it would take the heart out of them. It was at that moment John rushed into the hall and came to stand beside his brother. 'I wanted to be beside you.'

'But what...?'

'Never fear, Richard, I have checked the upper floors. The Yeo brothers are in place on the first floor, Digby and Robinson are on the roof and all is prepared. I just wish James had managed to get here.'

'Thank you, John. You have grown into a man today and I am proud to have you with me...although I would rather you weren't here. I am sorry not to have sent you with Elizabeth and the children and, if God is with us, James will be safe elsewhere.'

In the poor light filtering through the gaps in the window shutters, Richard saw his young brother shudder. 'I would not have wanted to leave you. With James not being here you would have been alone...and...and that would have been wrong.'

John thought that, knowing James, if he had known what was happening, he would have done everything he could to have been with them at that moment to defend their home. He would not have run away, but he stayed silent. Richard had enough to concern him.

'Hmm. James should have been here by now,' Richard agreed, gravely. 'I can only hope he...'

His comment was interrupted by a roar from the mob. It sounded as though they were cheering something. Richard's blood ran cold as a terrible thought occurred to him. Could that be something to do with James? He clenched his fists around the hilt of his sword with his right hand and his dagger in the left.

Harris had obviously had the same awful thought. 'I am certain Master James will be safe, my lord.' He tried to sound reassuring but, he too, was becoming anxious about the young master.

Chapter Twenty Nine

The moment they reached the hills that formed the backdrop to the woodland behind the manor, James heaved a sigh of relief as he gave the complaining monk a final tug to where a widespread veil of ivy hung down from a ledge above. Brother Matthew, gasping for every breath and bent double, was astounded to see James disappear under the heavy swathe of intertwined creeping tendrils and foliage. In the distance, the shouts of the men and the excited howls of the pack grew louder.

'For pity's sake..., James...,' Brother Matthew managed to mumble. 'They're almost at us, boy. What...?'

James reappeared, held the ivy curtain to one side and with an exaggerated bow invited Brother Matthew into a darkened opening in the hillside.

Brother Matthew, clearly still suffering with the pain in his side, struggled to get his breathing controlled, said: 'James, its...a...a tunnel inside the hill, but...how...when?' The look of bewilderment on his face made James laugh. 'My word,' said Brother Matthew. 'The Lord does work in mysterious ways, doesn't he?'

'I don't believe the Lord actually had anything to do with creating this tunnel, Brother Matthew.'

'Do not blaspheme, James!'

James pointed to a hidden lever high up near the right hand side of the door lintel that only those who knew about it would find, it was so well concealed. 'Since I discovered this tunnel, I have kept the lever and door hinges oiled. They were quite stiff to begin with. But please do not dawdle, we must get inside and close the door. The ivy seems to fall back into place as soon as the door is shut.' The hounds were so close now. James was thankful the men had kept them on leashes instead of letting them loose or he and Brother Matthew would have been caught some time ago. 'Now, quickly, get inside and I can close the door behind us.'

Brother Matthew did not need to be told again and, moving more quickly than James would have expected, he darted through the doorway. James followed, took a last look outside and, satisfied they were now safe from the mob who were too far away to see them through the drifting smoke, closed the door.

Inside a dim light glowed and the smell of damp earth reached their nostrils. For a moment Brother Matthew said nothing, shocked into silence by the sheer size and sturdy construction of the tunnel. He had walked through the woods for years, and had passed by these crags sometimes several times a day, never knowing this tunnel existed.

Strewn along the length of the tunnel and whatever was beyond, were a number of large boulder-like stones, some cut into cube shapes, clearly left over by whoever carried out the construction work. With a floor of compressed earth and half-buried old wooden slats, and the cobwebbed ceiling supported by timbers and tree-roots, the tunnel was wide enough for three men to walk side by side and high enough for anyone of average height to walk without stooping, and that certainly applied to Brother Matthew and James.

Brother Matthew looked down the tunnel, perplexed. 'There's air getting in here. I can feel a very slight draft, but I thought the air would be still and stale.'

James did not answer. He was standing at a set of wooden ledges concealed behind the door. On the lower shelf stood the lit oil lamp casting a dim light that allowed them to see for a few yards ahead.

On the upper shelf, Brother Matthew noticed two more oil lamps and a supply of long wax tapers on the shelf above. Reaching for one of the tapers, James held it to the flame until it caught light, then he lit the wicks in the other two lamps.

Brother Matthew gazed around in stunned silence until James offered him one of the lamps. 'When...how did...this?' His expression a muddle of excitement and curiosity. 'And where does it lead? Does the Earl know about it...and what is the reason you need to use such a secretive method of leaving and entering the manor?'

'We need to hurry but I will answer your questions as we go along. Come, Brother Matthew. The tunnel leads to my bed chamber, I found it by accident a few weeks ago when I was considering my future with Alice, and whether we would be content. I was standing in front of the fire, warming my hands, and vaguely staring at the mantle when I noticed, for the first time, how ornately the decorative ivy had been carved. I ran my hand across it and was astounded to hear a click, but even more astounded when a panel beside the hearth swung open. I took a lamp and went to investigate. And, no, Richard does not know about it...' Hearing the distant barking of excited dogs, he turned back to look at the door. 'No, he does not know yet but I suspect he will very soon.'

Muffled sounds from beyond the door reached their ears. The dogs were closer and the sound of the approaching ale and cider-fuelled pack of armed men was frightening, even though James and Brother Matthew felt they were now safe.

'We must go.' James took the monk by the elbow and urged him along at a more brisk pace along the tunnel.

'How...long is this tunnel?' Brother Matthew puffed. James was looking forward to getting to the end of his rescue attempt, but not looking forward to having to explain the tunnel and why he had been using it to Richard. That would be another matter entirely; but saving the life of the family monk was more important than whatever reprimand he would receive from his very honest and principled brother. It had not occurred to James yet that the family might be overwhelmed by the mob. They had the housecarls, the armoury, the gate in the surrounding walls should have been locked by now, so the household should be well protected behind the manor walls, and the kitchen stores were always well stocked. They could survive a siege for at least a week.

With his hand now on Brother Matthew's shoulder, James pushed the monk along. 'You asked how long this marvellous feat of engineering is. Well, it goes under the hillside, the rear courtyard, then into the manor. I have not taken measurements, but my estimate is a good half mile...maybe more.'

'Very well, we may have some way to go yet then, but go on, James,' urged Brother Matthew. 'What did you find then?' It was clear he was trying to keep his mind focused on something other than the danger he felt they might still be in.

James explained as they headed along the passageway, turning corners, brushing aside dust and cobwebs and earth-clogged tree roots that hung down from the ceiling, while weaving their way around the blocks of remaining unused building stones. 'From my bedchamber, a corridor leads to a wooden staircase and at the bottom, judging by the sounds and the warmth of one of the walls, the passageway skirted the kitchen close to the fireplace, and thence to a rough stone spiral staircase. After that there's another short tunnel to a wooden door that took me through to a large circular room that I can only assume was once used as a storeroom. Here, watch your step, Brother Matthew, the floor drops down suddenly.' He stepped ahead of the monk and lifted the lamp a little higher to indicated where the floor dipped.

'At the far end of the room I found another door that led me through to a wide, short corridor with a heavy wooden door, which we will soon be approaching. There was a large and heavy iron key in the lock. I tried it, it turned easily, and I found myself within this passageway. I found another key for that door so whenever I go in or out, I always leave the keys on the lintel above the door, so there is always one on either side. I am sure we are safe in here but to be sure, when we are through the door, I will lock it behind us and take the key through to the other side.'

'But how did you discover the opening mechanism when it's so well concealed?'

'Well, that was relatively easy. You see, from inside the tunnel, the device is easily found. It is only concealed from the outside. The other mechanism that opens the door to get back into my bedchamber, is a large wooden ivy leaf on the right hand side of the door. It just needs to be pressed.'

'God works in mysterious ways,' said the monk.

'You'll pardon me, Brother Matthew, I do not wish to deny God his rightful obeisance, but I do not believe He actually had any hand in the construction of this secret passageway. Although it is helping us now...Shhh!' They both stopped moving to listen as the noise of the mob was more clearly heard from beyond the tunnel entrance; they were very close now.

'Can we return to the questions I asked you earlier?' Brother Matthew clearly wanted to keep talking even though the effort of walking fast and talking at the same time was making him short of breath. 'Why? Do you use this method of leaving and entering the manor so often?'

James hesitated before speaking. 'I think this can wait until we are safely inside, Brother Matthew.' He seemed very reluctant to say any more, but the monk would not let the matter drop.

'There is something you are hiding from me, James, and I will go no further until you tell me the truth. Why do you have the need to steal out of the manor without anyone knowing so often that you keep a light burning in here?'

'I go to see a...friend, that's the truth of it.'

'But why in secret? Is it someone the Earl would rather you didn't see? A Protestant, perhaps?'

'Yes, no...but she...he. Oh it's no use.' James looked into the monk's eyes and said: 'Brother Matthew, you can hear my full confession any time but when I can, I slip out at night to see Audrey...

'Do you mean that young woman whose father owns the tavern! But you are betrothed, James! How could you go against your vows?'

'We can discuss this later Brother Matthew, but for now we need to get inside. And, no Richard does not know about the tunnel, and I am sure you will understand why, now that you have heard my guilty secret.'

'Yes, you're right,' said the monk. 'The dogs are quite close now.'

But they had only gone a few steps along when Brother Matthew said: 'The dogs! Surely they will pick up our scent and will find the door.'

'Don't worry, the lever is too well concealed for the mob to find it. They may find the door, but they'll never get in.' James prayed he was right.

'I do hope you're right.'

For the next few moments they walked together in unfriendly silence. The monk was clearly upset that James was involved in a clandestine romance. While James had so many conflicting thoughts running around his head: how would Richard react when he found out the truth? Did he, James, really want to go through with his marriage to Alice? She was pleasant enough, he liked her, and he understood the reality of marrying for business reasons...but, he thought he was in love with Audrey. And, of course, now there was the fear of the mob and could he get them both to safety?

A loud cracking sound from behind startled them both, followed by a loud shout of triumph that echoed along the tunnel.

'What in God's name was that?' Brother Matthew's eyes were wide with fear. James felt bile rise up into his throat. He unsheathed his sword.

'I am going back to take a look, but you continue without me. Just follow the directions I gave you and do not forget, the key is above the door, whatever happens, *do not stop.*'

'But...what about you, James?'

'Just go! Go now. I will join you as soon as I can, but I fear somehow they have found their way into the tunnel.'

Brother Matthew made the sign of the cross in a blessing as James headed back the way they had come, then he turned away and hurried towards the first door.

The sight that greeted James as he turned the corner made his blood run cold. Several men, some he knew well and had grown up with, were standing at the entrance to the tunnel.

Chapter Thirty

Holding the hem of his robe off the floor with his left hand and the oil lamp in the right, Brother Matthew stumbled over rocks and the uneven earth floor, as quickly as his bulk and aching feet would allow him, towards the door. As he finally saw the door, behind him he could hear angry voices. He called on God to protect James as his trembling fingers felt for the key above the door. He found it. With a shaking hand he pushed the door open and lurched through to the other side, swung the heavy door closed and, praying God would forgive him, he locked it again. In his terror, he had abandoned young James Maitland, his rescuer, to his fate.

-oOo-

'If yer din't wan' us ter find yer, yer should 'ave made sure the door were closed prop'ly, Master James. Once the dogs picked up yer scent an' brough' us yer, 'twas easy ter ge' in.' For all his bluster, Tom Cooper was unsure of what to do next. Although they wanted the monk, in his way stood young Master James. It seemed like only yesterday, he had played on the green with Tom's children and other youngsters in the village. James was well-loved by most people locally, and they were looking forward to his wedding. Now here he stood, alone, blocking their way.

'Wha' yer waitin' fer, Tom?' said William, as other members of the mob entered the tunnel to join them.

'Yer goin' ter 'ave ter let us by, Master James,' said Tom brushing aside a dangling tree root, he stepped closer to James. 'Come on now, me lad. You know me. I don' wanna cause yer no 'arm but yer goin' ter let us 'ave that' monk.'

'You know I cannot do that, Tom.' In the lamplight, James' face was ashen. His hand trembled as he slowly unsheathed his sword.

'Jest get 'im,' urged William, as more men pushed and shoved their way into the increasingly narrow space in the tunnel entrance.

James braced himself for the coming onslaught, took a deep breath, send a silent prayer to God and moved towards Tom and his accomplices. Tom hesitated just a little too long and William pushed him aside, followed by several more men who were not prepared to wait, regardless of who they faced. He was just one man, and a young and an inexperienced one at that. They could take him easily.

They rushed at James.

'*Nooo!*' screamed Tom. This had gone beyond anything he had intended. The monk was one thing, but hurting the Maitland family, who had been good local benefactors and employers, regardless of their religion, was quite another.

'Oi'd stay quiet if Oi was you, Tom,' William snarled, a crazed look in his eyes. 'If yer can't tek it, then per'aps ye'd better go 'ome. Leave this to us *men* an' the others tha' 'ave gone ter the fron o' the manor.' He turned to glare at James. 'Young Master Maitland 'ere'll be no problem ter the likes of us.'

Defeated and ashamed at having played any part in this madness, Tom felt bile rise into his throat as he realised it had all gone way beyond his control. William had arranged a second group to attack the manor that he had not known about. He was helpless to help James or the family. As he backed away through the crush of men trying to get into the tunnel he closed his eyes as they rushed at James. There was nothing he could do.

Just before he exited the tunnel, Tom turned to see William and three other men moving towards a terrified, but courageous James who stood his ground, sword ready. As Tom ran out into the darkness he heard cries followed by a heart-stopping scream. James may have taken one or two with him but he never really stood a chance. Alone, and at the edge of the trees, Tom fell to his knees, doubled up and retched.

-oOo-

Taking a moment to catch his breath and his heartbeat to slow, Brother Matthew leaned against the door. For a moment guilt overwhelmed him and he considered opening the door but then he heard the scream and made the sign of the Cross. 'May God bless his soul.' To die unshriven, without having prayers for the dying said, and without confession to receive God's Grace, was indeed a terrible death, according to Brother Matthew. There was no thought of James being so young, for his courage, or for the future that was now denied him. The monk only thought of the teachings of his Holy Order...and of his own safety. Soon the mob would be after him. It would not take them long to batter down the door.

Across the room was the door James had told him led to the staircase that would take him to the corridor past the kitchen and eventually up to the first floor. Once through that door, perhaps he could find a way of locking that one too. It was very likely now that the mob would find their way into the house by following the route he was about to take, but once in the manor, there would be the house carls and help.

Disappointment followed, as Brother Matthew found nothing to prevent the door from opening; no lock, no bar. Nothing. As soon as they got into the cellar, they would find their way inside.

Still clutching the hem of his robe and the lamp, Brother Matthew staggered up the twisting, stone staircase, struggling to get his breath, until finally he arrived at the last step. He stopped, listened. From below he could hear shouts and banging. They were still beyond the first door. Time was now on his side and being on a level, his heartbeat slowed and he was able to catch his breath as he stumbled and lurched along the corridor. The wall to his left felt warm and he could hear voices. If only he could attract their attention. Oh, why couldn't there be a door in this wall?

A little further along he came upon the second staircase. This one appeared straight but then it turned to the right and into another corridor, shorter, cobwebbed and dusty. At the end he held up his lamp and ran his hand over the right-hand wall. He could feel a crack that ran in a straight line down the wall. To the side he found a large carved wooden ivy leaf. He pressed it. For a moment, nothing happened.

Far below he heard shuffling footsteps. They had broken through the first door. They were on their way, staying as quiet as they could to take the manor by surprise.

A moment later, the terrified monk heard a loud click and to his great relief the door swung open. He darted through, burst into terrified tears in his panic to find the corresponding ivy leaf James had said was on the decorative plaster panel under the mantelpiece.

'Thank you, Lord,' he cried as he found it. He pressed hard and watched the door for a moment as it swung back.

He looked around and thought of James. Bearing in mind his current situation, it was irrational that his first instinctive thought was how fortunate James was to have such a large and comfortable room. Then he remembered the danger he was in. He had to find safety. There was little point in worrying about James any more.

Abandoning the no longer required oil lamp, he hurriedly left it on the mantelpiece and darted through the open door into the hallway, where he found two of the housecarls, the Yeo brothers, on watch at the front windows, surrounded by bags of arrows and tightly gripping their bows. They jumped in surprise as he approached them.

'Help me!' he gasped. 'For the love of God, help me!'

'Brother Matthew? Where did you come from?' Robert Yeo, the older brother ran towards him.

'Get me to the Priest Hole. Now! They are after me!'

'Who is?'

'The...mob is in two...two groups. One of them is close behind me...in the house! For pity's sake get me to safety now!' Robert realised by the sweat running down the pink face, the dirty and torn robe and the breathlessness, that the situation was critical. Where he had appeared from was unimportant for the moment; that could wait. Robert knew his duty; protect the monk. Getting him to safety was paramount, but something made him doubt the mob had split into two. Why would they do that? It didn't make sense. He also knew Brother Matthew for being the self-centred, arrogant, sullen man he had always been. It was more likely he was overplaying the situation to make sure his protection came before anything else.

'Yes, yes. Straight away, Brother Matthew.' He turned to his brother who had been watching with one eye while staying alert to what was happening at the front of the manor where a large mob was approaching. 'Daniel, I'll take Brother Matthew to the hole. You stay on watch.' He lowered his voice. 'He said summat about some of 'em 'ad got in the 'ouse but Oi don' see 'ow that can be an...'

'In the name of G...'

'...Roight. Sorry Brother Matthew, jest lettin' me brother know wha's 'appenin'. Oi'm comin'.' To Daniel, he said: 'Oi'll not be more than a couple o' minutes, so jest keep yer eyes on wha's 'appenin' out there an' once 'imself's in the 'ole, Oi'll let the Earl know 'e's 'ere.'

'Well, where'd 'e come from, then?'

'No idea, but then we was busy watchin' out the winder, so jest mustn't 'ave seen 'im come up the passageway.'

Brother Matthew was now impatient and angry. 'How much more time are you going to waste, you...you buff...'

'Roigh' then. Let's get yer ter the 'ole.' Robert took Brother Matthew by the elbow and hurried him along the hallway where, on either side of the hallway, family ancestors stared down from their portraits coolly witnessing the frantic scene taking place in front of them.

Robert stopped, hunkered down and unsheathed a long knife which he used to prise up a small section of floorboard. He reached in and tugged on a cord fastened to a hook.

'For pity's sake, *hurry!*' Brother Matthew paced up and down, casting anxious glances back along the hallway, sweat streamed down his reddened and blotchy face.

A low hanging portrait of the red-headed second Earl of Winterne swung open revealing a cavity wide enough to accommodate three men of average size, plenty of room for the portly monk. In his hurry to conceal himself, as he stepped over the threshold, he tripped on the hem of his robe and fell sideways into the chair.

Robert, satisfied Brother Matthew was safely ensconced within the hole, repeated the process and the portrait swung closed. Brother Matthew appeared to have forgotten him altogether. But, keen to get back to his brother, Robert was not concerned about not being thanked for this service.

There was no mechanism inside to open the door. It had been decided when the hiding place had been constructed, not to install an opening lever or button within the cavity, for the safety of the person hiding within. If they opened the door at the wrong time, they could be caught and the family severely punished. It was felt it would be wiser to leave it to a member of the household to let them out when it was safe to do so.

As the portrait door closed behind him, Brother Matthew closed his eyes, held his rosary tightly in his trembling hands, eased into the chair and waited for his breathing and his racing, throbbing heartbeat to quieten. Now he was safe from those who wanted to harm him, thanks be to God. Then the last image he had of James slipped into his mind. James was urging him to get to the door. He remembered the sacrifice James had made to get him to safety. It should have been James he thanked, not God. Did God actually have anything to do with saving his life? In the shelter of the hole and the moment of quiet, his faith in God and the teachings he had believed in all his life were now in question. If it had been James's decision to take such action, where did God fit in to that? No! He shook head. Of course God saved him. It was obvious. Everything came from God and He had sent James to be his rescuer. How could he have doubted God's involvement? But James had done something virtuous and noble, so why had God let James die if he was following God's instructions? Then it came to him. James was a sinner. He had been breaking his betrothal vows with that impious and shameless Audrey and now had died unshriven. Brother Matthew shuddered. To meet such an end was to go to Hell. And Poor Alice. When he was released from his hiding place, he would have to tell both her and Richard about how James met his end and where. Would they grieve for James when they learned about the tunnel and the reason he used it. Should he tell Alice? Yes. Both Richard and Alice deserved to be told the truth even if it tarnished their memory of James.

Should James have a decent funeral when he had died without having confessed and having his sins absolved? That was a difficult question. There had been no time for the prayers for the dying to be said, and could he take what James had told him about Audrey to be his last confession? Possibly. As far as he was aware, apart from this woman who had clearly led him astray, James had always led a decent and God-fearing life, but even so, he had not received God's forgiveness and therefore did not die in the state of God's Grace. Brother Matthew decided he would have to speak to his Abbot for permission to have James buried on hallowed ground. Not to have him buried in the family plot would only increase the family's anguish and, in view of James's heroism at the end, that was something Brother Matthew did want to contemplate.

The more he thought about it, the more upset he became, and he felt his heart beat increasing. The pain in his side he had felt earlier returned, but prayer would make that better and soon he would be released from his temporary confinement.

Having made sure Brother Matthew was comfortable inside the hole, Robert pulled the rug back over the floorboard, ensured there was no telltale sign, and ran back to his brother.

Chapter Thirty One

While Brother Matthew was making himself comfortable in the Priest's hole, William Hunter and his followers reached the end of the tunnel. To their disappointment all they found was a dead end. There was no sign of an exit. William raised his lamp high, moved it from side to side, and down the dusty stone wall studying every crevice for anything that might give a clue as to how they could get into the manor itself.

The two lamps, one held by William, the other held by Alfred, one of the manor farm hands, gave enough light to allow the men to see fairly well around them but it seemed that no matter how they tried, they could see no way of getting through the wall. Frustrated and angry, William finally accepted that, although Brother Matthew could only have gone along the same passageway, he must have known the way to get through. Or had he? Had they missed a turn off somewhere along the passage in their haste?

'Come on,' he ordered. 'Let's go back an' see if we'm missed summat.' He turned back and shoved Alfred along in front of him and the others in the group further back turned around and began heading towards the stairs.

When the group had first entered the passageway, Noah and Micah, the Weaver brothers, had moved along to the far end and so were behind William and Alfred as they turned back. As the light of the lamps moved away, although they could follow the lights, they were in a much darker part of the passage. It was then that Noah noticed a faint line of light showing at floor level of the wall to their left. Noah crouched down and felt a slight, but definite flow of air coming through a fine gap.

'William! Look here!' Noah called.

William turned and, together with the others rushed back to see what Noah had found. 'So there must be a way in an' we'm missed it.' He raised his lamp again to examine the wall to the left. 'Alfred, you tek a good look on t'other side.'

After a few minutes Alfred said: 'Look 'ere. There's a carvin' looks loike a leaf or summat.'

William pushed him out of the way. 'Let me by. Oi'm doin' this.' He tried to push the carving downwards. Nothing happened. Tried to push it up and again it had no effect.

'Why don' 'ee press it?' asked Alfred, rolling his eyes.

'Oi was goin' ter do tha' weren' Oi?' William pressed the carving and it moved inwards, with a slight rumble the door slid open and they piled into the room to find Brother Matthew's lamp still burning on the mantle. They were in the kind of bedroom they could only dream about and, for many of them, their entire home, if they had one, would fit into.

'Roigh',' said William, shushing his followers. 'We don' know wha's beyond tha' door so we go quiet loike.' He walked towards the door, opened it quietly, grateful for the shouting and the rattling of weapons their accomplices outside were making. Their noise would help to mask any sound they might make. He wanted to be sure of taking the family and their staff by surprise.

As he opened the door just a crack, he saw a man walk passed the door heading towards the far end of the landing. William slowly peered around the door to see one man at the end of the corridor by the window, and the other on his way to join him. Looking both ways William realised these two were alone and heavily outnumbered by his group.

'Now!' he commanded and a dozen or so armed and ferocious looking men burst out of the room and into the hallway. There followed a brief and bloody attack on the brothers who were overcome by the sheer number of opponents. Robert Yeo died within seconds, having been held by two men while another plunged a dagger into his heart. He had no time to fight back.

Daniel Yeo, having seen his brother die, rushed at William Hunter, determined to avenge the death of his brother, when Micah struck him across the head with a heavy cudgel. Daniel collapsed on the hallway floor close to the body of his brother.

William rolled his eyes. 'Well, tha' were damn clever weren't it?'

'Wass wrong, Willum? Oi jest saved yer loife, din't oi?'

'No. There was plenny o' us ter sort 'im out, yer damn fool, an' Oi wan'ed ter know where the monk were, din't Oi?' 'E can't tell me now yer killed 'im as well, can 'e?'

'Oh, sorry, Willum. Oi fought Oi was 'elpin', din't Oi?'

'Fool!' roared William. 'Come on, down them stairs. The fam'ly think there's only them outside the front. They don' know abou' us, do 'em?'

Chapter Thirty Two

Downstairs, with no knowledge of what had happened on the first floor, Richard, the Earl of Winterne, steeled himself against the onslaught to come. Putting his arm around the shoulders of his youngest brother, John, hoping it would give the boy strength, Richard found that instead, it was he who drew strength from John's stoic calm.

'All will be well, Richard,' said John, giving his brother a brave smile.

'I know it will, John.' He ruffled his brother's hair affectionately and wished the boy was safe, somewhere else.

On one side of Richard, Nell, the cook, still holding the ladle in one hand and a meat cleaver in the other, stood resolute and silent, and as formidable as any of the house carls. Richard smiled. If she fought with as much vigour as she ran the kitchen, their attackers would not stand a chance against her.

On Richard's other side, Harris, his hand wrapped tightly around the solid wooden quarterstaff, appeared very calm; his breathing steady, his face grim. Waiting by the window, one shutter at each window open just enough to peer through, the two house carls appointed to take their stand downstairs, Nathaniel Appleby and Peter Cobham, loaded muskets, matchlock pistols and, for Nathaniel, a crossbow, by his feet, and each with an unsheathed sword and long knife tucked into their belts.

The two footmen, Jack and Jonathan Parker, entered the hall silently, walked over to the long table where the weapons were placed and both selected a pistol and a quarterstaff. Richard nodded to acknowledge their courage in coming to stand with them.

With a sinking feeling in his stomach, Richard's thoughts turned to the still missing James. He prayed he and Brother Matthew were both safe. There had been no chance to try to find them and Richard fervently hoped James had decided to spend the evening with his betrothed. He had done what he could for everyone else, except of course, their monk. Hopefully, he had gone to earth somewhere, perhaps Minister Haywood would have taken him in. They may see religion differently, but the Minister was a good, charitable man and would not see Brother Matthew at risk of harm simply because of differences in their way of thinking.

A loud shout, the heavy sound of horse hoof-beats and a commotion outside amongst the mob alerted them to something happening. Richard turned to John. 'I believe the attack is imminent. It appears our assailants have brought reinforcements. Please, go to the kitchen while you have time,' he pleaded, ignoring the look of defiance on John's face, but John shook his head. 'No. *No!* I will not leave you.'

Richard placed his hands on his young brother's shoulders. The others in the room pretended they could not hear, could not see what was passing between the brothers and looked away; a silent agreement seemed to pass between them. They would all be happier if John was safely hidden.

Harris wished all along that John had gone with Lady Winterne and the children. This was no place for such a young lad. He had not said anything to the Earl at the time; John was most insistent that he stayed and, as a good servant, but although Harris felt it was not his place to tell the Earl what to do, he sincerely wished the young master would take advice.

Richard spoke quietly. 'The fire is out, the chimney will have cooled, and you can climb up inside where there is a ledge wide enough to sit on until this is over. Hide! For God's sake, John. Help me! I have enough to concern me without having to think about what might happen to you if you stay here.

'Master Harris,' Nathaniel beckoned from the window. 'Come, take a look. What think you?'

Harris hurried to the window and peered out. Nell, unable to wait, joined him.

'Oi can't mek out wha's 'appening Master Harris, but it seems to be roigh' rumpus.' Outside a number of riders had arrived and it seemed that the horde were running away.

Harris turned to Richard. 'My lord, it would appear young Master John need not hide after all.'

Richard and John ran to the window. 'Thank the Lord,' said Richard, clasping John close to him.

Chapter Thirty Three

On the first floor, William Hunter also heard the horses. He knew nothing about anyone on horseback coming to join them! Warily, he held up a hand and called for silence. Stepping over the body of Robert Yeo, he sidled up to the window frame and peered out. 'Get back in ter the tunnel!' he ordered. 'We're gettin' ou' of 'ere now!'

'Wha's wrong, then?' Harry Foster pushed his way through to William. 'An' why en't we goin' down?'

William grabbed Harry by the back of the neck and dragged him to the window. 'See. Thass why we en't goin' down there. They got comp'ny now, en't they?' He roughly shoved Harry to one side thrusting him against the wall. 'Get goin', all of yer.'

'What' abou' them two?' said Harry, rubbing his cheek. He had crashed into the wooden panelling with some force hitting his forehead and cheekbone. He pointed to the Yeo brothers.

'Wha' abou' 'em? They's dead en't they?' William grabbed Harry by the collar and dragged him back into the bed chamber. 'No-one's goin' ter know it were us wha' done it. Oi'll close the door arter we've all gone through an' no-one'll ever know we was 'ere.' Stepping back into the corridor, William went to close the door then remembered something. 'Oi'll 'ave tha' other lamp.' He picked up the oil lamp Brother Matthew had left on the mantlepiece. ' That'll come in 'andy ter gi' us some more light down them stairs. Some o' them steps're bloody unsteady.' He stepped back inside the tunnel, handed the lamp to Harry who held it high as William pressed the ivy leaf. The door swung closed.

'Bloody clever, tha' is.' William pressed his lips and nodded, clearly impressed by the handiwork. 'Tha' were a proper job by someone good at 'is craft. Come on, time we go' ou' of 'ere.'

It was a slower process going down the stairs than it had been when they ran up. The stairway was narrow, the steps a little too smooth and the tread smaller than the feet going down them. They could only go up, or down, in single file and each of them placed his feet sideways to stop them slipping and careering into the man in front.

Even so, it only took a few minutes before they were on the ground level, walking along the corridor and towards the winding staircase that led down to the large cellar. William brought up the rear with Harry just in front of him.

'Wha' 'appened ter Tom, then?' asked Harry as they walked a few paces behind the others towards the wooden door that gave entry back into the tunnel.

'Oi dunno. 'E weren't 'appy abou' wha we was gonna do ter tha' young Maitland lad. But Oi 'ad no choice, did Oi?'

'No, tha's roigh' William, you never did,' agreed Harry. William Hunter terrified Harry Foster. He always had, ever since they were boys. William had always been bigger, braver, more hot-headed and Harry had always done as William told him. But, after tonight, Harry had made up his mind, for once and for all, that he was leaving Winterne. Once he was away from William that night, he would pack his bag and head for Taunton to seek work and would never have to worry about William again. For the moment, though, William was still there.

Through the door and back into the dusty, stale tunnel, they turned a corner and Harry saw what had happened to James. He was clearly dead and some of the men who had been following behind William had laid one of the heavy cubed building stones onto his body. A little ahead of William, Harry paled and crossed himself then looked away. The lad hadn't deserved that. He hadn't really deserved any of it. He was just doing what he thought was right, and that was brave. Then Harry remembered that James had been due to get married soon. Poor lad. Harry moved on.

At the far end of the tunnel there were just a handful of men still to go through to the outside. One of them, was just setting down the oil lamp he had been holding on the shelf behind the door. The other lamp was still there.

'Yer moigh' as well put them lamps out now,' William called out. 'We'll leave this 'un as well. Won't need any outside an' there's no-one left in 'ere as it gonna need light no more.' He looked down at James. 'Roigh' 'Arry, get yersel' ou' an' leave me the lamp.'

Harry didn't need second telling. He scuttled out of the tunnel as fast as his legs and the condition of the tunnel floor would allow. Once outside, he ran. That was the last time Harry Foster was seen in Winterne.

William, still in the tunnel stared down at James' body. 'You lot got us in ter this! You 'elped tha' bloody monk ge' away from us ter safety an' now look at 'e.' The more he talked, the more angry he became, frustrated with not being able to catch the monk. 'Yer might be dead, young Master James but Oi can still stop tha' red-hair o' yourn lookin' pretty, so Oi can.' He kicked at the body. 'I allus 'ated you Maitlands. This be your own fault. Your father treated my ma badly. If 'e'd done roight by 'er this wouldn't never 'ave 'appened. She thought he loved her, but no, 'e never did. 'E jest used her. You grew up in tha' big ' 'ouse, in comfort, got fed good food while Oi wen' barefoot an' grew wi' nothin'. Me ma died when I was jest ten. Broken 'earted she were. 'Er sister took me in. She never cared neither but 'er 'usband, you'll remember 'im, 'e were the blacksmith. 'E trained me up ter tek over from 'im so Oi was able ter mek me own livin'. Bu' yer father...ha...*our* father never gev me a thought. Wass tha' yer say? P'raps 'e never knew...o' course, 'e bloody knew. 'E knew who Oi was alroigh but no' a penny came me way, no' a smile, never a gentle word from 'im. I used ter see 'im roidin' through the village an' 'oped he would one day acknowledge me as 'is son. But 'e never did. Ha! An' it weren't no riding accident he had...Oi'll wager none o' yer though' o' tha. Did yer?'

William leaned back against the wall and looked down at James' body, tilting his head this way, then that. Yer'll no' get' ou' o' 'ere wi' that' boulder on top o' yer, bu' it don' matter none, do it, 'cos yer dead en't yer, little brother? Tha'll 'urt 'im...oh no, it won' will it, 'cos 'e's dead too en't 'e? Oi killed 'im.' He crouched down on a level with James' head. I'm gonna ge' yer other big brother next. 'Twill be quite a thing to kill two Earls!' He stroked James' hair and smiled down at him. 'Yer were a pretty lad weren't yer? Not no more though an' let's jest mek it a bit worse.' He stood up and kicked at James' body. The more he kicked, the more enraged he became. He picked up a meat cleaver that someone had dropped earlier and, chuckling to himself, beheaded James kicking his head across the tunnel floor.

William, suddenly aware of the horror he had committed, came to his senses and ran to the door, leaving the still burning lamp on the ledge. Outside he remembered the lamp was still alight, baulked at the idea of going back inside but forced himself to return and smother the flame, then dashed away into the woods as though all the hounds of Hell were chasing him.

On hearing the horses arriving at the front of the manor, Tom Cooper, still hiding in the woods, realised their raid was over. He was convinced Master James had died but there was every likelihood the monk was now safe within the manor and it had all been for nothing. He also realised that anyone caught would more than likely hang.

He watched as, in twos and threes the men who had gone into the tunnel with him crept out. He saw two bodies being brought out but neither of them were Master James or the monk. James must have fought for his life and taken them with him. He stood at the edge of the trees making sure he could be seen by those who emerged from the tunnel and beckoned them to him. But there was no William. No-one had seen him for a while. Harry Foster came out alone. Tom called softly to him but Harry shook his head, and ran straight on.

Gathering the others in a circle around him, Tom took charge.

'Wha' 'appened inside?'

'We go' inside alroigh' but Master James 'e fought loike a demon 'e did,' said Dickon Moodie. 'But William made sure 'e was outnumbered an' 'e died. The monk go' away through a door an' we 'ad ter brek it down.'

'We wen' up the stairs, then along a passageway an' up some more stairs, then another short passage and William pressed summat an' a door opened an' we was in a bed chamber…'

'What abou' the monk?'

'We never saw 'im but the two guards was killed.'

Tom shook his head. 'More deaths? It weren't meant ter be loike tha. Wha were William thinkin'?' But he stopped, appeared to be thinking for a moment. 'So did yer see anyone else?'

Dickon shook his head.

'Roigh', so none of the Maitland household knows we was 'ere at all...an' let's keep it tha' way. Oi wan' yer all ter go 'ome. They was brough' in by William an...'

'Look! There 'e is now!'

They turned to see William standing at the door of the tunnel, looking all around, a wild look in his eyes and blood stains on his clothes. 'Tha's two of 'em gone' he shrieked before fleeing away into another part of the woods.

'Wha did 'e say?' asked Tom.

'Summat abou' two of em? Don' make no sense 'cos we know 'e didn't find the monk,' said Dickon, frowning.

'Well no matter. William'll turn up when 'e's good an' ready...but listen ter me an' listen well. Them Maitlands don' know we was 'ere, so whatever 'appens jest keep yer mouths shut. There's no tunnel, there's no way in ter the manor except through the proper doors. We was never 'ere...yer go' tha'?'

They nodded their heads.

'Then go 'ome. There's nuthin' we can do fer them as moight be caught at the front o' the manor, an' no-one can prove we was ever 'ere. Go 'ome an' say nuthin'.' He turned to Dickon. 'You come wi' me an' Oi want's two more o' yer ter 'elp us bury them two.'

Chapter Thirty Four

An hour or so after Elizabeth had arrived at her father's house in Wells with the children and their governess, the escort Richard had sent with her returned to Winterne Manor, together with her father's own housecarls, seven of them, the city constables and a group of volunteers; some twenty five armed men in all. And Elizabeth travelled with them.

As the mob ran off, Richard opened the door and embraced his wife who had saved the house from probable destruction and, for some the very great possibility of death.

Digby and Robinson, on their way down the main staircase from the roof, saw the Yeo brothers lying on the floor by the window and rushed to attend to them. Shocked to find Robert dead, the knife still in his chest and Daniel, who had been taken for dead by the invaders, still alive but unconscious, they carried them down to the ground floor and gently laid Daniel on the hall table.

Richard was about to send for a doctor when Harris intervened and leaned over Daniel to listen to his heart. 'My lord, Daniel has a head wound and it may take him a while to regain his senses but his breathing is good, his heart beats in a regular pattern and he is young and strong. If you send for the doctor, it is probable he will want to bleed him and, if you will excuse me, I would suggest that we avoid that course of action.'

'Then what do you suggest, Harris?'

'I believe, certainly from what I observed in my travels as a sailor when I was younger...'

Richard's eyebrows shot up. 'There really is more to you than we ever knew, Harris,...but go on please.'

'Yes, my lord. I believe that with rest, careful nursing, regular sips of ale to keep him hydrated that he may well recover. Perhaps young Kat could be persuaded...'

'Kat? The scullery maid?'

'Indeed, my lord. I believe they have become close and she would be the one to tend him most carefully.'

Richard smiled and gave the order to find a suitable room on the ground floor for Daniel and to find Kat. He would explain to Mistress Harper that Kat was to be exempted from all household duties until Daniel was well again. Perhaps, as Kat had been so helpful in warning them of the attack, and if Harris was right about them caring for each other, he should do something to make it possible for them to marry. But, first Daniel had to recover.

Once Daniel had been taken to what was to be his room for the time being, and Kat had joyfully received the news that she was to be his nurse, Richard called for Digby, Robinson and Harris to join him on the first floor where the Yeo brothers had been stationed.

Richard asked Digby and Robinson if they knew anything of what had happened there but, having been on the roof, they had no answer for him. With all the shouting going on outside, they had heard nothing from inside the house. Apart from blood stains on the carpet which were likely to have been from Robert Yeo, there was nothing that appeared to be out of place or curious. They looked into the bedchambers but nothing seemed amiss. They walked through the hall, but again saw nothing that would indicate anyone other than the Yeo brothers had ever been there.

'I believe we will have to wait for Daniel to recover before we find out what actually happened,' said Richard. 'Come. We shall take some wine together to thank everyone for all their efforts to get us through this ordeal.'

As they walked down the main staircase, Richard said, 'I must send a message to Squire Parker's house to find out if James is there and to the minister to enquire as to whether Brother Matthew found shelter with him. '

'I am sure that is what they will have done, my lord,' said Harris. 'But what happened to the Yeo brothers, is a mystery that will only be solved when Daniel awakes.'

Epilogue

Richard Maitland, Earl of Winterne

His home and most of his household having survived, Richard stood in front of the stained glass window and said a prayer for Lady Catherine.

In search of James and Brother Matthew, Richard, together with two constables from Wells, and Harris, went to investigate the fire at Brother Matthew's hut. This created another mystery. The ground around the hut was very dry, the undergrowth brown, brittle, and easily combustible. They expected the fire would have spread further into the woods. However, to their astonishment, the fire had been contained within the space of the hut and had not gone beyond the outline of the walls!

Although Richard, and later John, continued their investigations into the disappearance of James and Brother Matthew, no trace was ever found during their lifetimes.

Brother Matthew

Brother Matthew, at forty-five years of age, and very overweight after many years of inactivity and indulgence in favourite food and wines, had been subjected to a terrifying ordeal. He had been urged - in terror - to hasten through the woods, clamber up two flights of stairs and hide from enemies who wanted to kill him.

After settling into the chair, secure in the knowledge that he was safe, Brother Matthew felt the pulse throbbing in his head slowing, and his breathing returning to normal. He relaxed. Within minutes his heart began racing again, and he realised something was very wrong. Brother Matthew died of Apoplexy (Stroke) two hours after entering the monk's hole.

Daniel Yeo

Daniel was unconscious for two days. When he did wake, he appeared to be none the worse for his injuries other than having the most dreadful headache. But, to everyone's great disappointment, he could not recall anything that had happened after being sent to the first floor with his brother. He and Kat married a year later. They named their first son Robert, and their second, James.

William Hunter

When the mob had found the tunnel, they chopped away swathes of ivy covering the door. The door could then be clearly seen by any passer-by. When William Hunter had run into the forest, he left the door of the tunnel open. William was not seen alive again, but a little over two weeks later, his body was discovered caught in rushes on the bank of the River Axe.

Tom Cooper

Tom Cooper never revealed what he knew of the tunnel, but the burden of guilt of his involvement in the death of James Maitland, became too much for him. Several times he felt himself drawn into the woods to find the tunnel, but was never able to find it again. His body was found a few months later hanging from a tree in Winterne Woods.

The tunnel

No-one else from that mob who escaped through the tunnel into the woods that night ever mentioned what they had done, fearful of being arrested and hanged for their crimes. In their panic to get as far away from the manor as possible, they fled into the dark wood leaving the tunnel door open.

Apart from the attempts made by Tom Cooper to find the door, none of the others ever returned to that part of Winterne Woods. Instead they spent the rest of their lives trying to forget they were ever involved in something so shameful, so wicked.

Somehow though, a little after dawn the following morning, unobserved hands closed the door and, where the ivy had been wrenched away, new vines had grown back in a thick veil concealing the entrance. Perhaps that was why Tom Cooper was never able to find it again.

Part Four

1685
In the time of King James II
The Monmouth Rebellion

Chapter Thirty Five

The loud hammering on the front door of Captain Roger Wingfield's commandeered lodgings in the centre of the City of Wells, echoed down the long hallway. Unbeknown to Roger, it heralded the arrival of a messenger from Judge Jeffreys, Baron of Wem. Unfortunately for the captain, the messenger arrived while he was only halfway through his breakfast.

The pretty maid who had served Roger breakfast, smoothed the white pinafore that covered the front of her plain dark-grey dress, and tried to push a few escaping, strands of chestnut-red hair back into her white cotton mob cap, as she left the room to answer the door. Roger heard a male voice and a moment later, the maid walked back with a very breathless lad in a smart frilled white shirt and black breeches. Tendrils of his dark hair stuck to his forehead, and wet patches of sweat at the armpit bore witness to his exertion on a warm late Summer day. Dressed formally as he was, Roger guessed this was an official visit. The messenger leant against the door, his chest heaved as he attempted to regain his breath. Roger invited him to sit until he could manage to speak.

After a few moments the lad spoke, rushing out his words on each breath in.

'My apologies, Captain. I come…from His Lord…ship, the Baron of…Wem. Oh, thank you.' The young woman had handed him a cup of weak ale which he gulped down gratefully. 'It is very warm out there…and as you may realise…my message is urgent…so…I ran…all the way.' His chest no longer heaved, but trickles of sweat trailed down his face. He wiped them away with his sleeve. 'The Judge wishes to see you in his lodgings immediately, Captain.'

Roger had expected, but dreaded, the time when this command would come. He was not a seasoned soldier. His father had bought his commission in the Suffolk Regiment thinking it would give him a career, but that was only a few weeks ago and his experience was appallingly minimal.

Although having undergone a brief and, as he believed largely unhelpful training, he was not happy about his recent posting, or confident about dealing with the infamous, and much hated 'Hanging Judge'. His orders were to escort and protect Judge Jeffreys and the other five judges appointed by King James II. As the team of judges had only just arrived in Wells, Roger had not expected to meet him until later - the later the better as far as he was concerned. What he had expected was that the senior judge would need some hours to settle into the accommodation provided for him, and that Roger could be at ease for a few hours yet. He hoped that when they did meet, his inexperience would not be evident.

Not having expected to meet the senior judge until later, Roger had looked forward to a leisurely breakfast, and had made himself comfortable in the carver seat at the end of the long dining table, but now the time had come he decided to put a brave face on it.

'Very well. Thank you for making such an effort to pass on His Lordship's command. If the young lady here will allow, I suggest you sit here in the cool air of this house for a while and recover yourself.'

The girl nodded and smiled. 'And perhaps another cup of weak ale?'

The messenger nodded and gave a grateful smile. 'Thank you. I would like that, although I cannot stay long. His Lordship will require my services again soon, I am sure of that.'

According to all the reports Roger had heard, Judge Jeffreys had a reputation for being impatient, quick-tempered and not liking to be kept waiting. Roger put down his knife and, only having managed to eat a few mouthfuls of slices of ham, onions, rye bread and cheese, looked regretfully at the cup of cider beside his plate, shrugged his shoulders and, on his way to the door, asked the maid not to clear away his plate as he hoped, indeed expected, to return soon.

As he stood, he retrieved his sword belt and scabbard which he had left hooked over a peg at the back of the door, and hurried from the room. He was halfway down the long hallway when, as an afterthought, he turned back. The messenger had moved to sit in comfortable chair by the window and the maid was already busy clearing the rest of the table.

At the unexpected sound of his voice, the maid, who had her back to him, jumped out of her skin, and the messenger choked on his ale.

'I say, I'm very sorry. I did not mean to startle you both.' Even though he had apologised, and genuinely regretted their panicky reactions, he could not help being amused and smiled. 'I just wanted to say that, if I do not return within the hour, then please go ahead and clear the table.' Neither of them spoke, they just stared open-mouthed as he stammered another apology and left again. Although he tried to suppress his laughter, he could not help but chuckle as he headed for the front door.

On hearing Roger laughing as he went out of the door, the maid and the messenger looked at each other and grinned. Outside, the streets were filled with tense and unhappy people but for that moment, three of them had found something silly enough to lift their spirits.

In the hallway Roger snatched his hat and gold-trimmed crimson coat from the coat rack by the door, and dashed out into the street. As he passed the window, the maid watched him and gave a little smile as the departing handsome captain moved out of sight, while pulling on his coat and trying to adjust his white silk stock, tying it as tidily around his neck as he could whilst running, with his hat tucked securely under his arm.

Rushing down the centre of the cobbled street, he avoided the gutters on both sides of the road where running water washed away the human night-time waste thrown out of windows that overlooked the street. He fleetingly wondered why other largely populated areas did not follow this example. It was certainly cleaner than the few places he had already been sent to.

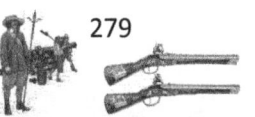

On reaching the judge's accommodation, he stopped to catch his breath, put on his hat and straightened the white silk stock around his neck a little. Another thing he knew by repute was that the judge did not approve of untidiness. His knock on the door was answered by a thin, hunch-shouldered and sour-looking, elderly man who was clearly resentful that his house had been taken over by the representatives of King James II and, although he denied it profusely, and there was no evidence, was undoubtedly a supporter of the Duke of Monmouth. The glowering man turned away and shuffled back down the hallway, weaving between wooden chests and a pair of armchairs that almost blocked the hallway, to the rear of the house where he was permitted to live, albeit in much reduced space than he had been used to before the arrival of the judge and his colleagues.

Captain Wingfield ran up the stairs two at a time until he reached the door of the first floor front room which the judge had chosen as his office. He took a deep breath, tucked his hat between his knees as he smoothed down his windswept blond hair, felt the black ribbon that held his cue – the longer lengths of his hair tied in a bunch – was in place, put his hat firmly on his head and knocked on the door. A few moments later he heard a gruff invitation to enter.

At the desk, sat the bewigged, senior member of the panel of judges commissioned by King James II to organise the identification of supporters of the Duke of Monmouth. Appointed to seek out the rebels, conduct the trials and administer what was considered to be appropriate punishments, the opinions of his five colleagues would be heard, but the man who sat behind the desk in the spacious, barely furnished and exceedingly tidy room, had the overall authority.

As Roger stood, courteously patient, he looked around the dimly lit wood-pannelled room, hoping to find something that might give him a reason to like the man he had been ordered to protect. The next day would see the last of the Assizes, and the reports of the horrific punishments handed down at Winchester the previous month, then in Salisbury, Dorchester, Exeter and Taunton in the following weeks, sickened him.

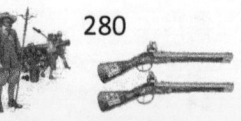

In Taunton alone there were over five hundred men imprisoned. Although it was true that the larger percentage were guilty of taking part in the rebellion, Roger thought it very likely that a few had merely had the bad luck to be in wrong place at the wrong time, and subsequently caught up in the turmoil after the battle at Sedgemoor. He wondered how many innocent farm labourers, carrying work implements, pitchforks and the like, had been arrested and hanged, having been unable to prove they had taken no part in the rebellion. Almost two hundred men had been hanged at Taunton with a further eight hundred sentenced to transportation to the West Indies where they were to be slaves for a minimum of ten years; if they lived that long. Although Roger had no sympathy with the late Duke, the judges having taken the view that anyone arrested was inevitably guilty, utterly sickened him.

So lost in his thoughts was he that he did not notice Judge Jeffreys had stopped reading the paper and was staring at him.

'Ah, I see I you are returned from your reverie, Captain,' the judge said, frostily.

With his mind still full of the horrors of tales of the previous Assizes, Roger sincerely hoped his face would not betray the loathing he had for the man in front of him. Putting his feelings to one side, Roger stood to attention and looked over the head of the judge into the sunlight that glimmered through the long window onto the judge's back.

'My apologies, my Lord. I did not wish to interrupt you until you had finished your business, and was thinking about the patrol my Lieutenant will be leading through the city very soon. It is his fir..'

'Good morning, Captain Wingfield. I trust you slept well,' Judge Jeffreys cut in.

'Yes sir, thank you, I...'

'Good. Glad to hear it,' the judge interrupted again. He clearly had no inclination or time for small talk, and went straight to the point of his request to see the captain. 'I understand that although distantly related to your commander, Lord Lichfield, your immediate family are from local stock, Bridgwater, I believe. So what do you know about the present Earl of Winterne, Lord Bartley Maitland?'

Not having been invited to sit down, Roger remained standing and thought for a moment while the judge staring fixedly at him. Roger hesitated before speaking; the question was unexpected. He had been told the judge would be direct in his manner, but he had expected a few moments of general conversation. As they had never met before and, as the judge's senior officer-in-charge, a few minutes of courteous, if not amiable discourse would have helped him to understand more about the man he was to work with, but, he now understood that was not going to happen.

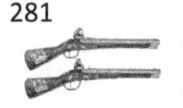

'Um, well they are a well-established family, my Lord. The Earl is well respected and a pleasant gentleman as I understand. I haven't met him personally, of course, but...but I have heard of nothing adverse about him or the other members of the family, and I have certainly never heard speculation that he is a Monmouth supporter.'

The judge swung his chair sideways, and turned away from the captain to look out of the window. 'And, from what you know...obviously,' he paused, appeared to gather his thoughts before he spoke again which Roger found to be disconcerting, even ominous, 'from what you've heard, of course...would you say that the Earl is loyal to the king?'

'Well, yes, sir. I believe so. May I ask if you have reason to doubt his loyalty?'

The judge swung back to look at the captain. 'Possibly, but to be honest with you I doubt everyone's loyalty.' He stood up and removed his wig. 'Damn thing!' he said throwing the wig onto the back of a wing-sided armchair. He scratched his head, then ran his hand over his bristle-like grey hair. 'It's far too hot to have to wear those things but they are considered fashionable, and now formality requires that I do.'

'May I ask my Lord, what prompts this doubt about the Earl?'

The judge looked down at some papers on the corner of the table and shuffled them along further into the centre of the desk. He looked up at the captain. 'Last evening I dined with the Bishop of Bath and Wells. What a delightful home he has at the palace here. Have you seen it yet?'

'Yes, indeed, my Lord. My men and I inspected the gardens on our arrival here a week ago when we had intelligence that there may be some fugitives from Sedgemoor hiding there. We had a report of a small number of men swimming the moat and scaling the wall.'

'Hmm. Did you find anything?'

'No, my Lord. There was no-one there.'

'Where did the report come from originally?'

The captain frowned. 'I cannot answer that, my Lord. One of my men was given the information, he came straight to me and we immediately went to investigate.'

'How long were you there?' Judge Jeffreys took his seat behind the desk again, steepled his fingers and stared, unblinkingly, at the captain.

Disconcerted by the piercing blue eyes, Roger Wingfield swallowed hard. Was the judge accusing him of something? 'About an hour, my Lord.'

The judge sat forward, leaned his elbows on the desk and rested his chin on his hands. 'Did your entire cohort accompany you?'

'Um...yes, my Lord.'

Judge Jeffreys looked away and shook his head. 'It did not occur to you, I suppose, that this may have been a ruse to keep you occupied behind the palace garden walls, while some of the rebels escaped from their hiding places in the city. An hour or so, whilst you and *all* your men were occupied behind the wall would have given them ample time to vanish into the woods and caves. If they are local, or have local people aiding them, the River Axe cave system or any of the tunnels I hear were excavated by monks in the past, could help them be miles away before you even left the gardens.' He looked up at the now disconcerted captain. 'I also understand some areas of the woods around here are so dense, they make superb hiding places.'

'Yes, my Lord.'

'Yes, my Lord? Is that all you have to say, Captain Wingfield?'

'Yes, sir...I mean no. my Lord.'

'I find this most disappointing.' He paused for a moment to look out of the window again until a few minutes had passed while Roger Wingfield stood to attention feeling mortified after being accused of failure. This was not the way he hoped his first meeting with the king's representative would go.

The Judge turned back to him. 'However, we have no proof that is what happened, it is merely an assumption of what might have happened.'

The captain allowed himself to relax a little. That was true. It was just supposition on the part of the part of the judge, and he wondered why this mean little man had put him through that.

'Now,' Judge Jeffreys began again. 'After what was a delightful meal with the Bishop, it being a very pleasant evening, I decided to walk back, with my two attendants. I slowed my pace and fell back a little, allowing them to walk ahead while I took note of the outstanding architecture of some of the buildings hereabout.'

'But...my Lord, was that wise? As you say there are still some rebels at large...'

The judge waved his hand in dismissal of Captain Wingfield's concern. He looked up at the captain from under his bushy, knitted eyebrows. ' As you point out that may have been a risky thing to do and, as it turned out, it was.'

'My Lord?'

The judge gave a thin-lipped smile and tilted his head slightly as he looked at the young, smartly dressed officer in front of him. 'I was just a few minutes away from this house when I stopped to look at the impressive architecture of the Cathedral, which I was quite taken with. For a small city, the residents here are very fortunate to have such a superb religious edifice. Do you not agree, Captain Wingfield?'

'Indeed, I do, my Lord.'

'But I digress. Whilst my attention was held by the design of the stained glass windows, I was unaware of a...a, well, I suppose what can only be described as a man, approaching from behind me. He did not speak and for a while I was unaware he was there, that was until I began to notice a very unpleasant smell and turned to see from whence it came. To my astonishment, I found this small, cringing, little rat-like man, standing far too closely to me, shuffling a filthy, battered felt hat between his hands and reeking of body odour and sour, filthy rag-like clothing. He kept his head down, seemingly unable to look at me, or frightened to do so.'

'Did he try to harm you, my Lord?'

'No. My attendants had finally noticed I was no longer with them, looked around and saw him approach me. They called out and began to run back but, as I surmised that he was not about to attack me, I shook my head to stop them from coming closer and trying to apprehend him. I wanted to find out what he wanted. With one eye on them through his downcast eyes – he did not appear to look at me at all – you know how these peasants keep their heads lowered when they speak to a superior, he muttered something about the Earl of Winterne hiding rebels in the tunnels. He knew where they were and for five shillings, he would take me to the place, but I had to go alone. Do you know anything about these tunnels?'

More concerned with the judge putting himself in danger, Roger reacted to the mention of the man wanting the judge to go somewhere...anywhere...without an escort. 'My Lord! I presume you don't intend to do what he said, do you?'

'No, of course not!' The judge snapped back. 'I know we do not know each other well, Captain Wingfield, but I would not have expected you to take me for a fool?'

'Um, no, my Lord. Of course...my apologies...' he appeared to be sincerely abashed, and looked down at his feet. 'I meant no offence, my Lord. Did he give you his name?'

The air between them crackled with tight-lipped tension. Judge Jeffreys broke the silence with a more conciliatory but belittling tone: 'You are young yet, Captain and, I assume, somewhat inexperienced, but I can assure you that I am not naïve, and I do have a certain amount of experience with the lower orders that includes rogues of many kinds. And, in answer to your first question, no, I am not going to do what he said. Why he wishes to cause trouble for the Earl is beyond me, but I did consider that perhaps he is one of the rebels and there is a plot to assassinate me. That is something I can believe. I want him…and any fellow conspirators… captured, and therefore, I do intend to meet him…'

Roger was about to protest, but the judge held up a hand to silence him.

'…but I will not be going alone. You and six of your men will come with me and, in answer to your second question, I insisted he gave me his name or I would have him arrested on the spot. He is Ned Wormald. Does the name mean anything to you?'

'No, I don't believe so, my lord, but I will see if I can find out anything about him. I will also select six of my men to form your escort.'

'Very well, do so. I have given this much thought and, like you, I believe it may well be a trap. You and your men will not wear uniform, but you will be armed.' The judge walked up and down the room as he spoke, not looking at Roger. 'You would stand out like a sore thumb in crimson, so please acquire peasants clothing in as a poor condition as you can find. There should be nothing to draw attention to yourselves, and you and will keep yourselves close by but concealed. I want him to believe I am alone. You will only reveal yourselves on my command.'

'I understand, my Lord. Where are you to meet this man and at what time?'

'It is a little over two miles away on the road due north of Wells, through Wookey Hole, towards Winterne Woods. He tells me there is a narrow cart track that leads to a small clearing where there is a hollow oak tree trunk, easily identifiable due to it being split by a lightning strike. I am to meet him there at thirty minutes past six of the clock tonight. I want you and your men to make your way there, following the cart track but hidden with the trees and undergrowth. You are to be concealed there waiting before

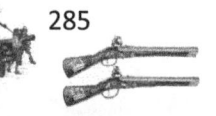

I arrive. Keep to the undergrowth and ensure you are not seen. If we are to apprehend this man and his accomplices, firstly, I do not intend to take any chances with my life and have him turn up early if I am unprotected and, secondly, I want to ensure we capture them all.'

'I understand, my Lord.'

'And in God's name, man, wear a hat! Something dark to cover that remarkably conspicuous blond hair of yours.'

Roger suppressed a smile. 'Yes, I will indeed, my Lord.'

A noise outside caught their attention and they both headed towards the windows. Looking down into the street below they watched as a platoon of some twenty-five soldiers of Roger's regiment, marched in a column of pairs, with the Second-in-Command, Lieutenant, Jack Thornton, at the head of the group.

While Roger and the judge watched from above, the reaction of most of the watchers on either side of the road came as no great surprise to either of them. No-one cheered the smartly dressed or well-drilled troop as they would have been by supporters of the king. Unaware they were being watched by the very man who could condemn them to death, two men, one holding the hand of a small boy, waited until the soldiers had passed by before spitting in their wake. The little boy, Roger estimated to be about five-years-old, looked up at the man Roger took to be his father, and made a childish attempt at spitting, but all he could manage was an inexperienced dribble. His father smiled and nodded his head in approval. The other man ruffled the boy's mousy-brown hair and smiled down at him. The delighted boy beamed and tried again. This time he managed to send his spittle to just beyond his toes, and looked up again in the hope of more praise. Instead, this time his father hunkered down to look him, eye to eye. It seemed to Roger that the man had just noticed two red-jacketed soldiers standing amongst the bystanders on the other side of the road. The other fellow had also spotted them and had begun to walk slowly away, never taking his eyes off the two soldiers. The boy looked across at the soldiers and his expression changed to one of fear.

Out of the corner of his eye, Roger peered across at the judge, hoping he had not seen the incident, and was relieved to see he was still watching the parade. The second Lieutenant, and the soldiers at the head of the column, had already passed out of view as they marched towards the

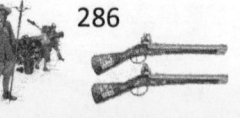

Cathedral. Roger felt sure the judge would have ordered the arrest of the men - and possibly the boy - if he had seen the incident. When he looked back, the three had vanished. He scanned the crowd for them, the two off-duty soldiers were still there, but he was thankful to see no further sign of the men and the boy.

Although he should not have been amused, Roger could not contain a little smile.

'Ahem.' Roger realised the judge had noticed after all and was glowering at him.

'My apologies, my Lord.'

'I do not expect our military to be welcome in this region as I believe that the misguided people locally revere the late Duke of Monmouth, but what good has it done them?'

Just then the door opened and a man similarly dressed as Judge Jeffreys in black and grey, but red-faced and sweating under a shoulder length lambs-wool wig, entered the room.'

'My apologies, my Lord,' he said. 'I wasn't aware you had company.'

'No need for apologies, Montague. The captain was just leaving.' He turned to Roger. 'Captain Wingfield, I no longer have any need of you for the moment, and therefore you are dismissed.' He sat down behind the desk and again steepled his fingers. 'You have your orders for later today, do you not?'

'Yes, my Lord and I have a few preparations to make.' He bowed. 'I shall have my men in place as arranged.'

'Very well. We will meet again later, Captain.'

On his way out of the house, Roger was unfortunate enough to meet the taciturn owner of the property who scowled at him and walked away muttering. But Roger was feeling cheerful. The little boy who had made him smile had obviously not been seen by the soldiers as they were still in the street, but now engaged in obviously flirtatious conversation with two pretty girls. In addition, the Cathedral clock had just chimed and he realised he had only been away from his lodgings for thirty-five minutes, which meant his breakfast should still be on the table.

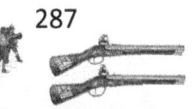

Chapter Thirty Six

Beyond the manor walls, very few fugitives from the ragtag militia who had fought for the Duke of Monmouth, and were finally beaten two weeks previously at Sedgemoor, were still at large. However, the labyrinth of tunnels under the Mendip Hills were useful hiding places for those who could still not return to their homes for fear of being arrested. Without receiving treatment, many of the injured now had wounds that were festering; some would be fatal. Most were starving, but all were scared to return to their homes knowing that the five judges appointed by King James II, the most brutal of them being Judge Jeffreys, were arresting anyone they suspected of supporting the Duke's ill-fated cause.

Two of these hungry and terrified men, had been found hiding in the hayloft of one of the Winterne Manor barns during the previous week. John Tanner, the steward, had taken pity on them and was taking food, linen strips, vinegar and honey to treat their flesh wounds, when he was spotted by the older of the two sons of the Earl of Winterne, twenty-year-old, Viscount Henry Maitland.

Having returned to the stables from his morning ride, Henry handed his mount's reins to a groom and was about to make his way back to the manor, when he spied John skulking around the barn door, looking very furtive before he entered.

His curiosity aroused, Henry waited a few moments giving the steward time to feel secure, then made his way towards the barn and listened outside. Hearing a voice speaking in a foreign accent coming from above, Henry slipped quietly into the barn, tiptoed over the straw to the ladder giving access to the loft, and quietly climbed up to find John handing out bread, cheese and weak ale to two fugitives in filthy and ragged uniforms. Henry immediately recognised the uniforms as belonging to the contingent of eighty-two men who had accompanied the Duke of Monmouth from the Netherlands in the abortive rebellion against the Duke's uncle, King James II.

Immediately understanding who they were and sympathetic to the cause, Henry showed himself and to everyone's relief, offered to help the two men. Sitting on the straw with the fugitives, he explained that the barns were not the safest place to hide as they could be searched at any time. He had somewhere far more secure to hide them. He further promised that, once the Assizes were finished, and most of the king's forces had been posted elsewhere, he would help them reach the coast.

One of them, who said his name was Hendrik, shook his head. He said they were both reluctant to leave the barn where they had been safe for the last five days, and introduced his companion as Caspar.

Henry frowned at John and stood up. 'You realise just what a devilishly dangerous risk you have taken, not only with your own life but, if these men are discovered my family will be implicated in treason.'

John nodded. 'Yes, my Lord.' He hung his head. 'I'm sorry, I just wanted to help. I regret I did not think of the possible outcome to yourselves. I found these men huddled between the hedge and the railings in the rear garden and wanted to help, but the only place I could think of was here.'

Henry sighed. 'I understand, John. You are good-hearted man and I know you sympathise with the rebels although, until now you have been so careful I saw nothing that gave away what you were doing. But, if I noticed your behaviour then so might one of the grooms, so you, and these men, must understand that they cannot stay here. You know as well as I do that some people will do anything for money and you may well be given away. The sooner we get them out of here and taken to where they can be looked after without being seen, the better. You *must* persuade them to do as I say. I have somewhere far safer for them. I must go now but be here at sunset and have them ready to move.'

John looked puzzled. 'But, my Lord…'

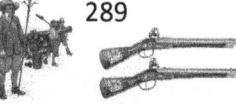

Henry walked towards the ladder and began to descend. 'No buts, John. I will help but this barn is not the place for them. My help will be on my terms only as I have to protect my family and our home. If you are caught hiding them here then I cannot support you. I urge you, for the sake of your wife and son, to trust me to take them to a safer place, or...' he shook his head, '...or, if not, I am sorry, John, you are on your own.'

'Yes, my Lord.' He turned to the frightened Dutchmen. 'You must do as his lordship says. He will not betray you.'

'John!' Henry called from the ground floor. 'Make sure they are well hidden and then I think you should return with me. 'As steward, your duties rarely requires you to be around the stables. To spend too much time here might raise questions.'

'Yes, my Lord.' John indicated that the two desperately frightened men should hide in the corner of the loft, hide themselves under the straw, and await his return. 'I am leaving you now. I will be back as the sun goes down. In the meantime, stay silent and try to get some sleep. Whatever you do though, stay still and do not move from this place.'

Soon after, Henry and John walked in strained silence through the field between the stables and the rear garden of the manor. At the gate, Henry halted, turned to John and said: 'Although I understand your motives for helping those men, and to some extent applaud your courage, there is a part of me that is furious with you for taking the risk with everything my family have built up over the centuries. I shall not tell my father. I fear he would dismiss you on the spot and where would that leave Mary and young Tommy?'

John looked down at his feet. 'I am sorry, my Lord. I acted alone and on impulse. I did not think of the consequences.'

Henry looked at the downcast man he had known for most of his life and said: 'Very well. Tell no-one...and I emphasise, you must tell no-one. Not Mary, *no-one!*'

'Oh no, my Lord. I have not and will not.' Taken aback by Henry's reply, John said: 'You should know I would not risk the lives of my wife and son.'

'Then as I said, I will help you but just this once. There can be no repeat of this. Have them ready to go at sunset and I will meet you at the barn. I'm taking them to a place in the woods where they will be safer than anywhere you could find for them. We will take a rarely used path and you will need me to guide you through it. I will now walk around to the front door, I can cut through one of the gaps in the outside wall.' He smiled. 'I was as distressed as anyone else when those cannon destroyed parts of the wall around the courtyard a few weeks ago but, I now consider that we actually got away with it lightly. That...skirmish...could have done a lot more damage and at least none of us were hurt. I actually thought your Tommy was extremely brave while that was happening.'

'He certainly was, my lord.'

'While we are involved in this exploit, you can call me Henry. We are conspirators in this and, if caught, we would both face execution. I think that makes us equals, John. In normal circumstances though, you had better revert to my title. Now, you slip back in through the kitchen. I believe, by now, Mary will be preparing supper.'

John gave a weak smile. 'Thank you, my Lord. It is such a relief to have your support and, believe me, I shall not jeopardise the security of the Maitland family again.'

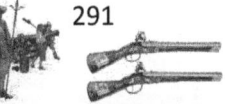

Chapter Thirty Seven

Later that morning, Jack Thornton, Roger's Second lieutenant returned to the house where Roger and other officers of the Suffolk Regiment were lodging. His men had finished their parade ensuring that the people of Wells were continually fully aware of their presence. They had now been relieved by another troop who were, at that very moment, marching around the green at the front of the Cathedral.

Jack found Roger, in the dining room reading his written orders. 'How did your meeting with Judge Jeffreys go?' he asked.

Roger put down the papers he had been going through. 'I found him quite loathsome if you really want to know.'

Jack nodded. 'That's what I thought.' He looked around. 'How can a man get a drink around here? I have a very dry throat. Shouting orders in the dusty heat, is thirsty work.'

'You could always see if the maid is around somewhere. She was in the kitchen a short while ago.'

Jack left the room to go in search of the maid. He came back a few minutes later. 'I found her. I also asked if there was somewhere private we could talk, Roger. I'd like to ask your opinion on something and I would rather not be overheard. She said we could use the library.'

'Very well. It sounds intriguing. Which is the library?'

'Apparently it's the room to the left of the stairs. Never been in there. Have you?'

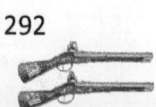

'Obviously not. I didn't even know they had one or I wouldn't have asked which it was, would I?' he replied, as a smile crept across his face. Jack's expression showed he had realised the absurdity of his question, shook his head and tutted at himself. 'Hmm, stupid of me.'

'Never mind,' said Roger still smiling. 'So lead on, let's go and have a look. What about your drink?'

'The maid is bringing it.'

Soon they were in the large wood pannelled room at the rear of the house with shelves from floor to ceiling, stacked with books. On the opposite wall was a large fireplace, the mantle as high as Roger's shoulder, with three thick pine logs in the grate that gave a fresh clean fragrance to the room. Above the mantlepiece hung a portrait of a stern-looking grey haired man, smartly and as far as Roger could tell, expensively dressed.

'I wonder who he is,' said Jack, just as the maid who had served breakfast, entered carrying a tray with two large cups and a jug of ale.

'That's my father,' she said, and her smile reflected in her emerald-green eyes as she put the tray down on a small ornate three-legged table. 'At present he is in a village on the other side of Glastonbury, Coxley. He is a doctor and is staying with friends, the vicar at Coxley, and his wife. The vicar had a nasty fall down the bell tower stairs and has broken bones. His wife is frail and unable to cope so father is staying until the vicar recovers.'

'Your father?' said Roger, completely taken aback. He looked over at Jack who seemed equally astonished. It appeared that he was not alone in thinking of her as anything other than a servant. 'So you're not a...'

'No, Captain Wingfield. I am not a housemaid,' she said with a smile and she removed the white lace mob cap freeing bunches of pretty ringlets, tied with cream pearly ribbons on either side of her head, to frame her face. Roger held his breath.

'I am Lady Veronica Cowley. After my husband died in the fighting at Axminster in June, I came here to look after my father. My late husband was Sir Christopher Cowley, our family are closely related to the Earl of Winterne.'

Roger breathed again.

'So that's how you pronounce Coxley...sounding like Cokesley,' said Jack. 'Oh dear, I told two men in our troop that they were wrong and it was pronounced as Cocksley. I must apologise to them.'

Lady Veronica laughed. 'There are a number of strange names and pronunciations in the west country, Lieutenant. You'll never get used to them all as you probably won't be here long enough.'

Roger cut in. 'Then please accept my apologies...once again, Lady Veronica, but why did you not correct me about your status?'

'I was having far too much fun, Captain.' Her smile dropped. 'You will have noticed that there is very little joy in this city at the moment.'

'Indeed, Lady Veronica. There is very little joy anywhere at present and I am sorry for your loss.'

'Thank you, but there is no need. I liked Kit...that's what we in the family called him, but it was not as if he was the love of my life.'

To Roger that seemed somewhat emotionless. She sensed that in his expression and moved a little closer. Her green eyes looked into his and he saw sincerity there.

'That may seem cold to you, but ours was an arranged marriage. We were distant cousins... were relatively...excuse the pun...' Roger smiled, '...friendly, but neither of us had any great desire to marry the other. It was purely a practical arrangement agreed to safeguard a piece of land for the family.' She turned away towards the bay window. Jack and Roger watched her glide across to the window seat where she made herself comfortable. The sun poured through giving a golden-red sheen to her hair, making Roger think of a halo. At a rumbling sound out on the street, Lady Veronica peered out. It was just a passing two-horse cart carrying logs. She turned back to Roger.

'I do miss Kit. Although distant cousins, we saw a lot of each other growing up, and I knew him well, or I thought I did. I was not the only person to be shocked when he turned against the king and joined the duke's forces. As lifelong Royalists his family were devastated, especially his mother. On the 10th of June he informed me that he was going to Lyme Regis to meet the duke when he landed, and he took twenty men with him. I never saw or heard from him again. It was not until a week after the skirmish at Axminster that I heard I had become a widow.'

Roger looked down at the floor, and nervously shuffled his feet wondering how to phrase his next question. Jack wondered why his captain seemed so...well... tongue-tied.

'Captain Wingfield?' Is there a problem, sir?' Lady Veronica tilted her head, her expression a combination of quizzical and amused.

Roger looked up to face her. 'Forgive me for asking, and you may choose not to answer, my lady, but may I ask which side you favour, Lady

Veronica?'

To his surprise, she smiled and seemingly took no offence at being asked what could be taken as a confrontational question. 'Let me be candid, Captain. I favour neither side. There are faults on both sides. To begin with the duke arrived with far too small an army. He was also vain, overconfident in his own abilities and I believe sulking, thereby leaving him open to flattery and exploitation by men who wanted to use him for their own ends.'

'Sulking?'

'Yes, indeed.' With a final glance out of the window she moved to an armchair near the fireplace. Jack was already sitting in the one opposite, so she indicated that Roger should pull up one of the fireside stools covered in the same damask rose satin as the armchairs and the window seat. 'I believe that the duke, having been brought up as one of King Charles' favourite children, although illegitimate, had hopes of being declared the monarch but, of course, with no legitimate children, the throne went to the king's legal heir, his brother. My belief is that the young duke, having been indulged all his life, and protestant, was talked into considering that he had a valid claim to the throne.

'On the other hand, King James has made no secret of his preference to the Roman Catholic religion and converted some time ago. He also believes in the divine right to rule and absolutism, meaning that he has the supreme authority and can over-ride our laws as he wishes. It is clear that the people do not want this, but he ignores any advice given on this matter. I hope and pray that I am speaking to sympathetic parties here, but I don't believe he will be our monarch for long.'

'For my part,' said Jack, 'you are indeed in safe company, my lady.'

'And you, Captain?' she turned her smiling eyes to him, waiting for his reaction.'

He hesitated for a moment, clasped his hands while he thought of an appropriate answer. He stood and rested his arm on the fireplace and looked down into the empty grate. She did not press him, but he was aware that Jack was studying him, awaiting his reaction. If Lady Veronica was a spy for Judge Jeffreys, then Jack had probably already put his head in a noose. On the other hand, she had given what his gut told him was an honest and appropriate point of view, and he dearly wanted to trust her.

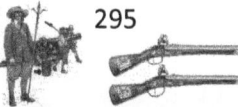

'My lady, firstly you must understand that from my position as a captain in the king's army, I have sworn to serve him.'

She nodded but showed no disappointment or fear of what he was going to say next.

'However, as a man I do see things I do not like.' He turned to watch her reaction. 'I feel the reprisals have gone much too far. The putting to death of Lady Alice Lisle sickened me. Whether she was aware that the two men she sheltered for that one night were Monmouth supporters, is up for question, but a lady of around seventy-years of age should never have been put through that distressing trial and subsequently executed.'

'At least Judge Jeffreys managed to persuade the king to commute her sentence to beheading instead of burning,' said Jack, staring at the floor. 'Do you think it's true that the king had a score to settle with her following her late husband's involvement with Cromwell in the execution of his father, Charles I? I would have thought he would have been satisfied when her husband was murdered by members of the King's Service in Switzerland. Did he have to take revenge on the old lady as well? Surely it would have been a more popular decision to have shown clemency to a lady of such an age.'

'That's true,' replied Roger, 'the judge did convince the king to change the manner of death to something quick and clean, and he should be lauded for that but, for everything else though, he follows the letter of the law to a very literal degree. Of course there's always the point that Judge Jeffreys knew that having her burnt at the stake would certainly have angered the populace. Her execution was disliked by the people and he may have thought changing the manner of her death might make him seem…more human? But in most other cases, where they may be mitigating circumstances, he ignores them. The appalling number of executions and transportation sentences over these last few weeks in Winchester, Salisbury, Dorchester, Exeter and Taunton, is nothing less than merciless…brutal. I also wonder how many of these men were not involved in the uprising at all.'

'Have you thought, gentlemen,' said Lady Veronica, 'that for each man executed or transported to the West Indies for ten years, there is likely to be a wife and children who will be left destitute? And how many of those men will ever return? Scurvy, gaol fever, disease brought on by their hard labour in the heat, and the treatment meted out to slaves in addition to the poor rations they will be provided with, will ensure that possibly only one in a hundred might return home...and to what?'

The Cathedral clock chimed three o'clock and Roger remembered he had a job to do. 'Lady Veronica, thank you for your candour and I assure you that what has been discussed here this afternoon will not leave this room, but I have to take my leave. I still serve judge Jeffreys and he has given me an order. There is something I have to do later for which I need to prepare.'

'Of course, Captain. I understand when duty calls.'

Roger turned to his second lieutenant. 'Jack, would you care to join me?'

Chapter Thirty Eight

Having selected five of the most reliable men in his command, and acquiring six sets of some suitable, but unfortunately somewhat smelly peasant clothing, including a dark woollen hat that would cover his hair – which he had painstakingly checked for lice - Roger and his team were ready to head out to the woods. Two of the men loaded up a small cart with bags of the clothing, covered them with a sheet and drove out of the temporary barracks on their assignment, to all appearances no different to any other. A few minutes later Roger and the other three men, marched out in uniform on what would look to the residents as just another regular patrol.

The two soldiers who had leisurely driven out of Wells, not wanting to attract an unnecessary attention, were waiting when Roger and the others arrived. Having changed clothes just inside the cover of the trees where they would be far less likely to be seen, Roger assigned one man to stay with the horses and the cart. They left their uniforms neatly folded on the back of the cart and headed further into the woods and towards the clearing, just as the sun began its descent.

With it being early autumn and still warm, the trees were still in full leaf, mostly green but some were just beginning to turn to reds, yellows and brown. The dense undergrowth of ferns and bracken, berry laden prickly brambles, and banks of tall grasses helped to conceal their movements through the woods. Soon they found the clearing. The scarred and split grey-brown hollow tree trunk stood alone close to the tree line, its branches broken and disintegrating.

While they waited, Roger ordered them to be silent and to stay completely still. Whatever it was that the weasely man wanted with Judge Jeffreys, the last thing he wanted was to scare him off. Around them the woods resounded with sounds. In the branches above their heads, song birds tweeted and hopped or flew from tree to tree, squirrels scurried about collecting and burying nuts, rabbits looked for juicy dandelions and groundsel, oblivious to the human newcomers. One, too busy eating and obviously unaware of possible danger, hopped within a few feet of one of the soldiers as he sat with his back to the trunk of a wide oak. He watched it as it came closer and closer. He hardly breathed, fascinated. Then, just a few inches away from his foot, it stopped eating, looked up and saw him. For a second they stared at each other, eye to eye, before the pretty grey rabbit turned tail and ran. For a moment the soldier had thought about rabbit stew, but he obeyed his orders to stay still and quiet, and the rabbit never knew how lucky it was that day.

Although the sun was going down, there was still enough of a glorious orange-red sunset casting deep purple-blue shadows over the Mendip Hills, to see clearly. One of the soldiers nudged Roger and pointed towards a movement in the treeline.

A small man, emerged from a gap between the trees. He looked cautiously around then ran towards the dead tree. Those of the soldiers who had been sitting upright, now lowered themselves onto their bellies on the ground to hide within the bracken, and slightly moved the fronds to one side to keep watch on the man.

They heard the whinny of an approaching horse. 'This will be the judge,' Roger whispered. 'Now stay alert. The judge's life may be at stake here.'

One of the soldiers pulled a face. Roger saw. 'Matthews, whatever your personal feelings are towards him, the judge is carrying out the king's command and working within the law. Keep your disapproval to yourself. You have sworn an oath to protect the king, and you will do your duty,' he whispered. He would not let his men see that he had some sympathy with the soldier's viewpoint.

Having been reproached, Matthews nodded. 'Yes, sir. Sorry, sir,' he mouthed.

They turned back to see the small man emerge from inside the shell of the tree. He walked up to the judge who had not dismounted. Roger and his men could not hear what was being said, but the man pointed back towards where he had come out of the trees, and began to walk that way. The judge, still on his horse made to follow but, looking at the man's gestures, Roger assumed he was telling the judge that the horse would not be able to get through the mass of trees and undergrowth. He seemed to be telling the judge that he should dismount and follow on foot. Initially Judge Jeffreys shook his head, clearly against the idea, but as he drew closer to the treeline, they saw him dismount and tether his horse to a tree, then they both vanished into the trees.

'Right,' said Roger. 'Let's go. We must stay close to the judge but without being seen. As I said before, we have no idea what this man is about or why he wants the judge to be here...alone.' He looked from one soldier to the next, then his gaze fixed on Matthews. 'This goes for all of you. Whatever you feel about the judge, remember we have a job to do and, as members of His Majesty's military force, we will carry out our orders. Do you understand?'

'Yes, sir,' came the whispered chorus of agreement.

'Right then, let's get on with it.'

They followed closely, but kept to the shadows with the judge kept in their sight. At one point, a frightened pheasant, disturbed from its feeding, flew out of the bracken making a loud two-note crowing sound, a little like a rooster. The little man and the judge looked around as Roger signalled for his men to drop to the ground. He peered over the bracken. Clearly satisfied there was nothing amiss, the man and the judge had begun to walk on. They rose up and followed.

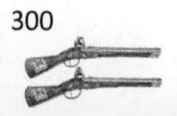

Chapter Thirty Nine

Henry Maitland excused himself from supper with his father, by saying that he had been invited to dine with his friend, Philip, the son of the Bishop. Priests of the Church of England had been allowed to marry following an Act by Edward VI in 1547.

Henry's father had been surprised at his sudden change of mind, and enquired as to whether there might be a young lady somewhere in the picture that his son preferred to say nothing about for the moment. Henry had neither agreed nor disagreed but had forced a little smile, giving his father the impression that he may have been correct. Satisfied the Earl gave Henry a knowing look and said no more.

A little while later, as Henry walked nervously through the rear garden of the manor, heading towards the stables, he wondered how he had managed to keep his nerve in front of his father. The sun was just beginning to go down beyond the hills and the time had come for him to keep his promise to John and the two Dutch soldiers.

Henry had chosen that time for two reasons. Firstly, of the two grooms who worked at the stables, one lived on the edge of Winterne Village, and the other, Bryn, had two rooms above the stables. At this time of day he would have gone for his supper, and it would be very unlikely that he would go back down to the stables for another two hours or so. That would be when he went to check on the horses for the night and made sure they had fresh water and hay. The other was that, with the woods so near to the stables, at that time there would be very few people about, giving them a good chance to slip into the woods unnoticed.

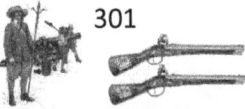

Henry was looking forward to getting this escapade over and done and not only because of the danger of being caught. There was a strange atmosphere in Winterne Woods. He always felt a little uncomfortable and tried to avoid walking through it when he could. He always had the uncomfortable feeling of being watched and constantly kept looking over his shoulder, but there was never any one...or any *thing* to see. There seemed to be an invisible force, whether good or evil he wasn't sure, but he knew many people felt the same. Local folk told tales of strange noises and that there were 'things' – which no-one ever gave a name to – that didn't want people in there. Even poachers went elsewhere, unless they were desperate enough to brave it out.

Some of the local farmers wives would always bake a small loaf at the same time as the family loaf, and left the small one out, "for the little folk" they said. Henry knew one woman who always left a hunk of cheese on the windowsill when she cut into a new one, and some bacon when she had smoked a new flitch. She, too said it was the little people who took them, but Henry thought it was more likely to be a cat or fox. But, on this evening, he had something more to think about than missing food and little people, and the woods would provide the cover he needed.

On arriving at the stables, he looked around to make sure Bryn was nowhere in sight. Satisfied Bryn was in his rooms, he slipped into the barn to find John, Hendrik and Caspar waiting for him.

'There's no-one about so now will be a good time to go.' He looked at the two Dutch soldiers. 'Are you both strong enough to walk a little over a mile?' They nodded. 'Then stay close to me. Keep listening for anything that might pose a threat but remember this, once we get to where we are going you will not have to be outside again. As far as I am aware, I am the only person alive who knows of this place. Even John knows nothing of it. Let's go but stay alert.'

Behind the stables was an open space of about one hundred yards between them and the treeline. Keeping to the shadows, and alert for any sign of movement, the four men scurried to the trees, halting for a few seconds when startled by the barking of Bryn's dog. The shutter at Bryn's window opened and they moved further into the shadows as he looked out. Seeing nothing, Bryn told the dog to be quiet and closed the shutter. Henry and John saw the fear in each other's eyes, gave a little smile of relief and the four moved on into the trees, where Henry realised he had been holding his breath. In the cover of the trees he breathed again. 'Stay close,' Henry ordered, 'and stay quiet.' Hendrik was the next in line, followed by Caspar. John was the last in line, his eyes watchful for any sign of impending danger.

Like any woodland, there were always the sounds of wildlife. From somewhere not too far away a fox gave its high-pitched bark, rabbits scuttled through the undergrowth rummaging about for their last meal of the day, crows cawed as they began to head to their tree-top roosts and, from somewhere in the distance came a strange bellowing noise.

Hendrik, trembling at being in the open again, jumped at the sound. The colour drained from his face and he stood stock still, looking this way and that in terror. Henry touched his arm reassuringly, told him not to worry, and explained it was the sound of a red deer stags fighting over a group of hinds, the females. Hendrik, inhaled, calmed, and they moved on.

After a while, Henry held up his hand for them to stop and signalled for them to drop to the floor. Ahead he had heard voices, something he had prayed would not happen. Crawling on their stomachs, they slithered a little closer. Just a few yards away they saw two men. One, short and thin, in a dirty shirt and baggy brown breeches, emerged from the trees very close to the place where Henry was planning to hide his fugitives. But it was the second man that terrified Henry.

'Keep still,' he whispered. 'It would have to be him, wouldn't it! With any luck, they will move on soon. We will just have to wait until they have gone.'

John crawled closer to him. 'Who is it?'

Henry looked surprised. 'Do you not recognise him?'

John shook his head. 'I don't think I have ever seen him before.'

'That's the Hanging Judge.'

'Oh, God help us,' said John.

'Yes, that's Judge Jeffreys, but what in heaven's name is he doing here?'

'There is something wrong?' whispered Hendrik.

'Yes, but we wait.'

'Oh Lord!' said John, lowering his head even further.

'What is it?'

'Take a look in the bracken beyond them, Henry.'

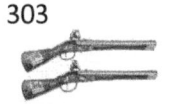

Henry peered through the long grass at the place to which John had pointed. At first he could see nothing, then a slight movement caught his eye. He concentrated on that spot and caught a glimpse of a few strands of blond hair straying from under a brown woollen hat. He saw the man the hair belonged to turn and speak. Clearly there were at least two men, possibly more watching the little man and the judge from the other side of the path. For the moment though, it seemed that he and the three men with him had not been spotted. They would stay still and wait; hopefully not for long, as full sunset was only about thirty minutes away. He wanted to get these men hidden before then.

While they watched, two more men broke from cover behind the judge brandishing wooden clubs and ran at him. The small man started to run away. Hendrik tried to see what was happening but Henry pushed him down, just at the moment when, with a shout, the blond haired man and four others darted from the undergrowth. One chased the small man, caught him and dragged him, crying back to where his colleagues, at the order of the blond haired man, were hauling back the two now captured newcomers.

'No! We stay low!' He pointed to John. 'This man has a wife and child. If he is caught aiding you he will be executed. Do you want that on your conscience?'

Hendrik did as he was told and held his countryman flat to the ground with his arm.

Having tied the hands of the three men and hobbled their ankles with ropes loose enough to allow them to walk a little, but not enough to run, the blond man removed his hat. 'It would appear, my lord, that this was indeed an assassination attempt.'

'It certainly would, Captain Wingfield.' He walked up to the weasely little man, who dropped to his knees. 'Me lord, they med me do it. Oi din't wan' ter, bu' they said they wud kill me if Oi din't do wot they said. 'Tweren't moi fault, 'onest, me lord.' He made a grab to cling on to the judge's legs, but he was kicked away. 'We were right not to trust this...this person,' said the Judge, wrinkling his nose at the pungent smell emanating from the captive. 'He can join the others awaiting trial tomorrow...and those...'

It was at that point that John sneezed. Henry and the two Dutchmen froze. John looked terrified. All nine men captors and captives, turned to look at where the sound had come from. Three of them started to walk towards the spot.

Henry was about to say: 'Run for your lives', when everything seemed to happen at once. The out-of-uniform soldiers sped up towards them, Hendrik and his companion got to their feet to run in one direction while John and Henry turned to go in another, but they had only gone a few feet when a rapidly moving thick grey mist filled the space between them and the judge and soldiers.

Henry made a lunge to grab Hendrik. John caught up with Caspar.

Henry said: 'Come. Somehow we have a chance. Follow me and be silent.' They could hear the soldiers shouting in the midst of the fog, calling to each other in confusion. The captain's voice called out.

'Don't let the prisoners escape!'

One of the soldiers called back that the prisoners were still hobbled and would not get far.

With his small group staying close together, Henry led them along the side of a crag and stopped at a thick veil of ivy vines. He pushed the heavy foliage to one side and disappeared under the cloak of green leaves. They heard a click, Henry poked his head out from the twining stems and beckoned to them. Through a thick wooden door, they found themselves in a tunnel where lit oil lamps, suspended from hooks on wooden supports at several places gave plenty of light to see ahead. Henry ensured the door was closed behind them and they heard a swishing noise from outside.

'That's the ivy sliding back into place, Henry explained. 'The door is completely hidden from view to all who don't know it's there.'

John looked around, open-mouthed. 'But...but, what is this place, Henry? Where are we?'

'My father has not looked at the drawn plans of the manor. I don't believe they ever interested him particularly, but I have. This tunnel and the room beyond, has been here for centuries but it is my guess that only a few have ever used it.'

'But where does it go?'

'I will show you that in a moment, but more to the point where did that mist come from? You do realise that, if it had not been for that, we would have been caught by the soldiers.'

'But they were not in uniform, how did you know they were soldiers?'

'Their mission this time was obviously covert as they were out of uniform, but I am sure I have seen that blond man before. But, now, let's get these gentlemen settled. I warn you though, you will see some unpleasant sights along the way.'

'But not as unpleasant as a hangman's noose, I think, Viscount Winterne,' said Hendrik. Caspar nodded, understanding.

Leading the way, Henry took them along the tunnel where they squeezed by the boulder that pinned down the headless remains of a man who died many years before. A little further along, they reached a thick wooden door that swung open at Henry's touch and found themselves in a wider area with two what of appeared to be cells on either side, and beyond that another wooden door.

Inside they found themselves in a large open room and, to their surprise five other men were already there. Two of them wore the same tattered uniform as Hendrik and Caspar. Caspar's eyes lit up.

'Jan!' he cried and ran to the other man. They embraced joyfully.

Hendrik explained that Caspar and Jan were brothers and that Caspar had thought his brother dead or captured. They had been separated at Sedgemoor and had not seen each since.

While the men, who had all eluded the king's soldiers, greeted each other, John looked around the room. Somehow, Henry had provided enough straw to cover the cold stone floor, food and blankets. The men who were already there seemed well fed and warm. He looked back at Henry, bewildered and astonished at the courage his young lord had shown.

'Henry, how did you do this? How long have these men been here? And that other door, where does it lead? Where on earth did that mist come from? And...oh, my God...what is that?' He seemed to be looking everywhere at once, but then pointed at a tall carved wooden box that stood against the back wall.

'I knew you would have lots of questions and I'll answer them all. Firstly, though that's what was called an Iron Maiden and that...' he pointed across the room, '...is a rack. Both instruments of torture. And, over there is what I assume is one of the victims.' He pointed towards a darkened corner of the room behind the door through which they had just entered.

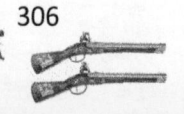

John walked over into the shadowy corner where something bulky was covered by a blanket. He pulled it off and gasped when he saw a skeleton, manacled to the wall, still with long strands of dark hair clinging to the skull and traces of desiccated skin. Henry walked over to join him.

'I have no idea who this was but either he was a member of the family, or was tortured by a member of the family. See, the ring with our family crest lies within his frame.'

'Does that mean he was made to swallow it?'

Henry nodded. 'It would certainly seem that way and it is my belief that it was one of my ancestors, Giles Maitland, from the time of our king's grandfather, the first King James of England and James VI of Scotland, who made this poor victim do so. Probably to emphasise he was vanquished.'

'But why would he do that?'

'Because he was quite mad. From the documents I have read, the king's fear of witchcraft was spoken of a great deal at Court, and Giles heard about it while at the palace of St James in Westminster when he attended the king's coronation. There have always been tales of witchcraft in the county. Men were accused and executed as well as women, although of course there were more women who suffered that terrible fate. Giles, it seems, became obsessed, perhaps even fanatical, with the idea of clearing the county of all witches. He set about finding like-minded men who believed as he did and anyone they didn't like, looked a little different, suffered at their hands. I think any excuse to make some poor person suffer was enough for Giles. He had many snatched, imprisoned and tortured...'

'...Until they confessed,' John finished the sentence. 'But I wonder how he managed to get these terrible things in here.'

'My guess is that he had them brought in through the tunnel in pieces and assembled them in here.'

John looked down at the skeleton again. 'I wonder who this poor creature is...was?'

'If I'm right,' said a deep, gravelly voice behind them.

Henry spun around. 'Father...I?'

'My lord?' said John, with a bow.

So deep in conversation were Henry and John, that neither had noticed the men in the far corner had stopped talking, or that someone else had entered the room. It was only when the Earl spoke that they became aware of the silence in the room. Henry was horrified to find his father, the Earl, standing behind them, glowering.

Every man in the room held his breath as he waited to see how the Earl would react, each one aware that his life was in the hands of a powerful member of the aristocracy.

'I'm...so sorry, Father...' Henry, clearly shaken at having been discovered, fell to his knees, head bowed.

'Get up, my boy,' the Earl smiled, as he reached down to help his son rise. 'I am not angry with you. In fact I applaud your actions. I just wish you had trusted me to help you.'

'Thank you, Father. I'm sorry not to have told you what we were doing.' Some of the cobwebs from the tunnel ceiling still clung to the back of the Earl's black doublet. Henry brushed them off with his hand.

The resemblance between father and son was remarkable but, being twenty years Henry's senior, Bartley had put on a little weight, his face was a little more jowly and his red hair and moustache were threaded with grey.

The Earl looked at Henry and John and smiled, then turned to look at the men they had hidden. He said: 'What I do not approve of are the actions of both sides. The duke was a fool. He had no legal right to the throne, but James has allowed his need for revenge to go too far. Jeffreys can tell himself he is only upholding the king's law, but he shows no mercy and does nothing to ensure that each man...or woman he is executing is in fact guilty of treason.' His eyebrows, knitted together in a deep frown, puckering his forehead.

'Now we must decide what we do next.'

'But...how long have you known?' Henry asked.

'A few days. I saw you taking food into your room and wondered why. I knocked on your door and received no answer, so went in. You weren't there. There was only one place you could have gone. Don't forget, your chamber was mine until I became the Earl. I followed you down and listened at the door.' He winked. Then walked around Henry and looked down at the skeleton.

'I found this room many years ago and have been down here several times. My father told me about Giles who he vaguely remembered from his childhood. He was terrified of him. He was a brute. I wanted to find out more about Giles, so I looked through all the family records.

'If I'm right, those unfortunate remains belong to a young man who had studied medicine in Italy. According to what I read, his skills were far beyond anything our doctors knew. He was a travelling monk, a good man from what I understand...and, don't look at me like that Henry, yes, I have read the manor documents, and the writings in the family bible that was begun by Catherine Hallett, wife of William, the creator of our lineage. And do not forget, I also had a father who told me what he knew from his father about our family.

'I found a small note folded in pages in another part of the family bible. It appears to have been written by Gerard, one of Giles's brothers, there was another brother, George but he only lived until he was a little over six years old. Gerard's note tells of a young monk named Antonius who had visited the manor and talked to my grandfather about his views on medicine. It seems grandfather approved, but Giles did not. He was vehemently against Antonius, hostile. According to Gerard's notes, after Antonius left the manor to return to Glastonbury Abbey where he was staying, he was never seen again. Gerard apparently did not know of the secret passage or this room, so had no knowledge of what Giles could have done, but he always suspected his involvement in the disappearance.'

The Earl, watched by all the hiding soldiers, continued. 'Yes, I am convinced this is Brother Antonius, a young and apparently brilliant Benedictine monk of whom Giles disapproved because of his superior medical expertise. Because his practices were innovative and had been learned abroad, Giles believed Antonius was in league with the devil, even though the poor man was clearly a worshipper of God.'

'What happened to Giles, Father?'

'He died in 1630 in unexplained circumstances. The only thing known from the family records is that his body was found on the circular lawn at the front of the manor by the fountain. There was not a mark on his body anywhere. No evidence as what...or who had killed him at just three and thirty years of age.' He turned away from the remains of Antonius to face the men waiting at the far side of the room.

'Now, about you men. My son has saved your lives, and I will not give you away. However, as you have already been here for a little while, you will have realised this is not a particularly comfortable existence for you, but you are alive, fed, sheltered and warm. I will do what I can to assist my son with your care. We will continue to feed you but, you must agree that you...to be honest, I'm sorry, but you stink, and you will need the...other ...um facilities.' He looked at Henry. 'I presume until now you have been waiting until the woods are quiet in the evening for that?'

Henry nodded.

'You will not do that again. With the soldiers now being aware of something untoward in the area, bearing in mind your narrow escape a short while ago, I do not consider your venturing outside for any purpose, at any time, to be safe. So far you have been fortunate. However, for obvious reasons I do not want anyone else to know you are here. The fewer people who know about you, the safer you, and we, will be. Tonight, when the family and servants are abed, one of us will take you, two at a time, through that door and along the corridor to the house. You will be taken to the small bathroom on the ground floor next to the kitchen where you will bathe, if you have lice, you will be given combs. You will be given clean clothing. If you have wounds they will be dressed. You *will* be silent! That is for your sake and for those who have helped you. Do you understand?'

The men nodded, solemnly grateful.

'Very well. You will be here until the troops have gone, then we will find a way to return you to your homes when it is safe.'

Two of the men crumpled onto the floor and cried relieved tears. Others looked joyful, and all understood the risks the Earl, the Viscount and the steward were taking to keep them safe.

-OoO-

Outside, the mist vanished as quickly as it had appeared and, although the sun had now set, the full moon gave enough light to see by. Although still thoroughly mystified at how the men they had caught sight of, before the haze materialised, had simply vanished, Roger wanted the judge to see he was fully in control, and ordered his men to remove the hobbles from their captives legs. They were to be walked back into the city and imprisoned while awaiting trial but, before leaving the woods, the soldiers would escort Judge Jeffreys back to the clearing where his horse was tethered. He would then accompany the soldiers and prisoners into Wells.

The moment Ned Wormald was free, he darted away from the solider holding him and threw himself at the feet of the judge.

'Lord Jeffreys, sir, Oi never lied. Oi beg yer ter believe it,' he cried. The judge took a step back. Wormald crawled after him. 'Oi din't know what them men was goin' ter do. Oi don't know 'em,' he pleaded to the stony faced judge. 'Yer must believe me, moi lord.'

The soldiers laughed at him, but Roger shut them up with an irritated glance.

'Why should I believe you? asked the judge. ' You led me here and they were here waiting. That seems very suspect to me. Would you not agree, Captain? These men had weapons which I assume they intended to use. That too is suspect. How did they know I would be here, alone, if you did not tell them? No, I believe it was planned between the three of you?'

By now Wormald was crying, his shoulder heaving with the effort, such was his terror. His begging and what seemed to be genuine pleading was almost convincing, Roger thought. But then he reasoned that any terrified man would be likely to behave in the same manner.

'You brought me here for one reason, did you not?' said the judge. 'You suggested you had evidence against the Earl of Winterne for harbouring fugitives. If you can produce that evidence, then I may consider sparing your life.'

'Oh, thank you, thank you, moi lord.' Wormald stood. 'Look, come wi' me, moi lord. I can show you. 'Onest I can. Oi don't know where tha' mist coom from, but Oi promise yer 'll see what yer lookin' fer over 'ere.'

He led the judge and Roger to the ivy-covered crag. 'This is it. 'Tis 'ere, moi lord.'

'Where? All I can see is ivy vines.'

Roger thought of Lady Veronica. She was a Maitland. If what Wormald was saying was true, how far into the family would the judge extend his self-styled justice?

'The door's under 'ere. Look Oi'll show yer.' He grasped a bunch of vines and pulled them to one side. 'Captain, would yer 'elp 'old this back, please?'

'So where is this door? asked the judge. Roger felt his heart pound.

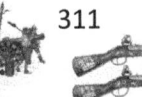

'Oi'm sorry, oi lord. Oi must've med a mistake. It's 'ere somewhere.' Wormald still seemed convinced but he was now clearly panicking. Nervous perspiration beaded his forehead and he looked around at the judge, then Roger, then at the other two captives guarded by the other soldiers. Above them in the trees an early evening owl gave a hoot that sounded a little like laughter.

Wormald moved along the side of the crag, sometimes buried under heavy trails of ivy while the rest of the company waited patiently. His panic increasing, the terrified man began laughing hysterically. 'But, Oi know it's 'ere…ha ha ha…'tis…ha…ha…'tis…*it is!* It mus be. Oi told the judge it were. Oi seen it…Oi did. Oi seen 'em goin' in…din't Oi?'

'I think that's enough, Captain. He's talking to himself now and its clear there's nothing here. The sun has set and it will take us a while to return to Wells…and, I don't know about you but I want my supper. The day will begin early and will end late tomorrow. No more of this nonsense. Get him dragged out of there and we will leave.'

Roger ordered two of his men to retrieve the frenzied Wormald, who seemed to have lost his mind. Roger almost felt some sympathy for him and wondered, if he stayed out of his senses, perhaps that would make it easier for him because the next day he would surely hang. Overall though, Roger felt a massive sense of relief. Lady Veronica was safe. He realised that he was far more concerned about her than the Earl and his side of the family and wondered why.

When they arrived at the clearing where Judge Jeffreys' horse waited for him, no-one realised they were being watched by three pairs of eyes. The owners of those eyes felt some sympathy for Ned Wormald, but the woods of Winterne belonged to them, and they alone decided the fate of those who entered their territory. They chose to support the Maitland family over who they had watched for centuries and, who to their minds, were doing an honourable thing. Wormald would have betrayed the Maitlands, and that would never do.

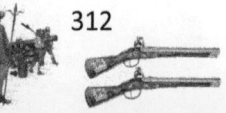

Chapter Forty

The next morning the crowd had gathered early. The space under the Market Hall was used as a temporary court and the scaffold, a long contraption with six nooses on a raised platform, had been erected outside. The mood of the crowd was angry, sullen and surprisingly quiet. No-one spoke. Roger would have preferred angry shouting; he would have expected that. But the silence, the stillness was disconcerting. From his elevated place on the steps of the Market Hall, he looked into the crowd, spotted the occasional nod or shake of the head, the odd covert hand signal between men. He walked towards Jack, and turned his back on the crowd as he quietly described three of the men he suspected of conspiring.

'I hope they will not be so foolhardy as to start anything. There are women and children here who are sure to be hurt if they incite trouble.' Even though he would do his duty, Roger hoped to God he would not have to. He fully understood every man and woman there realised that, even before their trial, the accused men had been condemned. His men were armed and well trained, but they were outnumbered by the mob. Any small spark could ignite a riot which would only end in more deaths.

Roger split his force of fifty men into two groups. The first, thirty-five men all told, with Roger himself in command, would be on duty outside. The smaller group of fifteen, including Jack, would be inside the court, at the doors and standing around the walls, all fully armed with muskets and swords.

The atmosphere was understandably tense. The soldiers were hated just as much as the judges, for they too represented the despised king. Roger knew that not everyone supported the late duke, but the brutal reprisals taken by the judiciary over the previous assizes in Hampshire, Dorset, Devon and Somerset, particularly by Judge Jeffreys, had sickened people. Although they were quiet at the moment, Roger sensed that he was sitting on a tinderbox. One little spark and the entire area could ignite.

A roar went up as the enclosed carriages holding the prisoners, came into view and the crowd moved in front to stop the horses passing. For a few moments Roger held his soldiers back, he had no wish to provoke the crowd into hostility, the situation was already precarious. To his relief it was the horses that broke up the blockade. Having become nervous with the mass of people pressing around them, one of the heavy carthorses pulling the first carriage reared up, its front hooves dangerously close to those people directly in front. With its neighbour already snorting and kicking out, the second horse joined in. The carriage began to rock, alarming the prisoners inside, and the people on either side who felt they might be in danger if the carriage tumbled over. Seconds later, the crowd moved back allowing the carriages through, and they proceeded to the cordoned off area, where the prisoners were led out and into the court.

Around fifteen minutes later, Jack emerged through the crowd, looking as though he wanted to be sick. He made his way directly to Roger.

'This trial is a travesty! I have never seen anything like it!' Jack's face was twisted with rage. 'Jeffreys is acting as though he is a prosecutor, not a judge. Damn him!'

'Calm yourself, Jack. Take a deep breath and then tell me what's happening.'

Jack's kindly brown eyes filled with angry tears. He blinked them back, and chewed his bottom lip as he took a moment to look up at the blue sky. Birds flew, long white clouds high up streaked the sky and looking upwards, all was right with the world but, as far as Jack was concerned, at ground level in the City of Wells, nothing was right. Hoping no-one other than his captain, who he knew to be compassionate, would see, Jack batted away his tears with his sleeve, and turned to Roger.

'Now tell me what's happening.'

'Did you know there were children amongst the prisoners. Little girls and boys, five of them, I would guess their ages are between six and nine years old. They are terrified.'

'But why are they there? What have they been...'

'Treason! Can you believe that, Roger? Treason at that age. These poor children have been ripped away from their families, imprisoned with all these men and charged with something they don't have the first idea of. They are utterly terrified. One poor little lad couldn't see over the witness box all he knew was that Jeffreys was shouting at him. The poor boy cried for his mother and...and Jeffreys shouted at him that he would never see his mother or home again. It was as though he actually enjoyed torturing the poor boy even further.'

'But what had he done?'

'It seems he was heard singing one of the rebel songs about the duke. He didn't even know what the words meant. He was just repeating what he had heard local men sing. God, Roger, these children are going to be transported to the West Indies, where our king's friends have plantations. Now look at the number of slaves they will have.'

'But didn't the other judges say anything in support of the children?'

'Oh, Montague and Wythens tried but Jeffreys pulled rank and shut them up. Pollexfen, Levinz and Wright all seem too scared of him. He has so much support from the king I'm guessing they feel they cannot go against him for fear of offending the king.'

'Stay here, Jack. Take my place here for a while. I am going inside.'

'Thank you, Roger, but please don't send me back in there. Friend of the king or not, if I go back in a might be tempted to kill him myself.'

Roger turned to go, but Jack touched him on the shoulder. 'Do you know how many prisoners they have in there today?'

Roger shook his head.

'Five Hundred and forty three! I can see you didn't realise it was so many either. *Five Hundred and Forty Three*! How many women and children, when their husbands, sons and fathers are executed or transported, will be left destitute after this, Roger? It's barbaric!'

Aghast at the number of victims, and the vindictive treatment they had received, Roger shook his head sadly, turned and walked into the courthouse. All prisoners held in Wells were dealt with that day. Although most were sentenced to death only eight were executed immediately. Of the others, some were sent straight away to ships for transporting to the West Indies, while others were left languishing in jail, most spent some months in gaol and died of gaol fever before transportation could be carried out. Like many of those who were executed during the Assizes, the eight men who were executed in Wells that day were hanged, drawn and quartered.

Roger later learned that Judge Jeffreys had trumped up false charges against a number of innocent men, and had taken bribes amounting to thousands of pounds to secure their freedom.

Epilogue

Roger Wingfield

Following the trial, Captain Roger Wingfield returned home to Bridgewater and resigned his commission in the Suffolk Regiment. His father was bitterly disappointed with his decision, until Roger described the horrors he had seen, and the lack of defence counsel for the poor. After Roger's detailed explanation of his experiences during his time with Judge Jeffreys, his father understood.

Roger married Lady Veronica Maitland very much against her family's wishes, but she stated that, as she had married before to please her family, she would now marry to please herself.

Some years later evidence was found that Jeffreys, and others close to him, had accused innocent men, threatening them with prison, execution or transportation, demanding bribes of thousands of pounds to allow them their freedom.

Roger studied Law, and became one of a small number of lawyers defending the ordinary man in English courts. He eventually rose to King's Counsel, serving the joint monarchs, William III and Queen Mary II, the daughter of King James II. Roger and Lady Veronica had two sons and one daughter. Both boys followed their father's footsteps in practising Law.

Lady Veronica Maitland

When the judges left Wells, Lady Veronica was horrified to discover the appalling situation that many women and children found themselves in with the loss of their menfolk. Calling on the goodwill of many of Somerset's society ladies, they set about securing enough labour from neighbouring counties, to bring in what was left of the cereal crops that should already have been harvested.

In addition, in larger villages where families were already close to starvation, they set up soup kitchens and, in some places where there was enough space, arranged for families without men to share accommodation and thereby help each other.

During this time, she and Roger Wingfield became closer and, in 1687 were married. Financially independent, Lady Veronica supported Roger during his years of studying.

George Jeffreys, Baron of Wem.

Having found favour with Kings James II, and subsequently made Baron of Wem in 1681, George Jeffreys was promoted to Chief Justice of the King's Bench and the Privy Council in 1683 and was, therefore given the position of senior judge at what became called The Bloody Assizes, following the Monmouth Rebellion in 1685. By way of reward for his efforts during that period, he was made Lord Chancellor.

With a reputation for brutality, Jeffreys was generally despised. In 1688 James II fled England for two reasons. The first was that the birth of his son, also named James, was felt to be threatening to protestants, who worried that this meant the beginning of a Roman Catholic dynasty. The second was that, when seven protestant bishops, who he had accused of sedition, were cleared, James felt that this was a direct threat to his authority as king. Riots against Catholicism ensued and James was persuaded to leave England to avoid another civil war.

Unfortunately for Jeffreys, he was left behind and waited a little too long before trying to escape to France. History has it that, dressed as a sailor while waiting in a public house in Wapping before joining a ship to take him to France, he was recognised by one of the few surviving victims of his courts. Jeffreys was taken to the Lord Mayor of London, who thought it better to have him imprisoned for his own safety as the mob hated him.

He ended his life at the Tower of London where he died of kidney disease and other health issues. His body was originally buried at St Peter

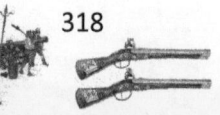

Ad Vincula at the Tower, then his remains were removed in the early 1690's to St Mary Aldermanbury in London. In World War II the church was obliterated by a German bomb during the Blitz of London. Nothing remains of Judge George Jeffreys.

Approximately thirteen hundred men were punished by being hanged, drawn and quartered or hanged, or transported to the West Indies.

The number of people who were executed at the order of Judge Jeffreys is slightly vague and dependent on who recorded them. These are the probable figures.

Axbridge 6	Bath 6	Bridgewater 12	Bridport 9	Bristol 8
Bruton 3	Castle Carey 4	Chard 12	Chewton Mendip 2	Cothelstone 2
Crediton 1	Crewkerne 10	Dorchester 13	Dulverton 3	Dunster 3
Exeter 14	Frome 12	Glastonbury 6	Ilchester 11	Ilminster 12
Keynsham 11	Langport 3	Lyme Regis 12	Milborne Port 2	Minehead 6
Nether Stowey 3	Norton St Philip 12	Pensford 12	Poole 11	Porlock 2
Shepton Mallet 13	Sherborne 12	Somerton 7	South Petherton 3	Stogumber 3
Stogursey 2	Taunton 24	Wareham 6	Wellington 3	Wells 8
Weymouth 12	Wincanton 6	Winchester 1	Wivelscombe 3	Wrington 3
Yeovil 7				

Hendrik and Caspar

Both Dutch soldiers were eventually smuggled out of the country, and returned home to The Netherlands where they were reunited with their families who had thought them dead. After a brief respite to recover their health and strength, they rejoined the army and returned to England with King William and Queen Mary. Both men spent a further two years in England and were able to renew their acquaintance with Earl of Winterne, Bartley Maitland and his son, Henry.

Jamie Scott, Duke of Monmouth

There is evidence that the duke stayed at Longbridge House in Shepton Mallet on the night before his final battle.

Sedgemoor was not the best site for a battle. On the 6$^{th\ of}$ July, the Duke of Monmouth's forces were crossing the marshy land, when they encountered the better trained and equipped army of King James II. Following the Battle of Sedgemoor, the duke, dressed as a woman was discovered hiding in a ditch, arrested and taken to London. History records that he begged his uncle, King James II, to show mercy and allow him to live, saying that he had been misled by others. The king allowed him to speak, according to some revelling in his nephew's misery, then condemned him to death.

On the 15$^{th\ of}$ July, the duke was beheaded, after several attempts, by Jack Ketch who was reputed to be the most inefficient executioner.

Whether true or not, there is a story that, following the duke's burial, it was discovered that there were no portraits of him. His body was removed from his grave, his head stitched back on, the portrait completed and reburied in the Church of St Peter ad Vincula at the Tower of London. His Dukedom was rescinded, but two of his titles, Earl of Doncaster and Baron Scott of Tindale, were subsequently bestowed on his grandson, Francis Scott, who became the 2nd Duke of Buccleuch.

Part Five

1848
In the Time of Queen Victoria
The Curse

Chapter Forty One

Eloise Rochester had her own set of pink and cream wallpapered rooms on the first floor of Number Fourteen, The Lane, Winterne, a rambling two-storey white-washed property owned by local banker and magistrate, Fredrick Rochester, and his wife, Constance.

One very large and sunshine-filled room had previously been the nursery for Eloise and her older brother Edward, who was now a Midshipman in the Royal Navy. As the children grew older, the room was divided by a partition. One side had been converted into a schoolroom where they were taught their lessons by a governess, Miss Chandler, who had left to be married when Eloise was ten years old. The other section of the room was now a snug sitting area with two small sofas and three small occasional tables upon which were potted houseplants, long arch-leafed Boston Ferns, sweet-smelling Jasmine, and, in the corner of the room adjacent to the window, a tall Aspidistra took pride of place.

When Miss Chandler, now Mrs Threlfall, left she had not been replaced. It was customary when a girl reached her tenth birthday, for her mother to continue her education. In this instance, the departure of Miss Chandler had coincided with Eloise reaching this milestone year, and Mrs Rochester had taken on the task of completing Eloise's education, schooling her in all the accomplishments required of a well-brought up young lady.

Edward, at twelve-years-old had continued his education within the Royal Naval College at Greenwich and at sea, confining his studies to all things related to progressing his career.

The first impression on entering the room was of light, airiness and calm contentment. In the grate, a cheery fire flickering brightly behind a secured gilt fireguard, radiated warmth throughout the room on such a cold late autumn day. Yellow beams shone through the diamond patterned leadlight glass windows, but the colour of the rays changed to pink and green as they streamed through the stained glass upper section of the windows depicting tulips with spear-like leaves.

The adjoining room was Eloise's bedroom with a comfortable, slightly wider than usual single bed with clean, crisp white linen sheets and under-pillowcase, and a pink shiny satin eiderdown embroidered with small cream flowers and a top pillowcase in the same material.

Against one wall were three pieces of matching furniture, a cream tallboy chest of drawers, a wardrobe and a washstand with a matching pink and cream floral basin and jug. Adjacent to the tall bay window, a dressing table with a mirror, a comb and bristle hairbrush set, several small open glass jars containing ribbons, hairpins, buttons and other small bric-a-brac sat neatly on white lace doilies. There was also one of Eloise's prized possessions, a closed tortoiseshell trinket box Edward had bought for her in a foreign port during one of his last voyages.

The only other item of furniture was a wide bookcase, so heavily laden the shelves were slightly bowed under the weight of the books thereupon. The décor of the room was finished off prettily by long velvet curtains in a deep rose-colour and a large rug, close in colour to the curtains, that left a ten-inch border of highly polished wooden floorboards all around the room, and several cream scatter rugs that continued the colour scheme of the rest of the room.

Several miniature framed paintings of flowers and woodland animals adorned the walls, and on the two armchairs and the window ledge were a number of dolls of various shapes and sizes.

Through the window the outlook was a pretty one. Tall trees, many now devoid of foliage were bare skeletons awaiting the time when they would burst into life again, mingled with pines, ferns, holly and variegated ivy and, in places where shade prevented the sun's waning warmth, a smattering of early frost tinted the grass a pearlescent white. It should have been a perfectly happy domestic scene but, for Fredrick Rochester, Eloise's father, standing by the door watching her play while being unobserved, it could not have been more distressing.

Eloise sat cross-legged on the floor playing with the most favourite of all her toys, a small rag doll with yellow wool hair and a lavender-coloured floral dress. She cuddled closely the pretty toy that gave her so much comfort, she cooed, gurgled and talked in nonsense words like any five-year-old child, while Mabel, the maid assigned to look after her, busied herself with preparing the small table ready for Eloise's lunch. The raised hoof-shaped scar on Eloise's forehead still appeared a livid red but her parents had been assured that, in time it would fade to a thin white line. Alas, the heavy-handed doctor at the Infirmary who had treated Eloise's wound, had used a clumsy method of stitching which had increased the size of what was now a very ugly scar.

Mabel became aware her employer was in the doorway and made a gesture inviting him in, he shook his head. Fredrick was waiting for a visitor, who he expected to arrive at any moment. Until then, he did not want to disturb his daughter from her play; she was happy and he was content not to disturb her.

Suddenly aware of a movement beside him, Fredrick turned to find Constance looking down at Eloise and trying to fight back the threatening tears. Watching Eloise play should have been a delight for them both, but Fredrick, an outwardly unemotional man, having been brought up not to show weakness or any display of sentiment, stood beside his wife resisting the impulse to put his arm around her shoulder, in case it weakened her resolve.

The ring of the doorbell went unnoticed by the couple, so pre-occupied were they both by their own thoughts. It was only when he heard the rattle of the housekeys that were hooked onto the belt of Mrs Burrows, the housekeeper, as she approached, that Fredrick turned.

'Your visitor has arrived, sir,' she said softly, 'and is waiting in the hall for you.'

Fredrick nodded. 'Thank you, Mrs Burrows. I shall attend him right away.' With one last look at Eloise, he tilted his head to give her a tender smile, which he knew she would not be aware of, then headed off to meet his guest.

Straightening his cravat and jacket as he headed down the stairs and along the blue and white-tiled hallway Fredrick made a great effort to contain his anxiety at seeing his visitor, even though he was a good friend. The conversation they were about to have would probably be the most difficult he would ever experience.

Mrs Burrows hesitated for a few moments to observe the obvious devotion Mrs Rochester had for her only daughter, while speculating on what had been and what might have been.

However, Eloise seemed unaware of anyone other than the doll. Before turning away, Mrs Burrows dabbed her eyes with a white linen handkerchief she had taken from her pocket, then straightened her shoulders, raised her head high, walked back along the long landing and descended the stairs, keys jangling at her waist.

Chapter Forty Two

'Good-day to you, Robert,' Fredrick shook the hand of Dr Robert Boyd, not only a good friend of the Rochester family but, more importantly on this occasion, the first Physician Superintendent of the County Asylum for Pauper Lunatics and now, at forty years of age, he had held this position for the last two years. Friends they may be but this was not a social visit.

Fredrick led Robert into his study, shut the door behind them and invited his brown tweed-suited visitor to sit in the armchair, while he poured a tot of single-malt whisky into each of two cut-glass crystal tumbler glasses, he handed one to his guest and took one to his own seat behind the heavy oak desk. 'I do appreciate how busy you are, so thank you for coming, Robert. You'll stay for lunch, of course? I know Constance will be pleased to see you.'

Dr Boyd, hitched up the knees of his trousers, to prevent the material bagging, eased himself into the armchair and lowered the plump cushion behind him onto the floor to allow him to sit back in the chair more easily.

'Are you sure, Fredrick? It may be that Constance will not be disposed to have me here any longer than necessary today, depending on what is decided.' He reached forward to take the offered glass. 'Thank you.'

With the low winter sun on the other side of the house, the study with its dark wood desk, fully stocked bookshelves and occasional tables, dark brown leather chairs, and heavy dark red velvet curtains was cold, dreary and dismal even though one of the maids had lit a fire which was flaming nicely in the grate. Even so, the gloom of the study matched Fredrick's mood.

'Well, Robert,' he began without looking at his visitor. 'Have you had any more thoughts about our last discussion? Is there anything that can be done for Eloise?'

Robert looked down at the glass in his hand and watched the whisky whirling as he swilled the glass around, pausing to find the right words. He looked up and shook his head, sadly. With his left elbow on the arm of the chair, he cupped his clean-shaven chin between his thumb and forefinger. 'As things stand at the moment, I have to say no. You have refused my suggestion of taking Eloise to see a specialist in London...'

'Bah! What good would it be to take the child away from her home.' Fredrick stood, turned his back on his friend and looked out of the tall window on to the long and late autumnal garden beyond.

'I understand how you feel...'

'Do you?' Fredrick snapped. He turned, glared briefly at Robert before his stern gaze relaxed. 'Oh my friend, I am sorry. This is no fault of yours...and I really do understand you are trying to do your best by Eloise. I should not be taking this out on you, but it would break her heart and ours to have her taken away and shut up in one of those...those...institutions so far away. No, Robert. She stays here.'

'I understand completely, of course,' said Robert. He took a sip of whisky. 'Some of these places are very bleak, but things are changing. Some physicians, like myself, are beginning to make some thrilling transformations in their environment and in therapies. I only wish I could do more but, since I took over the asylum, I have striven to make them more accommodating for our patients...but, I must be frank with you, Fredrick. I have had little experience with the injured brain. Most of my patients are, well...lunatics, but Eloise's condition is not the same. It is her injury that has affected her moods and turned her back into a child. I did not think for one moment that you would be prepared to send her away, but I had to mention it or I would not have been doing my duty by you...or Eloise. I do, though have another suggestion.'

Fredrick looked up, hope evident in his eyes. 'Yes, we'll try anything to make her life more bearable.'

'Then I suggest you employ a nurse to live in. I have someone in mind who you may like. She has a kind manner, is a good nurse with a gentle, caring disposition. Margaret is a widow of approximately middle thirties, has no children or other dependants, and I believe Eloise will like her.'

'That sounds like a capital idea. I will talk to Constance about it or, if you stay to lunch, perhaps you would like to broach it. I am inclined to think she will agree as she does not want Eloise to be taken away from us, and we certainly have the room for another person living in the house.'

'Actually, I am not sure I can spare the time to stay for lunch today, perhaps another time, but thank you for the invitation. Send me a message when you have discussed it and if Constance agrees. I will then approach Margaret.'

'In the meantime, I will continue to look for someone in the field who may be able to help. I have heard of someone in France...'

'France! Eloise is unable to travel to France! In Heaven's name man, think what you're saying!'

'You misunderstand me, Fredrick.' Robert said, calmly. 'The man I am thinking of is lecturing in London, Oxford and a few other places later this year. I shall be going to hear him and I suggest you come with me. I must insist though that I know everything if I am to help Eloise. You must not hide anything from me.'

For a fleeting moment a look of puzzlement and something else, flashed across Fredrick's face. He looked down, unable to meet his friend's scrutiny. It was clear he was not being entirely truthful.

'I take it there has been a development in Eloise's condition.'

Fredrick sat down, rested his elbows on the desk and covered his face with hands. The energy he had shown earlier seemed to suddenly drain away, leaving him stricken, overwhelmed. Robert waited. He had never seen his friend in such despair.

After a few moments, unable to look at Robert, Fredrick still looking down at the desktop, his head supported by his left hand, said: 'Eloise has begun having moments of rage.' He stood up, lifted his glass and took a large gulp of whisky as he stared out of the window again. Robert hesitated, unwilling to press for more information until Fredrick was ready. 'I had hoped it would only be one occasion but we have now had four of these...these incidents.' He turned back, put his glass down on the desk. 'I am at my wits end, Robert.'

'Good God man! Why didn't you tell me before? Of course, this puts a completely different bearing on the situation, you do understand that don't you?'

Fredrick nodded. 'Constance wanted to keep this news from you, but I now have the worry that Eloise may hurt someone. At fifteen years old, she is almost fully grown, almost adult and...and when she has one of these...um...episodes, she has thrown things, lashed out...has already caused minor injuries to one of our maids, Rose, who was so frightened she gave her notice without having another position to go to.'

'I can't say I'm surprised,' said Robert, with a frown.

'I gave Rose a very good reference and a month's wages to compensate her. Even gave her the names of two friends of ours who I know are looking for good domestic staff.'

'That seems very fair of you,' Robert said, tersely. As Rose was no longer within the household, she was not really of any great interest to him, he was far more concerned with his patient in the here and now.

'Now, going back to Eloise, you do realise that now I am aware of these developments, we can no longer consider Margaret moving into the house. Eloise will need more careful watching. It is likely, without treatment and the right sort of care, that these rages will increase in frequency.' He stood up, walked over to Fredrick. 'Understand this, I do not speak as your friend at this moment, but I offer my opinion as a psychiatric physician. In a psychotic rage, the patient becomes much stronger than one would anticipate. If Eloise remains at home, it may be that she will have to be locked up within two rooms. These changes in her nature will become more unpredictable and violent. Believe me, it will not be a nurse she needs but a guard, someone who may have to be stronger, possibly even more...physical, shall we say, than you and Constance can endure.'

Fredrick's face had become ashen. Fear and pain showed in his eyes. 'She was such a delightful little girl, Robert. So happy, talented, everyone loved her.'

Robert responded with a nod and a sad smile. 'I know. She was always such a polite, charming young lady. Her poetry was excellent, and she had such a delicate touch with water colours. The distress to you both of her losing those talents, and her potential, must be incalculable, but I feel that there is no longer any choice. It may be that, in time she will cease to know you both.

'In my hospital, she will have people around who will know how to calm her who she will learn to trust, and will care for her. None of my patients are locked up in windowless rooms that feel more like cold prison cells. None of my nurses look like gaolers. The rooms are decorated in restful pastel colours, with windows...albeit windows that only open a little, for their own safety. If she stays here, she would either have to be moved to the ground floor and the windows bolted shut to prevent her trying to escape.

'On the other hand, if she stays in her own two rooms, you would probably have to put bars on the windows in case she breaks the glass and tries to climb out. Either way she will feel stifled and imprisoned, and the outcome of that is that it could increase her rages due to frustration.

'Our patients have communal rooms where they can meet other patients suffering with a variety of conditions. You need not worry about Eloise coming into contact with the insane. They are housed in another part of the hospital. She will be given constant attention throughout the day and night, by a team she will get know. She will be encouraged to be creative, given pleasurable tasks to keep her busy and engaged, flower arranging, helping in the garden, we can let her have paints, canvasses and an...'

'...Did I tell you about her piano playing?' Fredrick interrupted.

'What about it?'

Fredrick smiled for the first time that morning. 'It's very strange and I don't understand it at all, but she can still play as well as she ever did.'

Robert looked down at his clasped hands for a moment. Then he looked up. 'That's very strange but I hope it's a good sign. Tell me what happens.'

'Eloise does not go to the piano of her own volition but if we take her to the stool, sit her down and lift the lid, she begins playing without looking at the keys. Her mind may have forgotten most things...um...regressed, is that the word? But it's as if her fingers remember the music and keys and they play for her.'

'Hmm. That's very interesting and maybe something positive we can focus on to help her. How does she appear while she's playing?'

'Distant. There's no expression on her face, no light in her eyes as there used to be when she played. She just stares ahead into the distance. She appears remote, detached.' His smile had slipped away, and Robert's heart went out to his friend as he saw that glimmer of a past remembered joy replaced by a forlorn hopelessness.

Robert was desperate to give the family something to hope for, but all his training and experience suggested that this situation was never likely to have a happy ending. Eloise was now probably as well as she was ever going to be...unless something miraculous happened.

'Fredrick, I will do everything I can to bring about an improvement in Eloise's condition. I will always be honest with you though. Being kicked in the temple by a horse's hoof may have caused irreparable brain damage, but we will do our utmost for her. You have my word. Would you like me to explain to Constance?'

Fredrick nodded. 'Yes, thank you. Constance likes you and will trust you to take care of our little girl. God knows it will break her heart but will be better coming from you. It will ease her mind a little knowing that Eloise is only a few miles away...will we be able to visit her?'

'Yes, visits will be encouraged when we think she has settled and is able to cope. They will be pre-arranged and, if we think it is not a good day, a note will be sent informing you not to come.'

Fredrick looked up at his friend. He knew the advice he was being given was sound. He knew in his heart that Robert was right. Eloise was becoming more than he or his wife could manage at home, nor could they give her the care or treatment she needed. He understood there was no choice but he was angry; angry at the people who had caused this pain and at himself. He lived with the guilt that he was not there to protect her when she needed him. Standing he paced up and down beside the window.

'Blast that damn thug! That Winterne boy...that Viscount...and...and his drunken cronies have turned my sweet girl into a...a...oh God, Robert...how do I tell Constance we are going to have to let her go? It will break her heart.'

'Believe me I do understand. I may not have children of my own, but I see this all the time with families handing their loved ones into my care, and I can only repeat, I will do everything in my power to help Eloise.' He put his hand on Fredrick's shoulder, trying to offer what little comfort he could.

A loud crash made them look up. It was followed by thump on the floor above and a scream.

'That's Constance,' cried Fredrick. 'Come on!'

Chapter Forty Three

The two men rushed out of the room into the hallway where they were met by Mrs Burrows, already hoisting up the hem of her long skirt in her haste to rush upstairs, and an anxious and wide-eyed Lily, one of the younger maids, who stood back to let them go first, clearly hesitant about going upstairs at all.

On opening the door of Eloise's sitting room, both men and Mrs Burrows stood, shocked, surveying the scene for a brief moment wondering what to deal with first.

Sitting on the floor with her back to the sofa, Eloise appeared to be in a kind of trance and, her hands clutching her precious doll, sat staring into the room, her eyes fixed on some point only she knew. She clearly had no awareness of anyone being there or of anything that had happened.

'Fredrick, look!' Robert exclaimed. He pointed to where Constance lay, just her feet showing from behind the sofa.

'Oh dear God...nooo!' Fredrick ran to his wife who lay unconscious.

'Dear Lord, what's happened here?' Robert gently pushed passed Fredrick to attend to Constance. He found her breathing to be erratic and her eyes were closed. He gently lifted her right eyelid, then her left and checked the dilation of her pupils in both eyes. The right pupil was considerably large than the left. 'It's possible she is concussed', he told Fredrick, ' and I don't like the look of that bruise that's developing on her temple. The bloody scratches are easily dealt with. We must get her to bed, make her comfortable and get those scratches cleaned and dressed to prevent infection.'

He looked around. 'I understood there was a maid here,' said Robert.

'Where is she?'

'Yes, but Constance? Is she going to be alright?'

'Yes. I'm sure she will but, where's the maid...Mabel is it?'

Fredrick nodded and patted Constance's wrist trying to rouse her, just as Mrs Burrows entered the room.

'Oh Heaven's above! What can have happened?' She ran to Eloise who did not react at her presence, not a blink, not a sign of recognition. 'Where's Mabel?'

'That's what I asked,' said Dr Boyd.

Just at that moment a groan was heard from the adjoining bedroom. The doctor and Mrs Burrows rushed to investigate only to find Mabel sitting on the floor, rocking, amongst a considerable amount of broken glass with blood pouring from a wound somewhere on the back of her head.

'What on Earth happened?' Mrs Burrows asked, but Mabel seemed too dazed to speak and continued rocking.

'Get some damp cloths, please,' said Doctor Boyd.

'Yes, sir, the bathroom is just two doors down. I'll be back in just a moment.'

'Thank you, Mrs Burrows.' She turned to go but the doctor called her back. 'Sorry, Mrs Burrows, but before you go, there are some other requirements I would like to leave in your customary efficient charge, please.'

Mrs Burrows nodded vigorously. 'Yes, Doctor.'

'First the cloths, then I need someone up here to help Mabel. Another of the maids will do. Then please get me some paper and a pencil. I need to get a message to the hospital urgently. When you've done that, pack some things that Mistress Eloise would want if she was going away for a few days. Clothes, hairbrush, night attire...you know the sort of thing.'

'I can't think she will be fit enough to take a holiday, Dr Boyd. I mean, just look at her,' Mrs Burrows questioned.

'No, you mistake my meaning. She is not going on holiday, she is going to my hospital. The lad who looks after the horses...'

'Oh, you mean George?'

'Yes, that's the one. When I have written my note, please ensure he gets it and he is to ride directly to the hospital. Now, *please*...this needs to be attended to with all haste.'

'Yes, sir.' Mrs Burrows darted out of the room. 'Lily! *Lily!!* Get yourself up here, now!'

Dr Boyd heard a distant voice answering and footsteps running up the stairs, followed by Mrs Burrows barking orders at the maid, and then the housekeeper's footsteps running back downstairs just as Lily arrived with a couple of damp towels, and was directed to help Mabel.

'Mind out for all the glass around her, won't you?' I'll attend to Mrs Rochester first, then will come to help you move Mabel. In the meantime, I would put a few of those rugs,' he pointed to the scatter rugs, 'over the glass to avoid you, or Mabel if she tries to move, from cutting yourselves.'

Robert then went back to join Fredrick who was on his knees beside his wife, still holding her hand and talking to her softly, trying to wake her, but there was still no response. 'Come Fredrick, let's get Constance to her bedroom and have her made comfortable. She will need those wounds cleaned and bandaged and, I need to examine that bump on her head.'

Chapter Forty Four

In the spotless ground floor kitchen at the rear of the house, Aggie McMurdo, the family's middle-aged capable, and rather feisty cook, who appeared to have eaten too many of her own cakes, stood at the doorway listening to the comings and goings on the floor above.

Bella, the kitchen maid had jumped nervously when they heard the crash and Aggie, with her no-nonsense attitude had snapped at her to pull herself together, explaining in very plain language that whatever was going on was none of their business, and ordering the trembling girl to bring the laundry in from the garden washing line.

Aggie hadn't meant to be quite so sharp with Bella, and perhaps she had sounded too short-tempered, but giving Bella something to do would help take her mind off whatever was going on. As soon as Bella headed for the back door, Aggie removed the pot of beef stew she had made for lunch, and set it down at the back of the stove, the pot was too hot to place anywhere else. She half-filled the gleaming copper kettle and put it on the bars above the enclosed fire inside the range. In her experience, after the kind of commotion she had heard coming from upstairs, it would be unlikely that anyone would want lunch but, at times like these, 'a nice wee cup o' tea' helped every situation.

Drying her hands on her stew-spotted pinafore, she darted to the doorway and peered round trying to find out what was going on, but scurried back in on seeing Bridie Burrows on her way down the stairs, and likely heading for the kitchen. Having become close friends, Aggie was the only person within the house who called Bridie by her first name. To everyone else, including Mr and Mrs Rochester, there was the customary formality of employer and senior servant, and first names were rarely acceptable.

Bridie might well be a dear friend, and would do anything for you, but even so Aggie didn't want her to think she had been snooping, so she slipped back into the kitchen before Bridie spotted her.

As Mrs Burrows entered she found a calm and outwardly uninterested Aggie, putting on a show of not having seen her approaching. Mrs Burrows gave a little chuckle. She was used to seeing Aggie nosing around trying to find out what was going on when she thought no-one was watching, and had seen the edge of Aggie's white mob cap with its lacy ruffle in the doorway as she made her way down the stairs.

'Did you hear what happened, Aggie? It was terrible,' said Mrs Burrows opening the two top buttons of the high-necked starched collar of her formal dress as she entered the kitchen. The cook turned to look at her with sympathy, but Mrs Burrows was well aware of Aggie's relief at not having to be involved with the goings-on upstairs.

Although Mrs Burrows had only been with family for a few short weeks, she and Aggie had liked each other on sight and had become good friends.

Aggie's husband, Archie, had been the Gamekeeper at a large country estate just outside Paisley in Renfrewshire. When he died following a shooting accident, the grief-stricken Aggie was further distressed when she was given just one week to vacate their cottage. With nowhere else to go, she had packed a carpet bag with her few possessions and travelled to Wells to stay with her sister, Flora, and her husband, Kenneth, while she tried to find some way to support herself.

Whereas Mrs Burrows, as housekeeper had overall responsibility of running the entire house smoothly, Aggie, was more than content with her realm in the kitchen and the fact that she rarely had to go beyond it. In her view Mrs Burrows was welcome to the rest of the house, Aggie didn't want it, thank you very much.

'Aye. Weel o' course young Lily did say something aboot it and' Ah'm no surprised it was bad. You'll tek a wee cup o' tea, Bridie?'

Mrs Burrows nodded. 'Yes, I will, thank you.'

The fire was lit in the range and the kitchen was warm with a combined smell of the remains of the beef stew that no-one had felt like eating still in the pot on the hob, a newly baked loaf that was cooling on a wire rack, coal in the scuttle on the hearth, chopped wood, smoke and the herbs drying in net bags above the range. The kitchen was, as always, utterly spotless. Gleaming copper pans hung from a rack over the table, with kitchen utensils suspended from another on the wall next to the range.

Mrs Burrows could see young Bella, the mousy kitchen maid, whose job it was to keep everything spotless leaving Aggie free to concentrate on feeding the family and staff, through the window, taking washing off the line to bring indoors where it would be hung on a wooden rack and hoisted high in an anteroom to finish drying.

Mrs Burrows reached out for one of the wooden chairs, pulled it away from the table and sat down dejectedly, the tears she had been holding back were not far away. What she had seen upstairs had upset her greatly. That poor child. Had she not been through enough?

She rolled back her sleeves to a little short of her elbows, as she watched Aggie McMurdo put a little cold milk into two porcelain china cups, stir the steaming brew in a matching teapot, then using a tea strainer to prevent tea leaves from slipping into the cups, she poured in the strong infusion. Setting the cups onto their saucers, Aggie reached around behind her to undo the bow that tied her crisp, spotless white pinafore and took it off laying it carefully over the back of one of the chairs, then carried one of the cups across to the well-scrubbed wooden table and put it down in front of Mrs Burrows. 'Would you like a slice of walnut cake as well?'

'No, thank you, Aggie, I don't think I could face anything to eat, but I'm ready for this I can tell you.' She allowed herself to slump into the hard-backed wooden chair and took a sip of tea. 'Poor little Miss Eloise, she had no knowledge of what was happening to her. Just allowed herself to be led along the hallway looking blankly ahead of her, still holding tight to that doll of hers.

'When we got upstairs to see what had happened, she just sat there, poor girl, just sat there on the floor staring into nothing. Lord knows how the Mistress is going to react when she awakes and finds Eloise has been taken to the hospital.'

'Hmm.' Aggie took her own cup of tea to the table and sat opposite Mrs Burrows trying not to make it obvious that she was studying her friend's face. She saw very plainly how tired she looked and pale, with dark circles under her eyes, and lips pressed in a thin line, but Aggie kept her thoughts to herself. She shook her head. 'Och, ah ken, Bridie. The wee lass'll ne'er ken where she is. She's home then she's no home. An' how's Mabel the noo?'

'Oh, bless her,' said Mrs Burrows. She took a mouthful of tea and put the cup back on the saucer. 'She'll be alright. Dr Boyd checked the bump on her head and the cut's not a big as he feared. He told me that a little blood goes a long way when it's from somewhere like the scalp, but she's got a nasty headache, bless her. I'm not sure about those scratches though. One or two looked pretty deep to me.'

'She'll no be scarred though?'

'Hmm, I'm not sure but let's hope not, not with that pretty face of hers.' She took another mouthful of tea and pushed the cup and saucer a little way forward. 'But Mabel won't be up to taking on her duties until at least tomorrow, or maybe the next day. Dr Boyd said she was to rest because she's in shock, whatever that means.'

'Aye. An' wha' aboot the Maister? How's he tekken aw this?'

Mrs Burrows shook her head. 'I have no idea how he's coping at the moment, but I wouldn't think it will be well. He's with Mrs Rochester. Hasn't left her side, not even to see Eloise away in the carriage. Dr Boyd went with her, and he had two men and a nurse with him.'

'Once they had Mrs Rochester into bed, I heard the doctor say she was concussed, needed rest and he would be back later this afternoon, or early evening to see her. In the meantime, the other nurse that came in the carriage from the hospital is staying with her.'

'Ha' yer finished wi' yer tea?'

'Yes, thank you, Aggie. I feel a little better now.' She stood up.

'An' where are ye off tae noo?'

'Both the rooms need cleaning up. We were too busy with seeing to Mrs Rochester, Eloise and Mabel but, now they're all attended to, and the rooms are empty, I need to make sure all the glass and oil from the lamps is cleaned up. With all of them broken it'll take some work to get the oil out of the rugs. Eloise threw three lamps at her mother before Mabel managed to get between them. That's when her face got scratched so badly.'

'Bu' wha' stairted it, Bridie? Thass wha' Ah'd like tae ken.' said Aggie, as she poured away the remaining tea from the pot and strained the tea-leaves for putting under the roses in the Spring.

'That was Mrs Rochester. According to Mabel, Mrs Rochester told Eloise to put her doll down and go to the table as lunch was about to be served, but Eloise ignored her. Mrs Rochester asked Mabel to bring one of Eloise's pinafores from her bedroom. As she headed into the bedroom, Mabel heard Mrs Rochester ask Eloise again in a very soft voice...no scolding, no raised voice, just very gentle, to hand over the doll and get up. Again, Eloise ignored her and carried on playing with the doll. Mabel wasn't sure what happened next but, she heard a crash and saw Mrs Rochester, holding the doll and backing away towards the sofa. It seems Eloise had got to her feet to get her doll back...Mabel said she reacted as if the Devil himself was inside her. She screamed at her mother, turned over one of the occasional tables and threw one of the lamps but missed her mother, then she picked up the second...in a rage it seems...and threw that one. Mrs Rochester had dodged that first one but not the next. She caught her mother a nasty blow with that one. It hit her on the forehead, and she fell behind the sofa with Eloise dropping to her knees beside her mother.

'At first, although she couldn't see what Eloise was doing behind the sofa, Mabel thought Eloise had gone to her mother to get her up, and she too went to help, but had a terrible shock when she saw Eloise had her hands tight around her mother's throat. That's when Mabel shouted at Eloise to stop. Eloise got up, ran at Mabel and caught her, slapping her face and digging her nails into her cheeks.'

'Och, the pair wee thing,' muttered Aggie.

'Well, Mabel managed to struggle free from Eloise, but she couldn't get passed her as she was in front of the door, so she ran into the bedroom, hoping to get out onto the verandah and down the fire stairs, when Eloise chased after her and threw the bedroom lamp. Mabel was trying to open the French windows when she was hit on the back of the head by the brass base of the lamp, and she thinks she blacked out for a few moments...'

'Ah'm no surprised. They things are heavy.'

'...because the next thing she knew was when Mr Rochester, the doctor and I arrived. Oh, there was so much glass around, Aggie. Of course, when Eloise threw the lamp, the glass cover smashed and after the base hit Mabel, part of it broke off and went through one of the French windows. It's an awful mess.'

'Aye, well iss nae wonner the pair wee lass has a headeck,' said Aggie. Shaking her head. 'Wha' goin' ons in this hoose, the day. An' that...that swine of a Viscount causin' aw this pain an' still runnin' loose. Iss no richt. Ah tell ye Bridie, tha' yin'll come tae nae guid.'

'Yes, well let's hope so,' replied Mrs Burrows.

But as she turned to leave Aggie thought she saw a look in her friend's eyes that made her shiver, and she realised that, although they got on well and Aggie liked Bridie Burrows very much, no-one actually knew a great deal about her. The only thing she knew for sure was that Bridie too was a widow and, as far as they knew had been a housekeeper in her previous employment in Wells. She had heard from Rose, who had now left the house, that when Mrs Rochester was looking for a new housekeeper, it had been a chap with the slightly odd name of Noel something...Elden...that was it, who was a friend of the butler at the manor, Mr Hastings, who had recommended Bridie. Mrs Rochester had taken to her straight away and trusted that if, Mr Hastings and Mr Elden said she was experienced and of sound character, then that was good enough.

But as she watched Mrs Burrows disappear onto the landing, Aggie lifted her linen cap and scratched her head. 'Ah'm no sure wha's goin' on wi' ye lass, bu' yeh had a strange look in yer eye. There's sumthin' yer hidin' an' tha's fer sure, bu' iss no business o' mine,' she said, quietly, before turning away and going back to her duties.

Chapter Forty Five

Rupert Maitland, Earl of Winterne, had been alone in the library for the entire morning and, below stairs the servants began gossiping, suggesting ideas on what was the matter until Mr Hastings, the butler, had put a stop to it, scolding them all for their prattle. Although there had been lots of conjecture about what was wrong, no-one actually mentioned the one issue they all believed, deep down, was causing his Lordship's melancholy; Lord Randolph.

After refusing breakfast, the morose Earl, his shoulders hunched and head down, headed directly across the hallway and shut himself away from everyone in the library. Although these occasions were a rarity, when his lordship had a serious issue to consider, or difficult decision to make, it was the library he made for and barring some emergency, the staff knew better than to him disturb him.

Enclosed behind the doors of his favourite room, the Earl stood looking down into the crackling log fire that burned brightly in the open fireplace, his left hand on the tall mantelpiece, his right hand cupped around the bottom of a crystal-cut bowl-shaped glass half full of brandy as he stared into the flames. Once again, his eldest son, Randolph, had brought trouble to the family and this time, Rupert could not just pay off the victim's family to make the scandal go away, as he had done so many times before. No, this time Randolph had gone too far on one of his drunken escapades. This time it was not one of the uneducated villagers who had suffered at the boy's hands. They had always either been too frightened to make a complaint, convinced any grievance against the old and aristocratic family would never be upheld, or pathetically grateful for any payoff in return for a promise to stay silent.

The girl had been with friends, innocently having a picnic in a field beside the river, when Randolph and his dissolute friends had ridden passed and had seen them. According to what Randolph had said afterwards, the girls were on Winterne Manor land and had, therefore been trespassing, but once again he was drunk, so were his friends, but it appeared not to the same degree that Randolph was. He had insisted he and his friends had merely trotted over to ask the girls, pleasantly, if they would mind leaving their land. He went on to say the Rochester girl had become rude and refused to leave. Her friends had agreed though, and were packing up the picnic things, getting ready to leave while attempting to placate Eloise and get her to leave, peacefully, with them. But she was not of a mind to do so and protested, screaming at them, rather hysterically, Randolph had said. What happened next Randolph had said was no fault of his own. Eloise had made a grab for the bridle, snatched it away from him and had begun pulling on it while shrieking at the top of her voice. The horse Randolph was riding had panicked, shied, reared and Eloise was accidently kicked in the forehead.

Unfortunately further enquiry amongst the friends who had been with Randolph at the time, and given their account of what happened had not agreed. So many differing versions had been told by his friends that, had the investigation been during a trial, it would prove them all to be unreliable. Two had since come to see the Earl in secrecy and admitted they had lied as they were frightened of his son.

The account given by each of the girls who had been with Eloise at the time, when interviewed individually, had all told the same story. That Viscount Randolph had ridden his horse very fast, and quite deliberately, directly at them. He appeared to be having trouble trying to stay on the horse and when he shouted at them he was slurring his words. The girls had scattered out of the way of the oncoming sixteen-hand high horse, Eloise had tripped and, as she tried to get up, in his drunken rage Randolph had charged at her, the horse had reared and kicked her in the forehead, whereupon she had collapsed onto the ground, insensible.

At that point one of his friends had seized the reins and dragged Randolph away, while two of the girls had run off towards the village for help. The Earl had discovered that it had been ten days before Eloise awoke from her coma. Her parents had been so relieved to see her awake, they failed to notice that something was wrong, but it soon became clear that Eloise was no longer the daughter they knew; she had regressed to a five-year old child.

No, this time he had injured a young girl of a good family, the daughter of a local magistrate and someone who intended to fight for justice for his child...dammit! Even so, he understood how the Rochesters would be feeling. Would he not feel exactly the same way if one of his own daughters, Frances or Charlotte, had been injured in similar circumstances? How could he defuse *this* situation?

Was it time he sent Randolph away for a while, perhaps to his cousin in Norfolk until people forgot, and how long would that take, if ever? But if he did get Randolph out of the way, how would that make him see the error of his ways? He and Gwendoline had been so thrilled their first child was a son, and heir to the estate. They adored him and gave in to his every wish, ignored the signs when he first showed a tendency for cruelty. The Earl thought back to the day when Randolph was just seven-years-old and had just mounted his pony for a riding lesson. Seeing some of the larger horses being made ready for their daily exercise, Randolph demanded the groom let him ride one that would have been far too powerful for him to handle.

The groom, Sam, calmly explained that his Lordship was too young and had not undergone enough training to control a horse of that size. Randolph had lashed out at the groom with his riding crop and cut the man's cheek. The senior groom, Philip, had snatched the crop away from Randolph and told him in no uncertain terms that there would be no riding lesson that day and he should apologise to the groom. Randolph not only refused, but using the mounting block he got off his pony and stormed out of the stable yard, snatching his riding crop from the hand of the senior groom as he passed.

Unfortunately that was not the end of the incident. On his way back to the manor, Randolph happened to see Sam's five-year-son playing happily on the grass while his mother was pegging out washing, completely unaware of Randolph being in the vicinity or of his temper. Randolph rushed at the unsuspecting boy and hit him several times on the back with the riding crop before the mother could intervene.

At the sound of the smaller boy's screams and his mother's furious shouts, Sam and Philip rushed to see what the noise was about. On seeing what Randolph was doing, Sam grabbed the riding crop out of his fist, smashing it on the ground and breaking it into three pieces. Philip then seized the belligerent and struggling Randolph, who kicked out and shrieked that his father would make them pay, and hauled him back to the manor, ignoring the punches and kicks that came his way from the headstrong and furious boy.

Rupert grimaced as he gulped down the last mouthful of the brandy in the glass, recalling that horrible incident. Perhaps if he had taken control, opposed Gwendoline's refusal to punish Randolph and teach him some discipline then, forced him to apologise and shown him that behaviour of that kind would not be condoned, that it was wrong to treat people that way, then perhaps the boy would have learned his lesson at an early age. But he didn't. He had given in to Gwendoline and her tears as she cuddled Randolph, and had simply given Sam a small financial compensation and suggested that maybe, as Randolph was so young, perhaps Sam and his wife could put the incident down to a child's tantrum.

But more similar incidents had followed and Gwendoline, even after her fifth child, had never ceased to protect and mollycoddle Randolph, to the detriment of her relationship with her other children of whom she was clearly fond, but did not have the all-consuming, smothering love she lavished on Randolph.

After Gwendoline died four years earlier, Randolph had spiralled out of control. He would spend most of his time either in taverns or gambling houses, running up debts which he expected his father to pay, chasing tavern maids and bullying anyone who was too old, too small or too weak to stand up to him. When he was at home, he would sleep for much of the day, or if awake, would drink vast amounts of wine, whisky or brandy, sometimes mixing all three throughout the drinking session, then abuse his younger sisters and brothers and the domestic staff. Before long the children stayed out of the way when Randolph was at home and, when he rang for a servant, it would always be one of the footmen or the butler, Joseph Hastings who attended him. Joseph refused to allow any of the maids to wait on Randolph whether he was alone or with friends.

The only person Randolph appeared to have the slightest bit of respect for was Joseph, to whom he was generally polite, especially when looking for support when pleading his case that - whatever awful thing he had done or been involved in, on any given occasion - was not his fault, and he would appear suitably contrite. The Earl had even been a little jealous of Joseph because Randolph seemed to regard him so highly. Even so he came to hope that perhaps the boy would learn something of decent behaviour from the butler. Sadly, as Randolph grew older, that one hope faded when it appeared that Randolph would try to avoid Joseph rather than see that look of disillusionment in the old man's eyes.

In the long run, the Earl knew it was time he came to terms with the fact that it was their fault the boy had become the monster he now was, but how did admitting that to himself help now?

On the oak sideboard, were a number of three-quarter filled crystal glass decanters, he picked up the one with brandy and refilled his glass for the third time. As he poured, his hand trembled spilling a few drops of the brown liquid onto the sleeve of his royal blue velvet smoking jacket. Putting the glass down he brushed off the drops and, for a moment stared, without really noticing anything, out of the window, too preoccupied was he. But he had come to a decision.

Beside the hearth a long, tasseled burgundy velvet rope hung from the ceiling, he gave it a tug then flopped wearily into a large and comfortable fireplace armchair and waited. A few minutes later, Joseph, opened the door and walked in.

A stern man who would have been taller had it not been for the rounded shoulders that gave the impression of a slight stoop, Hastings knew his place and was proud to serve the Earl and most of the family but, as with the other domestic staff, there was little love for Viscount Randolph. Those who had been with the Maitland family for some years had observed the firstborn son being spoiled, every whim being indulged, and he was never disciplined for rudeness or even bouts of cruelty.

The Earl barely looked in his direction. 'Ah, Joseph, I presume Lord Randolph has returned from his morning ride?'

'Um...no, my Lord. It would seem that his lordship did not return home last night. The chamber maid, Smith, reports that his bed has not been slept in.'

Without turning to look at him, the Earl replied, despondently: 'Ah,

Joseph. I believe I have made the biggest mistake in my life in the way I have indulged my eldest son. I was so proud when he was born.' Joseph made no answer. He had heard all this before. It was not his place to criticise or to agree with the Earl's own self-reproach.

The Earl looked down at his glass, took a large gulp draining the remains of the brandy, and held the glass out to the butler. 'Another small brandy, if you please, Joseph. Then that will be my fourth and, on an empty stomach, that is enough.'

Joseph walked over to the sideboard, took a small metal drink measure and poured two tots of brandy into the glass, but before he put the glass stopper back on the decanter, he could sight of himself in the mirror hanging on the wall. The dark circles surrounding his sunken eyes were evidence of the sleepless nights he had endured recently, and he could see by his prominent cheekbones and sunken cheeks that he too had not eaten enough. The worries consuming him had reduced his appetite; the cook had already noticed and tried to encourage him to eat more, but he had little interest in food and sympathised with the Earl on that point. But he would not turn to drink. That was not for him. Warming the brandy by cupping the glass in his hand, he carried it back to where the Earl appeared even more wretched than he had a few moments before.

'Is there anything more I can do, my Lord?' Joseph asked.

'Yes, have a sandwich of something sent up to me, please. I really must eat something, but I just could not face it earlier.' He looked up, 'Where are Lady Frances and Lady Charlotte?'

'They are in the sun lounge, my Lord, it is their music lesson.'

'And what about my other two boys, Simon and Ralph?'

'They are having their riding lesson, my Lord, but due back soon I believe.'

'Very well. When Randolph finally remembers where his home is, please send him directly to me.'

Joseph gave a slight bow. 'Yes, my Lord, and I will have a sandwich sent up to you immediately.'

The Earl did not reply, and Joseph left him to his thoughts.

Chapter Forty Six

Having waited patiently until the last of the servants had gone to bed, Mrs Burrows looked in on Mrs Rochester, who appeared to be sleeping peacefully in the care of one of Dr Boyd's nurses, who was to stay with her throughout the night until she was relieved by another nurse in the morning.

In the grate, the flickering flames of the log fire warmed the room casting small shifting shadows on the walls as the flames danced and curled, and a good supply of logs filled the brass box on the hearth.

The nurse was reading *Pride and Prejudice,* a book by Jane Austen in the light of an oil lamp on a small table beside her. Having removed her starched white cap and apron, which she wore over her pale blue uniform dress, and were now draped over the blue floral-pattern padded lid of the ottoman chest in front of the window, the nurse appeared very comfortable having settled herself in the cushioned rocking chair.

Mrs Burrows raised an eyebrow. In a hospital ward, nurses were expected to wear their full uniform throughout their duty hours. But then she conceded, the nurse was now in a residential home and not a hospital ward, in a warm bedroom, with just one patient who was unlikely to need a great deal of care during the night. In addition, it was doubtful if she would see anyone else until morning, and therefore perhaps it was more appropriate for her to be more...more relaxed, and continue the rest of the night without having to worry about hospital practice. Mrs Burrows had only been at the door for a moment or two when the nurse noticed she was there.

'Do come in,' the nurse whispered. 'You are unlikely to disturb her, she has had a small dose of laudanum and should sleep well tonight.' Noting the newcomer's austere, buttoned-up grey day dress, she realised that this lady was the housekeeper, Mrs Burrows, put her book down on the table and stood up. 'Allow me to introduce myself, I am Edith Sanders, senior nurse at the Infirmary and I believe you must be Mrs Burrows.'

'Yes, I'm Mrs Burrows...but please call me Bridie. I am so pleased to meet you and I'm relieved to hear Mrs Rochester is comfortable, poor lady. The family have been through a dreadful ordeal recently. She needs to feel stronger before she has to deal with the news that Eloise has been taken to the hospital. I believe Mr Rochester has already gone to the hospital. I didn't see him after we had cleared away the broken glass and cleaned the floor of oil.'

'Yes, he has.' Edith nodded and rocked. 'He left as soon as he was assured Mrs Rochester was taken care of and was in no danger.'

'Is that a good book?' asked Mrs Burrows, pointing to the book lying open on the table. 'I must admit to never having read anything by Jane Austen. I tend to prefer stories a little more frightening and at present I'm reading *The Legend of Sleepy Hollow* by Mr Washington Irving. I understand he was living here in England when the book was first published...Birmingham, I believe.'

'Oh, I do not like to be scared. I prefer something amusing, perhaps romantic and entertaining. I see enough of alarming things in my profession on a day to day basis.'

'Yes, I can understand that. Anyway, it has been very nice to meet you, but I was just heading down to the kitchen and wondered if you would like some warm milk or...'

Edith chuckled. 'Oh no. No warm milk for me, thank you. I have to stay awake tonight, but perhaps, if it's no trouble...a cup of tea?'

Mrs Burrows smiled. 'It is no trouble at all. I shall return shortly.'

'Oh, are there not servants who could do that for you? I don't want to put you out.'

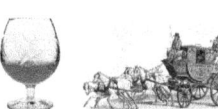

'Usually yes, there would be, but recently we lost one of our members of staff, Rose. Then today, Mabel was hurt...you know, during the incident, and Lily has worked hard helping with all the clearing up and she is always up early, bless her. She was very upset, so I sent her to bed early. Mrs McMurdo, our cook is always up at five-thirty, so she tends to go to her bed early. And, anyway it's no bother, I'm going there anyway.'

A short while later she was back with a tray upon which was a sterling silver tea service comprising a small steaming teapot, a milk jug, a cup and saucer, a small pot with some sugar and a teaspoon, a small jug with a lid with hot water to top up the teapot, and a plate of biscuits.

'Oh, Mrs Burrows...Bridie, you're so good to me. I do appreciate this. Here let me remove my book from the table and the tray can be set down there.' She put the book down on the windowsill and took the tray from Mrs Burrows. 'Are you not joining me?'

'No, Edith. It has been a very long and tiring day and I want nothing more than to remove my shoes and get to bed. I hope you have a good night.'

Edith looked around at her patient who was breathing easily and sleeping soundly. She turned back and smiled. 'Oh, I'm sure we will. Goodnight and thank you.'

Thirty minutes later Mrs Burrows returned to the room to find Edith sound asleep in the rocking chair. The teapot was empty and two of the biscuits had gone. She smiled and looked at the clock on the mantelpiece. 'Ten fifteen. Good, that gives me around five hours for what I need to do.'

Chapter Forty Seven

Bridie thought back to a few weeks before when she had first become involved in this complicated issue. When the raven arrived with a note wrapped around its leg, Bridie knew it could only be from her friend, Noel Elden, and that he would be in need of her skills. Throwing her cloak over her shoulders, she nudged her sleeping cat, Bandit.

'Come, my boy. It seems we're needed.'

Bandit yawned, stood up and stretched, arching his back and extending his front legs out in front of him, his tail pointing straight up. Bridie watched him. 'Are you ready, now? I am.' She headed towards the door while Bandit just sat and stared at her with his large, almond shaped jade-coloured eyes.

'You can always stay here if you're too tired, lazy cat,' she laughed, opening the door. 'Right, I'm going.'

Bandit dropped to the floor and ran out of the door before her, and had vanished into the woods before she had closed the door. She could not see him anywhere but was untroubled. He would jump out at her when he was good and ready. A few moments later he dashed out from under a drift of fallen leaves and sprang at her before running off again and jumping in and out of bundles of leaves. He was having a lot of fun, but Bridie was deep in thought about what Noel's problem was.

In the tops of the trees, crows cawed loudly as they headed back to their rookeries for the night, and the orange sun slid surprisingly swiftly behind the hills. Dark shadows filtered between the near-skeletal trees in the twilight and bats had just begun to emerge for their evening hunt.

At the sound of shuffling to her left, Bridie thought it would be Bandit playing in the leaves again, but then he appeared from the right, ears pointing sharply upward, eyes fixed on the point from whence the noise had come. He was ready for battle if need be.

A grunting, snuffling badger trundled into view from the undergrowth, ignoring them both while it searched for scarce food on the hard, cold ground of autumn. Reaching a tall silver birch tree, it stood on its hind legs and scraped at the bark with the long, sharp claws of its front paws until some of the fragile bark broke away and, to the badger's obvious satisfaction a meal of grubs proved to be worth the effort.

Bandit gave a sneer as much as to say that he would never lower himself to eat grubs. 'Think yourself lucky you don't have to. You're spoiled,' laughed Bridie. Bandit jumped up on to her shoulder and settled down in the hood of her cloak until they reached Noel's cottage, where the light that streamed out of the door, from flickering oil lamps and the hearty fire, showed he was waiting for them.

Noel reached out to greet Bridie with a hug, but stopped as Bandit, who was still in her hood jumped to the floor. 'You spoil that cat,' Noel laughed, watching Bandit pad snootily across to the fireside hearth rug.

'I have just told him that,' replied Bridie, smiling affectionately at the cat who was far more than a pet. He was her best friend.

Bridie sat in the comfortable armchair and waited to find out what it was Noel had wanted to see her about, while he made them two large cups of herbal tea. Once he had settled in the armchair on the other side of the hearth, she said, 'What was it you wanted to see me about?'

Noel pushed down his shaggy grey-white beard and took a sip from the steaming cup. 'You'll know about all the goings-on at the manor. The behaviour of the Viscount and so on.'

'Yes. I think everyone knows, but what does it have to do with me?'

'I have a friend who works at the manor,' he took another sip of tea. 'He came to see me earlier to ask my advice on how to stop it. Randolph's just hurt a young girl and her injury has probably damaged her permanently.'

'Oh, that is sad. What happened?'

'Let me give you the details as Joseph told it to me.' He sat back in the armchair watching Bandit grooming himself while he gave Bridie the story. 'As Joseph told me, the Earl had been so proud when his first son was born and had so many hopes and plans for the boy, but as little Randolph grew, the Earl's hopes for the future were shattered as the boy clung more and more closely to his doting mother, leaving the Earl ignored, belittled and undermined.

'Added to his disillusionment was that the Earl, who Joseph had initially respected a great deal, allowed his wife to chip away at his self-confidence and, from the strong and charismatic young man he had once been, the Earl has become nothing more than a shadow of the man he once was. It seems Lady Gwendoline had fought him on every occasion when the young Viscount needed discipline.

'When Lady Gwendoline died, Joseph had hoped to see the re-emergence of the Earl he once knew, but it seems to have been far too late for that. Although the Earl did make an attempt to bring Randolph into line, it was flouted, and Randolph carried on his disreputable way of life.

'The Earl then made an effort to reconnect with his younger children, a move Joseph observed with optimism, hoping the Earl had not left it too late. Sadly, this too proved to be a failure. Over their early childhood, the Earl had either been so preoccupied with the state of affairs concerning Randolph, or had stayed away from the manor as often as possible, accepting any invitation that would mean he could be elsewhere for as long as possible and, therefore, the four younger Maitlands barely knew him. Lady Gwendoline had also neglected them in favour of her firstborn, resulting in the children having far more regard for the domestic staff, their governess and later, for the two younger sons only, their tutor.

'During all the many years of serving the Earl loyally, Joseph had watched him diminish a little at a time and, following the incident with Eloise Rochester – the young girl I mentioned earlier - he had spent many long tormented nights agonising over what needed to be done, and had finally come to dreadful decision. Randolph had to die.'

Bridie nodded.

'Having come to that harrowing conclusion, on his next day off, Joseph came to see me to talk the matter over. He had no-one else he could talk to about it and felt I would give him good advice and, more importantly, keep the conversation between us. He had also been half-convinced that I would suggest something less extreme, and was taken aback when I agreed that it was probably the only course of action. Randolph is so corrupt, so wicked, and cares so little for anyone, or anything but his own pleasure, that it is too late for him to ever be redeemed.

'Well, of course, my agreement shook Joseph into fully understanding the enormity of what was being proposed, and like the Earl, he too found himself trying to find excuses for Randolph, desperately attempting to find a way back from the point we had reached, but I stood firm.

'He argues that the Viscount is young and perhaps could still be saved. He wanted us to think very seriously about what we were planning, and paced up and down, wringing his hands and chewing his bottom lip.

'It was at that point I took Joseph by the shoulders, led him to that armchair you're sitting in and pushed him gently down into it as I explained that, while I would never usually condone this kind of thing, it was too late for any other decision and told him that I have evidence Randolph is now involved with a coven of black witches. He is too far entrenched in evil.'

Bridie's eyebrows arched and Bandit stopped licking his paws.

'Well of course, Joseph was horror-struck. He went pale and groaned, buried his face in his hands as he told me that he had no idea things had gone so far. He went quiet...'

'...I can understand that,' said Bridie, before drinking more of her tea.

'He asked me if I had seen evidence of it with my own eyes. I had to tell him the truth. I had. It was then he agreed there could be no other decision and asked me what we should do next.'

'And I believe this is where I come in?'

Noel nodded. 'The Viscount's wickedness has gone beyond anything that can be condoned, Bridie. The so-called coven will be cleared from the woods, our friends will see to that. The people who lead this pack of fools are playing with things they cannot understand. Their followers are merely weak-minded people who believe membership will give them powers. Randolph is one of those. What will happen with him, being as dissolute as he already is, is that he will believe he is unassailable, invulnerable, that he is all-powerful and that makes him more dangerous than he already has been.'

'Yes, I can see that.'

'Joseph understood too and asked again what would happen next. I told him I would speak to you and that he could trust you as well as he trusts me. I told him you were a white witch...fire to fight fire, so to speak, I told him your name and said I hoped to be able to speak to you today.'

'Do you have a plan?'

'I have something in mind, but we need to discuss the situation and plan precisely what we are going to do, and I need your opinion on how to progress from here.'

'I will need to investigate the family, discover exactly how things stand and can then decide on the best action to take to make the...well, make it look like an accident. I have heard of the most recent incident with the Rochester girl and would like to, not only exact a natural justice, but see if there is some reparation, I can make...but, if I am accepted into the Rochester household, when this is over, I will need to disappear, and you can assure Joseph there will be no trace of his involvement.'

'Thank you. I know Joseph wants to stay with the younger children and I believe he should. Once this is over, they will need him.'

Chapter Forty Eight

With Edith unlikely to wake for a few hours, and having ensured the household staff were in bed and the house was quiet, Bridie Burrows put her plan into action. In Eloise's bedroom, she quietly unlocked the French windows and, outside on the verandah, wrapped a black woollen cloak around her, making sure that her silver-white hair was hidden. On such a clear moonlit night, her hair would show up like a beacon if she was seen.

Lifting the front hem of her austere uniform charcoal-coloured skirt, she tiptoed down the wrought cast-iron stairs. At the bottom she hesitated and looked around. The night-time sky was streaked with thin grey clouds that did little to hide the moon whose beams shone down brightly onto the fast settling frost. Satisfied, she slipped way into the trees and headed towards the woods constantly listening and looking, keeping to the shadows and close to hiding places.

A few minutes later she was at the edge of the woods. All was well. Then she heard it. A low growl that seemed to come from above her in one of the trees.

'Well, come on then,' she said, with a chuckle. 'I was expecting to see you before now.'

The sound of movement above made her look up into the branches of a nearby cedar tree, its leaves obscuring whatever it was that prowled there. She grunted as something heavy landed on her shoulder and she tottered under the sudden weight.

'Uh! Bandit, you're putting on weight. Noel is looking after you far too well!'

The grey cat, his jade coloured eyes reflecting the moonlight, rubbed his face against her cheek and purred loudly in her ear before laying down, draping himself across her shoulder and kneading her cloak with his claws. She stroked him fondly. 'Oh, I've missed you, my boy. Let's hope it won't be long before we can go home again and be together but, for now, there's something we need to do.'

The woods were anything but quiet at night, especially in the late autumn and winter months when the woodland floor was covered in a carpet of dead leaves. With no light other than the moon and stars, Bridie Burrows, with Bandit still clinging firmly to her shoulders, eyes closed and purring serenely, followed the winding paths through the tightly packed woods, kicking through the red, gold, brown and blackened fallen leaves that rustled under her feet. Bats flitted above her head, the movement of their wings creating fluttering sounds. Owls hooted, the high pitched barking yip of foxes and from somewhere nearby they heard the sniff and snort, and then a throaty growl of another badger as it shuffled away from them disturbed in its hunt for food by their presence.

Soon they arrived at a cave in the limestone hillside, its opening narrow and a little lower than Bridie's height. Bandit jumped down and preceded her inside. Although the cramped passageway was dark, they could see a small flickering light at the far end. 'Good, I see Noel is here already. The sooner we begin, the better.'

Noel stood up and cautiously looked above as he heard them approaching, his head almost touched the lowest part of the cave ceiling, his height being a little over six foot four inches. As it was, his collar length almost white hair, brushed the ceiling. Bridie, although tall for a woman, was several inches shorter and only reached Noel's shoulder. She smiled warmly as the firelight reflected in her dark blue eyes. 'Greetings, Noel, you're looking well.' She took both his huge hands and held them for a moment. 'Thank you for coming to help me tonight.'

'Bridie, Bandit. It's good to see you both,' his deep voice boomed, echoed around the cave. 'Although I cannot say that it is a pleasure this time…but it was me who asked for your help, and I *should* be here for you.'

Bridie gave a sad smile and moved closer. 'I see you had a dinner of roast chicken.'

Noel looked at her in puzzlement.

'You still have a little of it in that huge beard of yours. If you were planning to have any of it for supper, I would be careful if I were you, or Bandit will snatch it from you.' Bridie smiled. Bandit looked at the big man with renewed interest. Until Bridie mentioned it, he had not noticed the two fragments of chicken nestling in Noel's bushy, tousled white beard. With his huge size, hair and beard, and periwinkle blue eyes, people often said Noel resembled Father Christmas; they were closer to the truth than they realised.

'This viscount must be stopped,' said Bridie. 'He has hurt too many people. It cannot be allowed to continue. I have spent time with this broken hearted family...'

'...I know, I know, but is...it is a terrible step to take. Is there really no other way, Bridie? There are other members of his family to consider who have been innocent in all this... and I am afraid of the cost to yourself.'

Bandit mewed mournfully as though he understood every word. Bridie smiled down at him. He had been sitting quietly at her feet, but he gazed up at her, his jade coloured eyes looked directly into hers. He sprang up on to her shoulder, and lay down, the pieces of chicken now forgotten.

After settling Bandit comfortably, she looked up at her closest friend who towered inches above her. 'No, Noel. It is too late for leniency for the Viscount...and sadly for his father who must take responsibility for what his submissive and indulgent behaviour over the years has resulted in. The young ones and domestic staff will be safe, and I will warn the Earl of what is to come and suggest he makes arrangements for other members of the household. If he ignores me, as I feel he might, then I will make adjustments to ensure they are not harmed. Now, it is almost midnight, and we must begin. Do you have the items I requested?'

Noel bent down to pick up the linen bag at his feet and took out a long black feather, followed by a tall black candle and a small pouch. Bandit hissed and the hackles on the back of his neck stood up like bristles on a hairbrush. Bridie bent down to pick him up, but he continued staring at the candle and hissing furiously. He even struggled to jump down but she held on to him, talking to him softly and stroking him, trying to calm his obvious unease at the sight of these objects.

'You see, he doesn't like this any more than I do,' said Noel, and he looked away in distaste.

'This is no time to falter, Noel, and you too Bandit. We made a decision.

A hard one I grant you, but we need to put right a terrible wrong and for that we need to call upon a stronger power than we would normally use.'

'But what if it backfires on you, Bridie?' You know as well as I do that that can happen.' The puckered brows and worry lines around his firmly set mouth, which could just be seen through his thick grey beard, were obvious signs of concern for her welfare.

'Then it does, but It is a risk I am prepared to take. When you were asked to put a stop to this, you came to me, asked me to take up the position of housekeeper in the Rochester household to find out exactly what had happened that afternoon, and how poor Eloise was, and I did. She may never recover from what Viscount Randolph did to her. If I can bring about a recovery I will, but her attacker needs to be put out of the way first. She must never have to see him again or it will surely send her back into withdrawal. Once I have dealt with him and his weak, over-indulgent father, then I can work for her recovery.

'Dr Boyd means well, and he has had some measure of success but, for Eloise, some greater force is needed, and I will use all my powers of healing, do whatever it takes, whatever the outcome, to give her something back of her previous self.' She looked up at Noel imploringly. 'We have come this far, my friend. Please do not fail me now.'

Noel hesitated, part of him wanted to walk away, forget this had ever been suggested but, as he looked down into her earnest, pleading eyes he, albeit reluctantly, nodded his agreement. What Bridie was going to do was dangerous, there was no getting away from that, but it was in a good cause and, if it prevented anyone else from suffering at the hands of this young self-willed, wayward young man who had no regard for anyone, then so be it...as she had said, whatever the outcome. Bridie was skilled, knowledgeable, he wanted to believe she could manage her extreme task...as long as she carried out the procedure correctly. There could be no mistakes.

Chapter Forty Nine

At a small clearing in the wood, beside an ivy-vine draped hillside, Bridie and Bandit said their forlorn, but temporary farewells. Bandit was to return with Noel to his small, thatched cottage in the valley until Bridie was able to return to her home on the outskirts of Farnshall village on the other side of the woods, which would be when she had completed the task in hand.

'Come, Bandit,' said Noel, picking up the miserable cat who hissed at being manhandled, and lashed out with his paw, sharp claws ready to scratch. But Noel just gave a soft, sympathetic, chuckle. 'He really doesn't want to leave you, Bridie.' Noel held Bandit firmly but gently against his chest with his left hand while tenderly stroking the distraught cat, with the right.

Bridie moved closer and stroked the cat's head, giving him a gentle scratch behind his ears. 'I know, and I don't want to leave him either. We have already been apart too long.' She leaned forward to look Bandit in the eyes. 'But you know, don't you Bandit, that there are things I must do before we can go home.' The cat began purring and, although still being held by Noel, he stretched forward and rubbed his chin against her hand. 'Not long now, my boy, but you must go with Noel where I know you are safe and looked after.'

She looked up at the sky. 'Noel, the moon is beginning to lower. I must go now if I am to finish what needs to be done this night and return without risking being seen. Please, now take Bandit, and go home. I shall contact you soon.' She leaned forward and kissed the cat on his forehead. 'Oh, and please don't forget to send me that letter from my Aunt Florence, will you? I will need an excuse to be away from the house while I rest when all this is done.

'I'll remember. Take care, Bridie. Stay safe.'

Bridie nodded and watched as her huge friend and precious cat vanished into the darkness of the trees and smiled to herself at the sound of Bandit's continual sad mewling decreasing in volume as they moved further away. She reached out to push the swathe of ivy to one side revealing a hidden door. She reached up to pull on a concealed lever above the doorframe, followed by a barely heard clunking sound and the door swung open.

Inside, just behind the door, upon a shelf were two oil lamps. She removed the glass cover and, blew onto the wick. Instantly a flame appeared, and she replaced the cover. She had only been in this tunnel twice before, and knew she would have to pass the remains of two people who met their deaths within its walls, yet it held no fears for her. Neither of these souls meant her any harm.

The ceiling of the tunnel was shored up with wooden spars and tree roots and the rock-strewn floor was uneven and dusty. In places she had to circumvent large building blocks that had been left by those who had constructed the secret passageway.

She reached the place where a headless skeleton lay pinned down by a leg under one of the stone blocks, its skull a few feet away. The remnants of his clothing indicated that he would have lived, and died, within the Elizabethan era. On one of her trips through the tunnel, she had touched the head and received an image of a kind, red-haired young man who had died while trying to save someone's life. She sensed rage surrounding him, but did not believe it had emanated from him. To give him peace she had given him a pagan blessing.

She moved on, came to the door where, with a wave of her hand the heavy solid wooden door opened giving access to the small ante-chamber with two cells on either side. She swept passed them and into the main chamber where instruments of torture were still to be found. Bridie suffered intolerable pain each time she entered this room. It was as though the pain inflicted on those poor souls who suffered, and probably died within this room, had somehow permeated the walls and anyone as sensitive as she would feel it.

She moved on through the next door and, taking care to avoid the steps where chunks of stone had crumbled away, climbed the cobweb-draped winding stone staircase that ended at the long corridor running parallel with the manor kitchen. She could feel the dwindling warmth from the fireplace on the other wide of the wall, and pictured the dying embers in the wide grate. Holding the hem of her skirt and cloak away from the stone-dust strewn floor, she hurried on to the next set of steps, sweeping aside the gossamer cobwebs that had clung to the ceiling and walls, undisturbed for an unknown number of years. She briefly wondered whose footsteps she was retracing. Who was the last person to walk this mysterious path?

A fleeting image of a young man with red hair flashed through her mind and out again. Although the image slipped away as quickly as it had entered her mind, she *felt* it was the same young man whose skeleton lay in the tunnel. A sense of great unhappiness and loss spread though her, momentarily making her want to cry but she had a job to do and forced the sentiment away; she needed to concentrate on the task at hand.

Reaching the end of the passage, she lifted the lamp higher, found the image of an ivy leaf carved into the wall, set the lamp down on the floor, pressed the ivy leaf and stood back as the door silently opened into the room.

She found herself in a large and beautifully appointed bedroom, with a wide four-poster bed draped with luxurious gold-fringed deep blue silken curtains that matched the floor length curtains at the tall window. Instinctively she knew that this was the bedroom of Viscount Randolph. But he was not there. She knew where he was, he was at The Swan Inn in Wells, busy enjoying his time with tavern wenches, and his drinking and gambling friends. That suited Bridie very well. For what she had to do his absence was very convenient. But the room was not empty.

'Hello, Bridie. I see you have kept your promise.' Joseph Hastings emerged from the far corner of the room and walked towards her. 'I am pleased to see you and thank you for your commitment. When I spoke to Noel, I believed there was nothing that could be done but…but…I…'

Bridie reached out to lay her hand on his arm. '…Did you think I would fail you, Joseph?' Bridie interrupted. She smiled encouragingly, her eyes glinted, and Joseph caught a glimpse of her perfect, white teeth in the shaft of moonlight that shone through the open curtains.

'No, my dear. I know you understand why I turned to Noel for help, and

I am grateful to you both. The Earl is not a bad man, but he is weak. He will never gain control of the Viscount now, it is far too late and...well, unless something is done, when his Lordship dies, and I believe with the amount of brandy he is consuming and his loss of appetite, that day may not be too far away. Randolph will become the Earl of Winterne, and I cannot countenance that. If he has control of the Winterne Estate and the title, then I am sure all hell will break loose within this family and wherever else he goes. Randolph cares little for the younger members of the family, even though they are of his own blood, and cares even less for his father or, to her lasting disappointment, he cared almost nothing for his adoring mother. The boy has become a monster.'

Joseph's concerned frown was difficult to see with his back to the only light in the room, but Bridie didn't need to see it to know how sincere he was, and how worried.

Bridie understood Joseph's divided loyalties. To arrive at the decision to take action against the Viscount must have been incredibly difficult after having been with the family for years, and his long-term personal loyalty to the Earl. To have had to stand by, watching without comment, the Earl's frustration and growing ineffectuality as Lady Gwendoline spoilt and cossetted the little Viscount into thinking he could behave in any way he wanted, must have been exasperating.

And now the time had come. Bridie was there and Joseph was finally forced to face the fact that his terrible plan of action was actually going to happen. He shuddered at the thought. But Bridie was waiting, he could keep her waiting no longer.

'Are you ready to show me which room is the Earl's?' she asked.

'Yes...' he hesitated at the door. 'Promise me the Earl will not suffer.'

'The Earl will come to no harm at my hands. On that you have my word.'

'Very well...and thank you. Follow me.' Joseph opened the door slowly and peered out along the landing. 'There's no-one around. Come.' He led Bridie out of the room and to a door at the far end, where he stopped. 'This is his Lordship's room. I do not want to know how you are going to carry this out, so please...'

Bridie gave a soft chuckle. 'Did you think I was going to murder him in his bed?'

Joseph seemed a little bewildered. 'Um...no...no...of course not.'

'Good, because that's not why I am here at all, Joseph. You shall have your Earl for a little longer.'

'Then...why...what?'

'I am here to warn him only. I shall not even awaken him, but he will hear me. He will know what is to come and that it cannot be averted. The curse has been placed. The young ones will be saved, as will all the domestic staff. Your Earl will have time to make the necessary arrangements before he dies, hopefully peacefully in his sleep, but I have no control over how his demise will come about. You must understand though that it will come in the not too far distant future, so prepare yourself for that. It will be after the Viscount has died, and the Earl has suffered for the sorrow and anguish local people have felt due to his lack of strength.'

'I feel regret for the pain that will be caused to him.'

'Instead, Joseph, feel regret and sorrow for those who have suffered because of both of them. The Viscount directly and the Earl indirectly. It is over,' said Bridie, firmly.

Joseph nodded sadly as he opened the door to the Earl's room for her and she vanished into the dark as Joseph heard the Earl snuffling in his sleep. He closed the door behind Bridie and waited, on guard, hearing her muffled voice within.

A few moments later she reappeared. Joseph had waited for her while looking out of the window at the far end of the corridor, watching the moonlit mist edging eerily along the garden from the lake towards the manor. He turned as he saw Bridie approach.

'All is done,' she told him. 'The Earl will remember what has been said when he awakes, but will have no memory of from whence it came.'

Joseph gave the slightest of nods in acknowledgement. 'It is time for you to leave, Bridie. No-one is awake yet so you could leave by the back door, or will you use the tunnel again?'

'I will use the tunnel. Ending in the woods, it will hide me from anyone who might be awake early, and it will be a shorter distance to my employer's garden, and therefore less chance of being seen by anyone if I take that route. Now, be prepared for the Earl to send the younger boys away to school, and the girls to relatives in London to have their social education finished before being introduced into society. You will be expected to stay to maintain the manor as a home for them to return to, and for young Lord Simon who will become the next Earl. Some...some incidents will occur over the next ten years...'

'...Ten years?'

'Yes. That is how long this curse on the manor will last.'

'Why so long? What incidents?'

'The length of time is to ensure the Maitland family remember that they must never allow this to happen again. The incidents I cannot specify but you will know when they happen.' She laid a hand on his arm. 'Protect the young ones.' She turned away. 'Now I must go, and you must appear to have just arisen from your bed. Goodbye, Joseph. I doubt we shall meet again.'

Joseph did not move, unable to explain the sense of bereavement he felt as she disappeared behind the door. Something told him Bridie was right. They would not meet again.

As Bridie exited the tunnel, and ensured the door was concealed behind the blanket of thick, trailing ivy vines that hung down from the top of the crag above, the moon was waning, and the sunrise was a bright line behind the hills that could just be seen through the morning mist. She still had time to return to the house before the maids or Aggie awoke.

On the verandah, she removed her damp boots. The grass was heavy with dew, and she did not want wet tell-tale footprints left on the floor on her way to her room. The hem of her cloak and her skirt also had a darker damp edge. She would have to change her dress before heading downstairs. Closing the French window quietly, she walked through the bedroom and into the sitting room on tiptoes. At the door to the corridor, she listened for a moment for any movement. Hearing nothing, she opened the door slowly and peered out. There was no-one about, but she could just hear the scraping sound of the kitchen range being cleaned of yesterday's ashes. If that was Bella up and getting the range ready to lay and light the fire, Aggie would not be long after her.

With a speed that belied her age, plus having been up all night using her precious life force on mystical undertakings which had left her drained, Bridie somehow found enough energy to dart along to the staircase and run up to the servants' quarters on the top floor, narrowly avoiding been seen by Mabel who had just come out of the staff bathroom. She slipped into her own room without being seen, stripped off her cloak and dress and hung them both up at the side of her wardrobe where they could not be seen from the door. She had a quick wash at the sink in her room, changed her underclothes, put on a clean housekeeper's uniform-style charcoal dress. Then, after brushing her hair straight back, she pinned it tightly into a bun at the back of her head. Then she was ready for work. However, she wanted to make sure Mrs Rochester was still comfortable and stopped on the first floor to take a look. Entering the room, she found the nurse, Edith, awake and leaning over the still sleeping Mrs Rochester, while tucking in the bedcover.

Edith smiled and walked over to join Bridie at the door.

'How is she? Has she awoken at all?' asked Bridie.

'Yes, she briefly woke when Mr Rochester came in to see her on his return from the Infirmary. That would have been a little after midnight.'

At that time, Bridie realised, she had been in the cavern with Noel. 'Did Mr Rochester ask for me at all?'

'No, he said he just wanted to make sure Mrs Rochester was comfortable and that, as it had been a terribly long day and he was reassured with regard to Eloise, he did not want to disturb the household and was going straight to bed. I think he said something about being awoken at ten o'clock.'

'Thank you, Edith. I am pleased to hear he was going to get some rest. And, yes, Mrs Rochester seems peaceful. Did you manage to sleep at all?'

Edith shook her head and looked away briefly. 'Um, no. I don't sleep while I am on duty. Thank you for the tea, it revived me. If I am on duty through the night on one of the wards, there are always noises and other people around, and there is definitely no likelihood of napping but, here in a quiet house, a warm room there is always the possibility that we might nod off, but...no, no I didn't.'

'Oh, right. I'll just take your tray,' said Bridie, trying to look away to hide her smile. Either Edith did not realise she had slept or did not want to admit it. Either way, Bridie knew better, after all, the sleeping draft she had put in Edith's tea had definitely done its work, as Bridie had seen for herself.

'Do you know what time you will be relieved? I was just asking as I can have Bella bring you some breakfast on a tray if you would like anything.'

Edith said she would not be leaving until shortly after nine o'clock, and tea and toast with honey, if possible, would be very welcome.

Chapter Fifty

Downstairs in the Rochester house, Mr Rochester was having breakfast and reading his newspaper, while Mrs Rochester was taking her breakfast in bed. She was much improved, but had taken it very badly when she was given the news that her husband had agreed to Eloise being transferred to the Infirmary. She sobbed for some time, until she understood there had been no other choice, for them or for Eloise.

Even so, although she had met and liked, Dr Boyd, and understood his methods were second to none, Mrs Rochester found it difficult to forgive her husband, until Dr Boyd explained during his visit to check on her progress following her injury. He described how Eloise's brain had been damaged by its heavy contact with her skull, bruising and causing pressure, and how that injury could affect her moods making her irrational, contrary and, as they had seen unpredictably violent. She could also do herself some injury during one of these bouts of aggression and, therefore, she should be where she could be protected, and observed and, most importantly, given time to heal in a safe environment.

Constance had listened and finally understood that her daughter was not insane and, in time there was chance that some of her former personality could return, with careful handling, of course.

Bridie Burrows was in her small office next to the kitchen, going through the receipts from local shopkeepers and calculating the payments that were due, when Aggie walked in with a cup of tea for her.

'Ah Bridie, mah dear, yeh look sae tired an' pale ah though' yeh could dae wi' a wee cuppa.'

Mrs Burrows looked up from her paperwork and leaned back in her hard wooden chair. 'Aggie, you're so good to me. I'm grateful and you're right, I could do with this.' She reached out to take the big white cup that was used, without a saucer, by the staff. It was the family only who were served their tea in the floral china tea service.

Setting the cup down on the table, Bridie rubbed her eyes with the heel of her hands. 'I am tired. I have slept very badly since this business with Eloise. I keep worrying that perhaps I should have noticed something brewing, could have done something before it got to this point.'

'Och, away wi' yeh. There's no-one could have predicted what was tae come. Yeh tek on far tae much responsibility, lass. Yeh'll nae dae yersel' any guid frettin' aboot somethin' yeh cannae...'

Just at that moment, Mabel entered and handed an envelope to Mrs Burrows. 'The post has come, Mrs Burrows, and there's a letter for you.'

Aggie and Mabel looked at each other, puzzled. Mrs Burrows had never received a letter. Not many of the household staff did and, if they did get one it, was usually bad news.

Mrs Burrows reached out to take the envelope realising that both women were watching her, both frowning. She opened the envelope and took out a piece of white paper. 'Oh, it's from my Aunt Florence in Shepton Mallet.' She read the letter in silence with both women obviously dying to know what the note said.

'Oh dear,' said Mrs Burrows, putting the letter down on the table. She looked up at the two women waiting with evident curiosity to find out what the letter contained. 'It seems my aunt is very unwell, and wants me to go to stay with her for a few days. I must talk to Mr Rochester to ask his leave to attend her. I shall be back shortly.'

'Och, Bri...Mrs Burrows, ah'm sair sorry tae hear tha'.'

'But who will take your place while you're away, Mrs Burrows,' asked Mabel. She sounded a little nervous.

'That will have to be discussed with Mr Rochester, Mabel. I shall inform you on my return of the arrangements during my absence.'

In the dark wood pannelled dining room, made brighter by the autumn sun streaming in through the tall windows, Mr Rochester had finished his breakfast, and Lily had begun clearing away the remains of the food and the breakfast plates. With his now read newspaper lying on the table, Mr Rochester was about to leave the room when Mrs Burrows entered. Lily was just putting the condiment set back on the sideboard and turned to see why Mrs Burrows had come in, assuming it had something to do with a task Mrs Burrows wanted her to perform, but when the housekeeper simply nodded to her and approached Mr Rochester, she realised it had nothing to do with her and looked away trying not to show her interest, but she was listening, and Mrs Burrows was well aware of Lily's nosiness.

'If it is convenient, sir, I would be grateful if you could spare me a few minutes,' she asked.

He smiled, 'Of course, Mrs Burrows. Nothing wrong I hope?'

Mrs Burrows gave Lily a quick glance and suppressed a smile. 'I would rather talk in confidence, sir, if you don't mind.' Lily looked disappointed.

'Well, do come into the study, we can talk in private there.' Mr Rochester led the way.

In the study, Mr Rochester invited Mrs Burrows to take a seat. 'I'd rather stand if you don't mind, sir.' Mrs Burrows, as a domestic servant, even at a senior rank, was well aware of her position within the household, and it was not appropriate for her to sit in front of her employer as an equal would. Mr Rochester took his usual seat behind his desk. 'Is there something wrong, Mrs Burrows?'

'Yes, sir. I'm afraid there is. I need to ask for a few days leave of absence. I know this...'

Mr Rochester leaned forward. He noticed that Mrs Burrows looked very tired. She had lost the rosy bloom in her cheeks. Perhaps she should have some time off. 'It's not very convenient right now, Mrs Burrows, as I am sure you know. Mrs Rochester being unwell and with my daughter's situation. Is it necessary that you take leave at this particular time?' He frowned and stood up, turned to look out of the window, something she had seen him do a number of times before when faced with a problem.

'My apologies, sir. I do understand how difficult this may be at the moment, but I have received a letter informing me that my Aunt Florence, who lives in Shepton Mallet...you may remember I mentioned her when I first applied for this position...she is my only living relative...is very unwell and there is no-one else who could look after her.'

Without turning around, Mr Rochester asked, 'And is there anyone who could take on your duties while you are away?'

'Oh, indeed there is, sir. Mabel has assisted me, when necessary, with a number of tasks, she understands the accounts system, knows which suppliers are to be trusted, is capable of supervising Lily and understands the routine of the house. I have found her reliable and efficient and, excuse me for saying this, I have no reason to think she will do so but, should she ever wish to improve her situation and become a housekeeper herself, instead of senior housemaid, the experience of being responsible for the running of the house will stand her in good stead. In addition, she gets on well with Mrs McMurdo.'

Mr Rochester turned to face her. He was smiling. 'I see you have thought all this out, Mrs Burrows, and I have no wish to deprive your aunt of your company when she is ill...how old is she?'

'...sixty-four years of age, sir...and a widow.'

Mr Rochester clasped his hands behind his back and looked down thoughtfully. When he looked back up at the tidy, stern lady in front of him, he nodded. 'How soon would you wish to leave?'

'This afternoon, if that does not inconvenience you too much, sir. That would give me time to give Mabel her instructions for the running of the house during my absence.'

Again, he nodded, then smiled. 'How do you intend travelling to Shepton Mallet?'

'I shall travel on the mail coach from Wells to Shepton Mallet.'

'I would be happy to have George take you in the carriage if that would help?'

But Mrs Burrows shook her head. 'Oh no, sir. Thank you for the offer but that would take George away for too long, and you will need the carriage for visiting the Infirmary.'

'I appreciate that, thank you. However, I insist then that George takes you as far as Wells.'

For a brief moment Mrs Burrows appeared to be about to decline that offer as well, but then she inclined her head and said: 'Thank you, sir. I am most grateful.' She made a half turn to go. 'Now I must inform Mabel of her new position...'

'...Temporary position, Mrs Burrows,' Mr Rochester interrupted.

Mrs Burrows inclined her head and smiled politely, '...temporary position, of course, sir, and tell Cook that Mabel will be taking my place for a few days. Then I must pack a few things. I would like to say, sir, how much I have enjoyed my time within this house and in your employ.'

Mr Rochester gave a small chuckle. 'For Heaven's sake, woman, you sound as if you were leaving us permanently, not going away for a few days.'

Mrs Burrows smiled. 'Do I, sir? How silly of me?'

Chapter Fifty One

At the Infirmary later the following evening, the main lights were turned out in the ward, the patients had all been prepared for bed, and the smaller team of night staff had come on duty. A tall nurse with silver-grey hair, pulled tightly back in her clean, starched white cap that tied with a bow under her chin, blended in with the few other members of staff in the corridors. There were so many changes of staff that no-one reacted to seeing a stranger in the building.

The Infirmary was unusual in that, having a young and forward-thinking doctor in charge, the staff practiced a routine of cleanliness and hygiene. The walls were white-washed, the floor tiles in a black and white diamond pattern were spotlessly clean, but nothing could be done to prevent the strong and somewhat overpowering smell of carbolic soap that blended with the odour of cooked eggs, cabbage and, in one or two areas, vomit.

The nurse headed towards one of the main wards, walking quickly but quietly in a pair of soft-soled boots. In her arms she carried a pair of white folded sheets she had taken from a linen cupboard in the corridor, which gave her an air of validity, and of being busy. The double doors on the ward were just ahead but she turned right and headed along a smaller passageway toward the rooms reserved for the private patients and, making sure no-one was around to see her, she slipped into the private room where Eloise Rochester slept.

Eloise was asleep cuddling her favourite rag doll, her breathing laboured and irregular, as she lay in an iron-framed bed, between pure white linen sheets beneath a thick cotton pink coverlet. Her head rested on a white broderie anglaise edged pillowcase, her hair untied and spread out on the pillow. Apart from the erratic breathing Eloise appeared comfortable but it was probable she had been sedated.

On the bedside cabinet was an ornate vase of small flowered pink roses, which would have come from Mr Rochester's greenhouse. Their delicate perfume was noticeable as soon as one entered the room. In the far corner of the room the nurse saw a wheelchair and sincerely hoped it would not be needed for Eloise. Apart from a wooden chair on the other side of the bed, the only other item of furniture was a small wardrobe.

The nurse approached the bed and gently stroked the forehead of the sleeping girl without disturbing her. She looked down at the still red and raised hoof-shaped scar close to the right temple, and ran her hand over the wound so softly Eloise was unaware of her touch. The nurse knelt by the bed and whispered close to the girl's ear. Her hand, that a moment ago had been stroking the wound, stopped moving. She closed her eyes in concentration, willing her powers of healing to work where everything else had failed.

Eloise stirred in her sleep, called out for her mother, then settled again. The nurse continued her efforts, not letting her patient's momentary restlessness disturb her endeavours. Fifteen minutes, thirty minutes, an hour went by and it was clear the nurse was tiring but the patient, although asleep still, was looking better. There was a slight improvement in the pastiness of her complexion, a faint peach-tinge blushed her cheeks, where before she had looked sallow. Her breathing became more, steady and the redness of the scar had begun to pale, the swelling slightly less obvious.

But the nurse was weakening; her strength was ebbing with every minute she spent giving her life force to Eloise. She could feel she had done all she could, she had nothing left to give and it would be all she could do to leave the Infirmary and return to where she could rest.

Standing up, her legs buckled slightly, but she stood firm, put one foot in front of the other and headed for the door where she hesitated, 'Brigid give me strength.' She took a deep breath, and walked slowly and falteringly, until she heard footsteps heading her way from a passageway on the right. She drew herself up to her full height and managed to walk normally until the nurse who appeared at the end of the corridor passed her, and the exit was in sight.

In front of the door a number of cloaks were hanging on pegs, she removed one, too tired and too weak now to care who it belonged to and, relieved that her job was done, she left the hospital tottered to a small copse of trees where an almost purely black horse with a long soft mane and a perfect white diamond on its forehead, waited for her tethered to an almost leafless oak tree.

She unhooked the reins and the well-trained horse bowed down on its front legs to allow her to climb onto its back and without being given a direction. Soon they were in Winterne Woods, the nurse leaning forward in her fatigue, her head resting against the warm neck of the horse. She was vaguely aware of a pair of ravens flying overhead going in the direction the horse was taking her. She smiled. She loved ravens and wished for a moment that she had some to look after, then realised it was too late for that now and the thought saddened her.

From nowhere Bandit appeared and ran alongside the horse as it slowly walked, taking care of its passenger, until it reached its home, Noel's solitary cottage.

Bandit ran ahead, mewing loudly and was clearly relieved to see Noel come out to meet them. And he had company. Beside him were two small people whose height only reached that of Noel's waist.

When the horse stopped at the door, one of them moved forward to take the reins while Noel lifted the nurse, Bridie, off his back and carried her tenderly into the warmth of his sitting room where a fire blazed in the hearth, and the smell of a rabbit stew simmering in a pot over the fire was meant to revive the exhausted witch. Laying Bridie on the sofa, Noel prepared a herbal tea to which he added honey, nettle, ginger and dandelion, all of which were said to aid revival. While Noel was busy, the two elves put a pillow under Bridie's head, covered her with a blanket, then knelt beside her, quietly reciting an elven prayer. But when Noel returned to her with the brew, he could see Bridie was beyond any help of any kind. She was barely conscious. Her breathing shallow and difficult to draw. Bandit sat on the arm of the sofa staring at her, refusing to take his eyes off her. Noel understood immediately. It wasn't that the curse had rebounded on her, it was just that she had used the last of her strength for Eloise.

Bandit moved nearer and snuggled close to the side of her head on the pillow, he purred loudly into her ear. Bridie opened her eyes.

'Hello, my boy.' She tried to raise her hand to stroke him, but she was too weak. 'I want you to go with Noel. He will look after you.' She coughed and grimaced as though in pain. Noel tried to lift Bandit to take him away from her, but she whispered, 'No…please leave him…until.' A single tear rolled down from her right eye to the pillow.

'Noel, please look…uh…after him for me…uh…until I return. Then find me. Bandit, I shall not be far away.' She closed her eyes and took her last breath observed by a cat, two elves, two ravens who had perched on the window ledge, a black horse with a perfect white diamond shape on his forehead, and the closest, most eternal, friend she ever had.

Epilogue

Eloise Rochester

Eloise awoke from her deep sleep two days later. The nurse, Edith Sanders had asked to be assigned as the poor girl's chief nurse, and Dr Boyd had been happy to consign Eloise's care to her as she was one of his most efficient nurses. When Edith looked at Eloise's medical notes to see what had been recorded by the night staff, she was surprised to find there were no entries after midnight.

Realising something was very wrong, she asked one of the night nurses who was just going off duty if checks had been made on Eloise through the night. The nurse replied that she had seen a nurse sitting with Eloise at around midnight and she was still there an hour or so later. After that she had been busy in the main ward, and had not gone by Eloise's room again. She said she did not recognise the nurse but had assumed she was a new member of staff and, unfortunately her description was very vague. The only thing she could remember was that she had very pale silvery-grey hair.

With Eloise clearly appearing to have come to no harm, Edith felt it was more important to stay with her rather than continue to search for the mysterious nurse. It was a little later that morning when she began to see a change in Eloise even though she still slept. Edith called for Dr Boyd.

On examining Eloise, Dr Boyd was astounded at the baffling, but very welcome, change in Eloise's colour, pulse rhythm, and the lessening of the scar tissue on her forehead. There was no rational explanation for the change but as far as he could see her condition was improving.

At the Rochester's house, that evening, Dr Boyd explained to her now very hopeful parents that their daughter was, physically, looking better. He made no promises about her psychological health or the condition of the injury to the brain, but he would know more about that in a day or so when she awoke.

The following morning, while Edith was tidying the room, and preparing to give Eloise a blanket bath, a strange sighing noise came from the bed, and she turned to see Eloise awake and looking at her. She rushed to press the bell to call for assistance. Then calmly walked across to the bed and sat down on the bedside chair. 'Hello, Eloise. I'm your nurse, Edith. Dr Boyd will be here to see you in a moment. How are you feeling?'

Eloise tried to speak but her mouth was dry. Edith poured her a cup of water, lifted her head a little to help her take a few sips, then gently lowered her head onto the pillow and set the cup back down on the bedside cabinet.

Eloise looked at her. 'Where...where am I?'

'You're at the Mendip Infirmary and you're a patient of Dr Boyd's. I believe you have met him before at your home. You have been here a little over a week. How do you feel?'

With a knitted brow she said, 'I have a...a little bit of a headache and I am hungry.'

Edith laughed. 'Hungry...that's a very good...'

At that point, a nurse opened the door and peered in. 'Is it help yer wantin'?'

'Bridget, could you get Dr Boyd for me, please. He'll want to be here. Tell him Eloise is awake.'

'She's awake?' The nurse came into the room and stared at Eloise who smiled at her. 'Well, merciful Heaven, so she is. Oi'll go ter fetch Dr Boyd fer yer.' And she ran out of the room saying, 'Well thanks be ter Mary and Joseph...oh an' there's me runnin' when Oi'm not serposed ter.'

Eloise smiled and asked, 'Can I sit up a bit please? Maybe if you could plump up my pillows and help me up and why is my old rag doll in my bed? I haven't played with her for ages.'

'Not quite yet, young lady. Let's see what Dr Boyd says. If he agrees then we will.'

A few moments later footsteps were heard running along the corridor growing louder as they neared. The door swung open, and a breathless Dr

Boyd entered, smiling from ear to ear.

'Hello, my dear.' He noted immediately that her scar had reduced even more in colour and swelling, and where the rough stitches were, there was now hardly a sign of them, but he said nothing. He reached for her wrist and timed her pulse. It was regular and within a satisfactory pace. He sat by her bed and talked to her about how she felt, what she would like to eat and whether she felt strong enough to get up for a short walk around the room. She did.

Two days later, Eloise walked into the lounge of the hospital to find her parents waiting for her. After hugging them, she spotted a piano in the corner of the large room. 'May I?' she asked Dr Boyd. He nodded. 'You're very welcome.'

Eloise sat at the piano, flexed her fingers while Dr Boyd lifted the lid. Without sheet music, she began to play Debussy's *Claire du lune* from memory. She stumbled on a few notes here and there but continued until she finished the piece. By the time she reached the end, she had an audience of patients and nurses, most of whom were moved to tears – including Dr Boyd.

Over the next few weeks, Eloise continued to improve. To the great relief of her family, she was no longer the five-year-old child she had regressed to, and had no memory of the incident that caused her injury. There were no longer any aggressive outbursts and Eloise was able to return to the family home. Her parents thanked Dr Boyd for the wonderful progress Eloise had made, but of course, they had no way of knowing that it was not the good doctor's therapy that had brought Eloise back to them.

When Mrs Burrows failed to return to the family, Mr Rochester had investigations carried out around Shepton Mallet, but found no trace of her. Not knowing her Aunt Florence's surname, for a while he assumed it would be Burrows, but there was no Florence Burrows known in the town. After weeks of searching, he was forced to conclude that Mrs Burrows had simply vanished.

Randolph Maitland, Viscount Winterne

While Eloise had been in the hospital, at just nineteen-years-old and while hunting to hounds, Viscount Randolph was killed when the almost totally black horse, with a long soft mane and a perfect white diamond on its forehead, baulked at jumping a tall hedge and threw him over its head onto the cold hard ground on the other side, breaking his neck. At the time, his own horse being lame, a friend had loaned him the horse he had recently won in a card game at a local tavern.

The horse had run away, the other riders presumed it had run off in fright. When asked about the horse, the only thing the friend could recall about the person he had won it from was that had never seen him before and that he was very tall with white hair and bushy beard. That description was felt to be completely useless as it could fit any number of men in the area.

Very few people turned out for the funeral. The horse was never found.

Rupert Maitland, Earl of Winterne

On the morning after Bridie's nocturnal visit to his room, waking late after having had a disturbed night, the Earl awoke with a sinking feeling in his stomach. A sense of foreboding hung over him and, from somewhere, he seemed to hear a small voice in his head telling him to make arrangements for his younger children, to get them away from the manor.

All that day and the next day, while eating little and drinking brandy, he gave their future a great deal of thought. He was determined to have them sent away from the manor, utterly convinced they would be safer elsewhere, but where? He finally made the decision to send his daughters to stay with family in London to have their education 'finished'. They would learn social skills, how to behave in fashionable society and, when the Earl's cousin, Lady Eleanor Maitland, with whom the girls would be residing, felt that they were mature enough, at fifteen or sixteen years old, they would be presented at Court in the presence of Queen Victoria.

The Earl made arrangements for his younger sons as a matter of urgency, and Simon and Ralph left for Sherborne School for Boys, a boarding school founded in 1550. The school had an excellent reputation for their standard of education. It was also the type of establishment where they could take advantage of being able to make the acquaintance of sons from aristocratic and wealthy families. Making friends with boys of their own highborn class, or with monied people albeit originally from the lower strata of society, would give them useful connections for their future.

During the period when the Earl was pre-occupied with organising the future of his four younger children, he saw little of Viscount Randolph. Nor, he found, did he particularly miss his eldest son. While he was absent and there was no news of any recent unsavoury incidents, the Earl's appetite began to return, and he drank less to the relief of Joseph Hastings.

It was just a few days after the girls had left, that a breathless messenger arrived at the manor and gave Joseph the tragic news that the Viscount had been killed and his body was being brought home. The Earl then went into seclusion in the library, ultimately blaming himself for Randolph's appalling behaviour and death, leaving Joseph to make the necessary funeral arrangements.

Attending the funeral, the Earl leaned on Joseph as he walked through the crowd of villagers who were clearly not there to mourn the passing of Randolph Maitland. With respect for the Earl and his loss, the crowd stayed silent, although Joseph felt certain that had the Earl not been present, there would have been cheers; their sense of relief was almost palpable.

On his return to the manor, the Earl asked for pen, paper and envelopes and wrote letters to each of his four younger children, to his cousin, Lady Eleanor, to Joseph and to his lawyer. He handed all the sealed envelopes to Joseph asking him to ensure they reached their destinations, and told him not to open the envelope addressed to himself until after the Earl died. He then dismissed Joseph stating very clearly that he did not wish to be disturbed. Although Joseph found this very concerning, he could not disobey a direct command. As he walked away from the library, envelopes in hand and unease in his heart, he heard the key turn in the lock. He turned back and knocked on the library door.

'My Lord, is there anything I can do...anything you require?'

'No thank you, Joseph,' came the reply, slightly muffled by the solid wooden doors. 'I will ring if I need anything.' He sounded as though all was well, albeit maybe just a little the worse for brandy.

Reassured the Earl would call if he required attention, Joseph went back to his room next door to the kitchens, removed his jacket, undid his cravat and laid down on his bed while he looked through the envelopes to see who was to receive a letter. He was tired. One of the maids had set a fire in the grate and the room was warm. Soon he had drifted off to sleep and the envelopes had slipped from his hands to fall on the floor.

It was some hours later they found the Earl had disengaged the rope from the wire connected to the bell apparatus in the kitchen, and had hanged himself.

Noel Elden

With two homes to offer Bandit, a cottage in the woods and a second home with the elves who had only recently settled in their new residence, a cathedral sized cavern within the hillside, Noel Elden took Bandit to live with him. But Bandit too, had a place within the supernatural world. When his time came to die, he would be re-born and, through the centuries, would always be reunited with his soul-mate, she who had in her most recent life, been Bridie Burrows. In each of her incarnations, when she reached the age of five-years-old, Bandit would find her, and they would be together again.

Foreseeing his future, Noel knew the time would come when, in another identity, he would become a resident of Winterne Village and work within the manor estate and woodland. An immortal, who could never die or alter his appearance, it was vital Noel changed his location and name from time to time, to avoid awkward questions about his continued longevity when people locally were physically ageing and dying. To avoid any of the existing residents recognising him when he returned, he chose to stay away from Winterne for the next hundred years or so.

Although his cottage was concealed from human eyes, he was not isolated. He had many friends among the elven folk who had populated the woods and the limestone caves for centuries, but were rarely seen by humans. He had Bandit for the span of the cat's natural life, a family of ravens who kept him informed of going-ons in the area and, of course the woodland wildlife and his reindeer. At the end of each year, as Christmas approached, he found himself particularly busy and had no time to think about being the only human member of his community.

Soon after Bridie's death, a gathering of elves and animals – domestic pets and wild – met in a concealed clearing in Winterne Wood. They assembled around a knoll of natural, grassy appearance for Bridie's funeral. Hovering above the mound was a casket made of reeds intertwined with ivy, holly and the herb, Rosemary. The white flowers and red berries made Bridie's coffin look almost festive and the scent of the herb permeated the grove.

With Bandit sitting quietly at his feet, Noel spoke emotionally about the loss of their friend, but then continued by saying how much they looked forward to her next incarnation, and that those present should look out for signs that she had been reborn.

The ground beneath her coffin slid open revealing a tunnel like cavity below with shelves containing similar coffins. Bridie's casket slowly descended into the hollow and floated down until it slid sideways into a vacant space and settled. The gathering remained watching until the two sides of the mound silently slid to a close meeting in the middle, then in ones, twos or larger groups, they turned away to vanish into the woods, until everyone had gone leaving only Noel and Bandit to say their silent farewells.

'She gave her life for Eloise, Bandit,' Noel said, hunkering down to stroke the heartbroken cat. 'Be proud of her and do not grieve. You will be together again before too long.' He picked Bandit up and set him on his own broad shoulders. Bandit positioned himself, like a shawl draped across the big man's shoulders and hid his face under Noel's long hair. 'But, until that day, my boy, you will have to make do with me.'

Simon Maitland, Earl of Winterne

Having become the Earl of Winterne at just twelve years old, Simon Maitland depended a great deal on Joseph Hastings and gained from the butler's wealth of experience and wisdom. Simon's memories of his childhood estrangement from his father, the intolerable behaviour of his brother, Randolph, and Joseph's guidance, led to Simon growing into a kind and considerate lord of the manor. Through his common sense, humour and generosity, local people learned to forget their animosity, and regained their respect towards the Maitland family.

In 1876, following an occurrence with burst pipes during a particularly cold snap in January, water had run down from a second floor bathroom to an area of the first floor and seeped down to the ground floor hallway. Although immediate repairs were carried out, the Earl felt it would be wise to wait until the warmer weather in Spring, when windows could be opened, to carry out the necessary renovations; repointing and plastering, rotten wood removed and replaced with good new timber, and many smaller problems that needed to be attended to.

It was a warm day in April when the renovations began, starting on the first floor with the removal of old floorboards. Having stacked good new oak boards against the wall, Reginald Sykes, a local carpenter and his apprentice, Albert Browning, got down on their knees to rip up the old boards. They had been working for a little over an hour when, Albert discovered something attached to one of the joists.

'Mr Sykes, Oi think yer should coom an' tek a look a' this,' he said, puzzled.

'Wha' is it now, boy?' Reginald was always happy to answer what he considered to be 'serious' questions, but Albert had an annoying habit of slowing the flow of work with the most trivial things, and Reginald was finding it difficult to maintain his patience. After all, the Earl was paying him on completion of the work, not by the hour and time was money, after all!

'No, 'onest, Mr Soikes, Oi think yer need to see this. Oi don' wanna do nuthin' till you'm seen it.'

Reginald sighed noisily, and staggered to his feet, his knees complaining, and tottered over to where Albert was looking down into the gap between two joists.

'Alright then, what've yer found this time?' The older man looked down into the hole and frowned. He had never seen one of those before! 'Jest run down an' fetch Mister 'Astings, will yer lad. Oi think 'e needs ter 'ave a look a' this.'

A few moments later, John Hastings, the son of Joseph, who had replaced his father as the family butler when Joseph retired several years before, knocked urgently on the door of the study. The Earl, had been concentrating on finding a well-bred stallion to improve the bloodline of his horses, reluctantly invited John in. With his properties of the manor and the house in London, his political ambitions and his string of Arabian horses to care for, Simon had looked forward to a break in his busy schedule. Apart from the distant sounds of the work on the landing, the study was far enough away for the noise not to disturb his peace, and he was enjoying the time he could give to his hobby. As John entered the Earl grudgingly put down his papers but, being of good-nature, he smiled. 'I trust this is urgent, John.'

John raised his eyebrows. 'I cannot confirm that it is urgent, my Lord, but I do believe you will find it interesting. I wonder if you would be good enough to accompany me up to the first floor. Mr Sykes has something he would like your opinion on.'

'It sounds intriguing. Lead on, John.'

Upstairs he found the workmen looking into a hole where they had just removed an old and water-damaged floorboard. Reginald Sykes lifted his cap and scratched his balding head. 'Oi don' know wha' tha' is, me Lord. Ain't never seen nuthin' loike it.' He frowned as he stared down at the hook screwed into the floor joist, and the mildewed piece of thick cord looped over it, that continued under the skirting board below a low-hung portrait of the second Earl of Winterne.

The Earl hunkered down to touch the cord and gave it a small tug. Nothing happened. 'It looks old, but I think it feels fairly strong still. I'm just baffled as to what it could have been used for.' He looked up at John. 'Well, what do you think, should I pull harder?'

John grinned. 'Yes...as long as the house doesn't fall down, my Lord.'

The Earl laughed.' I wish Ralph was here. My brother may be younger than I, but he always knows the right thing to do.' He looked at Reginald, on his knees on the other side of the hole. 'What do you think, Reg?'

'It ain't fer me tell yer wha' ter do, my Lord, but curiosity would've got the better of me by now, an' Oi'd 'ave ter 'ave given it a tug.'

'Very well. Let's do that...and hope that all is well...'

'...And that it doesn't snap,' said John leaning forward to see better.

The Earl gave the cord a stronger tug than he had before. With a scraping sound, and to their great astonishment, the portrait of the second Earl swung jerkily open to reveal the emaciated skeleton of a monk, a prayer book on the floor beside his chair.

'My God!' said the Earl.

'What the...?' said John.

'My word,' said Reginald.

All four stared at the body for a few minutes, not knowing what to say or do. John was the first to speak. 'Do you think it is safe to have him moved, my Lord. I have read about bacteria living in cadavers.'

Without taking his eyes off the remains of the monk, the Earl said: 'I believe so. I, too, have read those reports, and I would think that anything that could spread disease from this poor soul would have died long ago. Look at that prayer book. It must be hundreds of years old. I would like to know more about who he was, John. Maybe there's something about him in the family bible.' He turned to John. Whoever he is...was...he deserves a proper burial. Would you send one of the servants to fetch Reverend Wilkins, please. He may know which order of monks this brother belonged to. I don't know whether he was a Catholic or Anglican monk. Once we know, we will know in which church to arrange his Christian burial.

Two weeks later Brother Matthew was finally laid to rest at St Michaels Church near Farnshall. The Earl, having found a little information in the back pages of the family bible about Brother Matthew, and his disappearance, and that of the then Earl's brother James, was able to give a eulogy. Sadly, there was nothing more ever discovered about what happened to either of them, or why Brother Matthew had never been released from the Priest Hole.

Winterne Manor

Bridie's curse began with the death of Randolph Maitland, and continued with the suicide of his father, the Earl of Winterne. Joseph was unnerved by the thought that it was going to last ten years, and dreaded what might still be to come. Although he was determined to be on guard, when each new misfortune occurred, it happened so quickly or so drastically, that all he could do was to try to put things right after the event, and wonder when the next one would occur.

The Earl had left authority for the management of the manor in Joseph's capable hands. Funds held by the Earl's lawyer were in place to pay the servants retained for the routine maintenance of the manor, or repairs of the building. But the curse did not end with the death of the Viscount and the Earl.

Over the years, heavy snows damaged the roof of the stables. A fire mysteriously broke out in a stone building used as safe storage area for the architect's plans and other documents that related to the manor.

Like many manor houses, at one time it had a stone-built wall surrounding the front courtyard. Much of that wall had been destroyed in the siege during Monmouth Rebellion, leaving a large quantity of rubble unused and left where it had fallen. Simon's father had instructed that this stone should be used to construct the other three walls of the store, the fourth being a part of the wall that remained intact. With a solid dry floor, a slate roof and a lockable door, it was thought to be a safer place to store documents rather than in the house which contained a great deal of wood, and therefore more prone to fire.

No-one knew, or admitted to knowing, how the fire in this store began, but the windows were broken – whether before by someone setting the fire, or from the heat once the fire had taken hold, no-one knew – and the solid wooden boxes containing the documents, were burnt to ashes.

During a lengthy period of heavy rain, rat's nests were found within the remains of the other side of the outer wall. The two manor gardeners were tasked with destroying the nests, which they did very efficiently but, unfortunately in leaning over the nests to destroy them, their actions released the airborne Hantavirus which they inhaled while they were working. This led to them both suffering severe breathing difficulties, and eventually death due to organ failure.

For two years running, the crops in the manor farm fields failed, but adjacent farms had successful harvests and, during one of those years, a fungus disease affected the trout in the lake killing at least three-quarters of the stock.

During a terrible storm, shortly after Randolph had been interred, lightning struck the Maitland family stone-built mausoleum in the cemetery of the church at Winterne, where the remains of many of their ancestors lay, cleaving the roof in two. This incident terrified many of the superstitious villagers who, of course, blamed the curse.

The Honorable Ralph Maitland, youngest son of the late Rupert Maitland, was sent home from Sherborne School for Boys after contracting a serious bout of Measles. Tended by the family doctor, Ralph did recover, but was left with partial hearing in one ear and completely deaf in the other.

Other incidents happened that the manor staff attributed to the curse. A swarm of wasps built their nest in one of the chicken houses, terrifying the chickens who stopped laying eggs. But some episodes may simply have been accidents. One example was, when one of the housemaids was standing on a ladder to replace newly laundered curtains, she slipped and fell breaking her leg. Of course, the curse was blamed for that as well.

Selene Fern

Five years after the death of Bridie Burrows, a little girl sat on a swing in her back garden on the edge of Godney village, sobbing. It was her fifth birthday and her old cat, Samson, had died two days before, leaving the child desolate.

Her mother, Sybil, watching from the kitchen window of their cottage, had tried to console her but nothing comforted the bereaved child. She walked over to the table, took up the bread knife and the two-tiered round cottage loaf she had made earlier that day. The aroma of fresh-baked bread made her feel hungry. She cut two thick slices, buttered them and spread a thin layer of honey, from their own beehive at the far end of the garden, on them both. Walking over to the dresser, she took down two tea-plates, put one slice on each, then put the bread away in a large white tin and put the lid on it. Turning back, she looked at the end of the table where, almost a year ago, there would have been a third place set.

Shortly after enlisting in the army – one of the Gloucestershire regiments - Terrence, her husband, had been sent to a place called Crimea. Mrs Osmond, the nice lady at the village school, had shown her where it was on a map, but that didn't help. It was too far away to take in.

Sybil hadn't wanted him to go but, he thought it was his duty as an Englishman to fight for his country. But why was it his country when it was all the way out there? It still didn't make sense, no matter who she talked to. She knew, deep down, in her heart of hearts, that he was never coming home. So now there was just her and the girl, her strange little daughter who was more interested in her books than dolls. Selene had very few friends as she spent more time watching the animals and birds in the garden, than wanting to go and play. She recalled the summer's day last year when Mrs Osmond had called to buy some apples, and had seen Selene reading. Sybil smiled remembering the look on Mrs Osmond's face when, in answer to her question about how old Selene was, Sybil told her that she was almost five-years-old and had been reading for a year, and that her father had taught her before he joined the army.

Mrs Osmond then invited Sybil to enrol Selene at her school even though she was still not yet aged five, and had offered to give her private lessons in English, Mathematics and Science for two hours, twice weekly after school. Although it was a wonderful offer, Sybil had declined as she had no money to pay for lessons. To which Mrs Osmond declared that she would be happy to teach Selene for a couple of loaves and some apples or honey in payment, and the deal was struck.

That had been a few months ago and Selene had made wonderful progress. Although she was the same age as the other first year children, in some subjects she was already working to the standard of children two years older than herself, and Mrs Osmond had great hopes for her.

And then there was that nice Mr Elden, the woodcutter from the other side of Godney. Whenever he was this way, he would stop for a cup of tea and spend time pointing out different plants, herbs, and so on, and tell Selene what they could be used for, healing and the like. Selene was learning so much.

Sybil just hoped that neither Mrs Osmond, nor Selene would be disappointed when she reached ten years old, and schooling stopped for girls. As far as Sybil could see, there were very few opportunities for girls, even though there was a woman on the throne for a change.

'Oh well,' Sybil sighed. She turned away from the table to put the kettle on to boil when, through the window she noticed a slight movement in the grass close to the hedge. Whatever it was, was heading quickly towards her daughter. Leaving the kettle on the table Sybil rushed out of the back door to find her daughter running towards it. Sybil screamed, 'No, Selene, don't...!'

But it was too late, the little girl had picked up something grey, cuddling it under her chin and smiling as she walked towards her worried mother.

'Look Mama, it's a kitten.' She held him towards her mother. 'Hasn't he got pretty eyes? They're green.'

The kitten looked directly at Sybil. His eyes reminded her of a Chinese vase she had seen in a museum once, and she remembered it had been made of Jade. She crouched down to stroke his forehead. 'Yes, what a pretty little thing he is.'

'Can we keep him?' Selene looked so hopeful, and she was such a well behaved, kind child, who had always had a way with animals and birds, even the bees would fly around her, settle on her without her being frightened of being stung and, of course, she was missing Samson dreadfully; they both were.

Sybil looked around, wondering whether there was someone in the lane who owned the kitten, but there was no-one in sight. She looked down at Selene. This was the first time she had smiled since Samson had died. How could she say no to her? Her daughter looked at her so pleadingly from deep blue eyes, so dark they were almost black, with puffy red eyelids caused by all her crying.

'If no-one claims him, then yes, you can keep him.'

'Thank you, Mama.' She lifted the purring kitten to face her, and he reached out a little paw to play with a strand of her long blonde hair that had come loose from the red ribbon holding it back. She laughed and cuddled him closer. 'You see, you can stay. Mama said you can stay. Isn't that wonderful? I *know* no-one is going to claim you. You came here just for me, didn't you?' The kitten purred loudly in her arms. 'You see, Mama, he knows he's come home.'

Her mother frowned, wondering what her daughter could be talking about. 'What are you going to call him?'

'Bandit. His name is Bandit.'

'Why Bandit? Where did you get that name from?'

'It just came to me. I don't know why. I'm going to show him to Mr Elden when he next visits. I'm sure he'll be surprised.'

Part Six

1992

The Knave
To Buy a Manor

Chapter Fifty Two

Harriet lowered her sunglasses, pulled down the sun visor above the windscreen, and checked her appearance in the mirror. Done, she delved into her cream leather handbag, retrieved her peachy-coloured lip gloss, pulled off the top and applied a little of the gel across her lips. Satisfied, she slid the top back on, put the tube back in the bag and snapped the catch closed, slipped her sunglasses back into place and smiled at the man beside her.

'I don't know what you're worried about,' he said. 'You know you look beautiful and it's for them to impress us, not the other way around.' He patted her knee and smiled at her tenderly. 'We're the ones with the money, remember.'

With scarlet long-nailed fingers she tidied a stray lock of red-gold hair that had blown across her face and tucked it behind her ear. 'Just tidying up and making sure I don't look a mess with this breeze blowing my hair about. And be kind, Jerry, they may be in a difficult position...eager to sell, but we need to create the correct impression, that we're in a position to buy.'

'I think he'll already be well aware of who we are. You can bet your bottom dollar he'll have done his homework and looked us up. They'll already know plenty about us and, my dearest, the roof may be down, but we're sheltered by the windscreen, so your hair has hardly been touched and anyway, windswept is a look many of the top models are trying to achieve.'

She laughed. 'And how does a fabulously wealthy property-owning businessman know anything about trendy models, may I ask?'

'Ahh...but did you know Lady Winterne was a well-known model in her younger days. You see, I did my research on them.'

'Yes. She was well known but that was years ago. Isn't it sad how fortunes can change? The manor's been in the Maitland family for centuries and I'm sure they must love it. When you see those photographs, how could they not love it, especially with all that heritage.'

'Perhaps they do, but they're not the first members of the aristocracy who have had to sell ancestral homes due to Death Duties and so on, and he said the financial crash a few years ago hit them hard.'

His wife nodded slowly. 'I know. I just think it's terribly sad.' She thought for a moment. 'Jerry, I suppose *our* money *is* safe?'

He smiled and put his hand on her knee. 'Yes, Harriet, my love. It's totally safe. My investments have not been in stocks and shares. I've been considerably more careful. I only go for *safe* commodities.'

She lowered her sunglasses and turned her emerald-green eyes to gaze at him adoringly. She leaned closer, wrapped both her arms around his left arm and nestled her head on his shoulder. 'Is anything really safe though?' she whispered. If he heard her, he gave no sign of it.

'I'd put my arm around you but driving with one hand could be a bit risky if we meet something coming the other way. I don't think I've ever driven on roads this narrow before and the Roller is just too wide. I should have checked before we left Bristol and, if I'd realised they were B roads, we could have taken one of the smaller cars. If we do buy this 'pile', remind me to get us *both* smaller run-arounds.'

'Maybe so, but it'll impress the Maitlands...sorry, the Earl of Winterne and his wife.'

Flashes of blazing sun bounced off the burgundy-coloured Rolls Royce Corniche convertible as it purred along the narrow winding lanes. High hedges, half-concealing fields of ripening cereal crops, bordered the left side of the road. At intervals, the hedgerows were replaced by towering sturdy trees whose branches reached across the road forming a canopy with those on the other side.

As they drove into one of the tree-lined tunnels where only dappled sunlight broke through the shadow, Jerry frowned. 'Although it's nice to get out of the glare, I wonder if these trees are on Manor land?'

'Why, what's wrong with them?'

'Well, look up. Firstly, when you drive into these shaded areas where the branches over-reach the road, your eyes are used to the glare and, if you're wearing sunglasses you suddenly drive into the gloom, and your eyes have very little time to react. Plus with all these bends and the lanes being so tight, it could be dangerous, especially at night. It's like driving into an unlit tunnel. There's so many of them spreading across the road they're like a roof above us.'

'But surely the headlights of oncoming traffic would let you know there's something around the corners...'

'Yes, that's true, but eyes still take a second or two to react to changes in light...and...then you'll turn another corner and find the tunnel stops suddenly and, in daylight, you're back in the glare again. At night, there are too many people who don't bother, or don't remember to dip their headlights and that's dangerous too. Some of them are blinding when they're coming toward you, or even in the rear view mirror.'

Harriet looked up. 'Yes, I see what you mean about the lights and some of those branches look pretty heavy. I was just enjoying the moments of shade...but, if one of these came down...'

'That's the other point I was coming to. If a damaged or dead one fell onto a car during a storm or in a bad winter when it's snow-laden, someone could get killed.'

'Jerry, be careful, I think I saw a flash of silver up ahead through the hedge. I think there's something coming the other way. Look there's a farm gate up ahead.'

Jerry sped up and made it to the gate in time to pull off the road and onto the rutted farm vehicle access to the field. The driver of the silver Honda Civic waved his thanks as he passed by. Jerry waved back and they drove on.

'Gosh, Jerry. These roads are much tighter than I thought they would be. I'm glad I'm not driving. They seem to have got a lot more narrow since we left the A361. I hope there are more places for vehicles to pull in if we need them again. At least being Sunday, the traffic has been fairly light and we haven't been stuck behind a tractor, thank goodness.'

'I don't think we have that much further to go now and don't forget, you wanted to use the Corniche, my darling. Mind you, it's my first one of these beauties so I *am* being careful. She has a special place in my heart already. What time is it?'

She looked at her gold Rolex watch. 'One-forty-five. Is it much further?'

'Ah, then we're almost there. Another five minutes or so. They're expecting us at two o'clock and I always like to arrive for an appointment a little early. Ten minutes is fine.'

Shortly after, they turned a corner to find the wooden gates of Winterne Manor on their left, weather-beaten and peeling square wooden panels displayed the once-blue family crest on both gates.

'If we do buy the place, they'll have to go,' he said as he reached in the glove compartment for his mobile phone. 'I'll install motorised wrought iron gates...and,' giving her a huge grin he said, 'Perhaps we could look for our own family crest. What d'you think about that?'

She laughed and reached up to pull the sun visor down again. Sitting back she ran her fingers through her hair to tidy it again, she gave him a sideways look. 'A family crest...the *Atkins* family crest? Do you know anything about genealogy?'

'No. Do you?'

She laughed. 'No. Nothing at all. You'd need to get someone to do the research for you to see what they can find about both our family trees.'

He turned towards her with an affectionate smile. 'Well, why not? Ours might be new money instead of inherited wealth, but I'm pretty sure we have an awful lot more of it than the Earl does right now.'

A few seconds later the right gate was opened by a middle-aged stocky man who chomped on what was left of a cheese and pickle roll as he walked towards them. He indicated they should stop while wiping a splodge of pickle on his baggy overalls. Jerry stopped the car.

'Mr an' Mrs Atkins, is it?' he said, stroking the grey stubble on his chin with one hand while wiping the last crumbs away from his heavy purple lips with the other. He did not look at Jerry or his wife, but stared enviously at the high-status vehicle.

'That's right. The Earl is expecting us.' Jerry's eyes narrowed. Courtesy cost little and clearly this man had none.

'Yeh. 'E said ter expect yer both. If yer just drive up ter the top o' the driveway an' pull up by the founten, the Earl and Lady Winterne'll meet yer there.'

'Thank you, Mr...?'

'Bragg.'

'Well, *Mister* Bragg, do you live in the gatehouse here?'

Bragg raised an eyebrow, seemingly surprised at the question. 'No. Oi got a farm just outside the village, but Oi 'elp out aroun' the manor when needed. Iss a bit of a part-toime job, loike, so Oi'm sure we'll meet agen.'

Don't be too sure of that, thought Jerry, but he nodded. 'I'm sure we will.'

Without looking back at the surly Bragg as he walked back to the gatehouse, Jerry drove slowly along the tarmacked avenue towards the manor. Neither of them spoke as they surveyed the lead-up to the manor which, as yet was still hidden by trees. This gave them time to take in the tall border of summer-flowering rhododendrons with their abundant pink, yellow and white blooms, on their left, and a promenade of equally spaced red maple trees standing tall on a verge of long grass on the other. Behind the trees, a metal railing bordered a large field, at the top of which the roofs and stone chimneys of two cottages peeked over the top of a hedge at the far end of the field.

'This is lovely,' said Harriet. 'The rhododendrons are a delightful way to greet any visitors we may have and this driveway must be half a mile long.'

'So far, the only thing I've seen that I didn't like was...'

'Bragg,' interrupted Harriet.

Jerry smiled. 'I'm glad we agree on that because, if we do take this place over, he goes. Right?'

She nodded. 'I hate to see anyone put out of work but, he's not exactly an asset is he? Do you think if we offered to train him he...'

Jerry laughed. 'Train him? You must be joking! Does he look to you like the type who would let himself undergo a training course?'

Harriet gave a sad smile. 'Well...I just thought...'

'My darling, you're one in a million. You always want to help people, but Mr Bragg strikes me as the type who will always go his own way. To be honest, I'm surprised the Earl keeps him on.'

A little further along the road widened at a slow bend where another narrow road turned off to the right.

'I'm guessing that leads down to those two cottages we saw,' said Jerry.

But Harriet wasn't listening. She was staring straight ahead. 'Jerry. Stop the car!'

Following his wife's gaze, Jerry understood what had overwhelmed her and saw why she wanted a few moments just to stare. Ahead of them the road encircled a round grass lawn with an idle stone fountain. Beyond stood the manor. Harriet stood up, rapt by the sight ahead. Jerry smiled. He thought she would like the manor but had not realised just how much seeing 'in the flesh' would affect her. They had both seen the photographs, so she knew what to expect, but her reaction was more than he had hoped for.

On the circular green where the fountain stood, a number of large rocks, some of a size that could be called small boulders were piled up close to the fountain, and another stack lay in front of the right corner of the manor. A further heap of these large stones, Jerry noticed were almost hidden under the drooping branches of a weeping willow a little way off towards the other side of the house. He added that to the ever growing list of questions he was mentally storing up to ask the Earl.

It was quite clear the building needed a considerable amount of work, but Harriet saw beyond that. The honey-colour Cotswold stone manor with its black and white Elizabethan style extension took her breath away.

'Oh, Jerry. It is beautiful. The children will love it.' She turned to look at him, tears of joy glistened in her eyes but she blinked them away. 'Oh, Lord. Now I need to do my make-up again!' She laughed as she sat back down and Jerry started the Corniche up again just as the wide front door opened and two people, they took to be the Earl and Lady Winterne, appeared on the broad front steps to meet them.

'Oh dear,' said Harriet, whispering.

'What's wrong?' Jerry smiled and waved at the couple waiting for them.

'The Countess Winterne is just like I imagined she would be. Shoulder length blonde bob hairstyle, linen shirt, jodhpurs and riding boots!' Then she too smiled as they approached the front door of Winterne Manor.

'Oh, and look, the Earl is leaning on a walking stick. I would have though he was too young for one of those yet.'

Jerry eased the car to a halt a little way from the steps and, just as they were about to open the doors, Harriet leaned slightly towards Jerry. 'Do you know, on closer look, she seems familiar. I have a funny feeling we've met somewhere before.'

'Probably seen her in magazines.'

'No. No, I'm sure it's somewhere we've both been at the same time.' As they stepped out of the car. Harriet said: 'It'll come to me. I never forget a face.'

Chapter Fifty Three

Over the next few hours, the Earl Maitland, the red-haired Earl and his wife, Lady Winterne, gave Jerry and Harriet an extensive tour of the grounds and the house. They began by leading them through the perfectly tended lawn that sloped gently down the trout-filled lake which was concealed from view from the house by the trees. Lady Winterne walked down to the lake with them while the Earl, leaning on his walking stick preferred to wait where the ground was level. Harriet removed her cream leather sling-back to walk barefoot on the lawn. The springy grass tickled her feet. Lady Winterne, who was wearing flat shoes, kept her's on.

Along its banks, long fringes of weeping willows trailed down to the edge of the water dangling into reed beds where nesting moorhens paddled in and out of the spear-shaped leaves of the marginal bank-side reeds. In areas where the movement of water was slow and gentle, brightly coloured damsel flies and dragonflies hovered above broad waxy lily pads surrounding pink and cream blooms.

A pair of swans, closely followed by their brood of grey-feathered cygnets glided along leaving a V-shaped wake in the water behind them. On such a glorious day, Harriet thought the scene was idyllic, and she knew Jerry must have been impressed as, taking a quick glance in his direction, she saw he stood transfixed, taking in the scene but he made no comment, seemingly silenced by its tranquillity. Harriet was convinced the lake, and certainly this part of the garden, would look just as beautiful at any time of the year, no matter what the weather. Harriet imagined the view in frost and snow; it would look magical.

Jerry walked over to join her on the bank. 'Have you noticed something missing?' he said, watching a black water bird with a red and yellow beak and forehead, guiding its brood from the bank into the water, alarmed at the humans who had obviously gone a little too close to the nest for comfort.

'No. What do you mean? I can't see anything missing. It's beautiful.'

Jerry smiled. 'I didn't say see something missing, did I?' he teased.

For a moment, she looked puzzled. Then looked at him. 'Noise.'

'Exactly. There's no sound of traffic at all.'

'Heavenly,' sighed Harriet.

The only sounds were the birdsong above them, the buzzing of insects, the gentle lapping of the water against the bank, and an occasional 'plop' as a fish jumped from the water trying to catch a fly, and slipped back under the surface.

Tightly-packed flowering rhododendron bushes, deep-red leaved beech trees and silver birches mingled with mature oak and ash trees, and this area of the property surprised the couple, not only with its tranquil splendour but, knowing how the Earl was struggling for money, Jerry wondered how he could afford to maintain the garden to such a perfect standard. Jerry added that to his list of questions for the Maitlands after the tour.

On hearing of Harriet's keen interest in horses and riding, Lady Winterne suggested they visit the stables next. Harriet eagerly accepted the suggestion even though she knew Jerry was keen to get a look inside the manor itself. Understanding her enthusiasm, with a slight frown he indulged her; it wasn't as if he wasn't going to get inside the manor, and they had plenty of time.

Lady Winterne gave them the choice of walking through the back garden and field, or driving to the stables. Harriet said she was happy to walk. Jerry raised an eyebrow but, again, accepted his wife's decision.

At first sight, Jerry and Harriet were impressed by the size of the two stables blocks and the yard itself, but were surprised to find only two horses in the first stable block stalls next to each other, peering inquisitively at them, over the lower half of the wooden doors.

'Come and meet my girls, Mrs Atkins,' said Lady Winterne. It was the first time Harriet had seen her smile. She thought about inviting Lady Winterne to call her by her first name but, bearing in mind that this was not a social visit, decided against it.

'The bay, here, was a race horse and she was very fast, but an injury stopped her racing and she was going to be put down, poor thing.' Lady Winterne gently stroked the horse's neck and in return the mare nuzzled into her neck. 'Her racing name was *Rose of the West,* but we just call her Rosie, don't we girl?'

'So what happened?' asked Harriet. 'How did she come to be with you?'

'A friend of ours is a local racecourse vet and was called out to do – you know, the deed - as it were but, when he got there, although he agreed she should no longer be used for racing, he knew the injury to her leg would heal in time and would not prevent her from being ridden. As she was still quite young and healthy, he refused to put her down and bought her on the spot, took her home to his small stable yard and with time, care and exercise, her injury healed completely. We went over to visit one day and he said he was looking for a home for her...the rest is history, as they say.'

While they were talking, the grey mare in the next stall kept extending her neck over the half-door, nudging Lady Winterne with her nose and making a funny little nickering noise, clearly attention seeking. It was very evident to Harriet that both horses were much loved and they both knew it.

'And who is this demanding lady?' she asked, stroking the muscular neck of the grey mare.

'Ah, now this is Argent.' Lady Winterne reached into her trouser pocket and pulled out a packet of polo mints. Both horses reached forward eagerly and were rewarded when she popped a mint into their mouths. 'She's ten years old and nothing but trouble, aren't you, my girl?' The horse nodded her head making both women laugh, so the horse did it again. 'I'll be back in a little while girls.' Lady Winterne patted them both and the women turned away to join their husbands, aware of both horses watching them go.

It was then that Harriet noticed how much taller the Earl was than Jerry, he had a more athletic build and a healthy look about him. She had never really noticed before, but Jerry had definitely put on a little weight around the middle over the last year or so, and his face had lost that firmness it once had; too many business lunches, and too little time for exercise was beginning to show. It occurred to her that buying the manor just might be the answer. Maybe they should get a couple of dogs for Jerry to walk. That would give him exercise, fresh air and a break from all those hours in the office or travelling. Having these beautiful surroundings to walk in would be relaxing for him and mean he had no excuse for not having gentle exercise, and after all, she was only thinking about his future health.

She even wondered if she could get him riding, that was something he had little interest in...but with their own string of horses...well, who knew what might happen. She gave a little smile: now that would be a marvel.

In her eagerness to meet the horses, Harriet had only given a cursory look around the stable yard, and had not spotted just how much had to be done to bring the stable blocks and yard into good repair. On leaving the horses, she looked around and began to see signs of neglect and dilapidation. Flecks of green paint littered the ground, small chunks of wood had splintered away from the door and from the beam above it. Some of the brickwork was chipped away, and the blackened timbers under the eaves were evidence of rain damage.

Jerry, however, not having had the horses as a distraction, had plenty of time to inspect the premises carefully. He had been making a mental note of the repairs needed at the stable-yard if they did buy the manor, and was totting up an approximate cost as they went along. Harriet may not have had time to appreciate the full situation, but he had and the estimated repair bill was growing higher all the time.

The two blocks clearly needed considerable repair work. The first block, although still in use and inhabited by the two mares, had four empty stalls. Two seemed in fairly good condition, but the two at the far end were unusable due to collapsed ceiling beams, and another with broken flagstones and extensive damage to the door. Scattered around outside were pieces of grey slate that had obviously fallen from the roof and, in one corner close to the apex, Jerry looked up and spotted a hole about fifteen centimetres wide that would very likely be the cause of some of the signs of damp. Patches of dark mildew and a raised green-black mould spread along the white-washed walls from the ceiling to the floor.

The other block was completely derelict and required total renovation. Jerry thought it might be better to tear it down and re-build. However, he was pleasantly surprised on finding that the building housing the tack-room and office were in fairly good shape. Another bonus was that the yard was a generous size, although it did need a good clean, weeding and in places, the ground resurfaced.

The Earl took in Jerry's dissatisfied frown and decided it was time to steer him away from the off-putting issues, and led him towards the two barns, pointing out as they walked, another small, white-washed cottage behind the second block. It was pretty, had a white picket fence and a thatched roof, which Jerry guessed had been re-thatched within the last couple of years.

Jerry stopped to look at the cottage. 'Who lives there?' he asked.

'No-one now, but previously it was our stable manager who gave riding lessons. We're keeping it aired and we inspect it every month. There don't appear to be any problems with it being empty for now.'

'Hmm. Nice little place. How long since anyone lived there?'

'A little over a year. We had to let Stephanie go when we couldn't afford the repairs as we were running at a loss, and the yard became unsafe.'

'Is it rented, when its occupied?'

The Earl thought Jerry seemed hopeful about getting an income from the property. He was quite clearly a business man. 'No, but the salary has been reduced to reflect the free accommodation.'

Jerry hid his smile. No wonder the Maitlands had gone broke. Definitely not business-minded.

They moved on across the yard to the linked barns. Inside the first one, to Jerry's great surprise he discovered it was in a far better condition than the stable blocks. The concrete floor was strewn with old straw with a several large, square bales of hay in one corner. In the opposite corner an old green tractor stood beside three paint-peeled and rusting wheelbarrows, and various gardening implements, a scythe, hoe, rake, watering cans and a green plastic coiled hose. Jerry looked up at the wooden ceiling where wisps of straw poked out from the edges of a wide, and open, trapdoor which was accessed by a sturdy built-in wooden ladder. Jerry held both sides of the ladder and tried to shake it. It did not budge. He turned to the Earl. 'That looks safe enough.'

'Both barns are the same size and style,' the Earl said, 'so there's probably no need to go into the second one.'

Jerry wondered if there was something to hide. 'Is it alright with you if I take a look above?'

The Earl nodded. 'Yes, absolutely. Go ahead. The steps are secure.'

Jerry was halfway up the ladder when several pigeons, disturbed by his presence, slapped their wings together in warning, then flew down and out through the door, just as Lady Winterne and Harriet entered, forcing them to duck to avoid being hit by the panicky birds. Harriet watched Jerry reach the top of the ladder and pull himself up on to the upper level where he had a good look around before. He looked down at her.

'Managed to drag yourself away from the horses then,' he grinned.

Harriet looked up. 'You be careful up there.'

'It's alright. I'm coming down.' Gripping the sides of the ladder tightly, Jerry, climbed back down and put his arm around Harriet's shoulder. He looked at the Earl. 'The roof looks watertight, the floorboards are sound and there's nothing wrong with the ladders. Does the equipment come with the sale?' He nodded towards the tractor and the other gardening and farm equipment.

'Yes, of course. Do you want to take a look in the other barn?'

As the Earl had said, the second barn was styled in exactly the same way and, on a brief inspection, Jerry was happy it was in the same condition as the first.

If the Earl was aware of Jerry looking around with a more critical eye than he would have wished, he gave no sign of it. Jerry wondered if he was banking on the more optimistic attitude that Harriet was displaying.

As they continued their walkabout, Jerry matched his walking pace to that of the Earl's slower, limping gait. Jerry pointed to the entrance.

'I see you have access to the road and there's plenty of room for parking in the yard, but knowing how narrow some of the roads are here, which road is it? I want to know if its wide enough for horse trucks and delivery vehicles.'

'Yes, we have all sorts of vehicles in and out of here. The road is wide enough for some of the larger horse trailers and when you turn right out of here, about half a mile down the road there's a turn off that takes you back onto manor land, past two cottages on the right, and then just after a left bend there are two more cottages on the left. You'll probably have noticed them on the way up our driveway. Three of the cottages are occupied by employees.'

'Do they pay rent?'

'Two of them do, but its' what we call a 'peppercorn' rent as they work for us.'

'OK, I can continue that...if we buy. What about the other one?'

'Ahh. Now that's a different story. Arthur and Gwen Sykes.' The Earl smiled broadly. 'They have lived here for years. Arthur's been the gardener here for more years than I can remember. They don't pay rent,'...Jerry frowned... 'and he's our resident gardener who works for free, so the cottage is free. That was an arrangement made with my father, it's in writing and is to continue in perpetuity.' Jerry's turned down mouth turned back up again.

'For free...with all this to take care of?'

'Yes, he does have help sometimes with the heavier work. He and my father came to the agreement when Arthur was made redundant from British Factoring. The couple live on their pensions, grow their own fruit and vegetables, and sell any excess. Gwen still works as a cleaner at the pub part-time, and that supplements their income.'

The Earl turned away from the yard entrance and they started walking back to where their wives were still talking while making a fuss of the horses. 'Arthur and Gwen have been here all their married life,' the Earl continued. 'They've known each other since schooldays and they have family in the village. Everyone knows them here, and in the nearby villages. Wonderful characters. Arthur works every day...in all weathers, even though Gwen tells him he shouldn't at times.'

'Even in winter?'

The Earl chuckled. 'You just wait till you meet him!'

It was becoming clear the Earl had taken it for granted they would be buying the manor, but Jerry was still undecided. There was still a lot to see and, depending on the amount of work needed, he and Harriet might decide to haggle over the price or not to buy at all.

Seemingly oblivious to what was going through Jerry's money-oriented mind, the Earl continued to talk about their gardener. 'A little thing like bad weather wouldn't stop him. If he can't get out on the lawns, he's in the greenhouse.'

'How old is he?'

'To be honest, I don't actually know...hmm....well...he must be in his late sixties, perhaps early seventies. I'm not sure. My wife would know. She spends more time with him and Gwen than I do, even though I like the old boy, he's an...unusual,' the Earl turned to Jerry and smiled...'shall we say...quaint character.' He looked back to where their wives were standing in the doorway of the tack room. 'If you've seen enough here, why don't we join the ladies and tour the house next.'

Jerry turned to look at Harriet and, from the expression on her face, she was thoroughly enjoying herself. He could see her mentally ticking boxes and nodding her head enthusiastically about something Lady Winterne was saying. She had mentioned to him on several occasions that she had a long held dream of running a riding stables where she could give lessons. Even their daughter, Meredith, lived and breathed horses, and at just five-years-old she was far more confident around them than he was.

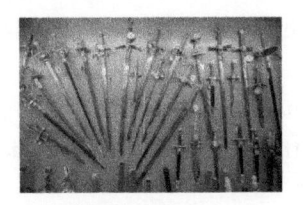

Chapter Fifty Four

On the return walk through the field to the manor house, Jerry shuddered as they passed an area of long grass between them and the trees. He felt as though someone had, "walked over his grave", but not being susceptible to spooky misgivings, he kept it to himself and walked on.

The Earl held the black wrought iron gate open, and Lady Winterne led the way into the tall hedge-bordered secluded garden. Harriet followed Lady Winterne down the path while Jerry waited for the Earl to close and lock the gate behind them.

'If everything we've just walked through is your own land, why do you lock the garden gate?' Jerry asked.

The Earl hesitated for a moment and looked away giving, what Jerry thought, was a swift, edgy glance back towards the field, then extended his right arm inviting Jerry to walk with him. 'Let's join the ladies, shall we? As for locking the gate,' he looked Jerry directly in the eye as if trying to underline his honesty, before looking away again, 'It's just something we've always done. I suppose it's a habit.' Jerry was convinced the Earl was holding something back. He decided to leave it for now but would try to find out more before they left.

'So just how large is this property?' Jerry asked, changing the subject. 'We took a look at the property details and saw the acreage, of course, but it's different when you can see the real thing.'

'It's a little over a thousand acres of woodland, lake, farmland and, you see those hills over there...'

Jerry shaded his eyes from the glare of the sun with his hand as he looked towards the range of wooded Mendip Hills that formed the background of the landscape, way beyond the stables.

'Well, some of our woodland extends onto the hillside in the distance, so that gives you an idea of the extent of land we own...and manage.'

Jerry lowered his hand. His mouth dropped open. 'All of...it?'

The Earl's brows knitted and he nodded vigorously. 'Yes, all of it. I thought you realised.'

Jerry looked a little shaken, and he turned away clearly deep in thought as he walked alongside the Earl towards the back door.

'I say, are you alright, Jerry?'

Jerry's frown turned into a little chuckle. 'Yes, oh yes. I am absolutely fine, thank you.' His chuckle turned into a full laugh while the Earl stood with a bemused look on his face, waiting for Jerry to move on again. Harriet and Lady Winterne turned wondering what all the laughter was about and hurried back to join their menfolk.

'Jerry? Are you alright?' asked Harriet, a puzzled frown on her face as she looked from the Earl to Lady Winterne and back to Jerry.

'Oh yes,' I'm fine,' said Jerry, when he finally regained control. 'Did you know how extensive this property was?' he asked her.

Harriet smiled. 'Well, yes. I had a pretty good idea. I thought you knew.'

'On paper I did, but seeing in it the flesh, so to speak, well that's another matter.' To the Earl he said, 'However do you manage all your woodland?'

The Earl led the group towards the house as he spoke. 'We have a woodsman by the name of Charlie Nowell, nice chap, big man, bushy beard...'

'...He looks a little like Santa Claus,' Lady Winterne cut in.

'Yes, he does.' The Earl gave a soft smile. 'In fact he sometimes plays Santa at the primary school Christmas party and at the department store in Wells. Our children used to think he really was Father Christmas, didn't he, Annabel? But what he doesn't know about forestry isn't worth knowing. If you do decide to buy I would seriously advise you keep him on. You won't be sorry.'

'And he's such a lovely man,' said Lady Winterne to Harriet. 'Everyone likes him and,' she smiled and lowered her voice, 'just between us, I don't know what will come of it, but he seems quite sweet on our local artist, Kathy.' Harriet wondered why Lady Winterne had whispered when there was just the four of them there, but then Lady Winterne leaned in a little closer, 'Bart doesn't like me gossiping,' she said. 'Then raised her voice to normal level. 'He's *friendly* with our local artist, Kathy Harrison. She makes pottery, has her own kiln etc., gives lessons and sells some of her produce locally, that sort of thing. She's very good. You'll see some of her work inside.'

As they walked down the path towards the back door, Lady Winterne pointed out the various plants and trees in the ornamental garden, detailed all the blossoming fruit trees in the orchard, and the herbs and vegetables being grown in the allotment and green houses.

Through the back door they entered a long magnolia-coloured painted room with wooden benches along both sides. Under the benches several pairs of wellington boots in various colours and sizes were set out neatly and above the benches, coat pegs with a number of green waxed jackets and two yellow shiny sou'wester rain coats hung, unwanted during the current warm and dry weather.

Through the next door they entered the long wide kitchen with its vaulted ceiling and magnificent fireplace. The white walls and green painted woodwork needed a little retouching here and there, but generally was not in too bad a condition, but Jerry decided that the old sink unit under the large three-pannelled window that overlooked the garden, would need to go, as would the ancient and coal-guzzling range. He added a refurbishment of the kitchen to his list of things that would need to change; the cost of renovations was growing higher all the time.

With a knowing smile passing between the Earl and his wife, Jerry and Harriet were guided through another door and up three steps into the hall.

Once into the hallway, they both gasped at the grandeur of the carved wood pannelled walls displaying an impressive collection of swords, axes and pikes and the two suits of armour standing guard at the bottom of the stairs.

'I know the agent's details included this...this...'

Jerry seemed to be lost for words for a change, thought Harriet.

'...superb display,' Jerry continued, '...but I hadn't realised just how magnificent a collection you had here, Earl Winterne,' said Jerry.

The Earl smiled broadly, lighting up his face. 'I'm sorry to say that most of this won't be included in the purchase.'

Jerry's face dropped. 'No? I thought it was.'

'No I'm afraid the agent made a mistake there.' He moved closer to the sword exhibit. 'You see much of this has been in the family for centuries. I could tell you in which battles a number of individual items were used, and by which of my ancestors. We did explain to the agent that there would be some items we just cannot leave behind.' It was clear Jerry was disappointed.

'Not even for a price?'

'No. I'm sorry. We are leaving my family's home, but those items that have personal relevance to me will be taken with us. I cannot leave all my heritage behind.' As he gazed fondly at the memorabilia gathered over the centuries, items that had been there throughout his childhood, his wife and Harriet exchanged glances. Harriet could see the pain in the Countess's eyes as she felt her husband's desolation at leaving the home he loved. For a few moments it seemed he was so absorbed in reflection, he had forgotten they had company.

'This is a beautiful piece,' the Countess pointed out a black leather scabbard taking pride of place in the centre of a circle of knives and their sheaths of various types and sizes. The case was embroidered with gold thread and decorated with sapphires and emeralds. It was certainly a spectacular item and, by speaking, the Countess had brought the Earl back to the moment.

The Earl turned back to his visitors. 'Sorry about that. I sometimes get a little pensive when I look at these beautifully preserved pieces. I have seen them every day of my life and heard all the stories that go with them. They are almost old friends...but, of course, we won't be taking all of them. Some, those that have no sentimental value for me, will be included in the sale.'

'As a matter of interest, where are you and Lady Winterne moving to?'

The Earl walked over to his stand by his wife. 'Annabel's parents live in France. They have a small chateau which is becoming too much for them to manage as they grow older...'

'...So we're going to live there, look after them and the chateau. It also gives us somewhere large with enough space to take some of the items precious to my husband...family keepsakes, so to speak.'

'Do you have children?' asked Harriet.

'Yes. We have to two boys and a girl,' said Lady Winterne. 'Our eldest, Richard, he's Viscount Winterne, but he rarely uses the title, is in the army...he's one month into a six month tour in Kenya. After that he has some leave owing. I think he's hoping we'll be at the chateau by then.

'Our daughter, Elvie, is at Sheffield University studying medicine – she wants to research tropical diseases and, James, our youngest, is at St Andrews University reading international politics, or something like that. He wants to go into the Diplomatic Corps.'

'He just wanted to be a spy,' laughed the Earl. 'Read all the James Bond books and couldn't get enough of 'Spooks' when it was on the television. So you see,' he continued, 'it doesn't really matter where we are. They aren't living at home anyway, and usually only come home during the holidays, which they can do in France. Plus they'll have the benefit of seeing their grandparents too.'

'And with their chosen career training, before long, they'll be off on travelling around the world and we won't see as much of them as we do now,' said Lady Winterne.

'How do they feel about your plans? Aren't they upset at all about their home being sold?' Harriet asked.

'Bless you, no,' the Earl smiled. 'They have agreed that selling and moving to France is the best course of action for us. We did think they might be worried about their inheritance, but they're clever enough to know that, with the cost of running this place and all our debts, there probably wouldn't be much left for them anyway. At least now, they'll know they'll have a chateau in France to fight over when we're gone, or to enjoy if they're wise.'

'Oh, Bart, let's not get too maudlin,' said Lady Winterne. 'I'm sure before we look around the house, you'd both like a cup of tea and a slice of Marjorie's cake. Marjorie Seymour, she's our cook, and a darned good one…but, before that, Mrs Atkins, how would you like to take a look at the ballroom?'

'Oh, I'd love to. Jerry, are you coming?'

Jerry shook his head. 'No, I'd rather stay here and look at this collection. A ballroom is a ballroom is a ballroom…if you know what I mean, but I have lots of questions about this magnificent armoury, if you'll humour me, Earl Winterne.'

'With pleasure,' said the Earl, and they watched their wives as they chatted away along the passageway and turned the corner, out of sight although they could hear their heels clacking on the wooden parquet floor tiles.

Chapter Fifty Five

Following Lady Winterne along a dark and dingy, dark wood panelled corridor, lined with countless pieces of art, many of them portraits of what Harriet assumed were ancestors, her first thought was that this passageway would need some decent lighting. Not being against an outside wall, the passage had no windows and the only illumination was from two small lights suspended at either end. It was clear this was a very unused part of the building that would need a complete overhaul if they did decide to buy the manor.

This depressing atmosphere was continued when they reached the very tall, heavy wooden double doors. While Lady Winterne stopped to take a large, and what appeared to be a very old-fashioned brass key from her jodhpurs pocket, Harriet gave a cursory glance around the wood-panelled walls and ceiling and noted the cobwebs and fine layer of dust that had gathered on the frames of the paintings.

After a brief struggle with the lock, and several increasingly exasperated sighs from Lady Winterne, they eventually heard a heavy clunk. 'At last!' she said, pushing open the right-hand door that groaned with the movement. 'These hinges haven't had to work for some time and they need oiling. Of course, as you can see it's been a very long time since we were last in here,' Lady Winterne said, apologetically.

Harriet's first impression on entering the ballroom was of claustrophobic Gothic gloom. There was musty, almost sour smell and she wrinkled her nose wondering whether she should breathe or not, a little unsure as to whether she was risking her health just being in there.

The room clearly needed sunlight and fresh air. From the clean, bright and tidy other areas of the house, to come into this fusty room that reminded her of something out of Charles Dickens' *'Great Expectations'*, was something of a shock. Harriet was relieved Jerry had not wanted to view it. She suspected that he would probably have wanted to walk away, no matter how much he had liked everything else he had seen. Not being the most imaginative of people, she thought Jerry would be totally put off any idea of purchasing if he saw it. They could easily have been in one of those old castles in a horror film, and it could well have been a step beyond which he would not be prepared to go.

'My apologies for the state of the place,' said Lady Winterne, 'I'm sorry to say this room has not been used in…oh, it must be years. We'd pretty much forgotten all about it…and between you and me,' she rolled her eyes, 'the few prospective buyers we've had have never got this far when they've been looking around. I think when they see how large the estate is…and how much work needs doing, it puts them off, but let me open a few of the curtains and you'll get a better idea of how it used to look in its heyday.' The sound of her boots beat a rhythm on the cold floor, and echoed around the almost empty room as she walked over to where a long pole, with a hook at one end, leant abandoned in a corner by the first window. Using it to reach up to the high curtain rails, Lady Winterne pulled along the heavy curtains at two of the windows, releasing long lying dust into the air as they swung open. She sneezed. 'Oh dear. We really shouldn't have let it get in this state, should we?' she said, sneezing again and, rummaging in her jodhpurs pocket for a handkerchief, she blew her nose and then moved on to the next window.

A few moments later, sunlight streamed in from four of the very tall windows, revealing dust motes swirling in the rays that filtered into the room between the long unopened, and sun-faded rose-coloured velvet drapes. Harriet turned in a full circle, finally able to see the room for what it could be.

The black and white tiled floor had seen better days, it was covered in a film of dust and some of the tiles were stained and chipped, but Harriet could see the potential. With replacement tiles, if they could find a match, or the whole floor replaced if necessary, the walls redecorated and new curtains, the ballroom would come alive again and be perfect for entertaining.

'Oh, you have a glitterball,' Harriet giggled. 'D'you know I've always wanted one of those. I used to watch *Come Dancing* on the television when

I was a little girl and fell in love with them.' She decided then that, if they went ahead and bought the manor, renovating this room would be a gloriously enjoyable project for her.

'I'll open a couple of these windows. It smells pretty awful in here doesn't it. I hope no-one's died and we haven't realised. If they have then they've been there for years.' Seeing Harriet's frozen face, she added: 'Just joking. Seriously, we cleared the last body out a few months ago before we put the manor on the market.'

The smirk on her face told Harriet that this too was in jest, and she smiled warmly. 'I like your sense of humour.'

'Do you have children?' Lady Winterne asked.

'Yes, we do, Lady Winterne.'

'Oh, please call me Annabel. I only use my title on formal occasions. Bart's pretty much the same really. It's just not necessary in normal situations.'

'And you must call me Harriet.' Harriet hesitated. 'May I ask you a question?'

'Yes, of course.'

'It's just me being nosey really, but Bart, is that short for Bartholomew?'

'No. His name's actually Bartley. It's a name that's been handed down here and there through the family. From the records we've seen, it goes right back to the fourteenth century. How old are your children?'

'Our daughter, Meredith's five and Jonah is just a year old.'

'Jonah? That's unusual.'

'Hmm. I can assure you that was not my choice.' Harriet scowled. 'I suppose I'm getting used to it now, but I prefer to call him JJ. While I was resting a few days after his birth, Jerry took it upon himself to drive to the Registrar's Office in Bristol and register his name as Jonah Jeremiah and, would you believe, came home all sweetness and light with a huge bunch of flowers for me, and very proudly announced what he'd done. I was pretty furious, I can tell you.'

'I would be too. It's not that I don't like the name, but you should have been included in the choice. What did you do?'

'What could I do? It was fait accompli. It was legal, and I...and JJ, were stuck with it. It's been the only real bone of contention between us since we got together, that and the fact that Jerry is away on business sometimes for so long the children forget what he looks like. Thankfully it doesn't happen too often, and I believe that with a home like this, he'll spend more time working from home instead of in his Bristol office and travelling.'

'Your husband's in property, isn't he?'

'Yes, that's right.'

'Buying and selling?' enquired Annabel.

'Yes, he buys old property, residential and commercial, has it renovated and sells it on. He also has a number of properties in Bristol that he rents out.'

'Residential?

'Yes, residential...apartments and town houses in the centre of the city, a few larger houses on the outskirts, and offices, bars and restaurants around the port and in the centre of the city.'

'And do you help with his work?'

At first, Harriet wondered why Annabel was asking so many questions but realised that, as they were prospective buyers of the manor, the Maitlands were perfectly entitled to know something about the people they would be dealing with.

'No, I have my own interests, riding, amateur dramatics, voluntary service and so on but, with the children I don't have as much time as I used to and, from time to time, I help my father with his accounts. He's an Orthopaedic surgeon at Bristol Royal Infirmary...'

'Not Mr Jamieson?'

Harriet smiled. 'Yes, that's him...that's my father. Do you know him?'

'Yes, he operated on my mother's back a few years ago and she's so much better. She absolutely idolises your father for giving her back her mobility without pain. And, do you know, I had a funny feeling we'd met before. I've been trying to think where from, but can only think it was at one of the charity events or something like that.'

'Yes, it's a pretty small world in the county society, and it's very likely we might well have bumped into one another before. I actually said to Jerry as we arrived that I thought I'd seen you somewhere before.'

Harriet thought it was a shame they had not met to talk before; there was something about Annabel she liked, something open, calm and amiable and, if they had more time she thought they could have become great friends.

'How does the Earl...I mean, Bart, really feel about leaving the manor?' she asked.

'Come,' said Annabel, 'let's have that tea and cake.' She took Harriet's arm and led her towards the exit. 'We can talk on the way to join the men. *That* has been the only real bone of contention between *us*.' She locked the door behind them. The key turned more easily this time. 'Bart, with this being his ancestral home, felt an obligation to keep the place going. I remember him saying, "We're not going to lose the manor on *my* watch." and resisted all our arguments, mine, the children's, our bank manager… everyone. He worked tirelessly trying to manage the place, carry out the repairs, you name it he worked on it…all hours…seven days a week…and then…'

'And then?'

Annabel stopped walking and turned to face Harriet. Tears welled in her eyes. 'And then he had his accident.'

'Oh dear. What happened?'

'He was driving home late one night after a meeting in Wells and fell asleep while driving on one of the bendy roads we have around here.' Harriet noticed Annabel's hands began shaking. 'The car went out of control, went off the road into a deep ditch and turned over. Of course, he was lucky, his seatbelt saved his life, but there was a nasty injury to his right leg and hip and he broke his right arm. The arm has healed fairly well, but the hip still gives him problems. It's improving but progress is slow and he'll have to use the walking stick for some time yet.

'This was a few months ago, and it was one of your father's registrars who operated on him that night. He's much better than he was but he's needed the walking stick ever since.' She gave a sad little smile and then started walking again, more slowly this time, opened the door and waited for Harriet to go through before continuing. 'I'll speak more quietly now. I don't want Bart to hear us.' She paused, inhaled. 'Anyway, after that shock and realising that he wasn't superhuman after all, the children and I were able to convince him that he couldn't go on the way he was and, for all his efforts, it wasn't making any difference. We were becoming more and more mired in debt, while he was killing himself trying to save the place for our family who don't actually want it. And, then of course, the situation with my parents cropped up and we felt we had no choice but to yield to the inevitable and sell. Then we can pay HMRC, clear ourselves of debt and head to the chateau.' She stopped beside the portrait of a woman in a Tudor-style headdress. 'You won't say anything to Bart about what I've just told you will you, Harriet?'

'No, of course not.' Harriet took Annabel's hand and squeezed it reassuringly. 'It was good of you to confide in me and my lips are sealed.'

'We'll join the men again,' said Annabel, 'and get off our feet for a little while for refreshments. 'It's a pity you won't meet Marjorie. She's one of the staff that has a cottage in the grounds. It's her day off, but she has left us a Victoria sponge and some madeira cake.'

After tea and cake in the large vault-ceilinged kitchen, Bart and Annabel led Jerry and Harriet back to the staircase where the suits of armour waited at the bottom of the stairs and, as they looked up to the landing they became aware, for the first time, of the large arched stained-glass window at the half-landing. The sun beamed down at them through the image of the blonde maiden in her white gown beside a pure white unicorn with a long white mane and tail, that looked at her adoringly.

'Oh, Jerry,' Harriet raised her hand to her open mouth and took an inward breath. 'That is so beautiful.' She looked at Bart. 'Do you know if she is anyone in particular, or just an exquisite work from imagination?'

Bart smiled. 'She tends to affect everyone like that when they first see her. She's actually one of my ancestors from the fourteenth century. According to the few records we still hold after the fire last century, she was the grandmother of the first Maitland children to be born in this house. Her name was Catherine Townsend and she died fairly young. Sir William Hallett, her husband, had this window made to commemorate her.'

'Hallett?' enquired Jerry. 'That's a pretty popular local name, isn't it?'

'Yes, that's right, it is, but our original Hallett was knighted at the Battle of Poitiers. We're not sure what he actually did but, according to the little information we have, he was an archer who must have done something special as he was knighted by the Black Prince personally, then given this manor as a reward by the then Earl of Salisbury, a close friend of the prince. William and Catherine only had one child who grew to adulthood, their daughter Isabelle, and it was she who married a Maitland. When William died all the property went to Isabelle and her husband. I wish we could take her with us...the window...I mean, but I don't think she would survive the journey,' he sighed, 'and she belongs here...in the manor...just where Sir William placed her to be seen by everyone.'

'What an incredible knowledge you have of your heritage. It must break your heart to be leaving all this,' said Harriet, softly.

'Yes and no,' replied Bart. 'Although I have lived here all my life, I am not entrenched in the past. We can take my family records with us and I have resigned myself to the truth, that we cannot afford to run this place, and I would rather someone who cares about it and who can look after it properly, take it over. I would love to take the window with me, but Annabel's parents have already said we can have a copy made at the chateau.' He raised his right hand. 'You see this ring. Well look at Catherine's left hand.'

Harriet and Jerry looked from his hand to the window. On the first finger of Catherine's right hand she wore a ring identical to Bart's. The insignia showed a dove hovering above crossed spears with a wolf underneath and set in a background of blue.

'That's our family crest, devised by William Hallett himself. Each image represents something. The dove is a symbol of the soul, and the Holy Spirit representing peace, gentleness and purity, the crossed spears show military affairs or gallant service in battle and the wolf implies courage and guardianship.

'There were just six of these rings ever made. We have still have four of them in our possession but I have no idea where the other two are, and it's my ambition to find them if I can. But, enough of that, come on, I'm sure you're keen to take a look around upstairs.'

An hour later, they had been given the guided tour of the upper two floors and had seen all they needed to. Very few of the rooms on the first floor were actually in use with just Bart and Annabel in residence and, in all there were seven large bedrooms, all with en-suite bathrooms. Three of them belonged to the absent children and were kept ready for when they returned. The Earl's office, Annabel's music room and the family library were all on the same floor. In addition, there were two more bathrooms and Harriet counted six shelved in-built cupboards. The walls would not have looked out of place in a portrait gallery, some of which Harriet recognised as being larger versions of those she had seen in the ballroom corridor.

At the far end of the corridor was a small staircase of just six steps where another very good sized room, light, airy and overlooking the back garden, seemed to be crying out for occupation. Harriet thought it would make a lovely room for Meredith when she was older and wanted a little retreat of her own.

The third floor rooms were mostly empty, neglected storerooms except for some small bare rooms with peeling paintwork and tiny windows. Annabel explained that these at one time would have been for servants. These were the only bedrooms they had seen that had no fireplaces.

After that there was nothing else to see. Annabel and Bart had given Harriet and Jerry almost four hours of their time, and Jerry was keen to get on their way so he and Harriet could discuss their thoughts, and he was relieved when they began their descent to the ground floor.

'Thank you for showing us around this magnificent home of yours. It's been a wonderful afternoon and we've both enjoyed it very much, haven't we Harriet?'

'Yes, indeed. It's been lovely, and I do hope we haven't taken up too much of your time. But, Jerry's right, it's time we were heading home.'

On the steps, Jerry turned to Bart. 'I meant to ask you, what are all these for?' he pointed to the three piles of cream-coloured stones.

'They are what remains of the wall and gatehouses that surrounded the manor. Over the centuries, the wall crumbled and, not being necessary for defence anymore, none of my ancestors bothered about repairs. Then, during the second World War, when the manor was temporarily used as army headquarters for...I think about six months, a couple of German planes, returning from having bombed Bristol, flew back over here and, seeing the number of military personnel and vehicles, strafed the area with twenty millimetre cannons. Several people were wounded but thankfully no-one was killed, but a lot of damage was done, to the manor and the wall. The house was repaired but whole chunks of the wall just fell apart, so it was left as it was. The cottages were built from those stones and these are all that remain and we're not sure what to do with them.'

'Right. So this place has seen even more action than I realised,' said Jerry, taking another look around the façade of the manor. Harriet thought he was now viewing the property with heightened appreciation and interest.

'It certainly has. During World War Two there was a prison camp not far from here at Penleigh, near Wookey Hole, for Italian prisoners of war. Like most green spaces, a lot of the manor land was turned over to the war effort for growing food. My grandfather spoke of a group of Italian prisoners who were brought in trucks from the camp to work here. Many of them were friendly, liked the area, found themselves girlfriends, and after the war ended and they were released, they married and never returned home.'

'Didn't the Italians become allies later in the war, after they ousted Mussolini?'

'Yes, that's right in nineteen-forty-three. By all accounts most of the prisoners here were very relieved not to be allied to Germany any more.

'But, back to the manor, we'll make sure you, or whoever does buy, will be given copies of all the records we have. There's been plenty of action here over the centuries, including the Monmouth Rebellion. The old place has a lot to tell, it's just that with one thing and another many of the original documents were destroyed.'

'Knowing so much about the manor, it must make it even harder for you to leave,' said Harriet. 'There's so much history, so much of your family here. It will be a wrench to leave it all behind.'

Annabel gave a sad smile and nodded.

Jerry said: 'Having that kind of history makes the place something very special. We'll obviously be giving it a lot of thought and I'm sure you'll hear, one way or the other, from one of us or the agent, in a couple of days.'

The farewells were made. Jerry and Bart shook hands while Annabel and Harriet hugged as though they were old friends, and then it was time to go.

As the Corniche purred away down the drive, Annabel turned to Bart. 'I liked her,' she said. 'Well, what do you think? Will they put in an offer?'

Bart gave a slight nod. 'Yes, I thought you did and she does seem nice, but...I'm not sure about him.'

Annabel gave him aa quizzical look. 'What aren't you sure about? I thought he was alright.'

He tilted his head, pursed his lips and gave a slight shake of the head. 'Oh maybe it's just me...my imagination. Just ignore me.'

Standing on the steps by the open door, they watched the Corniche until it disappeared around the bend and Bart took her hand and kissed it. 'Yes. I believe they will. I think he's more keen than he wanted to let on.'

'Did you tell him about the tunnel?'

Bart's eyes twinkled and he gave a playful smile. 'No. Why tell him everything? That's something he can find out for himself.'

Chapter Fifty Six

As they clicked in their seatbelts and Jerry fired up the Corniche, they took one long last look at the frontage of the manor with a completely different viewpoint than they had on their arrival. Neither of them spoke. With a last wave and a mouthed 'thank you', to Bart and Annabel, Jerry turned the car slowly back along the driveway. As far as he was concerned, the Earl and his wife, as they stood on the wide stone steps, were questioning whether they had made a sale or not.

Jerry had been very non-committal as they said their goodbyes. There were a number of things he and Harriet needed to discuss before he put in an offer for the manor. He had already made up his mind to buy, but wanted to see how much he could reduce the price. Even though he was cheerfully surprised with the extent of the land and buildings, and it was certainly a lovely property, he intended to use its neglected state, and the considerable amount of work to be done, to negotiate a lower price. He was an experienced and astute businessman, and knew the Maitlands were asking over the odds for the purchase, and would not expect anyone to meet their asking price.

'I had a nice chat with the Earl while you two were in the ballroom. What did you think of it by the way?'

'It's unused, old, stuffy and dirty,' she began. 'However, with a bit of TLC, it could be beautiful again...and they have a glitterball, how about that? Jerry thought she seemed more excited about that than at any time of their visit. Women could be very strange! 'What were you two chatting about?'

'I was asking about the cost of overheads in keeping an establishment like that and finding out a bit about the village. There's a post office and small supermarket, the pub...which apparently does good meals, the church - Reverend Driver has only been there a couple of years, does a good job and, according to Bart, has no intention of being moved on again. There's also a dentist, Joe Richards.'

'The village has its own dentist!'

'Uh-huh. Married with a couple of kids and lives next to that potter lady, they were telling us about, and apparently he's very good...private and NHS work done. Can't say I'm particularly interested in that but, there's a woman called Armistice Jenks who sounds like a character. Quite a few people avoid her if they can. Superstitious rubbish if you ask me. They think she's a witch.'

'She's a what?'

'Yes, you heard right, they say she's a witch,' Jerry grinned at the expression on Harriet's amused face. 'From what he was saying, she keeps herself to herself most of the time and she's a healer, so the locals call her a witch. I suppose it doesn't help her cause any that she makes herbal potions for people who want them, reads Tarot cards and so on.

'And..., it seems there was a curse put on the manor back in Victorian times.'

'A curse? How exciting. So, the old place has something sinister as well as all that wonderful history about it.'

'I know but they've heard two differing stories about it. One was about a farmer who had some land stolen by the church minister at the time, and the Earl was supposed to have backed him up. The story goes that the farmer refused to have his aunts...witches by all accounts...buried in the churchyard when they died and cursed the minister, and the manor.'

'But why would witches be buried in consecrated ground? That doesn't really make sense does it?'

'Well that's what I thought, but there's a lot of people around here who still believe that account. The other version, which sounds a little more plausible was that the Viscount, at the time, something of a ne'er-do-well by all reports, caused a grave injury to a young girl and tried to get his friends to lie about it. He had done some pretty awful things before and the locals decided enough was enough and brought in a witch to place the curse.

'Bart said the curse was supposed to have lasted a hundred years, and apparently there's a record of some awful things – the Viscount and his father died, there were plagues of rats, unexplained fires, floods, disease, and so on, but from what they've seen from the notes left in the family bible, it didn't last anything like that long. Gossip exaggerated it and extended it, and the slightest...accident, or whatever...the local villagers automatically blamed on the curse.

'He said he thought some people locally think it's still active but it's all nonsense. They never had any such problems...just the death duties and lack of income.

'Anyway, it seems the Earl's family eventually abandoned the manor and temporarily rented another large property on the outskirts of Glastonbury until they felt they could move back in.

'As you heard, a lot of records were lost in the fire and in 1942, of course, there was the strafing by the German Luftwaffe fighter-bombers that destroyed even more of the wall and some of the library...Bartley's grandfather had that rebuilt.'

'It really is fascinating,' said Harriet. 'What a wonderfully romantic place to live. Did Bart say anything else about the Monmouth Rebellion?'

'No, come to think of it, he didn't...we'd just started talking about it when we heard you both coming back to the hall. Maybe he meant to tell us more but forgot when we went for tea. That kitchen is pretty splendid isn't it? Should we keep the cook on?'

'Oh, yes. She'd lose her job and home otherwise and, the village is really beginning to sound interesting. Is there a doctor or a vet around?'

'Oh, yes. Doctor Brownlow. Someone else who's been here for years and doesn't want to move, and a vet, Dennis Hedges lives just outside of the village.'

'Good, that's good to know.'

At the end of the driveway, they nodded to Mr Bragg, who was slurping from a steaming mug as he opened the gate for them in the same surly manner he had previously shown. Then, to Harriet's surprise, Jerry turned left into the road instead of right.

'Where are we going?' asked Harriet.

'We're not in a hurry and I wanted to take a look at the village. How do you fancy having a meal in the pub garden while we talk.'

'Yes, fine with me.'

'Good. I didn't want to go all the way back to Bristol when, hopefully, we can make a decision this afternoon and go back to them with an offer... get this done. You're keen to buy aren't you?'

Harriet laughed, her small white teeth showing as she tipped her head back. 'Yes, I do and I think the children will love it, but I don't think I've ever known you so impetuous. You're usually so much more careful...'

'...I know,' Jerry cut in, 'but I don't want to lose it.' He laughed with her. 'We can be Lord and Lady of the manor and village...how about that?'

'That would be fun,' Harriet laughed and turned to look at her husband. But Jerry was not laughing. His mouth was set in a firm, hard line, his hands gripped the wheel a little more tightly than he would have done usually and, even though he was looking at the road ahead, there was a ruthless expression in his eyes. For a moment she caught a glimpse of something that frightened her. She felt a cold shiver run down her spine. Then he turned to look at her and he grinned. 'We'll have a great time. Come on, let's eat and we'll talk about what offer we're going to make.'

The old Jerry was back. Perhaps he had just been concentrating on the road. After all they hadn't travelled this way before and the road was narrow with lots of bends. Yes. That was it. There was nothing to worry about.

-oOo-

As the Rolls Royce glided towards Winterne Village, five figures slipped out of the hedge opposite the closed gates. One, a very tall, stocky man with a shaggy mane of grey hair and a full beard, stood on the grass verge watching the car drive away. His bright blue eyes, usually alight with fun and laughter, were troubled as he pondered what the future might bring.

His friends, three of whom barely reached the man's waist in height, sat on the verge looking up at him while they waited for him to speak.

One, his long blond hair tied with a green ribbon at the nape of his neck, seemed particularly on edge. He found it hard to sit still, his bright blue eyes looked from one face to another trying to judge their feelings.

The eldest, with dark grey-streaked, shoulder length hair, stood, brushed grass off his tan leather breeches and walked towards the tall man. 'I have a bad feeling about that man.' He looked around at the two seated companions. 'Any thoughts, either of you?'

The third sat quietly on the rise of the verge, half hidden by the hedge.

He shrugged, took off his green woollen beanie hat, releasing strands of curly brown hair to tumble across his shoulders. He looked gravely at the tall man and the smaller one standing beside him. 'I, for one, will be sad to see the Earl and his family leave. Our people have lived peacefully around the Maitlands for centuries…protected them when we could…'

'…Even though very few of them ever knew we existed,' the blond one added, miserably.

'True,' said his friend with the brown hair. 'But you asked for our thoughts, Jimander. I don't know why but I have a feeling that this man will bring trouble. Maybe not immediately but…'

'His arrival will bring change,' said the big man, 'and I agree, it's not going to be for the better. The woman though, is another matter. Time will tell, but I believe she's going to face ordeals she will eventually overcome and be the better for them.'

The fifth member of the group, a long-legged grey timber wolf lay down on the verge, his golden eyes narrowed, his nostrils flared, top lip curled back showing bared fangs as he watched the car head into the distance.

The big man turned away from the road and began to move towards the hedge. 'Come, my friends. There is nothing we can do to prevent what is to come. We just have to find a way to live with whatever the future brings.'

The wolf stood and walked behind his companions towards the hedge. As he reached the gap in the hedge, he looked back to the road but the car was now out of sight having turned a corner. He gave a low rumbling growl and the thick mane of hair on his neck bristled.

'Come on, let's go,' said his friend in the green beanie hat. 'There's nothing more we can do…for now.'

Author's Note

'From Knight to Knave' is the book I have wanted to write for the last three or four years. I always had the feeling that there were back stories that needed to be told. Why was the monk never released from the Priest Hole? Who built the tunnel? Who were the people whose skeletons were discovered in the tunnel and what happened to them? And who placed the curse on Winterne Manor and why?

In the case of the monk, I had the scene where James was urging the very unfit Brother Matthew to hurry, in my head for several years and it just had to be committed to paper. Now it's written, there is a little more space in my imagination for other things.

I cannot easily leave the world of Winterne behind and move on to other things. Once you have created characters and their community, they continue to live in your imagination, even if your thoughts begin to stray elsewhere. That being the case, I have already started work on a 'spin-off' with Morgan and Jericha, from 'Avaroc Returns' being the lead characters, which I hope to launch towards the end of 2021, or early 2022.

There will also be two more younger children's animal stories, illustrated by the wonderfully talented artist, Jess Hawksworth. I anticipate that these two books will also be launched towards the end of 2021.

I also have plans though for a more adult book. This will be a story of modern day smuggling set in the Canary Islands. However, this will probably not be available until 2022.

So, with this year's annual creative writing competition for 8 to 18 year old writers of Nottinghamshire – our thirteenth year – to work on as well, I am still keeping myself busy, and have no intention of slowing down.

In case anyone is wondering about the spelling of 'serjeant', I would like to explain that it was not until the 20th century that the 'j' was replaced by a 'g'.

About the Author

Jae was born in Isleworth, West London, then lived in Essex and Suffolk before spending the rest of her childhood in Sherborne, Dorset, near the Somerset border. During those happy years, a visit to Wookey Hole caves, and an inspiring History teacher, Gerald Pitman, sparked an interest in the history and myths surrounding the Mendip Hills. Another teacher, Anne Osmond, was equally inspiring with her love of literature, encouraging Jae in her first attempts at writing.

Later Jae moved back to London and began writing her first book – a story based on the life of Queen Hatshepsut – it was never finished and sadly it was lost during one of the family moves!

During the following years career, marriage and children became her priorities, Jae forgot her writing but was an avid reader, usually having more than one good book on the go; generally, historical or fantasy novels.

In her thirties, she moved back to the West Country to Butleigh in Somerset, just four miles from Glastonbury, and seven miles from Wells. She fell in love with the area all over again, but this was to be a short stay.

Later, Jae lived in Ayrshire for four years and there met and married her second husband, David, and lived in Dumfries for six years. Then in 1996, the family moved back to England settling in Nottingham where they have lived ever since. Jae's children, Rachel and Greg, are now grown up and she has two grandchildren, Erin and Finn.

Having originally written 'Silver Linings' in 2005 and self-published in 2006, Jae met two other self-published authors. Together they attended book festivals and other literary events and met a number of other self-published authors, all trying to find their way through the world of bookstores, journalists, publishers and agents.

In 2006 she founded not-for-profit New Writers UK and organised their first book festival in November that year. Participating were just eight very local authors. Having invited the Lord Mayor of Nottingham the Chairman of Nottinghamshire County Council, the Mayor of Gedling and a number of local journalists, New Writers UK was on its way.

NWUK has helped aspiring authors with advice, services and events in a membership of over one hundred writers throughout the UK and overseas.

In 2009, Jae initiated an annual Creative Writing Competition for Children and Young People of Nottinghamshire, which is now going into its thirteenth year. The competition is entirely free to enter.

Since writing her books and the formation of New Writers UK, Jae (under her given name of Julie Malone), has been a regular on local radio, runs a free to attend monthly creative writing workshop and was the Creative Director and main organiser of the Gedling Borough Arts Festival for four years.

In February 2015, Jae (as Julie) was thrilled to be presented with the 'Pride of Gedling' Award in the Public Servant category, in recognition of all her hard work in running creative writing classes, creative writing competitions and organising the Gedling Borough Council Book Festivals.

Of course, with the Corona Virus situation in 2020, many of Jae's outside activities have ceased, although for a while she was able to continue her writing group in a garden environment. Due to more restrictive regulations, that too has stopped for the time being. Once the vaccine is fully available and reduced infection rates allow more freedom of movement, the writing group will be re-established.

'Avaroc Returns' is the fourth book in the Winterne Series. The first, second and third volumes are 'Silver Linings', 'Queen of Diamonds' and 'Fool's Gold', all of which have received excellent reviews.

Jae has also written a series of animal story books for younger children, 'Lorna and the Loch Ness Monster', The Raven and the Thief' set at the Tower of London, 'Blue Teaches A Lesson', Mrs Pringles Needs a Nurse' and 'Tib and Tab Make A Friend'. At least two more books in this series will be available in late 2021.

To contact Jae please email her at jaemalone.author@gmail.com, visit her website www.jaemalone.co.uk, or contact her through her Jae Malone Facebook or Instagram pages.

Jae is a member of the Society of Authors (SoA) and the National Association of Writers in Education (NAWE) and holds a current Enhanced Disclosure and Barring Service Certificate

Earlier volumes in 'The Winterne Series'

Volume 1 'Silver Linings'

At fourteen years old, Sam Johnson has a fairly peaceful way of life; he has the company of life-long friends and lives in a pleasant house on the outskirts of Nottingham. He even finds school hassle-free, usually. In fact, there is only one thing that spoils Sam's life; for the last five months his father has been working in South Africa and Sam misses him, a lot. Thankfully with Christmas in a few weeks, Steve Johnson is due to come home for the holidays. But an unkind twist of fate changes Sam's life, literally overnight. He has to leave his comfortable surroundings and friends behind, and move to a quiet country village, to stay with an aunt he hardly knows, and an uncle he has never met before. Within a very short time Sam discovers life in the picturesque village hides a darker side and his uncle has a secret. Over the next few weeks Sam makes both enemies and friends, and he discovers childhood fantasies can turn into reality.

Volume 2 'Queen of Diamonds'

Sam Johnson's first weeks in Winterne, just before Christmas were exciting, dangerous and magical. Four months later, he is settled and has made friends. Now all he wants is a quiet life to prepare for GCSE's. But knowing some of Sam's new friends, how likely is that? Jonah Atkins is now a reformed character since Sam saved his life during a cave-in, and the boys form an unlikely friendship. Harriet Atkins, Jonah's mother, deeply regretting everything Sam and his friend, Jenny, have suffered at the hands of the Atkins family, invites them both to choose a reward from a range of gifts.

Fate, again intervenes when their choices bring them renewed danger and Sam, Jenny and Jonah find themselves involved in someone's scheme to find hidden diamonds. Ghosts disappearing into bedrooms walls and mysterious figures in the wood are all part of this dangerous puzzle.

Once again, Sam needs the assistance of Charlie and his extraordinary friends, including the local witch, in the second instalment of the Winterne trilogy.

Volume 3 'Fool's Gold'

The quiet village of Winterne has had more excitement over the last months than it has had in years. In this third volume of 'The Winterne Series' as the end of year Prom approaches, Sam discovers Jenny's been keeping secrets from him and an exotic visitor arrives putting an old friend in danger. Elven family history, a threat to a Queen and a missing elf all become entangled in this tale of greed and retribution. Above ground there is danger and finally a confession from one person. Below there is a wedding, conflict and betrayal. And all before the Summer begins! Who is Elêna? Why has she come to Winterne? And how far will she go to achieve her ambition.

Volume 4 'Avaroc Returns'

Driven by obsessive greed, Queen Ellien's uncle, Avaroc, plots to seize her crown by starting a war between elf clans. He will stop at nothing, including murder and kidnapping, bringing despair to Winterne. Charlie, Halmar, Sam, Jenny, Morgan, and her cousin, Jericha, unite against him. Loyalties are tested to the limit and sometimes keeping your enemies close isn't the best plan...

Jae is currently writing an presently untitled spin-off to 'The Winterne Series'. This is the first chapter.

Chapter One

The latest in a very long line of reincarnated and gifted female witches over five centuries, fifteen-year-old Morgan Landers sometimes found it difficult in coping with her past lives. Some of these women had no memory of who they had been before, but others…take Armistice Jenks for instance…Morgan's last regeneration, could recall certain incidents from former live, and found it very satisfactory that justice had been served on those who had put them through ordeals and trials in the past.

Morgan was somewhat different though, and had clear and vibrant memories of several of these women in addition to her own talents. Like Armistice, she was a healer, but she could also communicate by thought, and had the ability to 'see' incidents taking place elsewhere. She also had an innate ability to bring joy, that had become evident even before her birth into the miserable and broken family in which she would find herself.

The downside to all this, was that there were times when she clearly saw and felt the joys and sufferings of some of her preceding existences. One such was Mary Hicks of Huntingdon. Morgan was sometimes tormented by visions of Mary begging for the life of her daughter, Elizabeth, but being forced to watch while her daughter was hanged before she too was executed in the same manner.

Another two ill-fated women were Mary Fuller and Thomasine Shorte. They were accused of witchcraft and hanged. But others were able to live quiet lives without attracting the attention of those who had a grudge against them, but those were not the incarnations who troubled her by materialising in her mind.

On these rare but very often extreme occasions, she needed to get away to the peace and silence of Winterne Woods, partly to calm herself, but also to hide the effects from her family. They knew, of course, that Morgan was different to other girls in the village, but loved her as a free spirit; she was the joy of their lives, and they made allowances for her occasional strangeness.

One thing remained the same in all the reincarnations: Bandit, the grey cat with jade coloured eyes. He and, whichever incarnation was living at the time would always find each other. Of course, Bandit the cat, would never live as long as his human companion, but when his natural time ended, he would reappear as a kitten and the two would be reunited.

On this particular morning, after a troubled and disturbing night when Morgan had tossed and turned in her bed for hours, she had awoken late with the images and voices of several women from her past lives whirling through her mind leaving her exhausted. Now she needed peace and the only place that gave her that tranquillity was Winterne Woods. Thankfully, after dressing and going downstairs, she had no explanations to make as no-one was in; the family had already left for their daily routines, but Bandit quietly followed her down the stairs. As he slept in her bedroom, he was aware of how troubled her night had been and was not going to let her slip away without him. Moments after she closed the back door behind her, he slipped through the cat-flap trailing after her at a discreet distance, understanding her need for solitude but caring enough to want to be there if she needed him; and he sensed that very soon she would.

Once Morgan reached the haven of the woods, her mood quietened, the panic attack diminished, and she could breathe easily again. Having so many tormented women inside her head at one time had been overwhelming. Thankfully these incidents were rare. Usually, when they did happen it would be just one or two entities, and sometimes it could even be quite amusing for Morgan when they talked together using her as a way of communicating a three-way conversation; but when they came in multiples, it was anything but entertaining.

The further into the woods she was, the more Morgan relaxed. She was aware of Bandit following a few metres behind her and was comforted to know he was there, bless him. She knew how much he cared about her and loved him in return, but she had not acknowledged him yet. She would stop soon.

The path she took, through an assortment of evergreen fir trees, their branches thick with needle-like leaves and the deciduous trees now in bud, had left the base of their trunks surrounded by a carpet of dead leaves from last Autumn. The path led her towards an outer edge of the woodland where she could look down on farm fields where seedlings of cereal crops were pushing through the earth. Above her the treetops were alive with birdsong, small animals scurried through the undergrowth, and the perfume of wild cherry, hawthorn and rowan blossom carried on the soft breeze infused her with the pure joy of being alive; all her night-time torments vanished.

Watching, Bandit knew where she was heading for; her favourite seat was a fallen tree trunk and she was definitely heading in that direction. He would get there before and wait for her. Being sheltered by the trees but situated where the sun could reach it, the trunk felt warm and when Morgan arrived, Bandit was lying down basking in the sunshine.

'I thought you'd be here,' she said, smiling. 'Thank you for following me. I'm glad to have your company.' She sat down beside him.

Bandit purred, stood up and stretched lazily then climbed on her lap and curled up, contentedly watching the early emerged butterflies and occasional ladybird that came within view. They sat silent and content for a few minutes looking down on the burgeoning greenery in the fields below, the flocks of birds above, the lone kestrel or sparrow-hawk hovering above and the moving vehicles travelling on the road in the distance.

A tree-lined lane led off the main road and Morgan thought she recognised Rachel Seymour's old black Volvo Estate as it turned off the road and into the lane. 'Must be heading to Bragg's. That won't be much fun. I can't imagine him being a good patient, can you, Bandit?'

Then something in her attitude changed and a faraway look came into her eyes. Bandit had seen that look before. Someone was trying to come through to her again. Who was it this time?

'Now, what do you want?' Morgan asked, but there was no-one around. 'Hi Armistice. How are you?'

Bandit sensed rather than heard the reply.

'I'm pretty good all in all, but I wanted to know what's happening with my house? It's been empty for fifteen years and it really is time someone took it over. It'll become dilapidated if it's left much longer. Oh, hello Bandit. How's my favourite cat?'

Bandit purred and rubbed his chin against Morgan's cheek. Armistice was no-one to be scared of and she had lived such a long life, that he had been with her through more of his reincarnations than anyone else.

'But you know Charlie has been looking after the house and it's still in a pretty good condition,' Morgan answered.

'Yes, I know and I'm grateful, but it just doesn't seem right.'

'Maybe not, but the house itself has to take some of the blame for it still not having anyone living there. Charlie tried telling it we have someone who would like to live there and she's family, so would fit in.'

Armistice chuckled. 'Why? What's it done?...and who are you talking about?'

'My cousin, Jericha, of course. She's been living with us for a while now but wants her own place and your house is perfect. Whenever the Estate Agents arranged for someone to visit, there would be an awful smell, or the place would be infested with ants or even mice and they left...in a hurry. In the end the agents stopped taking people around!'

'Smell? What kind of smell?'

'Well...you know that horrible stink when male cats have been spraying their scent around?'

Bandit raised his head and looked at Morgan quizzically.

'Oh...no offence Bandit,' she laughed and stroked the top of his head. 'I know you don't do that sort of thing.'

Bandit looked smug, lowered his head to rest his chin on his front paws again and Morgan was convinced she could see a shadow of a smile on his face.

'Oh, yes, that smell. No wonder people were put off. You're going to have to do something about it. The house needs someone living in it,' insisted Armistice.

'Me! Why should it be down to me to do something about sorting out your house?'

'Because you're the new me, of course. The house will know you. You have to show it who's boss...me, I mean you...of course.'

'Hmm. I needed something else to do, didn't I, Bandit? As if revision and exams coming up...and that lot not letting me sleep last night.' Morgan rolled her eyes. So did Bandit. 'Anyway, how are things where you are?' Morgan asked, trying to change the subject. She had never quite become comfortable with her conversations with Armistice, rare though they were, it was very odd to be talking to your former self and have her image swirling around in your mind while you were trying to think of things to say; it didn't exactly make for a relaxed chat, but this time anyway Armistice seemed to have plenty to say.

'*Oh, do stop feeling sorry for yourself, dear,*' Armistice said in her usual forthright manner. '*Many of your visitors last night have been through so much worse.*'

'Yes, I know but...'

Bandit, bored now by all the talking, missed hearing what Morgan said next as he became distracted by a sudden movement in the grass close to where they were sitting. He lowered himself into a crouching position, his attention now firmly fixed on whatever was causing the blades of grass to bow and bend. Tail switching from side to side and ears pointed straight up, he stared intently and uttered a low growl – ignored by Morgan as she continued her conversation with the otherworldly Armistice. A few seconds later a grass snake slithered into view, its yellow collar clearly identifying its species.

Bandit sat up straight and watched as the snake glided through the undergrowth obviously heading towards the newly filled ponds further into the trees. At this time the frogs, toads and newts would be spawning, and the snake was probably hungry after its winter hibernation. Bandit let it go but kept gazing after it until it vanished into the thicker undergrowth on the other side of their tree trunk seat.

'So what is it you want me to do?' Morgan was saying.

'*Just go there now...*'

'Now? Why now?'

'Because this has gone on far too long, you're only a few minutes away and as you're just sitting around, you clearly have spare time on your hands. So let's not waste any more of it.'

'You should come with me.'

'Silly girl. I'll be there anyway. I'm inside you.'

'I wonder how you would have coped if we were like other humans and once we die we'd go to one of the two other places.'

'At least this way I don't have to bump in to that Elêna.'

Bandit growled on hearing that name and his hackles rose like a bird's crest. The memory of how Armistice died clearly still imprinted on his soul in this life. Morgan reached out to stroke him and his hostility eased slowly.

'Do you know what happened to her?'

'Oh yes. Piggy gave me all the news when he passed over. He was there you know, when Wolf followed her into the river cavern. When he saw Wolf come out with his head hung low and blood on his chin, he thought Wolf had killed her. I think they all did but, of course, he didn't. She slipped, fell in, went under and was swept away in the force of the water. I'm sure she's gone to that place beginning with 'H'.'

'They both begin with 'H'...in fact, they both begin with an 'H' and 'E'.'

'Well, she'll have gone to the hot one. I wonder if she ever found that god she was looking for...Tlaloc...was it?'

'I shouldn't think so. She was clearly deluded...deluded and dangerous.'

'Well, let's not worry about her now. It's time to get to the house.'

'Yeah, yeah, OK.' Morgan stood up and turned to go. Bandit appeared to be dozing in the sun. 'Are you coming or should I collect you on the way back?' Morgan asked him.

He opened his eyes slowly, yawned, stretched and jumped down.

'Nice of you to join me,' she said. 'I wasn't looking forward to visiting the house alone but it knows you and that might help.'

'It knows me too, and I'll be with you,' Armistice said.

Can she see the look on my face? Morgan wondered.

'Yes, of course I can. You can't fool me, young lady. I know this wouldn't be your first choice of what to do today and, I'm sure after last night, you'd rather not have anything to do with any of us for a while but you, I mean we, have to get this housing thing sorted out.'

'OK, OK. I agree and I'm sure Jericha will like the house. After all the time it's been empty, the price is very low, and she'll like that too.'

If anyone had been watching, they would have seen a teenage girl, seemingly talking to an accompanying grey cat and taking a casual stroll through the woods. Nothing strange about that. Was there?